John Mortimer

Rumpole à la Carte

VIKING

VIKING

Published by the Penguin Group
27 Wrights Lane, London W8 5TZ, England
Viking Penguin, a division of Penguin Books USA Inc.
375 Hudson Street, New York, New York 10014, USA
Penguin Books Australia Ltd, Ringwood, Victoria, Australia
Penguin Books Canada Ltd, 2801 John Street, Markham, Ontario, Canada L3R 1B4
Penguin Books (NZ) Ltd, 182–190 Wairau Road, Auckland 10, New Zealand
Penguin Books Ltd, Registered Offices: Harmondsworth, Middlesex, England

First published 1990
10 9 8 7 6 5 4 3 2 1

Copyright © Advanpress Ltd, 1990

Printed in England by Clays Ltd, St Ives plc
Filmset in $11\frac{1}{2}/13\frac{1}{2}$ pt Monotype Plantin

A CIP catalogue record for this book is available from the British Library

ISBN 0-670-83284-7

To Ann Mallalieu and Tim Cassell

Contents

Rumpole à la Carte

I suppose, when I have time to think about it, which is not often during the long day's trudge round the Bailey and more down-market venues such as the Uxbridge Magistrates Court, the law represents some attempt, however fumbling, to impose order on a chaotic universe. Chaos, in the form of human waywardness and uncontrollable passion, is ever bubbling away just beneath the surface and its sporadic outbreaks are what provide me with my daily crust, and even a glass or two of Pommeroy's plonk to go with it. I have often noticed, in the accounts of the many crimes with which I have been concerned, that some small sign of disorder – an unusual number of milk bottles on a doorstep, a car parked on a double yellow line by a normally law-abiding citizen, even, in the Penge Bungalow Murders, someone else's mackintosh taken from an office peg – has been the first indication of anarchy taking over. The clue that such dark forces were at work in La Maison Jean-Pierre, one of the few London eateries to have achieved three Michelin stars and to charge more for a bite of dinner for two than I get for a legal aid theft, was very small indeed.

Now my wife, Hilda, is a good, plain cook. In saying that, I'm not referring to She Who Must Be Obeyed's moral values or passing any judgment on her personal appearance. What I can tell you is that she cooks without flights of fancy. She is not, in any way, a woman who lacks imagination. Indeed some of the things she imagines Rumpole gets up to when out of her sight are colourful in the extreme, but she doesn't apply such gifts to a chop or a potato, being quite content to grill the one and boil the other. She can also boil a cabbage into submission and fry fish. The nearest her cooking comes to the poetic is, perhaps, in her baked jam roll, which I have always found to be an emotion best recollected in tranquillity. From all this, you will gather that Hilda's honest cooking is sufficient but not exotic, and that happily the terrible curse of *nouvelle cuisine* has not infected Froxbury Mansions in the Gloucester Road.

So it is not often that I am confronted with the sort of fare photographed in the Sunday supplements. I scarcely ever sit down to an octagonal plate on which a sliver of monkfish is arranged in a composition of pastel shades, which also features a brush stroke of pink sauce, a single peeled prawn and a sprig of dill. Such gluttony is, happily, beyond my means. It wasn't, however, beyond the means of Hilda's cousin Everard, who was visiting us from Canada, where he carried on a thriving trade as a company lawyer. He told us that he felt we stood in dire need of what he called 'a taste of gracious living' and booked a table for three at La Maison Jean-Pierre.

So we found ourselves in an elegantly appointed room with subdued lighting and even more subdued conversation, where the waiters padded around like priests and the customers behaved as though they were in church. The climax of the ritual came when the dishes were set on the table under silvery domes, which were lifted to the whispered command of *'Un, deux, trois!'* to reveal the somewhat mingy portions on offer. Cousin Everard was a grey-haired man in a pale grey suiting who talked about his legal experiences in greyish tones. He entertained us with a long account of a takeover bid for the Winnipeg Soap Company which had cleared four million dollars for his clients, the Great Elk Bank of Canada. Hearing this, Hilda said accusingly, 'You've never cleared four million dollars for a client, have you, Rumpole? You should be a company lawyer like Everard.'

'Oh, I think I'll stick to crime,' I told them. 'At least it's a more honest type of robbery.'

'Nonsense. Robbery has never got us a dinner at La Maison Jean-Pierre. We'd never be here if Cousin Everard hadn't come all the way from Saskatchewan to visit us.'

'Yes, indeed. From the town of Saskatoon, Hilda.' Everard gave her a greyish smile.

'You see, Hilda. Saskatoon as in *spittoon*.'

'Crime doesn't pay, Horace,' the man from the land of the igloos told me. 'You should know that by now. Of course, we have several fine-dining restaurants in Saskatoon these days, but nothing to touch this.' He continued his inspection of the menu. 'Hilda, may I make so bold as to ask, what is your pleasure?'

During the ensuing discussion my attention strayed. Staring idly round the consecrated area I was startled to see, in the gloaming, a distinct sign of human passion in revolt against the forces of law and order. At a table for two I recognized Claude Erskine-Brown, opera buff, hopeless cross-examiner and long-time member of our Chambers in Equity Court. But was he dining tête-à-tête with his wife, the handsome and successful Q.C., Mrs Phillida Erskine-Brown, the Portia of our group, as law and order demanded? The answer to that was no. He was entertaining a young and decorative lady solicitor named Patricia (known to herself as Tricia) Benbow. Her long golden hair (which often provoked whistles from the cruder junior clerks round the Old Bailey) hung over her slim and suntanned shoulders and one generously ringed hand rested on Claude's as she gazed, in her usual appealing way, up into his eyes. She couldn't gaze into them for long as Claude, no doubt becoming uneasily aware of the unexpected presence of a couple of Rumpoles in the room, hid his face behind a hefty wine list.

At that moment an extremely superior brand of French head waiter manifested himself beside our table, announced his presence with a discreet cough, and led off with, '*Madame, messieurs*. Tonight Jean-Pierre recommends, for the main course, *la poésie de la poitrine du canard aux céleris et épinards crus*.'

'*Poésie* . . .' Hilda sounded delighted and kindly explained, 'That's poetry, Rumpole. Tastes a good deal better than that old Wordsworth of yours, I shouldn't be surprised.'

'Tell us about it, Georges.' Everard smiled at the waiter. 'Whet our appetites.'

'This is just a few wafer-thin slices of breast of duck, marinated in a drop or two of Armagnac, delicately grilled and served with a celery remoulade and some leaves of spinach lightly steamed . . .'

'And mash . . .?' I interrupted the man to ask.

'*Excusez-moi?*' The fellow seemed unable to believe his ears.

'Mashed spuds come with it, do they?'

'Ssh, Rumpole!' Hilda was displeased with me, but turned all her charms on Georges. 'I will have the *poésie*. It sounds delicious.'

'A culinary experience, Hilda. Yes. *Poésie* for me too, please.' Everard fell into line.

'I would like a *poésie* of steak and kidney *pudding*, not pie, with mashed potatoes and a big scoop of boiled cabbage. *English* mustard, if you have it.' It seemed a reasonable enough request.

'Rumpole!' Hilda's whisper was menacing. 'Behave yourself!'

'This . . . "pudding"' – Georges was puzzled – 'is not on our menu.'

'"Your pleasure is our delight". It says that on your menu. Couldn't you ask Cookie if she could delight me? Along those lines.'

'"Cookie"? I do not know who M'sieur means by "Cookie". Our *maître de cuisine* is Jean-Pierre O'Higgins himself. He is in the kitchen now.'

'How very convenient. Have a word in his shell-like, why don't you?'

For a tense moment it seemed as though the looming, priestly figure of Georges was about to excommunicate me, drive me out of the Temple, or at least curse me by bell, book and candle. However, after muttering, '*Si vous le voulez. Excusez-moi,*' he went off in search of higher authority. Hilda apologized for my behaviour and told Cousin Everard that she supposed I thought I was being funny. I assured her that there was nothing particularly funny about a steak and kidney pudding.

Then I was aware of a huge presence at my elbow. A tall, fat, red-faced man in a chef's costume was standing with his hands on his hips and asking, 'Is there someone here wants to lodge a complaint?'

Jean-Pierre O'Higgins, I was later to discover, was the product of an Irish father and a French mother. He spoke in the tones of those Irishmen who come up in a menacing manner and stand far too close to you in pubs. He was well known, I had already heard it rumoured, for dominating both his kitchen and his customers; his phenomenal rudeness to his guests seemed to be regarded as one of the attractions of his establishment. The gourmets of London didn't feel that their dinners had been entirely satisfactory unless they were served up, by way of a savoury, with a couple of insults from Jean-Pierre O'Higgins.

'Well, yes,' I said. 'There is someone.'

'Oh, yes?' O'Higgins had clearly never heard of the old adage about the customer always being right. 'And are you the joker that requested mash?'

'Am I to understand you to be saying,' I inquired as politely as I knew how, 'that there are to be no mashed spuds for my delight?'

'Look here, my friend. I don't know who you are . . .' Jean-Pierre went on in an unfriendly fashion and Everard did his best to introduce me. 'Oh, this is Horace Rumpole, Jean-Pierre. The *criminal* lawyer.'

'*Criminal* lawyer, eh?' Jean-Pierre was unappeased. 'Well, don't commit your crimes in my restaurant. If you want "mashed spuds", I suggest you move down to the working-men's caff at the end of the street.'

'That's a very helpful suggestion.' I was, as you see, trying to be as pleasant as possible.

'You might get a few bangers while you're about it. And a bottle of OK sauce. That suit your delicate palate, would it?'

'Very well indeed! I'm not a great one for wafer-thin slices of anything.'

'You don't look it. Now, let's get this straight. People who come into my restaurant damn well eat as I tell them to!'

'And I'm sure you win them all over with your irresistible charm.' I gave him the retort courteous. As the chef seemed about to explode, Hilda weighed in with a well-meaning 'I'm sure my husband doesn't mean to be rude. It's just, well, we don't dine out very often. And this is such a delightful room, isn't it?'

'Your husband?' Jean-Pierre looked at She Who Must Be Obeyed with deep pity. 'You have all my sympathy, you unfortunate woman. Let me tell you, Mr Rumpole, this is La Maison Jean-Pierre. I have three stars in the Michelin. I have thrown out an Arabian king because he ordered filet mignon well cooked. I have sent film stars away in tears because they dared to mention Thousand Island dressing. I am Jean-Pierre O'Higgins, the greatest culinary genius now working in England!'

I must confess that during this speech from the patron I found my attention straying. The other diners, as is the way with the English at the trough, were clearly straining their ears to catch every detail of the row whilst ostentatiously concentrating on their plates. The pale, bespectacled girl making up the bills behind the desk in the corner seemed to have no such inhibitions. She was staring across the room and looking at me, I thought, as though I had thoroughly deserved the O'Higgins rebuke. And then I saw two waiters approach Erskine-Brown's table with domed dishes, which they laid on the table with due solemnity.

'And let me tell you,' Jean-Pierre's oration continued, 'I started my career with salads at La Grande Bouffe in Lyons under the great Ducasse. I was rôtisseur in Le Crillon, Boston. I have run this restaurant for twenty years and I have never, let me tell you, in my whole career, served up a mashed spud!'

The climax of his speech was dramatic but not nearly as startling as the events which took place at Erskine-Brown's table. To the count of '*Un, deux, trois!*' the waiters removed the silver covers and from under the one in front of Tricia Benbow sprang a small, alarmed brown mouse, perfectly visible by the light of a table candle, which had presumably been nibbling at the *poésie*. At this, the elegant lady solicitor uttered a piercing scream and leapt on to her chair. There she stood, with her skirt held down to as near her knees as possible, screaming in an ever-rising scale towards some ultimate crescendo. Meanwhile the stricken Claude looked just as a man who'd planned to have a quiet dinner with a lady and wanted to attract no one's attention would look under such circumstances. 'Please, Tricia,' I could hear his plaintive whisper, 'don't scream! People are noticing us.'

'I say, old darling,' I couldn't help saying to that three-star man O'Higgins, 'they had a mouse on that table. Is it the *spécialité de la maison?*'

A few days later, at breakfast in the mansion flat, glancing through the post (mainly bills and begging letters from Her Majesty, who seemed to be pushed for a couple of quid and would be greatly obliged if I'd let her have a little tax money on account), I saw a glossy brochure for a hotel in the Lake District. Although in the homeland of my favourite poet, Le Château Duddon, 'Lakeland's Paradise of Gracious Living', didn't sound like old Wordsworth's cup of tea, despite the 'king-sized four-poster in the Samuel Taylor Coleridge suite'.

'Cousin Everard wants to take me up there for a break.' Hilda, who was clearing away, removed a half-drunk cup of tea from my hand.

'A break from what?' I was mystified.

'From you, Rumpole. Don't you think I need it? After that disastrous evening at La Maison?'

'Was it a disaster? I quite enjoyed it. England's greatest chef laboured and gave birth to a ridiculous mouse. People'd pay good money to see a trick like that.'

'*You* were the disaster, Rumpole,' she said, as she consigned my last piece of toast to the tidy-bin. 'You were unforgivable. Mashed spuds! Why ever did you use such a vulgar expression?'

'Hilda,' I protested, I thought, reasonably, 'I have heard some fairly fruity language round the Courts in the course of a long life of crime. But I've never heard it suggested that the words "mashed spuds" would bring a blush to the cheek of the tenderest virgin.'

'Don't try to be funny, Rumpole. You upset that brilliant chef, Mr O'Higgins. You deeply upset Cousin Everard!'

'Well' – I had to put the case for the Defence – 'Everard kept on suggesting I didn't make enough to feed you properly. Typical commercial lawyer. Criminal law is about life, liberty and the pursuit of happiness. Commercial law is about money. That's what I think, anyway.'

Hilda looked at me, weighed up the evidence and summed up, not entirely in my favour. 'I don't think you made that terrible fuss because of what you thought about the commercial law,' she said. 'You did it because you have to be a "character", don't you? Wherever you go. Well, I don't know if I'm going to be able to put up with your "character" much longer.'

I don't know why but what she said made me feel, quite suddenly and in a most unusual way, uncertain of myself. What was Hilda talking about exactly? I asked for further and better particulars.

'You have to be one all the time, don't you?' She was clearly getting into her stride. 'With your cigar ash and steak and kidney and Pommeroy's Ordinary Red and your arguments. Always arguments! Why do you have to go on arguing, Rumpole?'

'Arguing? It's been my life, Hilda,' I tried to explain.

'Well, it's not mine! Not any more. Cousin Everard doesn't argue in public. He is quiet and polite.'

'If you like that sort of thing.' The subject of Cousin Everard was starting to pall on me.

'Yes, Rumpole. Yes, I do. That's why I agreed to go on this trip.'

'Trip?'

'Everard and I are going to tour all the restaurants in England with stars. We're going to Bath and York and Devizes. And you can stay here and eat all the mashed spuds you want.'

'What?' I hadn't up till then taken Le Château Duddon entirely seriously. 'You really mean it?'

'Oh, yes. I think so. The living is hardly gracious here, is it?'

On the way to my place of work I spent an uncomfortable quarter of an hour thinking over what She Who Must Be Obeyed had said about me having to be a 'character'. It seemed an unfair charge. I drink Château Thames Embankment because it's all I can afford. It keeps me regular and blots out certain painful memories, such as a bad day in Court in front of Judge Graves, an old darling who undoubtedly passes iced water every time he goes to the Gents. I enjoy the fragrance of a small cigar. I relish an argument. This is the way of life I have chosen. I don't have to do any of these things in order to be a character. Do I?

I was jerked out of this unaccustomed introspection on my arrival in the clerk's room at Chambers. Henry, our clerk, was striking bargains with solicitors over the telephone whilst Dianne sat in front of her typewriter, her head bowed over a lengthy and elaborate manicure. Uncle Tom, our oldest inhabitant, who hasn't had a brief in Court since anyone can remember, was working hard at improving his putting skills with an old mashie niblick and a clutch of golf balls, the hole being represented by the waste-paper basket laid on its side. Almost as soon as I got into this familiar environment I was comforted by the sight of a man who seemed to be in far deeper trouble than I was. Claude Erskine-Brown came up to me in a manner that I can only describe as furtive.

'Rumpole,' he said, 'as you may know, Philly is away in Cardiff doing a long fraud.'

'Your wife,' I congratulated the man, 'goes from strength to strength.'

'What I mean is, Rumpole' – Claude's voice sank below the level of Henry's telephone calls – 'you may have noticed me the other night. In La Maison Jean-Pierre.'

'Noticed you, Claude? Of course not! You were only in the company of a lady who stood on a chair and screamed like a banshee with toothache. No one could have possibly noticed you.' I did my best to comfort the man.

'It was purely a business arrangement,' he reassured me.

'Pretty rum way of conducting business.'

'The lady was Miss Tricia Benbow. My instructing solicitor in the V.A.T. case,' he told me, as though that explained everything.

'Claude, I have had some experience of the law and it's a

good plan, when entertaining solicitors in order to tout for briefs, *not* to introduce mice into their *plats du jour*.'

The telephone by Dianne's typewriter rang. She blew on her nail lacquer and answered it, as Claude's voice rose in anguished protest. 'Good heavens. You don't think I did *that*, do you, Rumpole? The whole thing was a disaster! An absolute tragedy! Which may have appalling consequences . . .' 'Your wife on the phone, Mr Erskine-Brown,' Dianne interrupted him and Claude went to answer the call with all the eager cheerfulness of a French aristocrat who is told the tumbril is at the door. As he was telling his wife he hoped things were going splendidly in Cardiff, and that he rarely went out in the evenings, in fact usually settled down to a scrambled egg in front of the telly, there was a sound of rushing water without and our Head of Chambers joined us.

'Something extremely serious has happened.' Sam Ballard, Q.C. made the announcement as though war had broken out. He is a pallid sort of person who usually looks as though he has just bitten into a sour apple. His hair, I have to tell you, seems to be slicked down with some kind of pomade.

'Someone nicked the nail-brush in the Chambers loo?' I suggested helpfully.

'How did you guess?' He turned on me, amazed, as though I had the gift of second sight.

'It corresponds to your idea of something serious. Also I notice such things.'

'Odd that you should know immediately what I was talking about, Rumpole.' By now Ballard's amazement had turned to deep suspicion.

'Not guilty, my Lord,' I assured him. 'Didn't you have a meeting of your God-bothering society here last week?'

'The Lawyers As Christians committee. We met here. What of it?'

'"Cleanliness is next to godliness." Isn't that their motto? The devout are notable nail-brush nickers.' As I said this, I watched Erskine-Brown lay the telephone to rest and leave the room with the air of a man who has merely postponed the evil hour. Ballard was still on the subject of serious crime in the facilities. 'It's of vital importance in any place of work, Henry,' he batted on, 'that the highest standards of hygiene are maintained! Now I've been instructed by the City Health Authority in an important case, it would be extremely embarrassing to me personally if my Chambers were found wanting in the matter of a nail-brush.'

'Well, don't look at me, Mr Ballard.' Henry was not taking this lecture well.

'I am accusing nobody.' Ballard sounded unconvincing. 'But look to it, Henry. Please, look to it.'

Then our Head of Chambers left us. Feeling my usual reluctance to start work, I asked Uncle Tom, as something of an expert in these matters, if it would be fair to call me a 'character'.

'A what, Rumpole?'

'A "character", Uncle Tom.'

'Oh, they had one of those in old Sniffy Greengrass's Chambers in Lamb Court,' Uncle Tom remembered. 'Fellow called Dalrymple. Lived in an absolutely filthy flat over a chemist's shop in Chancery Lane and used to lead a cat round the Temple on a long piece of pink tape. "Old Dalrymple's a character," they used to say, and the other fellows in Chambers were rather proud of him.'

'I don't do anything like that, do I?' I asked for reassurance.

'I hope not,' Uncle Tom was kind enough to say. 'This Dalrymple finally went across the road to do an undefended divorce. In his pyjamas! I believe they had to lock him up. I wouldn't say you were a "character", Rumpole. Not yet, anyway.'

'Thank you, Uncle Tom. Perhaps you could mention that to She Who Must?'

And then the day took a distinct turn for the better. Henry put down his phone after yet another call and my heart leapt up when I heard that Mr Bernard, my favourite instructing solicitor (because he keeps quiet, does what he's told and hardly ever tells me about his bad back), was coming over and was anxious to instruct me in a new case which was 'not on the legal aid'. As I left the room to go about this business, I had

one final question for Uncle Tom. 'That fellow Dalrymple. He
didn't play golf in the clerk's room did he?'

'Good heavens, no.' Uncle Tom seemed amused at my
ignorance of the world. 'He was a character, do you see? He'd
hardly do anything normal.'

Mr Bernard, balding, pin-striped, with a greying moustache
and a kindly eye, through all our triumphs and disasters
remained imperturbable. No confession made by any client,
however bizarre, seemed to surprise him, nor had any revel-
ation of evil shocked him. He lived through our days of murder,
mayhem and fraud as though he were listening to 'Gardeners'
Question Time'. He was interested in growing roses and in his
daughter's nursing career. He spent his holidays in remote
spots like Bangkok and the Seychelles. He always went away,
he told me, 'on a package' and returned with considerable
relief. I was always pleased to see Mr Bernard, but that day he
seemed to have brought me something far from my usual line
of country.

'My client, Mr Rumpole, first consulted me because his
marriage was on the rocks, not to put too fine a point on it.'

'It happens, Mr Bernard. Many marriages are seldom off
them.'

'Particularly so if, as in this case, the wife's of foreign
extraction. It's long been my experience, Mr Rumpole, that
you can't beat foreign wives for being vengeful. In this case,
extremely vengeful.'

'Hell hath no fury, Mr Bernard?' I suggested.

'Exactly, Mr Rumpole. You've put your finger on the nub
of the case. As you would say yourself.'

'I haven't done a matrimonial for years. My divorce may be
a little rusty,' I told him modestly.

'Oh, we're not asking you to do the divorce. We're sending
that to Mr Tite-Smith in Crown Office Row.'

Oh, well, I thought, with only a slight pang of disappointment, good luck to little Tite-Smith.

'The matrimonial is not my client's only problem,' Mr
Bernard told me.

' "When sorrows come," Mr Bernard, "they come not single spies, But in battalions!" Your chap got something else on his plate, has he?'

'On his plate!' The phrase seemed to cause my solicitor some amusement. 'That's very apt, that is. And apter than you know, Mr Rumpole.'

'Don't keep me in suspense! Who is this mysterious client?'

'I wasn't to divulge the name, Mr Rumpole, in case you should refuse to act for him. He thought you might've taken against him, so he's coming to appeal to you in person. I asked Henry if he'd show him up as soon as he arrived.'

And, dead on cue, Dianne knocked on my door, threw it open and announced, 'Mr O'Higgins.' The large man, dressed now in a deafening checked tweed jacket and a green turtle-necked sweater, looking less like a chef than an Irish horse coper, advanced on me with a broad grin and his hand extended in a greeting, which was in strong contrast to our last encounter.

'I rely on you to save me, Mr Rumpole,' he boomed. 'You're the man to do it, sir. The great criminal defender!'

'Oh? I thought *I* was the criminal in your restaurant,' I reminded him.

'I have to tell you, Mr Rumpole, your courage took my breath away! Do you know what he did, Mr Bernard? Do you know what this little fellow here had the pluck to do?' He seemed determined to impress my solicitor with an account of my daring in the face of adversity. 'He only ordered mashed spuds in La Maison Jean-Pierre. A risk no one else has taken in all the time I've been *maître de cuisine*.'

'It didn't seem to be particularly heroic,' I told Bernard, but O'Higgins would have none of that. 'I tell you, Mr Bernard' – he moved very close to my solicitor and towered over him – 'a man who could do that to Jean-Pierre couldn't be intimidated by all the judges of the Queen's Bench. What do you say then, Mr Horace Rumpole? Will you take me on?'

I didn't answer him immediately but sat at my desk, lit a small cigar and looked at him critically. 'I don't know yet.'

'Is it my personality that puts you off?' My prospective

client folded himself into my armchair, with one leg draped over an arm. He grinned even more broadly, displaying a judiciously placed gold tooth. 'Do you find me objectionable?'

'Mr O'Higgins.' I decided to give judgment at length. 'I think your restaurant pretentious and your portions skimpy. Your customers eat in a dim, religious atmosphere which seems to be more like Evensong than a good night out. You appear to be a self-opinionated and self-satisfied bully. I have known many murderers who could teach you a lesson in courtesy. However, Mr Bernard tells me that you are prepared to pay my fee and, in accordance with the great traditions of the Bar, I am on hire to even the most unattractive customer.'

There was a silence and I wondered if the inflammable restaurateur were about to rise and hit me. But he turned to Bernard with even greater enthusiasm. 'Just listen to that! How's that for eloquence? We picked the right one here, Mr Bernard!'

'Well, now. I gather you're in some sort of trouble. Apart from your marriage, that is.' I unscrewed my pen and prepared to take a note.

'This has nothing to do with my marriage.' But then he frowned unhappily. 'Anyway, I don't think it has.'

'You haven't done away with this vengeful wife of yours?' Was I to be presented with a murder?

'I should have, long ago,' Jean-Pierre admitted. 'But no. Simone is still alive and suing. Isn't that right, Mr Bernard?'

'It is, Mr O'Higgins,' Bernard assured him gloomily. 'It is indeed. But this is something quite different. My client, Mr Rumpole, is being charged under the Food and Hygiene Regulations 1970 for offences relating to dirty and dangerous practices at La Maison. I have received a telephone call from the Environmental Health Officer.'

It was then, I'm afraid, that I started to laugh. I named the guilty party. 'The mouse!'

'Got it in one.' Jean-Pierre didn't seem inclined to join in the joke.

'The "wee, sleekit, cow'rin, tim'rous beastie",' I quoted at him. 'How delightful! We'll elect for trial before a jury. If we can't get you off, Mr O'Higgins, at least we'll give them a little harmless entertainment.'

Of course it wasn't really funny. A mouse in the wrong place, like too many milk bottles on a doorstep, might be a sign of passions stretched beyond control.

I have always found it useful, before forming a view about a case, to inspect the scene of the crime. Accordingly I visited La Maison Jean-Pierre one evening to study the ritual serving of dinner.

Mr Bernard and I stood in a corner of the kitchen at La Maison Jean-Pierre with our client. We were interested in the two waiters who had attended table eight, the site of the Erskine-Brown assignation. The senior of the two was Gaston, the station waiter, who had four tables under his command. 'Gaston Leblanc,' Jean-Pierre told us, as he identified the small, fat, cheerful, middle-aged man who trotted between the tables. 'Been with me for ever. Works all the hours God gave to keep a sick wife and their kid at university. Does all sorts of other jobs in the day-time. I don't inquire too closely. Georges Pitou, the head waiter, takes the orders, of course, and leaves a copy of the note on the table.'

We saw Georges move, in a stately fashion, into the kitchen and hand the order for table eight to a young cook in a white hat, who stuck it up on the kitchen wall with a magnet. This was Ian, the sous chef. Jean-Pierre had 'discovered' him in a Scottish hotel and wanted to encourage his talent. That night the bustle in the kitchen was muted, and as I looked through the circular window into the dining-room I saw that most of the white-clothed tables were standing empty, like small icebergs in a desolate polar region. When the Prosecution had been announced, there had been a headline in the *Evening Standard* which read GUESS WHO'S COMING TO DINNER? MOUSE SERVED IN TOP LONDON RESTAURANT and since then attendances at La Maison had dropped off sharply.

The runner between Gaston's station and the kitchen was the commis waiter, Alphonse Pascal, a painfully thin, dark-eyed young man with a falling lock of hair who looked like the hero of some nineteenth-century French novel, interesting and doomed. 'As a matter of fact,' Jean-Pierre told us, 'Alphonse is full of ambition. He's starting at the bottom and wants to work his way up to running a hotel. Been with me for about a year.'

We watched as Ian put the two orders for table eight on the serving-table. In due course Alphonse came into the kitchen and called out, 'Number Eight!' 'Ready, frog face,' Ian told him politely, and Alphonse came back with, '*Merci*, idiot.'

'Are they friends?' I asked my client.

'Not really. They're both much too fond of Mary.'

'Mary?'

'Mary Skelton. The English girl who makes up the bills in the restaurant.'

I looked again through the circular window and saw the unmemorable girl, her head bent over her calculator. She seemed an unlikely subject for such rivalry. I saw Alphonse pass her with a tray, carrying two domed dishes and, although he looked in her direction, she didn't glance up from her work. Alphonse then took the dishes to the serving-table at Gaston's station. Gaston looked under one dome to check its contents and then the plates were put on the table. Gaston mouthed an inaudible '*Un, deux, trois!*', the domes were lifted before the diners and not a mouse stirred.

'On the night in question,' Bernard reminded me, 'Gaston says in his statement that he looked under the dome on the gentleman's plate.'

'And saw no side order of mouse,' I remembered.

'Exactly! So he gave the other to Alphonse, who took it to the lady.'

'And then . . . Hysterics!'

'And then the reputation of England's greatest *maître de cuisine* crumbled to dust!' Jean-Pierre spoke as though announcing a national disaster.

'Nonsense!' I did my best to cheer him up. 'You're forgetting the reputation of Horace Rumpole.'

'You think we've got a defence?' my client asked eagerly. 'I mean, now that you've looked at the kitchen?'

'Can't think of one for the moment,' I admitted, 'but I expect we'll cook up something in the end.'

Unencouraged, Jean-Pierre looked out into the dining-room, muttered, 'I'd better go and keep those lonely people company,' and left us. I watched him pass the desk, where Mary looked up and smiled and I thought, however brutal he was with his customers, at least Jean-Pierre's staff seemed to find him a tolerable employer. And then, to my surprise, I saw him approach the couple at table eight, grinning in a most ingratiating manner, and stand chatting and bowing as though they could have ordered doner kebab and chips and that would have been perfectly all right by him.

'You know,' I said to Mr Bernard, 'it's quite extraordinary, the power that can be wielded by one of the smaller rodents.'

'You mean it's wrecked his business?'

'No. More amazing than that. It's forced Jean-Pierre O'Higgins to be polite to his clientele.'

After my second visit to La Maison events began to unfold at breakneck speed. First our Head of Chambers, Soapy Sam Ballard, made it known to me that the brief he had accepted on behalf of the Health Authority, and of which he had boasted so flagrantly during the nail-brush incident, was in fact the prosecution of J.-P. O'Higgins for the serious crime of being in charge of a rodent-infested restaurant. Then She Who Must Be Obeyed, true to her word, packed her grip and went off on a gastronomic tour with the man from Saskatoon. I was left to enjoy a lonely high-calorie breakfast, with no fear of criticism over the matter of a fourth sausage, in the Taste-Ee-Bite café, Fleet Street. Seated there one morning, enjoying the company of *The Times* crossword, I happened to overhear Mizz Liz Probert, the dedicated young radical barrister in our Chambers, talking to her close friend, David Inchcape, whom she had persuaded us to take on in a somewhat devious manner – a barrister as young but, I think, at heart, a touch less radical than Mizz Liz herself.★

★ See 'Rumpole and the Quality of Life' in *Rumpole and the Age of Miracles*, Penguin Books, 1988.

'You don't really *care*, do you, Dave?' she was saying.

'Of course, I care. I care about you, Liz. Deeply.' He reached out over their plates of muesli and cups of decaff to grasp her fingers.

'That's just physical.'

'Well. Not just physical. I don't suppose it's *just*. Mainly physical, perhaps.'

'No one cares about old people.'

'But you're not old people, Liz. Thank God!'

'You see. You don't care about them. My Dad was saying there's old people dying in tower blocks every day. Nobody knows about it for weeks, until they decompose!' And I saw Dave release her hand and say, 'Please, Liz. I *am* having my breakfast.'

'You see! You don't want to know. It's just something you don't want to hear about. It's the same with battery hens.'

'What's the same about battery hens?'

'No one wants to know. That's all.'

'But surely, Liz. Battery hens don't get lonely.'

'Perhaps they do. There's an awful lot of loneliness about.' She looked in my direction. 'Get off to Court then, if you have to. But do *think* about it, Dave.' Then she got up, crossed to my table, and asked what I was doing. I was having my breakfast, I assured her, and not doing my yoga meditation.

'Do you always have breakfast alone, Rumpole?' She spoke, in the tones of a deeply supportive social worker, as she sat down opposite me.

'It's not always possible. Much easier now, of course.'

'Now. Why *now*, exactly?' She looked seriously concerned.

'Well. Now my wife's left me,' I told her cheerfully.

'Hilda!' Mizz Probert was shocked, being a conventional girl at heart.

'As you would say, Mizz Liz, she is no longer sharing a one-on-one relationship with me. In any meaningful way.'

'Where does that leave you, Rumpole?'

'Alone. To enjoy my breakfast and contemplate the crossword puzzle.'

'Where's Hilda gone?'

'Oh, in search of gracious living with her cousin Everard from Saskatoon. A fellow with about as many jokes in him as the Dow Jones Average.'

'You mean, she's gone off with another man?' Liz seemed unable to believe that infidelity was not confined to the young.

'That's about the size of it.'

'But, Rumpole. *Why?*'

'Because he's rich enough to afford very small portions of food.'

'So you're living by yourself? You must be terribly lonely.'

' "Society is all but rude," ' I assured her, ' "To this delicious solitude." '

There was a pause and then Liz took a deep breath and offered her assistance. 'You know, Rumpole. Dave and I have founded the Y.R.L. Young Radical Lawyers. We don't only mean to reform the legal system, although that's part of it, of course. We're going to take on social work as well. We could always get someone to call and take a look at your flat every morning.'

'To make sure it's still there?'

'Well, no, Rumpole. As a matter of fact, to make sure you are.'

Those who are alone have great opportunities for eavesdropping, and Liz and Dave weren't the only members of our Chambers I heard engaged in a heart-to-heart that day. Before I took the journey back to the She-less flat, I dropped into Pommeroy's and was enjoying the ham roll and bottle of Château Thames Embankment which would constitute my dinner, seated in one of the high-backed, pew-like stalls Jack Pommeroy has installed, presumably to give the joint a vaguely medieval appearance and attract the tourists. From behind my back I heard the voices of our Head of Chambers and Claude Erskine-Brown, who was saying, in his most ingratiating tones, 'Ballard. I want to have a word with you about the case you've got against La Maison Jean-Pierre.'

To this, Ballard, in thoughtful tones, replied unexpectedly, 'A strong chain! It's the only answer.' Which didn't seem to follow.

'It was just my terrible luck, of course,' Erskine-Brown complained, 'that it should happen at my table. I mean, I'm a pretty well-known member of the Bar. Naturally I don't want my name connected with, well, a rather ridiculous incident.'

'Fellows in Chambers aren't going to like it.' Ballard was not yet with him. 'They'll say it's a restriction on their liberty. Rumpole, no doubt, will have a great deal to say about Magna Carta. But the only answer is to get a new nail-brush and chain it up. Can I have your support in taking strong measures?'

'Of course, you can, Ballard. I'll be right behind you on this one.' The creeping Claude seemed only too anxious to please. 'And in this case you're doing, I don't suppose you'll have to call the couple who actually *got* the mouse?'

'The couple?' There was a pause while Ballard searched his memory. 'The mouse was served – appalling lack of hygiene in the workplace – to a table booked by a Mr Claude Erskine-Brown and guest. Of course he'll be a vital witness.' And then the penny dropped. He stared at Claude and said firmly, '*You'll* be a vital witness.'

'But if I'm a witness of any sort, my name'll get into the papers and Philly will know I was having dinner.'

'Why on earth *shouldn't* she know you were having dinner?' Ballard was reasoning with the man. 'Most people have dinner. Nothing to be ashamed of. Get a grip on yourself, Erskine-Brown.'

'Ballard. Sam.' Claude was trying the appeal to friendship. 'You're a married man. You should understand.'

'Of course I'm married. And Marguerite and I have dinner. On a regular basis.'

'But I wasn't having dinner with Philly.' Claude explained the matter carefully. 'I was having dinner with an instructing solicitor.'

'That was your guest?'

'Yes.'

'A solicitor?'

'Of course.'

Ballard seemed to have thought the matter over carefully, but he was still puzzled when he replied, remembering his instructions. 'He apparently leapt on to a chair, held down his skirt and screamed three times!'

'Ballard! The solicitor was Tricia Benbow. You don't imagine I'd spend a hundred and something quid on feeding the face of Mr Bernard, do you?'

There was another longish pause, during which I imagined Claude in considerable suspense, and then our Head of Chambers spoke again. 'Tricia Benbow?' he asked.

'Yes.'

'Is that the one with the long blonde hair and rings?'

'That's the one.'

'And your wife knew nothing of this?'

'And must never know!' For some reason not clear to me, Claude seemed to think he'd won his case, for he now sounded grateful. 'Thank you, Ballard. Thanks awfully, Sam. I can count on you to keep my name out of this. I'll do the same for you, old boy. Any day of the week.'

'That won't be necessary.' Ballard's tone was not encouraging, although Claude said, 'No? Well, thanks, anyway.'

'It *will* be necessary, however, for you to give evidence for the Prosecution.' Soapy Sam Ballard pronounced sentence and Claude yelped, 'Have a heart, Sam!'

'Don't you "Sam" me.' Ballard was clearly in a mood to notice the decline of civilization as we know it. 'It's all part of the same thing, isn't it? Sharp practice over the nail-brush. Failure to assist the authorities in an important prosecution. You'd better prepare yourself for Court, Erskine-Brown. And to be cross-examined by Rumpole for the Defence. Do your duty! And take the consequences.'

A moment later I saw Ballard leaving for home and his wife, Marguerite, who, you will remember, once held the position of matron at the Old Bailey.* No doubt he would chatter to her of nail-brushes and barristers unwilling to tell the whole truth. I carried my bottle of plonk round to Claude's stall in order to console the fellow.

* See 'Rumpole and the Quality of Life' in *Rumpole and the Age of Miracles*, Penguin Books, 1988.

'So,' I said, 'you lost your case.'

'What a bastard!' I have never seen Claude so pale.

'You made a big mistake, old darling. It's no good appealing to the warm humanity of a fellow who believes in chaining up nail-brushes.'

So the intrusive mouse continued to play havoc with the passions of a number of people, and I prepared myself for its day in Court. I told Mr Bernard to instruct Ferdinand Isaac Gerald Newton, known in the trade as Fig Newton, a lugubrious scarecrow of a man who is, without doubt, our most effective private investigator, to keep a watchful eye on the staff of La Maison. And then I decided to call in at the establishment on my way home one evening, not only to get a few more facts from my client but because I was becoming bored with Pommeroy's ham sandwiches.

Before I left Chambers an event occurred which caused me deep satisfaction. I made for the downstairs lavatory, and although the door was open, I found it occupied by Uncle Tom who was busily engaged at the basin washing his collection of golf balls and scrubbing each one to a gleaming whiteness with a nail-brush. He had been putting each one, when cleaned, into a biscuit tin and as I entered he dropped the nail-brush in also.

'Uncle Tom!' – I recognized the article at once – 'that's the Chambers nail-brush! Soapy Sam's having kittens about it.'

'Oh, dear. Is it, really? I must have taken it without remembering. I'll leave it on the basin.'

But I persuaded him to let me have it for safe-keeping, saying I longed to see Ballard's little face light up with joy when it was restored to him.

When I arrived at La Maison the disputes seemed to have become a great deal more dramatic than even in Equity Court. The place was not yet open for dinner, but I was let in as the restaurant's legal adviser and I heard raised voices and sounds of a struggle from the kitchen. Pushing the door open, I found Jean-Pierre in the act of forcibly removing a knife from the hands of Ian, the sous chef, at whom an excited Alphonse

Pascal, his lock of black hair falling into his eyes, was shouting abuse in French. My arrival created a diversion in which both men calmed down and Jean-Pierre passed judgment on them. 'Bloody lunatics!' he said. 'Haven't they done this place enough harm already? They have to start slaughtering each other. Behave yourselves. *Soyez sages!* And what can I do for *you*, Mr Rumpole?'

'Perhaps we could have a little chat,' I suggested as the tumult died down. 'I thought I'd call in. My wife's away, you see, and I haven't done much about dinner.'

'Then what would you like?'

'Oh, anything. Just a snack.'

'Some pâté, perhaps? And a bottle of champagne?' I thought he'd never ask.

When we were seated at a table in a corner of the empty restaurant, the patron told me more about the quarrel. 'They were fighting again over Mary Skelton.'

I looked across at the desk, where the unmemorable girl was getting out her calculator and preparing for her evening's work. 'She doesn't look the type, exactly,' I suggested.

'Perhaps,' Jean-Pierre speculated, 'she has a warm heart? My wife Simone looks the type, but she's got a heart like an ice-cube.'

'Your wife. The vengeful woman?' I remembered what Mr Bernard had told me.

'Why should she be vengeful to me, Mr Rumpole? When I'm a particularly tolerant and easy-going type of individual?'

At which point a couple of middle-aged Americans, who had strayed in off the street, appeared at the door of the restaurant and asked Jean-Pierre if he were serving dinner. 'At six thirty? No! And we don't do teas, either.' He shouted across at them, in a momentary return to his old ways, 'Cretins!'

'Of course,' I told him, 'you're a very parfait, gentle cook.'

'A great artist needs admiration. He needs almost incessant praise.'

'And with Simone,' I suggested, 'the admiration flowed like cement?'

'You've got it. Had some experience of wives, have you?'

'You might say, a lifetime's experience. Do you mind?' I poured myself another glass of unwonted champagne.

'No, no, of course. And your wife doesn't understand you?'

'Oh, I'm afraid she does. That's the worrying thing about it. She blames me for being a "character".'

'They'd blame you for anything. Come to divorce, has it?'

'Not quite reached your stage, Mr O'Higgins.' I looked round the restaurant. 'So, I suppose you have to keep these tables full to pay Simone her alimony.'

'Not exactly. You see she'll own half La Maison.' That hadn't been entirely clear to me and I asked him to explain.

'When we started off, I was a young man. All I wanted to do was to get up early, go to Smithfield and Billingsgate, feel the lobsters and smell the fresh scallops, create new dishes, and dream of sauces. Simone was the one with the business sense. Well, she's French, so she insisted on us getting married in France.'

'Was that wrong?'

'Oh, no. It was absolutely right, for Simone. Because they have a damned thing there called "community of property". I had to agree to give her half of everything if we ever broke up. You know about the law, of course.'

'Well, not everything about it.' Community of property, I must confess, came as news to me. 'I always found knowing the law a bit of a handicap for a barrister.'

'Simone knew all about it. She had her beady eye on the future.' He emptied his glass and then looked at me pleadingly. 'You're going to get us out of this little trouble, aren't you, Mr Rumpole? This affair of the mouse?'

'Oh, the mouse!' I did my best to reassure him. 'The mouse seems to be the least of your worries.'

Soon Jean-Pierre had to go back to his kitchen. On his way, he stopped at the cash desk and said something to the girl, Mary. She looked up at him with, I thought, unqualified adoration. He patted her arm and went back to his sauces, having reassured her, I suppose, about the quarrel that had been going on in her honour.

I did justice to the rest of the champagne and pâté de foie and started off for home. In the restaurant entrance hall I saw the lady who minded the cloaks take a suitcase from Gaston Leblanc, who had just arrived out of breath and wearing a mackintosh. Although large, the suitcase seemed very light and he asked her to look after it.

Several evenings later I was lying on my couch in the living-room of the mansion flat, a small cigar between my fingers and a glass of Château Fleet Street on the floor beside me. I was in vacant or in pensive mood as I heard a ring at the front-door bell. I started up, afraid that the delights of *haute cuisine* had palled for Hilda, and then I remembered that She would undoubtedly have come armed with a latchkey. I approached the front door, puzzled at the sound of young and excited voices without, combined with loud music. I got the door open and found myself face to face with Liz Probert, Dave Inchcape and five or six other junior hacks, all wearing sweat-shirts with a picture of a wig and YOUNG RADICAL LAWYERS written on them. Dianne was also there in trousers and a glittery top, escorted by my clerk, Henry, wearing jeans and doing his best to appear young and swinging. The party was carrying various bottles and an article we know well down the Bailey (because it so often appears in lists of stolen property) as a ghetto blaster. It was from this contraption that the loud music emerged.

'It's a surprise party!' Mizz Liz Probert announced with considerable pride. 'We've come to cheer you up in your great loneliness.'

Nothing I could say would stem the well-meaning invasion. Within minutes the staid precincts of Froxbury Mansions were transformed into the sort of disco which is patronized by under-thirties on a package to the Costa del Sol. Bizarre drinks, such as rum and blackcurrant juice or advocaat and lemonade, were being mixed in what remained of our tumblers, supplemented by toothmugs from the bathroom. Scarves dimmed the lights, the ghetto blaster blasted ceaselessly and dancers gyrated in a self-absorbed manner, apparently oblivious of

25

each other. Only Henry and Dianne, practising a more old-fashioned ritual, clung together, almost motionless, and carried on a lively conversation with me as I stood on the outskirts of the revelry, drinking the best of the wine they had brought and trying to look tolerantly convivial.

'We heard as how Mrs Rumpole has done a bunk, sir.' Dianne looked sympathetic, to which Henry added sourly, 'Some people have all the luck!'

'Why? Where's your wife tonight, Henry?' I asked my clerk. The cross he has to bear is that his spouse has pursued an ambitious career in local government so that, whereas she is now the Mayor of Bexleyheath, he is officially her Mayoress.

'My wife's at a dinner of South London mayors in the Mansion House, Mr Rumpole. No consorts allowed, thank God!' Henry told me.

'Which is why we're both on the loose tonight. Makes you feel young again, doesn't it, Mr Rumpole?' Dianne asked me as she danced minimally.

'Well, not particularly young, as a matter of fact.' The music yawned between me and my guests as an unbridgeable generation gap. And then one of the more intense of the young lady radicals approached me, as a senior member of the Bar, to ask what the hell the Lord Chief Justice knew about being pregnant and on probation at the moment your boyfriend's arrested for dope. 'Very little, I should imagine,' I had to tell her, and then, as the telephone was bleating pathetically beneath the din, I excused myself and moved to answer it. As I went, a Y.R.L. sweatshirt whirled past me; Liz, dancing energetically, had pulled it off and was gyrating in what appeared to be an ancient string-vest and a pair of jeans.

'Rumpole!' the voice of She Who Must Be Obeyed called to me, no doubt from the banks of Duddon. 'What on earth's going on there?'

'Oh, Hilda. Is it you?'

'Of course it's me.'

'Having a good time, are you? And did Cousin Everard enjoy his sliver of whatever it was?'

'Rumpole. What's that incredible noise?'

'Noise? Is there a noise? Oh, yes. I think I do hear music. Well . . .' Here I improvised, as I thought brilliantly. 'It's a play, that's what it is, a play on television. It's all about young people, hopping about in a curious fashion.'

'Don't talk rubbish!' Hilda, as you may guess, sounded far from convinced. 'You know you never watch plays on television.'

'Not usually, I grant you,' I admitted. 'But what else have I got to do when my wife has left me?'

Much later, it seemed a lifetime later, when the party was over, I settled down to read the latest addition to my brief in the O'Higgins case. It was a report from Fig Newton, who had been keeping observation on the workers at La Maison. One afternoon he followed Gaston Leblanc, who left his home in Ruislip with a large suitcase, with which he travelled to a smart address at Egerton Crescent in Knightsbridge. This house, which had a bunch of brightly coloured balloons tied to its front door, Fig kept under surveillance for some time. A number of small children arrived, escorted by nannies, and were let in by a manservant. Later, when all the children had been received, Fig, wrapped in his Burberry with his collar turned up against the rain, was able to move so he got a clear view into the sitting-room.

What he saw interested me greatly. The children were seated on the floor watching breathlessly as Gaston Leblanc, station waiter and part-time conjuror, dressed in a black robe ornamented with stars, entertained them by slowly extricating a live and kicking rabbit from a top hat.

For the trial of Jean-Pierre O'Higgins we drew the short straw in the shape of an Old Bailey judge aptly named Gerald Graves. Judge Graves and I have never exactly hit it off. He is a pale, long-faced, unsmiling fellow who probably lives on a diet of organic bran and carrot juice. He heard Ballard open the proceedings against La Maison with a pained expression, and looked at me over his half-glasses as though I were a saucepan that hadn't been washed up properly. He was the last person in the world to laugh a case out of Court and I would have to manage that trick without him.

Soapy Sam Ballard began by describing the minor blemishes in the restaurant's kitchen. 'In this highly expensive, allegedly three-star establishment, the Environmental Health Officer discovered cracked tiles, open waste-bins and gravy stains on the ceiling.'

'The ceiling, Mr Ballard?' the Judge repeated in sepulchral tones.

'Alas, yes, my Lord. The ceiling.'

'Probably rather a tall cook,' I suggested, and was rewarded with a freezing look from the Bench.

'And there was a complete absence of nail-brushes in the kitchen handbasins.' Ballard touched on a subject dear to his heart. 'But wait, Members of the Jury, until you get to the –'

'Main course?' I suggested in another ill-received whisper and Ballard surged on '– the very heart of this most serious case. On the night of May the 18th, a common house mouse was served up at a customer's dinner table.'

'We are no doubt dealing here, Mr Ballard,' the Judge intoned solemnly, 'with a defunct mouse?'

'Again, alas, no, my lord. The mouse in question was alive.'

'And kicking,' I muttered. Staring vaguely round the Court, my eye lit on the public gallery where I saw Mary Skelton, the quiet restaurant clerk, watching the proceedings attentively.

'Members of the Jury' – Ballard had reached his peroration – 'need one ask if a kitchen is in breach of the Food and Hygiene Regulations if it serves up a living mouse? As proprietor of the restaurant, Mr O'Higgins is, say the Prosecution, absolutely responsible. Whomsoever in his employ he seeks to blame, Members of the Jury, he must take the consequences. I will now call my first witness.'

'Who's that pompous imbecile?' Jean-Pierre O'Higgins was adding his two pennyworth, but I told him he wasn't in his restaurant now and to leave the insults to me. I was watching a fearful and embarrassed Claude Erskine-Brown climb into the witness-box and take the oath as though it were the last rites. When asked to give his full names he appealed to the Judge.

'My Lord. May I write them down? There may be some

publicity about this case.' He looked nervously at the assembled reporters.

'Aren't you a Member of the Bar?' Judge Graves squinted at the witness over his half-glasses.

'Well, yes, my Lord,' Claude admitted reluctantly.

'That's nothing to be ashamed of – in most cases.' At which the Judge aimed a look of distaste in my direction and then turned back to the witness. 'I think you'd better tell the Jury who you are, in the usual way.'

'Claude . . .' The unfortunate fellow tried a husky whisper, only to get a testy 'Oh, do speak up!' from his Lordship. Whereupon, turning up the volume a couple of notches, the witness answered, 'Claude Leonard Erskine-Brown.' I hadn't know about the Leonard.

'On May the 18th were you dining at La Maison Jean-Pierre?' Ballard began his examination.

'Well, yes. Yes. I did just drop in.'

'For dinner?'

'Yes,' Claude had to admit.

'In the company of a young lady named Patricia Benbow?'

'Well. That is . . . Er . . . er.'

'Mr Erskine-Brown' – Judge Graves had no sympathy with this sudden speech impediment – 'it seems a fairly simple question to answer, even for a Member of the Bar.'

'I was in Miss Benbow's company, my Lord,' Claude answered in despair.

'And when the main course was served were the plates covered?'

'Yes. They were.'

'And when the covers were lifted what happened?'

Into the expectant silence, Erskine-Brown said in a still, small voice, 'A mouse ran out.'

'Oh, do speak up!' Graves was running out of patience with the witness, who almost shouted back, 'A mouse ran out, my Lord!'

At this point Ballard said, 'Thank you, Mr Erskine-Brown,' and sat down, no doubt confident that the case was in the bag – or perhaps the trap. Then I rose to cross-examine.

'Mr Claude Leonard Erskine-Brown,' I weighed in, 'is Miss Benbow a solicitor?'

'Well. Yes . . .' Claude looked at me sadly, as though wanting to say, *Et tu*, Rumpole?

'And is your wife a well-known and highly regarded Queen's Counsel?'

Graves's face lit up at the mention of our delightful Portia. 'Mrs Erskine-Brown has sat here as a Recorder, Members of the Jury.' He smiled sickeningly at the twelve honest citizens.

'I'm obliged to your Lordship.' I bowed slightly and turned back to the witness. 'And is Miss Benbow instructed in an important forthcoming case, that is the Balham Mini-Cab Murder, in which she is intending to brief Mrs Erskine-Brown, Q.C.?'

'Is – is she?' Never quick off the mark, Claude didn't yet realize that help was at hand.

'And were you taking her out to dinner so you might discuss the Defence in that case, your wife being unfortunately detained in Cardiff?' I hoped that made my good intentions clear, even to a barrister.

'Was I?' Erskine-Brown was still not with me.

'Well, weren't you?' I was losing patience with the fellow.

'Oh, yes.' At last the penny dropped. 'Of course I was! I do remember now. Naturally. And I did it all to help Philly. To help my wife. Is that what you mean?' He ended up looking at me anxiously.

'Exactly.'

'Thank you, Mr Rumpole. Thank you very much.' Erskine-Brown's gratitude was pathetic. But the Judge couldn't wait to get on to the exciting bits. 'Mr Rumpole,' he boomed mournfully, 'when are we coming to the mouse?'

'Oh, yes. I'm grateful to your Lordship for reminding me. Well. What sort of animal was it?'

'Oh, a very small mouse indeed.' Claude was now desperately anxious to help me. 'Hardly noticeable.'

'A very small mouse and hardly noticeable,' Graves repeated as he wrote it down and then raised his eyebrows, as though, when it came to mice, smallness was no excuse.

'And the first you saw of it was when it emerged from under a silver dish-cover? You couldn't swear it got there in the kitchen?'

'No, I couldn't.' Erskine-Brown was still eager to cooperate.

'Or if it was inserted in the dining-room by someone with access to the serving-table?'

'Oh, no, Mr Rumpole. You're perfectly right. Of course it might have been!' The witness's cooperation was almost embarrassing, so the Judge chipped in with 'I take it you're not suggesting that this creature appeared from a dish of duck breasts by some sort of miracle, are you, Mr Rumpole?'

'Not a miracle, my Lord. Perhaps a trick.'

'Isn't Mr Ballard perfectly right?' Graves, as was his wont, had joined the prosecution team. 'For the purposes of this offence it doesn't matter *how* it got there. A properly run restaurant should not serve up a mouse for dinner! The thing speaks for itself.'

'A talking mouse, my Lord? What an interesting conception!' I got a loud laugh from my client and even the Jury joined in with a few friendly titters. I also got, of course, a stern rebuke from the Bench. 'Mr Rumpole!' – his Lordship's seriousness was particularly deadly – 'this is not a place of entertainment! You would do well to remember that this is a most serious case from your client's point of view. And I'm sure the Jury will wish to give it the most weighty consideration. We will continue with it after luncheon. Shall we say, five past two, Members of the Jury?'

Mr Bernard and I went down to the pub, and after a light snack of shepherd's pie, washed down with a pint or two of Guinness, we hurried back into the Palais de Justice and there I found what I had hoped for. Mary Skelton was sitting quietly outside the Court, waiting for the proceedings to resume. I lit a small cigar and took a seat with my instructing solicitor not far away from the girl. I raised my voice a little and said, 'You know what's always struck me about this case, Mr Bernard? There's no evidence of droppings or signs of mice in the kitchen. So someone put the mouse under the cover deliberately. Someone who wanted to ruin La Maison's business.'

'Mrs O'Higgins?' Bernard suggested.

'Certainly not! She'd want the place to be as prosperous as possible because she owned half of it. The guilty party is someone who wanted Simone to get nothing but half a failed eatery with a ruined reputation. So what did this someone do?'

'You tell me, Mr Rumpole.' Mr Bernard was an excellent straight man.

'Oh, broke a lot of little rules. Took away the nail-brushes and the lids of the tidy-bins. But a sensation was needed, something that'd hit the headlines. Luckily this someone knew a waiter who had a talent for sleight of hand and a spare-time job producing livestock out of hats.'

'Gaston Leblanc?' Bernard was with me.

'Exactly! He got the animal under the lid and gave it to Alphonse to present to the unfortunate Miss Tricia Benbow. Consequence: ruin for the restaurant and a rotten investment for the vengeful Simone. No doubt someone paid Gaston well to do it.'

I was silent then. I didn't look at the waiting girl, but I was sure she was looking at me. And then Bernard asked, 'Just who are we talking about, Mr Rumpole?'

'Well, now. Who had the best possible reason for hating Simone, and wanting her to get away with as little as possible?'

'Who?'

'Who but our client?' I told him. 'The great *maître de cuisine*, Jean-Pierre O'Higgins himself.'

'No!' I had never heard Mary Skelton speaking before. Her voice was clear and determined, with a slight North Country accent. 'Excuse me.' I turned to look at her as she stood up and came over to us. 'No, it's not true. Jean-Pierre knew nothing about it. It was my idea entirely. Why did *she* deserve to get anything out of us?'

I stood up, looked at my watch, and put on the wig that had been resting on the seat beside me. 'Well, back to Court. Mr Bernard, take a statement from the lady, why don't you? We'll call her as a witness.'

★

Whilst these events were going on down the Bailey, another kind of drama was being enacted in Froxbury Mansions. She Who Must Be Obeyed had returned from her trip with cousin Everard, put on the kettle and surveyed the general disorder left by my surprise party with deep disapproval. In the sitting-room she fanned away the bar-room smell, drew the curtains, opened the windows and clicked her tongue at the sight of half-empty glasses and lipstick-stained fag ends. Then she noticed something white nestling under the sofa, pulled it out and saw that it was a Young Radical Lawyers sweatshirt, redolent of Mizz Liz Probert's understated yet feminine perfume.

Later in the day, when I was still on my hind legs performing before Mr Justice Graves and the Jury, Liz Probert called at the mansion flat to collect the missing garment. Hilda had met Liz at occasional Chambers parties but when she opened the door she was, I'm sure, stony-faced, and remained so as she led Mizz Probert into the sitting-room and restored to her the sweatshirt which the Young Radical Lawyer admitted she had taken off and left behind the night before. I have done my best to reconstruct the following dialogue, from the accounts given to me by the principal performers. I can't vouch for its total accuracy, but this is the gist, the meat you understand. It began when Liz explained she had taken the sweatshirt off because she was dancing and it was quite hot.

'You were *dancing* with Rumpole?' Hilda was outraged. 'I knew he was up to something. As soon as my back was turned. I heard all that going on when I telephoned. Rocking and rolling all over the place. At his age!'

'Mrs Rumpole. Hilda . . .' Liz began to protest but only provoked a brisk 'Oh, please. Don't you Hilda me! Young Radical Lawyers, I suppose that means you're free and easy with other people's husbands!' At which point I regret to report that Liz Probert could scarcely contain her laughter and asked, 'You don't think I fancy Rumpole, do you?'

'I don't know why not.' Hilda has her moments of loyalty. 'Rumpole's a "character". Some people like that sort of thing.'

'Hilda. Look, please listen,' and Liz began to explain. 'Dave

Inchcape and I and a whole lot of us came to give Rumpole a party. To cheer him up. Because he was lonely. He was missing you so terribly.'

'He was *what*?' She Who Must could scarcely believe her ears, Liz told me. 'Missing you,' the young radical repeated. 'I saw him at breakfast. He looked so sad. "She's left me," he said, "and gone off with her cousin Everard."'

'Rumpole said that?' Hilda no longer sounded displeased.

'And he seemed absolutely broken-hearted. He saw nothing ahead, I'm sure, but a lonely old age stretching out in front of him. Anyone could tell how much he cared about you. Dave noticed it as well. Please can I have my shirt back now?'

'Of course.' Hilda was now treating the girl as though she were the prodigal grandchild or some such thing. 'But, Liz . . .'

'What, Hilda?'

'Wouldn't you like me to put it through the wash for you before you take it home?'

Back in the Ludgate Circus verdict factory, Mary Skelton gave evidence along the lines I have already indicated and the time came for me to make my final speech. As I reached the last stretch I felt I was making some progress. No one in the jury-box was asleep, or suffering from terminal bronchitis, and a few of them looked distinctly sympathetic. The same couldn't be said, however, of the scorpion on the Bench.

'Ladies and gentlemen of the Jury.' I gave it to them straight. 'Miss Mary Skelton, the cashier, was in love. She was in love with her boss, that larger-than-life cook and "character", Jean-Pierre O'Higgins. People do many strange things for love. They commit suicide or leave home or pine away sometimes. It was for love that Miss Mary Skelton caused a mouse to be served up in La Maison Jean-Pierre, after she had paid the station waiter liberally for performing the trick. She it was who wanted to ruin the business, so that my client's vengeful wife should get absolutely nothing out of it.'

'Mr Rumpole!' His Lordship was unable to contain his fury.

'And my client knew nothing whatever of this dire plot. He was entirely innocent.' I didn't want to let Graves interrupt my flow, but he came in at increased volume, 'Mr Rumpole! If a restaurant serves unhygienic food, the proprietor is guilty. In law it doesn't matter in the least how it got there. Ignorance by your client is no excuse. I presume you have some rudimentary knowledge of the law, Mr Rumpole?'

I wasn't going to tangle with Graves on legal matters. Instead I confined my remarks to the more reasonable Jury, ignoring the Judge. 'You're not concerned with the law, Members of the Jury,' I told them, 'you are concerned with justice!'

'That is a quite outrageous thing to say! On the admitted facts of this case, Mr O'Higgins is clearly guilty!' His Honour Judge Graves had decided but the honest twelve would have to return the verdict and I spoke to them. 'A British judge has no power to direct a British jury to find a defendant guilty! I know that much at least.'

'I shall tell the Jury that he is guilty in law, I warn you.' Graves's warning was in vain. I carried on regardless.

'His Lordship may tell you that to his heart's content. As a great Lord Chief Justice of England, a judge superior in rank to any in this Court, once said, "It is the duty of the Judge to tell you as a jury what to do, but you have the power to do exactly as you like." And what you do, Members of the Jury, is a matter entirely between God and your own consciences. Can you really find it in your consciences to condemn a man to ruin for a crime he didn't commit?' I looked straight at them. 'Can any of you? Can you?' I gripped the desk in front of me, apparently exhausted. 'You are the only judges of the facts in this case, Members of the Jury. My task is done. The future career of Jean-Pierre O'Higgins is in your hands, and in your hands alone.' And then I sat down, clearly deeply moved.

At last it was over. As we came out of the doors of the Court, Jean-Pierre O'Higgins embraced me in a bear hug and was, I greatly feared, about to kiss me on both cheeks. Ballard gave me a look of pale disapproval. Clearly he thought I had broken all the rules by asking the Jury to ignore the Judge. Then a cheerful and rejuvenated Claude came bouncing up bleating, 'Rumpole, you were brilliant!'

'Oh yes,' I told him. 'I've still got a win or two in me yet.'

'Brilliant to get me off. All that nonsense about a brief for Philly.'

'Not nonsense, Leonard. I mean, Claude. I telephoned the fair Tricia and she's sending your wife the Balham Mini-Cab Murder. Are you suggesting that Rumpole would deceive the Court?'

'Oh' – he was interested to know – 'am I getting a brief too?'

'She said nothing of that.'

'All the same, Rumpole' – he concealed his disappointment – 'thank you very much for getting me out of a scrape.'

'Say no more. My life is devoted to helping the criminal classes.'

As I left him and went upstairs to slip out of the fancy dress, I had one more task to perform. I walked past my locker and went on into the silks' dressing-room, where a very old Q.C. was seated in the shadows snoozing over the *Daily Telegraph*. I had seen Ballard downstairs, discussing the hopelessness of an appeal with his solicitor, and it was the work of a minute to find his locker, feel in his jacket pocket and haul a large purse out of it. Making sure that the sleeping silk hadn't spotted me, I opened the purse, slipped in the nail-brush I had rescued from Uncle Tom's tin of golf balls, restored it to the pocket and made my escape undetected.

I was ambling back up Fleet Street when I heard the brisk step of Ballard behind me. He drew up alongside and returned to his favourite topic. 'There's nothing for it, Rumpole,' he said, 'I shall chain the next one up.'

'The next what?'

'The next nail-brush.'

'Isn't that a bit extreme?'

'If fellows, and ladies, in Chambers can't be trusted,' Ballard said severely, 'I am left with absolutely no alternative. I hate to have to do it, but Henry is being sent out for a chain tomorrow.'

We had reached the newspaper stand at the entrance to the Temple and I loitered there. 'Lend us 20p for the *Evening Standard*, Bollard. There might be another restaurant in trouble.'

'Why are you never provided with money?' Ballard thought it typical of my fecklessness. 'Oh, all right.' And then he put his hand in his pocket and pulled out the purse. Opening it, he was amazed to find his ten pees nestling under an ancient nail-brush. 'Our old nail-brush!' The reunion was quaintly moving. 'I'd recognize it anywhere. How on earth did it get in there?'

'Evidence gets in everywhere, old darling,' I told him. 'Just like mice.'

When I got home and unlocked the front door, I was greeted with the familiar cry of 'Is that you, Rumpole?'

'No,' I shouted back, 'it's not me. I'll be along later.'

'Come into the sitting-room and stop talking rubbish.'

I did as I was told and found the room swept and polished and that She, who was looking unnaturally cheerful, had bought flowers.

'Cousin Everard around, is he?' I felt, apprehensively, that the floral tributes were probably for him.

'He had to go back to Saskatoon. One of his clients got charged with fraud, apparently.' And then Hilda asked, unexpectedly, 'You knew I'd be back, didn't you, Rumpole?'

'Well, I *had* hoped . . .' I assured her.

'It seems you almost gave up hoping. You couldn't get along without me, could you?'

'Well, I had a bit of a stab at it,' I said in all honesty.

'No need for you to be brave any more. I'm back now. That nice Miss Liz Probert was saying you missed me terribly.'

'Oh, of course. Yes. Yes, I missed you.' And I added as quietly as possible, 'Life without a boss . . .'

'What did you say?'

'You were a great loss.'

'And Liz says you were dreadfully lonely. I was glad to hear that, Rumpole. You don't usually say much about your feelings.'

'Words don't come easily to me, Hilda,' I told her with transparent dishonesty.

'Now you're so happy to see me back, Rumpole, why don't you take me out for a little celebration? I seem to have got used to dining *à la carte*.'

Of course I agreed. I knew somewhere where we could get it on the house. So we ended up at a table for two in La Maison and discussed Hilda's absent relative as Alphonse made his way towards us with two covered dishes.

'The trouble with Cousin Everard,' Hilda confided in me, 'is he's not a "character".'

'Bit on the bland side?' I inquired politely.

'It seems that unless you're with a "character", life can get a little tedious at times,' Hilda admitted.

The silver domes were put in front of us, Alphonse called out, '*Un, deux, trois!*' and they were lifted to reveal what I had no difficulty in ordering that night: steak and kidney pud. Mashed spuds were brought to us on the side.

'Perhaps that's why I need you, Rumpole.' She Who Must Be Obeyed was in a philosophic mood that night. 'Because you're a "character". And you need me to tell you off for being one.'

Distinctly odd, I thought, are the reasons why people need each other. I looked towards the cashier's desk, where Jean-Pierre had his arm round the girl I had found so unmemorable. I raised a glass of the champagne he had brought us and drank to their very good health.

Rumpole and the
Summer of Discontent

Change and decay in all around I see. Our present masters seem to have an irresistible urge, whenever they find something that works moderately well, to tinker with it, tear it apart and construct something worse, usually on the grounds that it may offer more 'consumer choice'. Now, many things may be said of the British legal system, but it seems odd to me that it should be run as a supermarket, round which you trundle a wire wheelbarrow and pick up a frozen packet of the burden of proof or a jumbo-sized prison sentence, with 10p off for good behaviour. By and large, I have always thought there is little wrong with the system and all the criticism should be levelled at the somewhat strange human beings who get to run it, such as the mad Judge Bullingham, the sepulchral Judge Graves or Soapy Sam Ballard, Q.C., the less than brilliant advocate whom an incalculable fate has placed in charge of our Chambers. However, in the summer of which I speak, all sorts of plans were afoot, in Equity Court as well as in Parliament, to streamline the system, to give solicitors the doubtful privilege of appearing before Judge Graves, to abolish all distinctions between barristers and solicitors and to elevate solicitors to the Bench. So the Old Bailey hack, skilled in the art of advocacy, which is his daily bread, would be in danger of extinction. Well, the best that can be said of such plans is that they do something to reconcile you to death.

In that same summer, strikes seemed to spread like the measles. One day the tubes didn't run, on another the postman didn't deliver (to my great relief, as I was denied the pleasure of those sinister brown envelopes from Her Majesty). In due course the infection spread to the legal profession and even into the matrimonial home; but I mustn't anticipate the events which began with that more or less simple case of manslaughter, which I think of as the Luxie-Chara killing, and which turned out to be one of my more interesting and dramatic encounters with homicide.

The scene of the crime was a large garage, yard and adjacent office premises in South London. A huge notice over the open gateway read: ERNIE ELVER'S LUXIE-CHARAS. TOILETS. DOUBLE-GLAZING. VIDEOS. HOSTESS-SERVED SNACKS. SCHOOLS, FAN CLUBS AND SENIOR CITIZENS' OUTINGS SPECIALLY CATERED FOR. At the window of an upstairs office Ernie Elver, the owner of the business, a large, soft-eyed man with a moustache, a silk suit and a heavy gold ring, was squinting down the sights of a video-camera, recording, for posterity and for ultimate use in the Old Bailey, what had become a common scene that summer in England.

A small crowd of about twenty pickets was guarding the gates. It consisted mainly of middle-aged coach drivers, but there were a number of young men among them, and a particular youth in a red anorak was joining vociferously in the protest. The object of the picket was to stop the coaches, driven by non-union men, from leaving the garage. The officer in command of the posse was a tall, gaunt fellow, named Ben, but known affectionately as 'Basher', Baker, a prominent shop steward of the National Union of Charabanc Drivers and Operators (N.U.C.D.O.). The incident began when a coach was driven out of the garage and towards the gateway to be met with cries from the pickets of 'Bash the blacklegs!', 'Kill the cowboy bastards!', 'Scrag the scabs!' and suchlike terms of endearment.

As the coach reached the gateway, Ben Baker stood in front of it with an arm upraised, saying, 'Halt, brother. I wish to reason politely with you as to why you should not cross this picket line in an officially recognized dispute.' This invitation to a debate had no effect whatsoever on the driver. The coach surged forward. Ben stood his ground until the Luxie-Vehicle was almost upon him, then he stepped aside with the unexpected agility of a bull-fighter and was seen to stoop suddenly, perhaps as though picking something up from the ground. Seconds later, the windscreen of the coach was shattered by a hard object, flung with considerable force. The driver was seen twisting the wheel and he then crashed into the gatepost, where the coach came to a full stop. When the door was pulled open, the driver was found to have been cut on the head and neck by flying glass. An artery had been severed and within minutes he was dead.

The police car arrived in a surprisingly short time. Although, when it stopped by the crashed coach, the band of pickets had diminished and the younger men had scarpered. As the dead coach driver was removed by the ambulance men, who had come on the scene, Basher Baker was standing near the body, singing 'The Red Flag':

> 'Then raise the scarlet standard high!
> Within its shade we'll live or die.
> Tho' cowards flinch and traitors sneer,
> We'll keep the red flag flying here.'

He was immediately arrested and later charged with the manslaughter of the coach driver. In due course, and thanks to our old legal system still being in operation, Basher was able to obtain the services of the most wily and experienced member of the Criminal Bar.

Dramatic events were also taking place in our Chambers in Equity Court. Work was a touch thin on the ground at that time and I used to drop into Chambers to do the crossword and as a temporary refuge from domestic bliss. I arrived a little late one morning to be told by Henry, our clerk, that a Chambers meeting was taking place and that they were waiting for me. Accordingly, I went up to Soapy Sam Ballard's room to find that some sort of boardroom table had been installed. Our Head of Chambers was seated at the top of it with Claude Erskine-Brown, now apparently restored to favour, at his elbow. Among those present were Uncle Tom, our oldest inhabitant; Mizz Liz Probert, the well-known young radical barristerette; her friend Dave Inchcape; the greyish practitioner Hoskins and one or two others. 'Not another Chambers meeting?' I asked with some displeasure as I joined the group.

'In the new age of efficiency at the Bar,' Ballard told me, 'it might be more appropriate to call it a "board meeting".'

'Quite right.' I took a seat next to Uncle Tom. 'I must say, I feel bored to tears already.'

'I'm afraid yours is a voice making jokes in the wilderness.' Claude, back at the top, was at his most pompous. 'We at Equity Court decided, while you were away doing your stint of minor crime in the North of England . . .'

'It was gross indecency. In Leeds.' It was also my last serious case and it seemed a long time ago.

'We have decided to put our full weight behind the Government's plans to drag the English Bar into the twentieth century.' Erskine-Brown spoke as though he were making a statement in the House, and was almost overcome by the gravity of the occasion.

'There was a man called Whympering in Chambers in Fountain Court,' Uncle Tom reminded us. '*He* told them he was going to drag the Bar into the twentieth century. So he bought a new automatic coffee machine instead of the old kettle they used in the briefs cupboard . . .'

'Please, Uncle Tom!' Ballard's mind was clearly on higher things than electric kettles. 'We have decided that, to give the consumer a real service, we are going to run Equity Court on strictly business lines. You may look on me as Chairman of the Board. Claude Erskine-Brown is Managing Director. He will be speaking to our new ideas on possible partnership with solicitors.'

'And how will your new ideas be answering him back?' I inquired. 'Rudely, I hope!'

'The Office Italiano.' Uncle Tom was still remembering things past. 'That was what the machine was called. It was meant to brew up the sort of inky black stuff you used to get at foreign railway stations.'

'We're going to start by working proper business hours.' Erskine-Brown began to outline a bleak future. 'Nine to six and no more than an hour for luncheon! And there'll be a simple form for you to fill in each week. So we can monitor each member's productivity.'

'How do we monitor your productivity, Claude?' I asked, purely for information. 'By the number of years in chokey you manage to achieve for your unfortunate clients?'

'The up-to-date Office Italiano machine exploded, destroying a number of original documents, including three wills!' Uncle Tom was determined we should hear the end of his story. 'There was a most terrible stink about it. Poor old Whympering was sued for negligence.'

'We're aiming for a more streamlined, slimmed-down operation here at Equity Court.' Claude ignored the interruption and then tried, unsuccessfully, to be witty. 'Do you think *you* could manage a slimmed-down operation, Rumpole?'

'Very amusing, Claude. But do try to remember, *I* tell the jokes at Chambers meetings.'

'I hope, in the future, we can get through our business in an atmosphere of quiet efficiency,' Soapy Sam Ballard rebuked us, 'without too many jokes.'

'No jokes at all, if you have anything to do with it, Bollard.' I wasn't to be put down, but then neither was Uncle Tom. 'He had to leave the Bar,' he told us, 'and take up chicken farming in Norfolk.'

'Who had to leave the Bar?' Hoskins, as usual, was a few lengths behind.

'This fellow Whympering who introduced the new coffee machine. They went back to the old kettle on the gas ring. Far more satisfactory.'

'I think I went into the law because I wanted to be a barrister.' This was from young Inchcape, who earned my immediate approval. 'I don't want an office job, quite honestly.'

'Times change, Inchcape,' Ballard told him. 'We've got to change with them. Now, to get back to Claude's paper.'

Hoskins, however, was troubled. 'I'm not sure we want solicitors joining us,' he said. 'Do we need the competition? I speak as a man who has four daughters to bring up and jolly well needs every brief he can get hold of.'

'I suppose, Hoskins, it's just possible that some solicitors have got daughters too.' It was one of Ballard's better lines but Mizz Liz Probert, who had been frowning thoughtfully, piped up, 'If we're making these changes . . .'

'Oh, we are, Probert,' Ballard told her firmly. 'The Lord Chancellor expects it of us. Very definitely.'

'Carry on, Elizabeth. We'd like to hear your contribution. Don't be shy.' Claude smiled at her in the sickly and yearning manner he reserves for young ladies.

'Then why don't we become a really *radical* Chambers?' Liz suggested, and this triggered off more memories from Uncle Tom. 'This fellow Whympering was a bit of a radical. Wore coloured socks, from what I can remember.'

'I mean, why don't we concentrate on civil liberties?' Liz's intervention was clearly going down like a lead balloon at the board meeting. 'Stop the Government using the Courts for another spot of union-bashing. My Dad knows a union leader who's been arrested. That's just the sort of case . . .'

'Defending trades unions?' Ballard looked pained. 'I don't think that's quite the sort of image we want to give Equity Court.'

'I'm afraid I agree.' Claude was soaping up to Sam Ballard. 'Arguing cases for the Amalgamated Sausage-Skin Operatives, or whatever they are. Not quite the name of the game at this particular moment in history.'

'Oh, really, Claude! You're a barrister, aren't you? You belong to the oldest trade union of the lot,' Liz gave it to him straight, 'cram full of restrictive practices.'

'Well, really, Elizabeth! Isn't that just a little bit hard on a fellow?' Erskine-Brown smiled at the young radical with all his charm, but I applauded her aim. 'Got you there, old darling!' I told him. 'Mizz Liz Probert has scored a direct hit. Below the water-line!'

That evening, when I made my duty call at Pommeroy's Wine Bar for a glass of Château Fleet Street, my alcohol level having sunk to a dangerous low, I came upon our clerk sitting alone at the bar and looking extremely doleful. 'Why so pale and wan, fond Henry?' I asked politely, and I must say his answer surprised me. 'To be quite honest with you, Mr Rumpole, I am seriously considering industrial action.' At which point I advised him to consider another drink instead and instructed Jack Pommeroy to put a mammoth-sized Dubonnet and bitter lemon, Henry's favourite refreshment, on my slate. At this, my clerk paid me an unusual tribute, 'You're a generous man, Mr Rumpole.'

'Think nothing of it, Henry.'

'If only there were other gentlemen in Chambers as generous as you, Mr R.'

'Meaning, Henry?'

'Meaning Mr Erskine-Brown.'

'To name but a few?'

'Ah, there, Mr Rumpole. You've put your finger on it. As is your way, sir. As is your invariable way.' I was quite overcome by my clerk's tribute and I tended to agree with his general conclusions, 'Old Claude was behind the door when they handed out generosity.'

'It's not that, sir. It's his business plan. To slim down Chambers, Mr Rumpole.' At which, my unhappy clerk lowered his nose towards the large Dubonnet.

'Never trust anyone who wants to slim down anything, Henry.' I raised my glass in a general salutation. 'God rot all slimmers!'

'He's suggesting taking me off my percentage, sir. And putting me on wages! He says a clerk should be a constant figure on their new balance sheets. Should I withdraw my labour?'

'Industrial action by barristers' clerks?' I was doubtful. 'It sounds a bit like a strike by poets or pavement artists. Hardly going to bring the country to its knees.'

'Too true, Mr Rumpole. Too very true. So I'd be grateful of your opinion.'

'My opinion, Henry, is this. You and I are the last of the freelancers.' I came out with a speech I had been polishing for some time. 'We're the knight errants of the law, old darling. We rode the world with our swords rusty and our armour

45

squeaking. We did battle with the fire-breathing dragons on the Bench and rescued a few none too innocent damsels in distress. We don't fit anyone's business plan or keep office hours or meet productivity targets. We can't offer the consumer any choice but freedom or chokey. It may well be, Henry, that our day is over.'

'Over, Mr Rumpole?'

' "From too much love of living." ' I gave him a choice bit of Swinburne at his most melodious:

> 'From hope and fear set free,
> We thank with brief thanksgiving
> Whatever gods may be
> That no man lives forever,
> That dead men rise up never;
> That even the weariest river
> Winds somewhere safe to sea . . .'

'There now, does that cheer you up, Henry?'

'Not very much, sir. If I have to be extremely honest.'

He had, however, perked up considerably about three hours, and numerous large reds and Dubonnets, later, when we filtered out into Fleet Street. I was still in a moderately melancholy mood, however, and lamenting life passing, as I gave my clerk, and the rest of the bus queue, my version of Walter Savage Landor, which went, so far as I can remember, as follows:

> 'I strove with everybody that was worth my strife;
> I loved the Bailey and the Uxbridge Court;
> I warmed both hands before the fire of life;
> It sinks, and you and I are off, old sport.'

As the bus crawled towards Gloucester Road, I was conscious that it was somewhat later than usual. Accordingly, as soon as I let myself into the mansion flat, I called out, as cheerfully as possible, 'Hilda! Hilda!' I repeated the cry as I searched through the sitting-room, the bedroom and finally entered the kitchen. This room was in an orderly condition and showed no signs of anyone being about to prepare anything like dinner.

As I surveyed this discouraging scene, I heard the front door open and my wife joined me. Something in her manner suggested that the welcome was unlikely to be warm. She asked me what I was doing and I said I was looking for the note.

'Which note?'

'The one that says "Your stew's in the oven".'

'There isn't one.'

'Why not?'

'Because there isn't any stew in the oven.'

'Chops, then. Actually, I'd prefer chops.'

'There aren't any chops in the oven either.'

At this point I opened the oven door and found that it was, as she had predicted, empty. All the same I was determined not to make trouble. 'Well, if you'd like to run something up, I don't really mind what it is,' I told her. Her answer, I have to confess, astonished me. 'Rumpole, I'm not going to run anything up. I waited for you until eight o'clock. Then I went out for a bridge lesson with Marigold Featherstone.'

'I'm sorry. There was a problem in Chambers,' I explained. 'I had to commiserate with Henry.'

'Oh, I expect you did.' I'm afraid I detected a note of cynicism in Hilda's voice. 'And I suppose that meant carousing with him too.'

'I had to carouse a bit,' I explained, 'in order to commiserate.'

'Daddy would have drawn the line at carousing with his clerk.'

'Your Daddy wasn't much of one for carousing with anyone, was he?'

'Let's hope you drew the line at singing. This time.'*

'No, of course we didn't sing. Things have got past singing. Although I did recite a bit of poetry. Look, Hilda. You don't feel like turning your hand to a little cookery?'

'No, Rumpole. I'm finished with cooking for you, when you don't come home until all hours. I'm sorry, this is the end of the line.'

* See 'Rumpole and the Barrow Boy' in *Rumpole and the Age of Miracles*, Penguin Books, 1988.

'You're not leaving home?' I did my best to exclude any note of eager anticipation from my voice.

'No, Rumpole. I am not leaving home. I am taking industrial action. Withdrawing my labour!'

'Hilda! Not you too?' I looked at her in astonishment. I had not yet seen She Who Must Be Obeyed in the role of a shop steward.

'It's not what you know, but who you know that matters', as my learned friend Claude Erskine-Brown is fond of saying, although the fact that he was so well acquainted with Miss Tricia Benbow, the fair instructing solicitor, got him into quite a bit of trouble lately. I knew Mizz Liz Probert pretty well, and she knew her father, Red Ron Probert, the much-feared and derided Labour Councillor, even better. Red Ron had lots of lines out to members of the trades union movement, including that well-known libertarian Ben Basher Baker of N.U.C.D.O., and this chain of friendship landed me and Liz Probert briefs for the Defence in the Luxie-Chara case. Accordingly, we made a tryst with the client and met in the interview room at Brixton, where Liz, Mr Bernard, our solicitor, and I sat around the Basher hoping to hear something to our, and his, advantage. Our client was the sort of man who always seems to be suffering from a deep sense of injustice. His beaky nose and tuft of unbrushed, receding hair, combined with a paunch and long, thin legs, gave him the appearance of a discontented heron. 'Brother Rumpole, Sister Probert, the brother from the solicitors' office.' He started off, as though he were addressing the strike committee, 'Comrades and brothers.'

'You make it sound like a case in the Family Division,' I told him.

'Brother Rumpole' – Ben looked at me suspiciously – 'I was assured you was taking on this case as an expression of your solidarity with the workers' struggle and the right to withdraw labour.'

'Let's say I'm doing it as an expression of *my* right to do cases that don't bore me to extinction,' I told him. 'And above all, of course, to irritate Brother Bollard.'

'Who's Bollard?'

'No one of the slightest importance. Don't worry your pretty head about him, my old darling.' And then I started to cross-examine the client quite energetically. 'Now let me put the case against you, Mr Baker. Manslaughter!'

'Me kill someone? That's a joke, that is.' The Basher gave us a hollow laugh.

'"Manslaughter in jest; no offence i' the world?" There's evidence that as the unfortunate coach driver, now deceased, was being carried to the ambulance, you were heard intoning some ditty about the people's flag being deepest red.'

'"The Internationale", Brother,' the client instructed me. 'We sings it at social events. It's just like "Auld Lang Syne".'

'Or "Somewhere over the Rainbow"?' I suggested, and then went back to the attack. 'At one stage of the negotiations you told your employer, one Ernest Elver . . .'

'Ernie the Eel, we call him. He's that slippery.' Ben Baker's intervention was not encouraging.

'You told Elver that if your demands were not met, it might well lead to death?'

'The patience of my executive committee was exhausted.' His answer sounded like a statement on the six o'clock news. 'Elver was employing non-union cowboys to drive kids on outings. They didn't know the road and they didn't know the vehicles. There was going to be an accident sooner or later.'

'Is that what you meant?' I wasn't convinced.

'I swear to God!'

'Are you a religious man, Mr Baker?'

'No. Of course, no. Load of codswallop.'

This fellow was clearly going to be a walkover for prosecuting counsel, so I warned him, 'Then try and be careful how you give your evidence. In this industrial dispute, I suggest you behaved with total disregard for the law.'

'We never!'

'You were on a picket line with more than six people.'

'That's not a law. That's a code of practice.'

A little knowledge of the law is a dangerous thing, especially for clients. I warned him again, 'Please, Mr Basher . . . Mr

49

Baker. Let's leave such niceties to Mizz Probert. She has the legal textbooks. Neither you nor I have got time to read them. Do you deny you were with more than six people?'

'Some other brothers turned up. To give us extra support, yes.'

'Brothers from your place of work?'

'Not necessarily.'

'Or brothers you'd never seen in your life before?'

'Some of them was. Yes. We needs all the help we can get.'

'Even illegal help?'

'I . . . I suppose so.'

'Even the help of a brick chucked through the window of a moving charabanc?' I was doing it better than anyone we were likely to have prosecuting us, but Basher came back at me with 'I never did that. I swear it.'

'A witness named Jebb was on the picket line. He says he saw you throw it.'

'Then he's a bloody liar.'

'Not a brother, eh? Possibly a more distant relation.' I sifted through my brief and found the forensic evidence. 'Down at the local nick you were examined forensically . . .'

'They took a liberty!' I had clearly touched the button marked 'civil rights', but I went on regardless, 'Distinct traces of brick dust were found on your shirt, your trousers and hands.'

'I'd been doing building in my back garden, hadn't I? A man's got to do something when he's out of work.' It wasn't the greatest explanation in the world, and I made so bold as to give him the retort cynical. 'So you indulged in a little brick-laying?' I said. 'How extremely convenient.'

Not much later, when Mizz Liz Probert, Mr Bernard and I were making our way towards the gatehouse of the nick, crossing that wasteland where screws stood about with Alsatians, and a few trusties planted pansies in the black earth, my radical junior said, 'So you think he's guilty?'

'Not at all, Sister Liz,' I told her. 'I know he's innocent.'

'Innocent?'

'No criminal's going to stand around singing "The Red

Flag" over his victim's dead body,' I explained. 'Not in the presence of the Old Bill, anyway. You wouldn't get the Timsons behaving like that, would you?'

'If he's innocent we might get him off at the committal.' Mr Bernard was on the verge of a dangerous train of thought.

'Our only chance of getting him off is before a jury, Brother Bernard. We say as little as possible at the committal.'

'All the same, I'd like you there, Mr Rumpole.' I didn't at once follow our instructing solicitor's drift and I said, as jovially as possible, 'Would you, Brother? Always ready to oblige.'

'You see, I might need a few tips,' Mr Bernard said, and I must confess I was puzzled, so I asked, 'Tips, Brother Bernard?'

And then the man revealed all. 'I thought I'd do the advocacy in the preliminary hearing,' he said. 'Bit of a dummy run for the Lord Chancellor's changes, when we solicitors can appear in the highest Courts of the land. So if you'll sit behind me, Mr Rumpole.'

'Behind you, Brother?' I could only give a sigh of resignation and quote Swinburne again: ' "That even the weariest river/ Winds somewhere safe to sea" '.'

Change, as I have said, and also decay, in all around I see. True to the Lord Chancellor's fearless and totally misguided shake-up of the Bar, Mr Bernard was encouraged to represent Ben Baker before the South London stipendiary magistrate, a small, pinkish, self-important, failed barrister of mediocre intelligence. The Prosecution was in the hands of a deeply confused young man from the Crown Prosecution Service who kept losing documents. Detective Inspector Walcroft, the officer in charge of the case, sat listening and taking notes, clearly pained by the poor performances on offer. And, if you can believe it, Horace Rumpole, star of the Penge Bungalow Murders and leading actor in so many dramas down the Bailey, sat mum and junior to his instructing solicitor. After enough evidence had been given to send a canonized saint for trial, Mr Bernard, against all my advice, arose in order to argue that the

51

case should be thrown out. 'And so far as the brick dust on our client's trousers goes,' I heard him saying, 'we have a complete answer!'

'Don't tell the Old Bill what it is.' I whispered a terrible warning, as I saw D. I. Walcroft preparing to note down our defence. 'The truth of the matter is perfectly simple,' Bernard banged on regardless, 'my client was building a wall in his back garden.' I saw the D. I. write this down with a smile of cynical amusement, and the Beak suggested that where the brick dust came from was surely a matter for the Jury. But Bernard had the bit between his teeth and said there was no evidence to commit the Basher to trial.

'But, Mr Bernard' – at least the perky little magistrate knew the rudiments of his job – 'we have the statement of a Mr Gerald Jebb who actually saw your client hurl the brick.'

'Clearly an unreliable witness.' Bernard was enjoying himself. 'If you recall, he couldn't even remember how many pickets there were between him and my client. Or how they were dressed, or . . .'

'The time of high tide at Dungeness?' I suggested in a whisper and the Bench weighed in with 'Whether or not Mr Jebb is a reliable witness is also a matter for the Jury.'

'But, sir! What about the presumption of innocence?' Bernard had a stab at pained outrage.

'Very well, Mr Bernard. What about it?' The Beak was clearly bored, and my solicitor chose this inopportune moment to attempt a Rumpolesque peroration, complete with gestures. After all, he's seen me do it often enough.'With the evidence in doubt, my client is entitled to be acquitted!' he boomed majestically. 'That is the golden thread which runs through British justice. We are all of us innocent until you can be certain sure we *must* be guilty. And I put it to you, sir. In my humble submission. My contention is. You couldn't find my client guilty on a charge of non-renewed dog licence on the vague and unsatisfactory evidence of this fellow Jebb!'

'Not now, old darling,' I whispered to the fellow on his feet. 'We don't do that bit now. We save it for the Jury.' And the Magistrate clearly agreed. 'Mr Bernard,' he said through a prodigious yawn, 'your client will be committed for trial in the Central Criminal Court. Before a jury and a judge.'

'As you please, sir.' And Bernard hissed under his breath, 'And I very much hope he's a judge with no prejudice against trades unions.'

The moving finger wrote on the history of *The Queen* v. *'Basher' Baker* and spelled out the name of Mr Justice Guthrie Featherstone. Those familiar with these records will know that, many years ago, the Head of our Chambers was Hilda's father, C. H. Wystan. When old Wystan dropped off the twig I had hoped to have become Head, but a far younger man named Guthrie Featherstone, Q.C., M.P., 'popp'd in between the election and my hopes' and came to rule our roost at Equity Court. Guthrie was either a left-wing member of a right-wing party, or a right-wing member of a left-wing party – for the life of me, I can't now recall which. Whichever it was, I don't remember him ever coming out strongly in favour of the brothers on the shop floor. Guthrie was married to the formidable Marigold Featherstone, a handsome woman who managed to speak like a ventriloquist – you couldn't see her lips move. The Featherstones lived in Knightsbridge, which Marigold found convenient for Harrods, and had two perfectly acceptable children called Simon and Sarah. My wife, Hilda, greatly admires Marigold, takes bridge lessons with her and often complains to her about Rumpole.

For some reason the then Lord Chancellor took it into his head to make Guthrie, who suffered from a total inability to make up his mind about anything, a red judge. Clad in scarlet and ermine, Mr Justice Featherstone presided over his cases in a ferment of doubt, desperately anxious to do the right thing, fearful of the Court of Appeal, and frequently tempted to make the most reckless pronouncements which got him into trouble with the newspapers. Despite all these glaring character defects, there was something quite decent about old Guthrie. He often tried, in his nervous and confused fashion, to do justice, and he was, in every way, a better egg than Soapy Sam Ballard, Q.C., who succeeded him as Head of Chambers at Equity Court.

Having given the old darling the benefit of every conceivable doubt, I have to report that he was pretty shocked when the Prosecution opened a case of homicide on the picket line. He had an ancient and reptilian clerk named Wilfred who frequently fell asleep in Court. One morning, early in the trial, Wilfred was helping his master into fancy dress for the day's performance and they had something like the following conversation – the gist of which I owe to Wilfred's recollection, prompted by a pint or two of draft Guinness. 'We've got to watch the trades unions,' Mr Justice Featherstone started off. 'They're getting too much power again. Trying to run the country.'

'Getting too big for their boots, my Lord?' Wilfred suggested. To which Guthrie replied, laughing, 'And their boots are probably big enough in all conscience! Remember the Winter of Discontent, do you?' Here he referred to a strike of many trades, including that of grave-diggers, some years ago under another government. 'You couldn't even get buried then!'

'Terrible thing, my Lord,' Wilfred clucked with disapproval.

'Oh, yes, Wilfred. A terrible thing. Not that I want to get buried. Not yet awhile, anyway. I don't particularly want to go on a chara. But people do. And they should be given the opportunity.'

'Very good, some of these charas, I believe, my Lord,' Wilfred pointed out. 'They have toilets.'

'Yes. Oh, yes, I dare say they do. Not that I suppose I'll ever find out. I can't quite picture Lady Featherstone aboard a chara!'

'No, my Lord. I can't picture it myself,' said Wilfred, joining in the judicial mirth.

'Think they're above the law, these union bosses do.' Guthrie became serious again. 'What's the country coming to, Wilfred? The Summer of Discontent, that's what I call it.'

'What it brings to mind, my Lord,' Wilfred suggested, 'is the French Revolution.'

'Does it, Wilfred? Well, yes. I suppose it does. Well, let me tell you this. Rumpole's not getting away with it again.'

'With the French Revolution, my Lord?' Ideas were flowing a little too fast for Wilfred.

'Don't be silly! With manslaughter! You know there's a sort of legend grown up round the Bailey. Old Rumpole gets away with it every time. Even my wife, even Lady Featherstone, thinks Rumpole can twist me round his little finger!'

'Very astute lady, if I may say so, my Lord.' Wilfred had a healthy respect for Marigold.

'That's as may be, Wilfred. But old Rumpole is not getting away with this one. I tell you, I've taken a good look at Union Boss Baker. And I don't like what I see. I intend to pot him good and proper' – at this, his Lordship imitated a man playing billiards – 'in off the red! At least he won't be able to go on strike in prison!'

It was at this point that, after a brief knock, another judge, considerably senior in years and experience to Guthrie, named Sir Simon Parsloe, blew into the room to discuss what he called the 'dotty schemes the Lord Chancellor's got to reform the Bar'. Stowing away Guthrie's mufti jacket and hat, Wilfred was privy to a plan for a few top judges to rise early and meet in Mr Justice Parsloe's room in the Law Courts to discuss the best way of foiling the lunatic scheme which would have solicitors appearing in the top Courts, solicitors sitting on the Bench, 'solicitors in the House of Lords, if we're not bloody careful, overturning our judgments' – to adopt the vivid language of Sir Simon Parsloe – 'and,' he added, 'we judges have got to take some sort of action.' 'You don't mean' – poor old Featherstone was aghast – 'our jobs are at risk?'

'Well, who knows? Anything can happen. Can you make yourself free, Guthrie?'

'They'd better try and stop me!' Our judge was uncharacteristically decisive. 'Sound fellow!' Parsloe departed with a vague salute and Guthrie turned to confide in his clerk. 'Jobs at risk!' He seemed close to tears. 'Can you believe it, Wilfred? The Summer of Discontent, I tell you. That's what I call it.'

The Prosecution of Ben Baker was in the hands of Soapy Sam

Ballard, Q.C., with Claude Erskine-Brown as his learned junior.
It seemed that this pair were quite ready to do trades union
cases, so long as they weren't on the side of the workers. That
morning, Ballard called Gerald Jebb, who was Basher Baker's
contemporary and a fellow member of N.U.C.D.O. Mr Jebb
was a small, cheerful man with a turned-up nose who looked
like a grey-haired schoolboy. I feared that he was the most
dangerous of all adversaries, an honest witness. Ballard took
him through the events of the fatal day, until he reached the
point when my client got hurriedly out of the way of an
advancing Luxie-Coach. Then he asked Mr Jebb, 'From your
position on the picket line, did you see the defendant Baker
stoop down?'

'My Lord' – I rose slowly to my hind legs – 'I didn't know
that leading questions were allowed. Even in cases against
trades union officials.'

'Leading questions are not allowed in any case, Mr Rumpole,' my Lord said. 'As you know perfectly well. Yes, carry
on, Mr Ballard.' I subsided, clear in the knowledge of which
side Guthrie was on.

'I'm obliged to your Lordship.' Ballard was in a particularly
servile mood. 'Yes. What did you see Baker do?'

'He stooped down and picked up a brick, my Lord. Then he
hurled it at the coach driver.' Jebb gave us the facts with
effective reluctance.

'Did he hurl it hard?' And although I rumbled a warning
'Don't lead, Mr Ballard!' the witness supplied the answer. 'He
hurled it with full force, my Lord.'

'He hurled it with full force at the driver,' Guthrie repeated
with great satisfaction as he noted the evidence down. Ballard
subsided, well satisfied, and I rose to cross-examine, with no
very clear plan of campaign. 'Mr Jebb. You said you saw my
client stoop to the ground.' I began quietly as the Jury clearly
liked Mr Jebb and would have hated to see him bullied.

'Yes, I did.'

'Hadn't he just jumped out of the path of a charabanc
travelling at speed?'

'He had got out of its way. Yes.'

'Wasn't the driver doing his best to kill *him*?'

'I'm not sure what he was doing,' Jebb answered perfectly fairly. It was a slim chance but I jumped on it. 'Just as you're not sure what my client was doing when he stumbled and stooped to the ground?'

'He has given evidence that he saw your client pick up a brick and hurl it, Mr Rumpole.' Guthrie was quick to the witness's aid in a time of not very great trouble.

'I'm sure my learned friend Mr Ballard is most grateful to your Lordship for that intervention,' I said to Guthrie with an irony that I was afraid might be lost on him. And then I turned to the witness. 'Oh, one more thing, Mr Jebb. When the police arrived on the scene you said nothing about seeing Mr Baker throw the brick. You made your first statement' – I picked it up and looked at it – 'some three weeks afterwards. Why was that?'

'I didn't want to get Basher into no trouble.'

'Well, you've got him into trouble now, haven't you? Why did you change your mind?'

'Because I thought I should tell the truth.'

Judge and jury loved that answer and it was clear I was getting absolutely nowhere with Brother Jebb. Accordingly I asked to postpone the rest of my cross-examination to the next day. I said I was waiting for some further inquiries to be made, when what I meant was that I was waiting for a touch of inspiration. Rather to my surprise, both Guthrie and Soapy Sam agreed to have Mr Jebb back at the end of the prosecution case, but before he was released his Lordship got one in below the defence belt. 'Just a moment before you go, Mr Jebb. You just referred to the defendant as "Basher". The Jury might like to know how he got that nickname?' And although I naturally objected, I was rapidly overruled and the witness answered the Judge's question to devastating effect. 'Because he was always talking about bashing people what took the boss's side, my Lord.'

'Thank you, Mr Jebb. That was extremely helpful.' His Lordship was effusive, but the answer had been about as helpful to me as a cup of cold poison. And then Guthrie made the announcement which, like a stone thrown into a lake, would make waves in an ever-expanding circle.

'Mr Ballard. Mr Rumpole. I shan't be able to sit this afternoon.'

'Oh. May we ask why, my Lord?'

'No.'

'No?'

'I mean, well, yes. Yes, of course. It's an urgent matter. A matter of public duty. I will rise now.' And he was off like a rabbit out of a trap. Mizz Liz Probert was gone almost as quickly, saying she couldn't chat about the case as she had a lunch fixed with young Dave Inchcape. Then my learned opponent Claude Erskine-Brown appeared beside me, staring after Liz with a look of sickly yearning on his face. 'It's the contrast, isn't it,' he babbled, 'between the strict white wig and the impish little face? No disrespect to your cross-examination, Rumpole, but I couldn't take my eyes off her.'

'How's your wife, Erskine-Brown?' I tried to bring the great lover back to reality with a bump.

'Philly?' He seemed to have difficulty remembering the name. 'Doing a rather grand corruption in Hong Kong. We see so little of each other nowadays.'

'So you want to invite Mizz Liz Probert to the Opera again?' I had, of course, got it in one.

'She'd never come,' Claude answered dolefully. 'She doesn't really like me very much, does she? I mean, the way she told me off at the Chambers meeting! Look. I don't want you to get the wrong idea, Rumpole. What I have in mind is merely a social event, entirely innocent. You believe that, don't you?'

'Oh, yes. Everyone's innocent until they're proven guilty.' And then an idea occurred to me, which had in it more than my usual high per cent of brilliance. If it could only be made to work, it might solve a number of problems. 'I have, perhaps,' I told him, 'a little influence with my former pupil, Mizz Liz Probert. She sometimes takes my advice.'

'Do you think you could advise her, Horace?'

'Of course, I couldn't connive at anything but a purely musical evening.' I sounded as pious as Soapy Sam Ballard.

'Purely musical, I promise you. Scout's honour.'

'I'll do my best.' I gave him a boy scout's salute. 'And do a good deed for somebody every day.' And then I scuttered off in the direction of lunch, satisfied with a good deal of ground well prepared.

Women, it seemed to me, make a great mystery about such simple tasks as cooking the dinner. After Hilda withdrew her labour, there I was in the kitchen, peeling the potatoes, with a saucepan of water bubbling, ready to receive them. (There is, after all, no very great skill required in the boiling of water.) The chops were warmly ensconced under the grill and cooking well. Another saucepan was steaming for the inundation of the frozen peas. I took these out of the fridge and it would be a matter of moments, I thought, before I had them open and swimming. Then I ran up against a problem in what, up to then, had seemed the simple art of cooking. Those selling frozen peas clearly regard them as being as precious as jewels or krugerrands; enormous precautions are taken to prevent a break-in and the packet is covered with tough, seamless and apparently impregnable cellophane. I tried to rip off this covering. I tore at it with my teeth, I worried it as a dog worries a bone, but all in vain. Finally I stabbed it with a sharp knife, causing a fusillade of frozen green bullets to ricochet off the cooker and adjacent walls. One of them hit the overhead light with a most melodious twang. At last I got a reasonable proportion of the elusive vegetables into hot water, but I was distracted by a 'whoosh' and a sheet of flame which shot out at me from under the grill. Naturally I had covered the chops with fat to ensure a sound cooking and, it seemed, this substance was dangerously inflammable. I had never invested in a fire extinguisher, but, with great presence of mind, I remembered the siphon on the sitting-room sideboard. It was a matter of moments to search for it, and, returning, to direct a powerful stream at the blaze.

Strangely enough the soda water also appeared to be

59

inflammable, because it strengthened rather than diminished the blaze. Then it occurred to me to turn off the grill, and I was beating the dying conflagration with a wet dishcloth when Hilda, who had been out when I started cooking, arrived upon the scene, coughing at the cloud of smoke in what I thought was an exaggerated manner and asking if she should call the fire brigade.

'No longer necessary,' I assured her, 'I'm just cooking the dinner.'

'Oh, really?' She was examining the charred chops critically. 'I thought you were arranging your interesting collection of fossils.'

'Hilda,' I protested, 'I've had absolutely no training in this line of work.'

'Perhaps you should have thought of that before you decided to stay out all hours.'

'Be reasonable. Couldn't we refer the matter to the conciliation service, A.C.A.S.? Or at least discuss it over beer and sandwiches, like they used to in the good old days?'

Then the front-door bell rang and Hilda went to answer it, after advising me that if I put the potatoes on immediately, I could have them for pudding. She was back in short order, with a figure familiar to me, but not to her. 'Can you believe it?' Fred Timson said. 'Mrs Rumpole and I have never had the pleasure, not after all these years you've been working for the Timsons.' Fred was the undoubted chief of the Timsons, that large clan of South London villains who, by their selfless application to petty crime, had managed to keep the Rumpoles in such basic necessities of life as sliced bread, Vim, Château Fleet Street and the odd small cigar. Luxuries might depend on an occasional well-paid dangerous driving or a long-lasting homicide, but the Timsons, in their humble way, gave us solid support. They were the sort to breed from.

'Fred!' I greeted him. 'Good of you to drop in.'

'Well, I happened to be in the vicinity. Not getting up to any naughtiness, Mrs Rumpole,' he assured Hilda. 'I wasn't doing over the downstairs or nothing. And I come on the off chance you and your old ball and chain might be sat in front of the telly. Also I have a bit of info which may be of interest in that job what you're doing at the Bailey, Mr R.'

Fred has a far from villainous appearance. He is cheerful, a grandfather, and wears the sort of tweed jackets and cavalry twill trousers a bank manager might sport in the pub at weekends. None of the Timsons is first class at their jobs, but in his day Fred was a fair to average safe-blower. Despite his look of respectability, She Who Must Be Obeyed was eyeing one of our best customers with deep suspicion. When I invited Fred to stay for a bite of supper, she announced that she was off for a bridge evening at Lady Featherstone's, where, no doubt, she could keep going on the cheesy bits provided. 'I think it's a little much,' she said as I saw her out of the front door, 'having the criminal classes calling here at all hours!' And although I told her there was absolutely no violence in Fred's record and he was an old sweetie, she didn't seem in the least mollified.

I returned to the kitchen and poured out a hospitable Pommeroy's Ordinary for each of us. 'I looked for you at your place of business, Mr Rumpole, but your boy Henry said as you were out shopping for groceries. I said I found that hard to believe.'

'Difficult times, Fred. What's called the Summer of Discontent. Got yourself into a bit of trouble, have you?'

'No. Not at the moment. Cor! This wine!' He made a disapproving face. 'Bit rough, isn't it?'

'Liquid sandpaper,' I agreed. 'But you get used to it.' I was worried by his apparent idleness. 'What's the matter? *You're* not on strike, are you?'

'Course not. Matter of fact, I thought I might help you for a change, Mr Rumpole.'

'Oh, yes?'

'Thought I might tell you about our holiday. In Marbella.' He sat at the table and I felt a pang of boredom at the prospect before me. 'Oh, really? Want to show me the snaps?'

'To be quite honest, I brought one along. You see, our enjoyment was just that little bit ruined by the arrival of this shower.'

And then he carefully removed a photograph from his wallet and showed it to me. I saw a coach by a white wall in sunshine, with a number of people, including a familiar, scowling young man in a red anorak, grouped about it. 'Good heavens! Isn't that the clan Molloy? Your rival firm in South-East London?'

'Not rival, Mr Rumpole. The Timsons wouldn't stoop to their way of doing business. But it's the Molloys all right, including young Peanuts. That case you is on, as is reported in the paper, it's manslaughter, isn't it? I thought you might just be interested in the Molloys' vehicle.'

I examined the picture more closely and the words painted on the coach. I could make out: ERNIE ELVER'S LUXIE-CHARAS. COMPLETE WITH TOILETS AND DOUBLE-GLAZING. And, then, I was delighted to see young Peanuts Molloy. 'Bless you, old darling!' I thanked Fred.

'They said as they got lent the chara for a free holiday by the firm concerned. And you'll notice the grey-haired old party with his arm round Peanuts' Aunty Dolly.'

'My God, I notice him!' It was none other than the honest witness in person. Whoever is in charge of the universe clearly felt that it was time to do old Rumpole a favour.

'Gerry Jebb,' Fred confirmed it. 'What used to drive get-aways for Peanuts' father. Know what I mean?'

'Fred, you're a treasure. Please. Stay for supper.'

'I don't think so, Mr R.' Fred glanced at the chops on offer. 'Look, why don't we attack a Chink?' He stood, ready to be off.

'What *are* you talking about?'

'Go for a Chinese.' It was simple and offensive, like all the Timsons' jokes.

'You want a radical Chambers, Mizz Liz? Only way we'll get it is to persuade Claude Erskine-Brown to stop trying to be a whizz kid and go back to the old ways. Then Equity Court'll be a place fit for freelancers to live in again. We can ride forth like the knights of old and rescue the brothers in distress.'

I was walking with Mizz Liz down to the Old Bailey the next morning and putting into operation stage one of my master plan to prevent Chambers slipping off into the twenty-first century.

'Who's going to persuade Claude?' Liz asked reasonably.

'The person who has the greatest influence on him. The Member of the Bar he'd do anything to impress.'

'You mean, you?'

'No, you! Tell him you liked him better when he was an old-fashioned sort of barrister, keeping up the best traditions of the Bar and taking snuff. Tell him he was much sexier like that. It'd sound better, coming from you.'

'Rumpole!' Mizz Probert was shocked. 'Are you suggesting I exploit my femininity?'

'In a good cause, old thing! And can you think of a better? Also you might put up with a little Wagner, in the interests of justice.'

So we proceeded on towards the workplace. And that was not the only useful conversation I had that morning, for when I had got robed and come downstairs I found Wilfred, Guthrie's old clerk, hovering about the door of the Court. I asked him if the Judge was honouring us with his presence, after having taken yesterday afternoon off. 'Bless you, yes, Mr Rumpole.' Wilfred looked at me with sleepy, crocodile eyes. 'We're not going on strike yet.'

'On strike?' I pricked up my ears.

'We think it might come to it,' Wilfred told me. 'That's what our judge was saying. If the Lord Chancellor wants to put up solicitors over our heads. We may have to take action, Mr Rumpole.'

'Quite right, Wilfred, I'm sure.' I sounded deeply understanding. 'So yesterday afternoon . . .?'

'Just a taster, Mr Rumpole. Just to show the public we're not to be pushed around. Of course, there *was* a meeting.'

'A union meeting?'

'A meeting of judges, Mr Rumpole. Some very senior men was there,' Wilfred couldn't help boasting, 'including us.'

'Of course! The brothers. Have you ever thought of that, Wilfred? Judges and trades unionists always call themselves "brothers". It doesn't mean they like each other any more.'

'I must be off, Mr Rumpole.' Wilfred clearly didn't care for this line of thought. 'I must go and get us on the Bench.'

'Must be quite a heave for you. Some mornings.'

'And, Mr Rumpole. You will try not to twist us round your little finger, won't you? Because we're determined to pot you on this one. I thought we ought to warn you.'

'Very charming of you, Wilfred,' I said as the man went about his business. 'Very charming indeed!'

In Court that day we were treated to an entertainment. The place was plunged into darkness and television sets were placed among us on which Ernie Elver's home video played. We saw the pickets shouting at the gates, as the coach driven by the working driver approached them. I sat watching with the photograph Fred Timson had given me in my hand, and, at a vital moment, I reared to my hind legs and called 'Stop!' An officer in charge of the telly pressed a button and the picture froze.

'My Lord. I call on my learned friend, Mr Bollard . . .'

'Ballard!' Soapy Sam was not in the best of tempers that morning.

'Makes no difference. I call on him to make the following admission. That the young dark-haired man wearing the red jacket on that picket line is otherwise known as Peter "Peanuts" Molloy.'

'I don't suppose your learned friend has any idea.' Guthrie was unhelpful.

'Then let him ask the Detective Inspector in charge of the case. He'll very soon find out.'

Ballard had a whispered conversation with D. I. Walcroft and then emerged and admitted grudgingly, 'That would seem to be correct, my Lord.' It was a good moment for the Basher, but as he sat frowning in the dock it seemed that, like most clients, he had very little idea of what was going on.

After his movie show, Ernie Elver was called to give evidence, and, as a hard-pressed boss more sinned against than sinning, he clearly had the sympathy of his Lordship. As we got towards the end of his questioning, Ballard asked, 'Mr Elver. Throughout this industrial dispute was there any doubt in your mind who the leader was?'

'The man in the dock, my Lord.' Ernie had no doubt.

'Baker?'

'Yes, my Lord.'

'Did he say anything you remember during the negotiations?'

'Yes, my Lord. He said someone was going to get killed if it wasn't settled.'

'Someone was going to get killed.' Guthrie was taking another note with great satisfaction.

'Mr Elver. What was the man Baker's reputation, in industrial disputes?' Ballard's question caused me to rise with the outrage turned up to full volume. 'This is monstrous! If my learned friend's going to practise at the Bar, he ought to do a bit of practising at home. He can't ask questions about reputation!'

'I think we might leave it there, Mr Ballard.' His Lordship poured a little oil on troubled Rumpole. 'After all, the Jury have heard this man's nickname.'

Ballard sat down looking displeased and I rose to smile charmingly at the witness I hoped to devour.

'Mr Elver. This dispute at your charabanc garage was about your employing non-union untrained drivers?'

'That's what they said it was.' The big man in the shiny suit grinned at the Jury as though to say, Pull the other one, it's got bells on it.

'And my client took the view, rightly or wrongly, that if you employed these cowboys there might be an accident. Someone might get killed?'

'I wanted to offer the public a wider choice.' Ernie Elver sounded like a party political broadcast and old Claude chimed in with a penetrating whisper, 'Consumer choice. That's the name of the game nowadays.'

'Oh, mind your own business, Mr Erskine-Brown!' I gave him a sharp whisper back. Then I turned to the witness with 'So you wanted to offer the public a choice between good drivers and bad ones who might not know the routes.'

'If you want to put it that way.' Ernie clearly didn't.

'Oh, I do,' I assured him. 'And I suggest that even the most gentle, mild-mannered man might take industrial action in that situation. Take his Lordship . . .'

'Mr Rumpole?' Guthrie woke up with a start the moment his name was mentioned.

'As you probably know,' I confided in Mr Ernie Elver, 'the powers that be have suggested that solicitors can get jobs as High Court judges. Appeal judges! Lords of Appeal!'

'Mr Rumpole!' His Lordship was about to draw the line. 'These questions are quite irrelevant!'

'Is your Lordship stopping my cross-examination?' Then I said to Mizz Liz in a deafening mutter, 'It's not a particularly long walk to the Court of Appeal.' At the mention of these dreaded words, his Lordship could be heard going into reverse. 'No. No, of course, I'm not stopping you,' he said hurriedly. 'But I fail to understand . . .'

'Then might I suggest you sit quietly, my Lord. All will become clear.' I was beginning to lose patience with his Lordship, and he came back with a rather sour 'Mr Rumpole. Don't get the idea that you can twist this Court round your little finger!'

'My little finger, my Lord?' I played the retort courteous. 'What an idea!' Then I resumed my conversation with Ernie. 'Solicitors who haven't spent a lifetime arguing in Courts might not be up to the job. That's the suggestion,' I told him.

'I didn't know.' Ernie looked as though he might have thought that solicitors were ladies of the street who probably were unsuited to the work in the Court of Appeal.

'Well, you know now, Mr Elver. And that suggestion caused even such a reasonable, sensible, moderate man as his Lordship to go on strike.'

'On strike, Mr Rumpole?' His poor old Lordship could contain himself no longer. 'What can you be talking about?'

'Yesterday afternoon, my Lord' – I tried to keep as calm as possible – 'I seem to remember not very much work was done. Was not your Lordship on strike?'

'No, I was not on strike!' The Judge gave his desk a moderate, middle-of-the-road sort of thump. 'Simply withdrawing your labour?' I smiled sweetly.

'As I told the Court, I had to go to an important meeting' – Guthrie was making the mistake of defending the charge – 'with a very senior judge and brother judges from the Chancery and the Family Division.'

'Of course. The shop stewards. And what was the discussion about?'

'Mr Rumpole!' the Judge asked with deep suspicion, 'are you cross-examining me?'

'Cross-examining your Lordship? Perish the thought!' Of course I was, and on I went. 'I can understand that if the Judges are in dispute with their employers it may be a delicate matter. Better kept secret.'

'I don't think it's any secret that certain changes have been proposed in the legal system.' As a witness, his Lordship was proving almost too easy to handle.

'Cowboys on the Bench, my Lord?' I suggested.

'No, but perhaps' – he searched for a tactful way of putting it – 'persons whose training may not entirely fit them for the Bench.'

'And if they get there? *Can we expect further industrial action?* Down the Old Bailey?' Poor old Guthrie was now really in deep water. 'It's a possibility,' he said. 'We hope wiser counsels will prevail.' And then he tried to swim for the shore. 'Mr Rumpole, we have had quite enough of this. High Court judges are not, and never have been, members of a trades union.'

'Is that a legal proposition, my Lord,' I asked, 'or a subject of debate?'

'Will you please return to the question we have to try? Did your client commit manslaughter?'

That was not one I felt like answering just yet, so I turned back to the witness. 'Mr Elver. I was just venturing to point out that reasonable people may withdraw their labour when their jobs are threatened. I'm sure his Lordship would agree.'

Elver didn't care to answer that, but Guthrie couldn't resist it. He leant towards the witness and said, 'Surely that's a reasonable proposition, Mr Elver?'

'I suppose so.' Ernie was disconcerted by a judge who was suddenly talking like one of the brothers.

'And you wanted to make it look as *unreasonable* as possible?' I asked him.

'Why would I want to do that?'

'Childishly simple, Mr Elver,' I told him. 'Because if you could prove there were more than six pickets you could get an injunction. If you could prove there was violence and intimidation you could get the union fined large sums of money. You could get rid of that thorn in your flesh, Mr "Basher" Baker, and employ all the cheap cowboy labour you wanted.'

'But there *was* violence on the picket line,' Ernie protested.

'Of course there was! Because you put it there. Usher, give that to the witness.' What I passed up was the photograph Fred Timson had given me of the Molloys on holiday. 'You know the Molloy family, don't you?' I asked as Ernie looked at it with some reluctance. 'I'm not sure,' he said, after a considerable silence.

'Come on, Mr Elver,' I encouraged him. 'You employ Gerry Jebb. He's one of the clan. They're a pretty hard firm of criminals, the Molloys. Well known to the Inspector in this case. You hired the Molloys, didn't you, no doubt through Jebb, to swell the picket line and create as much violence as possible? Then, when you'd arranged the performance, you went and filmed it all from your office window.'

'Baker was in charge of the picket line,' Ernie insisted.

'In charge of the peaceful pickets, yes. He didn't know the new arrivals, those he took for sympathetic workers from other firms. They were your gang of hired troublemakers. Weren't they?'

'Mr Rumpole. Are you suggesting this witness planned the death of the driver?' Guthrie, as usual, looked puzzled.

'Oh, no, my Lord.' I explained, careful to allow for the slow pace of the judicial mind, 'No doubt he was as surprised as anyone when young Peanuts Molloy, who probably threw the brick, went too far. But it was a blessed opportunity to get the awkward Mr Baker into real trouble.' Then I asked the witness, 'How much did it cost you to get Jebb to give that perjured evidence?'

'My Lord, I object.' Ballard rose plaintively. 'There's no basis whatever for that suggestion!'

'Or did you get the whole package for a free holiday in Marbella?' Ballard's interruption was worth ignoring. 'Just take a look at that photograph. Is that one of your Luxie-Charas in Spain?'

'It seems to be,' Ernie had to admit.

'Do you see Mr Jebb there?'

'Yes.'

'I have asked the Prosecution to admit that the man in the red jacket is Peanuts Molloy. Was that a free holiday? A present from your firm?'

'I don't think so.' Ernie saw the dangers ahead, and I snapped at him, 'Can you produce evidence that your coach was paid for by the Molloys?'

'Maybe not.'

'Why not?'

'Gerry Jebb had been with the firm a long time. I wanted to do him a favour.'

'So he did you a favour in return?'

'Mr Rumpole' – Guthrie was restive again – 'none of these serious suggestions was put to the witness, Jebb.'

'Your Lordship is perfectly right,' I agreed, now that I had plenty of questions to put to Jebb. 'That is why I have asked the Prosecution to have him back here tomorrow.'

'Very well.' Guthrie looked wistfully at the clock. 'I see it's a little early. But I will rise now.'

'Public duty, my Lord?' I wanted to help the old darling.

'Yes, Mr Rumpole. Public duty. You may put your case to Mr Jebb in the morning.'

'I'm very much obliged to your Lordship.' I bowed low and added, under my breath, 'Keep the red flag flying here!'

'Did you say something, Mr Rumpole?'

'I said what an interesting case we're trying here.'

For a full understanding of *The Queen* v. *Basher Baker*, we must now follow his Lordship into private life. My source for what follows is the account Lady Marigold Featherstone gave to She Who Must Be Obeyed. Further details were supplied by Wilfred, the faithful clerk, in whom Guthrie often confided. It's clear from all the evidence available that the 'public duty' for which he had risen 'a little early' was going back to the Knightsbridge flat for the purpose of resting up on the sofa with a cup of tea. While he was so engaged, his wife Marigold returned home with a full Harrods bag and a copy of the *Evening Standard*. I have done my best to reconstruct their dialogue from the information I have received, and my knowledge of the characters of the two Featherstones. Marigold's opening salvo did not augur well for his Lordship's continued repose. 'Working hard, Guthrie?' I think she may well have said, 'or are you taking industrial action?'

'Oh, Marigold' – Guthrie had no doubt awoken with a start – 'there you are! Well, hard day in Court. What's that you say about industrial action?' And I imagine that he slid somewhat guiltily off the sofa as Marigold announced, in awesome tones, 'I have been reading the paper.'

'Oh. Yes, of course. Got a bit about my case in it, has it? Interesting discussion about union law. But let me tell you this, Marigold. I'm going to pot the shop steward. Old Rumpole's not going to twist me round his little finger this time!'

'Aren't you fit to be let off the lead, Guthrie? Ought I to be up there on the Bench beside you all the time, telling you when to keep your mouth shut?'

'Why? They must have got it wrong. Let me see. What am I supposed to have said?'

Marigold didn't hand over the paper but read him the best bits: '"Industrial action is a possibility, says Mr Justice Featherstone, 53, if jobs on the Bench are open to solicitors".' Did you say *that*, Guthrie dear?' She must have smiled with misleading sweetness.

'Well, something like it, I suppose. Something quite like it.' The Judge was beginning to wilt under cross-examination and Marigold read on without mercy: '"The Judge agreed with Mr Horace Rumpole, counsel for Baker, that he had been 'withdrawing his labour' yesterday afternoon when he closed down his Court to attend a protest meeting of senior judges whom he called 'shop stewards'."'

'That's a libel! Rumpole called them that!' Guthrie felt he had a genuine grievance.

'Sounds a pretty accurate description, if you ask me. There's a leading article on page six.' And as she turned the pages, Guthrie said, in stricken tones, 'A leading article!'

'"Judges add to nation's misery",' his wife read out, and his protest rose to a quavering wail, 'Marigold. It's simply not *fair!*'

'"Train drivers, air-traffic controllers, local government workers, prison officers and drain-clearance operatives"' – Marigold carried on reading. 'What charming company you keep, Guthrie! – "have all managed to put the public through the hell of a Summer of Discontent. Now, if you go mad and strangle a porter when you've been waiting three days for a train at Waterloo, you won't even be tried for it, according to Mr Justice Featherstone, who also went on strike yesterday afternoon. Come off it, your Lordship! Drop the old Spanish practices and offer the public a decent service".'

'Marigold' – Guthrie felt he knew who to blame – 'it's entirely the fault of Rumpole.'

'Of course it is,' his wife agreed. 'Why can't you twist him round *your* little finger for a change? You're bigger than he is!'

'I shall deny it all! In Court.' His Lordship was adopting what might be called the Timson defence.

'Oh, do' – Lady Featherstone was cynical – 'then everyone will believe it. I had to read this paper at lunch in Harrods. In the Silver Grill! I was deeply humiliated.'

'Marigold. I'm sorry, but . . .'

'I bought you a present.' At this sign of affection I'm sure our judge was considerably relieved. 'Oh, darling,' he said, 'I knew you'd understand.'

'Oh, yes. I understand perfectly.' At which she opened her Harrods bag, took out a decisively checked cloth cap and plonked it on her husband's head. 'It's your flat 'at, Guthrie. Now you can go down the working-men's club and play darts over a pint of wallop with the charge hands. I'm going to my bridge class with Hilda Rumpole. Her husband may have his drawbacks, but at least she's not married to a shop steward.'

At this, Hilda told me, Marigold said she left the unhappy man alone. I see him looking at himself in the mirror, seeing the cloth cap, symbol of the working-class struggle, on his head, and uttering something really desperate like 'Oh, brother!'

Another direct result of Rumpole's advocacy was taking place in the crush bar of Covent Garden during a welcome interval in some opera by Richard Wagner whose music, as the late Mark Twain once said, is not as bad as it sounds. My learned friend Claude Erskine-Brown and the radical lawyer Mizz Liz Probert were crushed up against the bust of Sir Thomas Beecham. Claude was doing his best to pour her a glass of champagne without moving his arms and looking at her with the Erskine-Brown version of smouldering passion, and Liz was gamely twinkling back, noticing his bow-tie, watch-chain and conservatively tailored gents three-piece suiting. I do my best to reconstruct their conversation from the detailed account of Mizz Probert who, acting on the instructions of my good self, kicked off with, 'This is how I like you, Claude.'

'You do like me a little then, Elizabeth?' The dear old ass was suitably gratified.

'When you're the old English barrister.'

'Did you say, "old"?' Claude sounded miffed. 'I mean, I'm not "old" exactly.'

'Old-fashioned. That's what I mean.'

'Oh, I see. You like that, do you? I should've thought you wouldn't.'

'Oh, yes,' she assured him. 'It's the old-fashioned elegance I admire. The bow-tie and all that. It's rather sweet.'

'Actually it's an old Wykehamist bow-tie,' Claude said modestly.

'Is it, really?' Liz was less than impressed.

'I wouldn't wear it in the day-time. But it goes rather well with a great evening out like this!'

'You're charming when you look like a good old traditional barrister,' Liz told him. 'You know. The sort who takes snuff!'

'Snuff?' Claude was doubtful.

'Yes. Snuff.'

'You think I ought to take it?'

'As a simple working-class girl, Claude, I do find that sort of thing a wild turn-on.'

'Oh, do you, really? Snuff, eh? Well. I suppose I might give it a whirl.' Claude was ready for anything in the pursuit of love.

'Out of a little silver box, I'd find that irresistible. Oh, and stop trying to be a whizz-kid. Talking about slimming down and productivity targets. Sounds like some naff little middle manager in a suit. Horribly unsexy.'

'Elizabeth. Is that why you went off me?' The penny was dropping fast.

'And "consumer choice". Consumer choice is absolutely yuk! You know what I've always loved about you, Claude?'

'Loved?' The poor fellow seemed to have run out of breath. 'Please, Elizabeth. Tell me!'

'You being so square. And vague. And beautifully un-businesslike. And sort of dusty.'

'Dusty?' He frowned.

'In the nicest possible way. Dreamy, with all sorts of ideals. You do believe in freelance barristers, don't you, Claude?'

'I believe in them passionately, Elizabeth. Radical ones too, of course.' Men in love will say anything.

'Then would you mind saying so at the next Chambers meeting?' Liz got straight down to business. 'That is, if you're not too much in awe of Ballard.'

'In awe of Ballard! I'll show you if I'm in awe of Ballard. Elizabeth' – he tried to hold her hand – 'do you think we'll ever sing the love duet together?'

'Not now, Claude.' She released her hand.

'When?'

'Perhaps after the next Chambers meeting.' And then the bells rang and Wagner called them both to another, sterner duty.

Whilst these historic events were taking place, I slept the

73

peaceful sleep of the just and went off to the Bailey with a light step, ready to fire off my considerable ammunition at Mr Gerry Jebb, who was to be recalled as the last prosecution witness. But when a somewhat shaken Guthrie resumed his seat on the Bench, he was faced with nothing but a flustered and apologetic Soapy Sam Ballard. 'My Lord,' the discomforted Prosecutor started. 'I gave the Court an undertaking that the witness Gerald Jebb would return today. He was warned that he must be available. But I regret to inform the Court that Jebb has vanished.'

'Not unexpectedly,' I whispered for all the world to hear.

'Vanished, Mr Ballard?' The Judge clearly didn't believe in miracles.

'The Inspector thinks he has probably left the country.'

'Try Marbella,' I suggested.

'My Lord, the flight of this witness, for it must be described as a flight, must cast considerable doubt on his evidence,' Ballard admitted, and then threw in, 'if it can be described as evidence. Our inquiries have also disclosed that the defendant was in fact laying bricks in his garden, which could account for the brick dust on his clothing.' And Ballard concluded, 'I therefore feel that it would not be right for the Prosecution to persist with these charges.'

'Mr Rumpole?' His Lordship asked my view of the matter, so I rose politely. 'I'm sure we are all grateful to my learned friend. It's a wise decision. And I have no doubt your Lordship has other matters to attend to?'

'Oh, yes, indeed. I have an important meeting,' and Guthrie added, with some apprehension, 'with the Lord Chancellor.'

So Basher Baker was set at liberty and walked out, after a gruff 'Thanks, Brother Rumpole', to the world of pay claims and union meetings, and Mr Justice Featherstone prepared to face a higher tribunal.

Henry Fairmile had been a rather dusty, tall, scarecrow of a Q.C. and M.P., with a voice like dead twigs snapping in the wind. He had been an ultra-loyal member of his party and had been promoted, by way of such dull jobs as Solicitor-General and Attorney-General, to the woolsack and the splendour of the Lord Chancellor's office. Now in command of the Judiciary, Lord Fairmile developed a quirky and ironic sense of humour and he enjoyed teasing the Judges who had not taken much notice of him at the Bar. He also enjoyed discovering character weaknesses – drink, women or holidays in the Greek islands with young men in advertising – which would debar ambitious advocates from the Bench. He constantly lectured his colleagues on 'judgeitis', which he defined as pomposity and self-regard, whilst congratulating himself on his peculiar modesty for one who has, in his keeping, the great seal of the Realm. When the Government he served decided to reform the Bar, in the interests of consumer choice and the free market economy, he welcomed such plans as giving him ample scope to irritate the other judges. When the papers came out with news of Guthrie's industrial action, the Lord Chancellor sent for his striking Lordship, who naturally turned up in the office in the House of Lords in fear and trembling, fully expecting to be asked to hand in his resignation, as an alternative to being dismissed by a special act of Parliament. It was not, after all, the first time, that Featherstone J. had been hauled up before the Chancellor.*

When he arrived in the big room and saw the lanky old man sitting in his white bands and tailed coat, his gold-encrusted robe and purse and the long full-bottomed wig on stands ready for his appearance at the woolsack, he was surprised by the warmth of the Chancellor's welcome. 'Come along in, my dear old fellow. Drink? Beer and sandwiches.' The long-abandoned symbols of conciliation stood on a side table.

'That's very kind, but not at the moment. Look, Lord Chancellor' – Guthrie embarked on his long-prepared explanation – 'all that business about striking . . .'

'That's why I wanted to see you, Guthrie.' Lord Fairmile abandoned his usual pastime of fitting a large number of paper clips into a sort of daisy-chain and stood up, whether

* See 'Rumpole and the Tap End' in *Rumpole and the Age of Miracles*, Penguin Books, 1988.

Featherstone wanted it or not, to open a bottle of beer. 'I mean, we just fined the drain-clearance operatives a quarter of a million for not taking a ballot. Do you have that sort of money in your trousers? Do change your mind and take a small light ale?'

The Chancellor smiled and his ready hospitality gave Guthrie courage. 'Well,' he said and took the proffered glass, 'I think the Judges pretty well agree, Lord Chancellor, that if it *came* to a ballot, they might well take action.'

'Oh, dear. Oh, my ears and whiskers. I don't think the Cabinet's going to like that. The idea of all the Judges on a picket line with the local elections coming up. I don't think the Cabinet's going to be attracted by that. Got a cloth cap, have you?' Lord Fairmile gave himself a light ale.

'Well, Lord Chancellor, as a matter of fact I have,' Guthrie admitted.

'A little something to eat?'

'Beer and sandwiches? The way they settled disputes in the Labour Government.' Guthrie smiled as he took a sandwich which he found to be filled with Civil Service Class C hospitality fish-paste.

'Sometimes the old-fashioned ways are the best,' the Lord Chancellor admitted. 'Look here. I have no wish to quarrel with you fellows. And I don't really know why these solicitor chaps want to be judges anyway.'

'Quite agree.' Guthrie was further encouraged. 'They can make much more money sitting in their offices selling houses.'

'Or whatever it is they do.' The Lord Chancellor's voice was slightly muffled by a sandwich.

'Well, exactly!'

'In fact I don't know why anyone wants to be a judge. Unless their practice is a bit rocky. That your trouble, was it?'

'Certainly not!' Guthrie was hurt. 'I felt a call for public duty.'

'Well, I suppose your wife likes it. But no more talk about going on strike, eh? What do you say we leave the whole question of solicitors joining the Judges as one for the Judges to decide?'

'Absolutely super!' Mr Justice Featherstone's reaction was enthusiastic.

'I'm thinking along those lines,' the Head of the Judiciary told him. 'Good to talk to you, Guthrie.'

'Thank you, Lord Chancellor. It's been a most successful negotiation. May I tell my committee . . . I mean, my brother judges?'

'Of course! We'll probably put something rather vague through Parliament. Ought to keep everybody quiet. Now, then. Why don't you try the cheese and tomato?'

'It's all ended happily.' Guthrie was smiling with joy as he took the penultimate sandwich. 'I can't wait to tell Marigold!'

Not long afterwards we legal hacks in Equity Court met again round Ballard's boardroom table. Erskine-Brown, who was toying with a small, silver snuff-box which he tapped occasionally, interrupted Ballard's tedious speech about streamlining our Chambers business-wise, to increase productivity and market share, with the following, unexpected contribution. 'With all due respect to you, Ballard,' he said, 'aren't we in danger of throwing the baby out with the bathwater? We mustn't lose our freedom. Our eccentricity.' He looked at Liz. 'That's what makes us, us barristers' – he smiled modestly – 'so attractive. Ever since the Middle Ages we have been the great freelancers! The independent radicals! The champions of freedom and against tyranny and oppression wheresoe'er it might be! We must preserve, at all costs, the great, old British tradition!'

'Erskine-Brown' – Soapy Sam looked as though he had just sat down on a favourite armchair which had gone missing – 'am I to understand I can no longer count on your support, in getting Chambers efficient, business-wise?'

'No, Ballard,' Claude told him frankly. 'I'm afraid you no longer have my support on this one.'

'Does that mean we're not getting a new coffee machine?' Uncle Tom asked hopefully.

'Yes, Uncle Tom. I rather think it does,' I told him.

'Oh, good!'

'Let's stop trying to be a lot of whizz-kids,' Claude addressed the meeting. 'Talking about "slimming down" and "productivity targets". It makes us sound like awful little middle managers in suits. Yuk!' At this point he took a large pinch of snuff and broke down in hopeless, helpless sneezing, waving a large silk handkerchief.

'I say, you've got the most terrible cold!' Uncle Tom seemed deeply concerned.

I was looking at Liz, who was holding hands with Dave Inchcape under the table, something poor old Claude didn't see. Not for the first time I felt a distinct pang of sympathy for the chap.

That night I went home with a plastic bag, on which was written THEODORAKIS TAKEAWAY KEBABS, which contained what I feared was going to be my dinner. But in the hallway I smelt a magic perfume, a distinct whiff of roast beef and Yorkshire pudding. When I pushed open the kitchen door, there was Hilda preparing these delicacies, together with cabbage, baked potatoes, an apple tart with cream. The whole was to be washed down, I was delighted to see, with a bottle of Pommeroy's Extraordinary Troisième Cru.

'Has peace,' I asked, 'broken out?'

'Well, poor Marigold Featherstone! She was so upset when Guthrie went on strike. Do you know what she bought him? A cloth cap! Rather funny, really. But there are certain people at the top who just shouldn't strike. In the public interest. Judges and generals and well, and . . .'

'Decision-makers of all kinds?' I looked respectfully at Hilda.

'Well, I felt that going on strike was really not on.'

'Distinctly orf?'

'It's just not a thing that people like me and Guthrie should do.' She looked at me, I thought nervously. 'You wouldn't buy me a cloth cap, would you, Rumpole?'

'Perish the thought!'

'So, I thought to myself, it's a long time since you had Yorkshire pudding.'

'Thank you, Hilda.' I was truly grateful. 'Thank you very much.'

'You don't want it to get cold, do you? After I've been to all this trouble. Sit down, Rumpole, and have your dinner.' What could I do then but obey?

Rumpole and the Right to Silence

What distresses me most about our times is the cheerful manner in which we seem prepared to chuck away those blessed freedoms we have fought for, bled for and got banged up in chokey for down the centuries. We went to all that trouble with King John to get trial by our peers, and now a lot of lawyers with the minds of business consultants want to abolish juries. We struggled to get the presumption of innocence, that golden thread that runs through British justice, and no one seems to give a toss for it any more. What must we do, I wonder. Go back to Runnymede every so often to get another Magna Carta and cut off King Charles's head at regular intervals to ensure our constitutional rights? Speaking entirely for myself, and at my time of life, I really don't feel like going through all that again.

The hard-won privilege most under attack at the moment is a suspect's right to silence. Those upon whom the Old Bill looks with disfavour are, it is suggested, duty-bound to entertain the nick with a flood of reminiscence, which will make the job of convicting them of serious crimes a push-over. Now if I were to be arrested – a thought which lurks constantly in the back of my mind – and found myself, an innocent Old Bailey hack, confronted by Detective Chief Inspector Brush and his merry men, I should say nothing, saving my eloquence for a jury of common-sense citizens. And those accused of malpractices may have other reasons for silence apart from a natural shyness in the presence of the law. On the other hand, of course, they may be guilty as charged. These were the questions which confronted me during the Gunster murder case, when a pall of silence hung not only over my client but over some of those dearest, or at least nearest, to me.

Gunster University stands in a somewhat grim Northern landscape, far from the dreaming spires of Oxford or the leafy Cambridge backs. It seems to have been built in the worst age of concrete brutalism and looked, as Hilda and I approached it in a taxi from the station, like an industrial estate or an exceptionally uninviting airport. We had gone there to see young Audrey Wystan graduate in English. Readers of these reminiscences will know that, when it comes to breeding, the Wystans are up there with the rabbits and She Who Must Be Obeyed has relatives scattered all over the world. Were I to be shipwrecked and cast upon some Pacific island, I should not be in the least surprised to find that the fellow in charge of banana production was one of her long-lost cousins. 'Audrey is Dickie's daughter,' She had told me, and, when I looked blank, had explained, 'Dickie was Daddy's brother Maurice's oldest. Her mother was inclined to be flighty, but Audrey was always a clever girl. She has Daddy's blood, you see. And now she's got first-class honours in English. You never got first-class honours in anything, did you, Rumpole?' From all this you will gather that Hilda has a strong sense of family loyalty, and when she heard of young Audrey's success she felt she had to be in at the prizegiving, and, as crime appeared to be a little thin on the ground at that time of the year, I was brought along to swell the applause.

So far as entertainment value went, the degree ceremony at Gunster University ranked a little below a boy scout jamboree in the Albert Hall and a notch or two above a Methodist service in a civic centre. Its main fault was a certain monotony. When you have watched one young person doff a mortar board, shake hands and accept a scroll you have seen them all and you still have about a thousand more to get through. When it was the turn of the English students to file across the platform, their names were called by Professor Clive Clympton, tall, more powerfully built than your usual academic, with gingery hair, an aggressive beard and a resonant voice. When called, the students presented themselves in front of the Chancellor, Sir Dennis Tolson, Chairman of the Tolson's Tasty Foods chain, and the University's main source of finance in these days of decreasing government support. Sir Dennis was a small, plump, round-shouldered man with drooping eyes and a turned-down mouth who looked like a frog in some children's story-book who'd got dressed up in a mortar board and a black-and-gold embroidered velvet gown. Standing next to him, and dressed in similar academic robes, was Hayden Charles, Vice-Chancellor. Charles, apparently a distinguished economist, was slight, grey-haired and good-looking in a dapper sort of way. His smile seemed somewhat patronizing, as though the idea that these honours would help their recipients land a decent job in a merchant bank was really rather quaint.

When the ceremony was over young Audrey told us we were invited to the Vice-Chancellor's house, a handsome Georgian mansion, which stood on the edge of the campus like a good deed in a concrete world. Tea and sandwiches were being served in the big, marble-paved entrance hall, from which a staircase with a wooden balustrade curled up to the higher floors and a painted dome. Nibbling and sipping academics and their families packed out the place, and the party was being ably supervised by a grey-haired, competent-looking woman whom I later discovered to be Mrs O'Leary, the Vice-Chancellor's housekeeper.

'They're destroying the universities! The Government's condemning us to death by a thousand cuts.' Clive Clympton, the English Professor, was haranguing our group which consisted of my good self, Hilda, Audrey and a vaguely anxious-looking person with a purple gown continually slipping off his shoulders. He had introduced himself as Martin Wayfield, Head of Classics.

'You should see what they're doing to the law, Professor,' I said to Clympton, adding my pennyworth of gloom to the party.

'We're going to have nothing but computer courses and business studies. Our masters don't want literature,' the Professor told us.

'Or jury trials. Or freelance barristers. Or the right to silence.' I joined in the litany and earned a rebuke from Hilda, 'Ssh, Rumpole. You're not down the Old Bailey now.'

'The right to what?' The Professor seemed puzzled, so I explained. 'Silence. If you're accused, you can keep quiet and make the Prosecution prove its case. That's what they want to abolish. Bang goes freedom! Nowadays the law's supposed to work with business efficiency like a bank!'

'Most of the people reading English are going into banks.' Audrey, who seemed a bright and reasonably attractive young lady, despite her Wystan ancestry, joined in. And Professor Clympton's mouth curved in a mirthless sort of way over his beard as he said, 'What can you expect, Audrey, with a Vice-Chancellor like Hayden Charles who writes books about money?' He was looking across the hall to Charles, who was talking to Sir Dennis Tolson. Beside him was a well-turned-out, well-groomed female, who looked as though she might have featured on the cover of *Vogue* ten or fifteen years before. Audrey had told us that this was Mercy Charles, the Vice-Chancellor's wife.

'You know Sir Dennis, our Chancellor, is head of that great cultural institution, Tolson's Tasty Foods? And poor old Hayden has to spend most of his time licking the Chancellor's boots.' As Clympton said this, the housekeeper had drawn up beside him and was offering him a plate of what, I deduced from pursed lips, she might have hoped were cyanide sandwiches.

'But Professor Clympton' – Hilda was fair-minded as always – 'they do quite good frozen curries at Tolson's in the Gloucester Road.'

'Don't remind me!' I shuddered at the memory of an occasional evening when Hilda hadn't felt like cooking, and the gangling Martin Wayfield came into the conversation with a fluting protest. 'Perhaps they do, Mrs Rumpole. But they don't do Latin. Nothing's been said yet but I may be the last Professor of Classics the University of Gunster will have.'

'*Amo, amas, amat.* Wordsworth. The right to silence.' I joined in the lament. 'The bloom is gone, and with the bloom go I!'

'"*Eheu fugaces, Postume, Postume*",' Wayfield quoted.

'*Onus probandi, in flagrante delicto,*' I told him.

'What did you say?' The classical scholar seemed puzzled by my Classics.

'Sorry. That's about all the Latin I know,' I explained. 'But I do know Wordsworth.' And I recited, in what I thought was a very moving manner, some lines from the old sheep of the Lake District:

> 'Waters on a starry night
> Are beautiful and fair;
> The sunshine is a glorious birth:
> But yet I know, where'er I go,
> That there hath passed away a glory from the earth'

Far from being touched by this, Clympton looked at me as though I had made a joke in poorish taste. 'Wordsworth,' he barked with disapproval, 'ended up a Tory!'

'Perhaps,' I told him, 'but he can still bring tears to the old eyes.'

'The purpose of literature' – Clympton seemed to be conducting a seminar – 'is not to produce tears, but social change. Your precious Wordsworth betrayed the French Revolution.' Then he stopped lecturing me and sought other company. Mercy Charles was now standing alone, a still beautiful woman with long, soft hair and a smart dark-blue suit with golden buttons. The English Professor excused himself and went over to her, and Audrey said, 'Clive Clympton's a wonderful teacher. What do you think of him, Uncle Horace?' At which point I claimed the right to silence.

Later we were introduced to Hayden Charles, who spoke highly of Audrey's attainments and talked about the fellowship she was being offered. Hilda pointed out that she came from the sort of family to which brains had been handed out with the greatest generosity. I was also introduced to the head of Tolson's Tasty Foods, who held out his hand to me in a somewhat curious manner, with the first two fingers extended and the others tucked into his palm. I paid little attention to this at the time as I was watching Professor Clympton, all aggression drained away, talking to Mrs Charles in a gentle voice and with smiling eyes.

'Mercy Charles is pretty, don't you think?' Audrey said as we were leaving. 'Did you know she used to be quite a famous model?' Hilda frowned at me when I asked if that meant she was a model wife, or merely a model model.

Such were the characters in the drama which was played out on the evening of the graduation ceremony, in the Vice-Chancellor's home. After dinner, Mrs O'Leary was in the kitchen, engaged in polishing some of Charles's silver, the care of which was her particular pride. The kitchen door was a little open and it gave on to the paved entrance hall, which had been the scene of our tea party, so she was able to hear the sound of upraised male voices from the doorway of the Vice-Chancellor's study on the first floor. She distinguished the words 'licking the Chancellor's boots' and she was afterwards able to swear that they were shouted in Professor Clympton's voice. Then she heard Charles shout, 'You've gone mad! Totally mad!' and footsteps on the staircase, followed by the words she couldn't altogether make out in Clympton's voice. However, she was sure she heard an 'oh!' and then 'temporary' and finally 'more is'. This was followed by further incomprehensible shouting, a noise like wood breaking and a crash. There were then footsteps running across the marble, and the sound of the front door opening and banging shut.

When she got out into the hall, she first noticed that part of the wooden banister of the staircase was broken. And then beneath it she saw the slight, elegant figure of Hayden Charles lying on the blood-stained floor. She knelt beside him, held his wrist and called his name but he was past hearing her.

The next day, after the police had been called and made their preliminary inquiries, Detective Inspector Wallace and Detective Sergeant Rose, both of the local force, called on Professor Clive Clympton and asked him to account for his movements at around ten o'clock the previous evening. The Professor, who must have remembered what I had told him about the right to silence, said he had no intention of answering their questions. From then on, in all matters of importance concerning the Gunster case, he shut up like an oyster.

It wasn't only among those accused of crime that silence appeared to be golden. Shortly after the news of Hayden Charles's death had appeared in the papers, I was in my room in Chambers, preparing for an extremely tedious Post Office fraud due in the next day, when Soapy Sam Ballard, Q.C., the sanctimonious leader of our group of legal hacks in Equity Court, put his head round my door and said, 'You're working late.'

'Oh, no,' I told him. 'I'm just arranging my large collection of foreign postage stamps.' 'Are you, really?' 'No, of course not!' The fellow does ask the most idiotic questions. Undeterred by the coolness of my welcome, he made his way into the room, carrying, I couldn't help noticing, a moderate-sized zipper-bag covered in some tartan, and no doubt plastic, material.

'I just called in to put this away in my room,' Ballard said, as though it explained everything.

'This what?'

'This bag.'

'Oh, that.'

Ballard clearly had more in mind than introducing me to his bag, for he sat in my client's chair and prepared to unburden himself.

'I wanted to talk to you some time. I mean, Rumpole, how do you find marriage?'

'In my experience, you usually don't. It finds you. It comes creeping up unexpectedly and grabs you by the collar. How's Matey?' I was referring, of course, to Mrs Ballard for whom Soapy Sam had fallen whilst she was the Old Bailey matron, administering first aid to both sides of the law. 'You mean my wife, I assume?' Ballard guessed right. 'You remember the wonderful work she did at the Central Criminal Court?'

'She was a dab hand with the Elastoplast from what I can remember,' I assured him.

'Much loved, wasn't she, by all you fellows?'

'Well, let's say, highly respected.'

'Highly respected! Yes!'

When we had reached this accord, Ballard seemed stumped for words. He straightened his tie, crossed and recrossed his legs, pulled at his fingers until he seemed in danger of wrenching them off, and finally came out with, 'Rumpole, what's your opinion of secrets? In married life?'

'Absolutely essential.' I had no doubt about it.

'Is one entitled to keep things from one's spouse, for instance?' He asked the question after a good deal of finger pulling and, out of consideration for his joints, I was able to reassure him, 'As many things as possible. Everything you tell the other side just gives them material for cross-examination. That's the first lesson in advocacy, Bollard.'

'I wanted your opinion because of the slight, well, difference, that has arisen between Marguerite and myself.'

'Who the hell's Marguerite?' I was no longer following the fellow's drift.

'Marguerite, Rumpole, is my wife. The person you call Matey.'

'Oh, yes, of course.' My memory was now jogged. 'Why didn't you say so?' But here Ballard drew a deep breath and took me into his confidence. 'She called into Chambers, having been at her refresher course in sprains and fractures. She doesn't work now, of course, but she likes to keep her hand in. And Henry told her I'd already left. At five o'clock. And he thoughtlessly added that he imagined I'd gone home because I was carrying my "tartan bag". He meant this very bag, Rumpole. This one!' And to remove all doubt, he slapped the small item of luggage on the floor beside him. 'It's most unfortunate that Henry should have mentioned this bag at all,' he went on mysteriously, 'because I never take it home!'

'Oh, naturally not.' I had no idea what the fellow was talking about.

'And Marguerite keeps on asking where I was going with this particular bag,' he told me. 'I think, quite honestly, she's curious to know about what's inside it.'

'I'll look up some of the defences to a charge of carrying

house-breaking instruments.' I tried to comfort him with a helpful suggestion. 'Let's say you're doing evening-classes in locksmithery?'

'I've told her that there are certain things, even in married life, which a man is entitled to keep to himself.' He ignored my attempt to treat him like one of my more villainous clients and asked, 'Am I within my rights, Rumpole?'

'Your right to silence,' I reminded him, I hope, correctly, 'it's been yours since Magna Carta!'

'I'm glad you said that.' Soapy Sam seemed enormously relieved. 'I'm very glad to hear you say that, as a married man.'

'Of course, you can't stop the other side thinking the worst,' I warned him.

'Just at the moment,' Ballard admitted, 'that's exactly what she thinks. Really she needs something to take her mind off it. It would make a great deal of difference to Marguerite's happiness if she saw more of you fellows in Chambers.'

'She can see us at any time,' I told him. 'Not that we're much to look at.'

'No. I mean, I think it might be a terrific help if you and Hilda invited her to dinner at your place.'

'Is that what she'd like?' I was greatly taken aback.

'Well. Yes.'

'You're telling me in confidence that Matey would like to be asked to dinner in Froxbury Mansions?' I was still incredulous.

'Well, yes. She would.'

'Don't worry,' I promised him, 'I won't breathe a word to Hilda about it.'

'Rumpole!' Ballard gave a plaintive sort of bleat.

'Oh, well. Come if you want to!' I decided to humour the man. 'Dinner with She Who Must? Your Matey's got a curious idea of fun.' And then I could restrain my curiosity no longer and had to ask, 'What on earth *have* you got in that bag?'

'I think, Rumpole' – Ballard was standing firmly on his rights – 'that's a question I prefer not to answer.'

When I got back to the mansion flat I broke the news to Hilda.

'Ballard's invited himself and Matey to dinner,' I said. 'I fear for the man's sanity. He's carrying round a sort of tartan hold-all, the contents of which he refuses to divulge. It makes him look like a Scottish pox-doctor.' But She Who Must Be Obeyed had other news to impart. 'Do stop prattling, Rumpole,' she said. 'Just come along in and listen to what she's got to say.'

'Who's got to say?'

'Audrey, of course. She's got nobody but us to turn to.'

I found Audrey Wystan in the living-room. She was one of the apple-cheeked, dark-haired girls with the bright-eyed, enthusiastic appearance of those Russian dolls which come in various sizes. If you can imagine an apple-cheeked Russian doll on the verge of tears, that's how Audrey looked as I joined her. 'Thank God you've come, Uncle Horace,' she said in a shaky voice to me. 'They've arrested Clive.'

'Clive?'

'Professor Clympton. You remember?'

'Of course. The academic revolutionary.'

'He wants you to appear at his trial.'

At that moment I had only read about Hayden Charles's death in the paper and knew nothing of the questioning of the English Professor or of his possible involvement in the matter. So I said he had made a wise choice and asked, 'What sort of trial? Driving whilst tiddly?'

'They say it's murder. He thinks you'll understand.'

'About murder? Well, yes. A little . . .'

'No!' Audrey said with particular emphasis, as though delivering a message. 'He says you'll understand about keeping silent.'

So, accompanied by Mizz Liz Probert, as note-taker and general amanuensis, and Mr Beazley, a small, puzzled Gunster solicitor, who had probably up till then spent a blameless life conveying houses and drafting wills, I turned up in the interview room at Brixton prison to take instructions from the captive Professor. I was surprised by his presence there, as the crime had taken place in the North, but the trial was fixed at the Old Bailey. However, we started by discussing what seemed to be Clympton's principal concern. 'The right to silence,' he said, 'they haven't abolished it yet?'

'Not here, old darling,' I reassured him. 'Only in Northern Ireland, where we've handed the forces of evil a famous victory by allowing them to rob us of one of our priceless freedoms. Sorry, I'll save that for the Jury. You can still keep your mouth shut, if that's what we think you ought to do. Silence can't be evidence of guilt.'

'Audrey Wystan says you've won a lot of cases,' Clympton began doubtfully.

'I've won more murders than you've had degrees, Professor.'

'And you've got people off who refused to answer questions?' he asked, anxiously.

'When I thought it was right for them to do so. Yes.'

'It's right now.' His mouth closed firmly, his beard jutted. He seemed to have made up his mind.

'I'll consider that,' I told him, 'when I know a little more about your case.'

'I've decided already.'

In the ensuing quiet I pulled out my watch, lit a small cigar and told him that he had an hour of my time and if he wouldn't discuss the case perhaps he'd rather we talked about Wordsworth.

'If you like.' He shrugged his broad shoulders and looked sullen. I wondered why young Audrey, and perhaps Mrs Charles, found him so attractive, but men never know that about other men. Then I had second thoughts about the topic for the day. 'No, we shan't agree about Wordsworth. Let's discuss your Vice-Chancellor, Hayden Charles. A slightly built man who crashed through some worm-eaten banisters to his death on a marble floor. Pushed, no doubt, by a stronger opponent. You didn't like him?'

'I didn't like his money-mad politics, or his way of running the University.'

'And Mrs Charles?'

'She was a good friend.' The Professor sounded cautious. 'As a matter of fact, she reads a lot of poetry.'

'Read it together, do you?' I made so bold as to ask.

'Sometimes. Mercy's very bright, for an ex-model.'

'And I'm very bright for an Old Bailey hack. I can see a motive rearing its ugly head.'

'I don't understand.' I think he understood perfectly well, but I spelled it out all the same. 'Husband finds out about his beautiful wife's infidelity. Has it out with the lover in his study on the first floor of his house. A row develops and continues on the stairs. It becomes violent. The lover's bigger than the husband. He takes him by the throat, that's where there were bruises, finger marks but no finger-prints. The lover pushes the husband into the banisters. They're not built of reinforced concrete like the rest of Gunster University and they collapse. End of outraged husband. The lover runs out into the night. And that, my Lord, is the case of the Prosecution.' I ground out the remains of my small cigar in the top of the cocoa tin provided as an ashtray.

'The Prosecution can believe that if they want to,' the Professor said at last, with an unconvincing sort of defiance.

'And if the Jury believes it?'

'They won't have any evidence!' He was making the mistake of quarrelling with his defender, so I decided to confront him with the reality of the matter. 'I'll ask my learned junior to read us the statement of Mrs O'Leary, the housekeeper,' I said. Mizz Probert was quick to find the document in her bundle of papers and recited, 'Statement of Mrs Kathleen O'Leary. "I have been housekeeper at the Vice-Chancellor's house for ten years, and before that I worked for Mr and Mrs Charles in Oxford." Blah, blah, blah. "I have observed an intimate friendship develop between Mrs Charles and Professor Clympton." Blah, blah. "I heard quarrelling on the stairs shortly before 10 p.m. I heard Mr Charles's voice and another man's. All I heard the other man say clearly was something about 'licking the Chancellor's boots'. I am quite sure I recognized Professor Clympton's voice."'

'Do *you* think I said that, then?' the Professor challenged me and again I let him have the uncomfortable truth. 'It seems probable. That's exactly what I heard you say in the hearing of half a dozen other people that afternoon over tea and sandwiches. Don't worry, old darling. I'm not going to give evidence for the Prosecution. Someone else might, though.'

'Who?'

'Young Audrey Wystan, for one.'

'She won't.'

'You're very sure of her.'

'Oh, yes. Quite sure.' The Professor, I decided, was behind the door when modesty was handed out.

'The Professor of Classics?'

'Martin Wayfield's an old friend . . .' he began but I interrupted him.

'You were seen earlier by a young man called – What was his name? Peters?'

'Perkins. He'd just got a degree –' Mizz Probert found the statement with her customary efficiency and Clympton told us, with a good deal of contempt '– in business studies. He was one of Hayden Charles's favourites.'

'Christopher Perkins saw Professor Clympton at about 9.15 p.m. He seemed to be in a hurry,' Liz reminded us and I reminded the Professor, 'Mrs O'Leary heard the front-door bell ring at twenty to ten. Charles called out that he was going to answer it, so she didn't see whoever arrived. Was it you?'

'No,' Clympton said after a long silence.

'Then you have to tell us exactly where you went and what you did between nine thirty and just after ten, when Mrs O'Leary found the Vice-Chancellor dead.' But there was no answer. 'Say something to us, Professor,' I begged him. 'Even if it's only goodbye.'

After another long silence the Professor took refuge in literature. 'The sentimental approach to nature in Wordsworth's early poetry,' he told me, 'is his excuse for ignoring the conditions of the urban poor.'

'Say something sensible,' I warned him. 'Because if you don't, the Jury are going to find their own reasons for your silence, however much the Judge warns them not to.'

'Compare and contrast the deeper social message in George Eliot,' was all that Clympton had to say.

'Where were you that night, Professor?' I tried for the last time, and as he still didn't answer, I stood up to go. 'All right, then. Keep quiet. You're entitled to. But there's one line of

Wordsworth it might pay you to remember, "All silent and all damn'd!"'

I can't help experiencing a strong feeling of relief when I walk out of the gates of Brixton prison. It's a case of 'There, but for the Grace of God, stay I.' As we emerged that morning Mizz Probert said, 'What's he got to hide, do you reckon? Guilt?'

'Or he was tucked up somewhere with that ex-model girl you were talking about and he doesn't want to give her away,' Mr Beazley suggested.

'You soliciting gentlemen have got incurably romantic natures,' I told him. 'But there is one thing I can't understand about this case.'

'The silence of the Professor?'

'Not just that. The crime, if it were a crime, occurred up in Gunster, in the wilds of the North, your neck of the woods, Mr Beazley. All the witnesses are up there. But the Prosecution get him committed here in London and sent for trial at the Old Bailey. What's their exquisite reason for that?'

'Search me, Mr Rumpole.' My instructing solicitor was of no assistance.

'Shall we ever know, my Bonny Beazley?' I wondered. 'Shall we ever know?'

It was a time when everyone in Chambers seemed to be coming to me for advice, so that I felt I ought to start charging them for it. I was busily engaged in trying to think out some reasonable line of defence in the Gunster murder when my learned friend, Claude Erskine-Brown, put his head round the door to announce that his wife, Phillida, the Portia of our Chambers, was back from doing a corrupt policeman in Hong Kong.

'Then she can buy us a bottle of Pommeroy's bubbly on the oriental constabulary,' I suggested. 'We can celebrate!'

'Absolutely nothing to celebrate. In view of what she found when she got back.' Claude sat disconsolately in my client's chair and told me his troubles, as a non-fee-paying client. 'I'm afraid I had carelessly left two programmes for *Tristan and Isolde* at Covent Garden on the kitchen table.'

'Pretty scurrilous reading.' I understood the problem at once. 'Was our Portia shocked?'

'She asked whom I'd taken to the Opera.'

'Your wife can always get to the heart of a case, however complicated. She can put her finger on the nub!'

'Of course, I'd been with Liz Probert, as you remember,' Erskine-Brown confessed. 'We had a talk about the future of Chambers in the crush bar at Covent Garden.'

'And I'm sure that when your wife heard that, Claude, she decided not to press charges.'

'That's exactly the trouble, Rumpole. She didn't hear that. In fact, to be perfectly honest with you, I didn't tell her that. I told her I'd taken Uncle Tom.'

'You what?'

'I said I took Uncle Tom with me to the Opera.'

'Uncle Tom?' I couldn't believe my ears.

'Exactly.'

'To five hours of unmitigated Wagner?' It was incredible.

'I'm afraid so.'

'You must have eaten on the insane root,' I told the chap, 'That takes the reason prisoner.'

'Well, this is the point, Rumpole.' Claude suddenly became voluble in his own defence. 'I knew Phillida wouldn't have taken well to the idea of Lizzie and me drinking champagne in the crush bar. Although absolutely nothing happened. I mean, Liz bolted off down the underground almost as soon as the curtain fell. She even left me with her programme, which is why I had two. But on our way from Chambers earlier, we'd met Uncle Tom and he said it was his birthday, so he was off to buy himself a chop at Simpson's in the Strand, and Lizzie said what a pity we didn't have a spare ticket, so we could take him to the Opera as a treat. Of course we hadn't. But when Phillida asked me for an explanation . . . Well, Uncle Tom sprang to mind.'

'Erskine-Brown' – sometimes I despaired of the man ever becoming a proper, grown-up barrister – 'have you learnt nothing from your long years at the Criminal Bar? If you're going to invent a defence at least make it credible.'

'The point is' – he looked desperate – 'I'm terrified Philly's going to ask him.'

'Ask who?'

'Uncle Tom!'

'To another opera?' I was, frankly, puzzled.

'No, of course not. Ask him if he went with me. And if she does *that* . . .'

'You'll be in the soup. Up to the ears.' The situation was now crystal clear to me.

'Exactly. Unless he says he did.'

'You're not going to ask Uncle Tom to commit perjury?'

'I've got no influence over Uncle Tom,' Claude admitted, 'but *you* have, Rumpole. You've known the old boy forever. You can put it to him, as a matter of life and death. He's got to help a fellow member of the Bar.'

'No, Erskine-Brown.' I was shocked by the suggestion. 'Absolutely and definitely no! I will not enter into conspiracy with an elderly and briefless barrister to pervert the course of justice.'

'Is that your last word on the subject?' Claude was deeply disappointed.

'Absolutely my last word,' I assured him.

'You expect me to plead guilty?' He seemed to have reached the end of the road.

'Throw yourself on the mercy of the Court,' I advised him in as friendly a manner as possible.

'Rumpole, I know you call her Portia, but my wife's forgotten all about the Quality of Mercy. I came to you for advice.'

'You came too late. The moment was when she asked you about those two programmes.'

'What should I have done?'

'Claimed the right not to answer any questions,' I told him. 'Everyone else is doing it!'

At last the day arrived, awaited with a certain amount of grim foreboding, when Mr and Mrs Soapy Sam Ballard, on pleasure bent, arrived to dine with the Rumpoles in the Gloucester Road. Marguerite Ballard, the former Old Bailey matron, is a substantial woman who seems to move with a crackle of starch and a rattle of cuffs, and it's still hard to picture her without a watch pinned to her ample bosom. Her hair, done up in what I believe is known as a 'beehive' coiffure, looks as though it were made of something brittle, like candy-floss. So far as weight and stamina are concerned, she is one of the few ladies who might be expected to go ten rounds with She Who Must Be Obeyed. 'The wonderful thing about marriage, Hilda,' the ex-Matey said as we reached the pudding without any major disaster, 'I'm sure you'd agree, is telling each other *everything*. I bet when old Horace climbs into bed with you at night . . .'

'You don't care for baked jam roll, Mrs Ballard?' Hilda discouraged further inquiry into the secrets of the Rumpole marriage bed. 'Baked jam roll is on my naughty list, I'm afraid.' Matron pouted with disappointment. 'We've all got to watch our tummies, haven't we?'

'Marguerite is very keen on keeping fit,' Ballard explained. 'And I'm with her one hundred per cent. I've lost a good deal of weight, you know. You should see my trousers. They hang quite loose. Look!' At which point, he stood up and jerked his waistband in a distasteful demonstration.

'I was saying to Hilda, Sam,' Mrs Ballard banged on regardless, 'I bet when Horace climbs into bed with her, he tells her all the events of the day. And about all the little cases he gets as a *junior* barrister.'

'The little murders in provincial universities,' I agreed.

'I expect you'll be taking in a leader on the Gunster murder, won't you, Horace?' Ballard sounded hopeful.

'I expect not. The client seems to think I'm the world's greatest expert on the right to silence.' I looked at Soapy Sam. 'You're keen on that, aren't you? Silence?'

'When I was on duty down at the Old Bailey –' Marguerite was off again – 'everyone used to confide in me. All the way from the Recorder of London to the lads down in the cells. I think they found me wonderfully easy to talk to. "Matey," the old Recorder said more times than I care to remember, "you're the only person I feel I can really take into my confidence on the subject of my feet." Everyone seems to be able to confide in me except my husband.' And she repeated, at increased volume to Ballard, the refrain, 'I said everyone seems able to confide in me except you, Sam.'

'So good of you to have us to dinner, Hilda.' Ballard was clearly anxious to change the subject. 'It's really a fun evening. We'll have to fix up a time to return your hospitality.'

'Oh, please, don't put yourself out,' I begged him, but my voice was drowned in Marguerite's continued harangue. 'Sam's a new boy, of course. But we're old hands at marriage, aren't we, Hilda? When I was married to poor Henry Plumstead, who passed away, we told each other every little thing. We just knew all there was to know about each other. I'm sure old Horace would agree with that.'

'Old Horace isn't so sure.' And I gave them an example of the blessings of silence. 'You remember George Frobisher? Hopeless at cross-examination so they made him a circus judge. Before your time, Bollard. Anyway he wanted to marry this Mrs Tempest. Frightfully struck with her, George was. I happened to recognize her as an old client with a tendency to burn down hotels for the sake of the insurance money.'*

'The women he's known! Old Horace has been around, hasn't he?' Marguerite joked and was rewarded with a freezing look from Hilda.

'I took it on myself to let old George know about Mrs Tempest's past,' I told them. 'He never forgave me. I don't think I've ever forgiven myself. They'd probably have been quite happily married, provided he didn't leave the matches lying around. When it comes to a nearest and dearest, a profound ignorance is usually best.'

I could tell by the way Hilda stood up and cleared away the plates that she wasn't best pleased by my conclusion. She then retired into the kitchen to wash up and Matey insisted on coming with her to dry. I was left with our Head of Chambers who, no doubt still hoping for a brief, re-opened the subject of Gunster. 'Funnily enough, I had an old uncle who lived there.'

* See 'Rumpole and the Man of God' in *The Trials of Rumpole*, Penguin Books, 1979.

I didn't find the fact especially amusing, but he went on, 'Used to be an estate agent, but he had to give it up. He said you couldn't get anywhere in Gunster unless you were an Ostler. They practically run the show.'

'A what?'

'Ancient Order of Ostlers. Rather like the Freemasons, only more so. My uncle didn't hold with it, so they squeezed him out.'

'Did he say what they did, these Ostlers, or whatever they called themselves?' I felt a faint stirring of interest. 'Oh, all sorts of secret ceremonies, I believe,' Ballard told me. 'Mumbo-jumbo, Uncle Marcus said. And they had a peculiar handshake.'

'Like that?' I asked. I remembered something and extended my hand with two fingers stretched out and the others bent back.

'Yes, I rather think it was. Look, wouldn't you like my assistance as a leader in that case?'

'No, thanks,' I hastened to assure him. 'You've been a great help to me already. Ah, Hilda. Is that the coffee?'

She Who Must Be Obeyed had come back with Marguerite and a tray. Her face was set grimly, with the look of a jury returning with a guilty verdict, as she ignored me totally and merely asked Marguerite if she took sugar.

'I'm going up to Gunster tomorrow,' I told my wife, and, when she still ignored me, I repeated the news. 'Gunster, dear. It's in the North of England. I'll probably be taking my junior, Mizz Probert, with me. You won't mind that, will you, Hilda?' In the normal course of events this information would have set off an avalanche of protest from Hilda. Now she simply handed Ballard coffee and asked him, 'Are you still keeping busy in Daddy's old Chambers?'

'So I'll probably be away tomorrow night,' I intruded firmly into the conversation. 'You won't be lonely, will you?' My wife looked at me but said nothing at all. So far as Rumpole was concerned the rest was silence.

It was not until long afterwards that I discovered what had transpired in the kitchen. 'Sam is up to tricks,' Mrs Ballard had confided in Hilda, 'and your Horace is encouraging him.' When asked for further and better particulars, Matey referred to the mysterious zipper-bag which Sam left in his Chambers and was apparently ashamed to bring home. When asked about its contents by his wife he had replied, 'Old Rumpole takes the view that married people are entitled to a little privacy. Rumpole says we all have the right to silence, even in married life.' 'So you see,' Marguerite summed the situation up, 'it seems your Horace takes sides with husbands who get up to tricks.' This information was, of course, more than enough to cause She Who Must Be Obeyed to sever diplomatic relations with my good self.

Once again I was at Gunster and in the Vice-Chancellor's house. I stood on the stairway, by the broken banister, and shouted at the top of my voice, 'You spend your life licking the Chancellor's boots!' Then the kitchen door opened and Liz Probert came out, followed shortly by Mr Beazley. We had been able to make this experiment by kind permission of the local force and Hayden Charles's widow. 'You heard that?' I asked Liz.

'Clearly!'

'You could tell it was me?'

'Oh, it was you, all right. Just the sort of thing you would say!'

'Let's try it again. This time I'll come down the stairs after I've shouted and run across the hall.'

'Did you say "run", Rumpole?' Liz was incredulous.

'Well, move fairly rapidly.'

They went off to the kitchen again and I was left alone to repeat my performance and cross the hall. Then the front door was opened and Mercy Charles came into the house. 'You were kind enough,' I thanked her, 'to say we could inspect the scene of the crime.'

'It's rather a long inspection.' She still looked beautiful but the creases at the corners of her eyes, which had looked like the signs of laughter, now seemed the marks of tiredness or age. 'I know,' I sympathized with her, 'crimes take such a short time to commit and so terribly long to investigate. Do you think Professor Clympton killed your husband?'

She looked at me and, instead of answering, asked another question. 'Do you think you'll get him off?'

'The Professor won't tell me where he was on the night in question,' I told her. 'He's not being much help to me at the moment, imitating the oyster.'

'What do you want me to do about it?'

'He might just be keeping quiet to protect a lady's reputation,' I suggested. 'Rather an old-fashioned idea, I suppose. But it's possible, isn't it?'

'That Clive was in bed with me and he doesn't want to tell anyone? Is that what you'd like me to say? Then of course I will, if it'll be a help.'

'Is it true?' I had to ask her.

'What's it matter to you if it's true or not? You're a lawyer, aren't you? It's your job to get Clive off.'

She was looking at me, smiling, when Liz and Mr Beazley came out of the kitchen to join us. I asked then if they'd heard my footsteps going to the door and they said they had. 'You know Mrs Charles, of course?' And I instructed our solicitor, 'Please, Beazley. On no account take a statement from her.' We left the house then and Mercy was still standing in the hall, looking lonely and mystified – a woman who, as far as I was concerned, had just disqualified herself from giving evidence.

'What was all that about Mrs Charles and her statement?' Liz asked me as we crossed the Gunster University quadrangle, an area which looked like a barrack square for some bleak army of the future.

'It wouldn't have been the slightest use to us,' I told her. 'She'd have been torn apart in cross-examination. Silence may not always be golden, but it's worth more than lies. Lots of people need to learn that lesson including Claude Erskine-Brown.'

'Claude? What's he done?'

'Sssh! Don't say a word. I suppose it was my fault, really. I got him into it.★ Here we are at the library. At least books have to give up their secrets.'

The library was another concrete block. We went up in a lift to a floor which hummed with word processors and computers and even had shelves of books available. The presiding librarian was seated at his desk, a small, worried man, who seemed nervous of the machinery which surrounded him and was likely to take over his job.

'Sir,' I addressed him with due formality, 'I am engaged on a history of the fair city of Gunster. I wonder if you have anything on the Ancient Order of Ostlers?'

'Order of what?' The librarian frowned as though he didn't understand me.

'Ostlers. Men who look after horses, although I don't think there's many grooms among them now. I would say there are more chairmen of committees, planners, property developers, chief constables, even, dare it be said, heads of universities. Important people in the long history of Gunster.'

'I'm quite sure we haven't got anything like that.' The man was almost too positive. I managed to sound amazed. 'Your library is silent on this important subject?'

'Nothing about it at all. In fact I've never heard of these grooms or whatever it is you're talking about.'

'Mr Rumpole?' I heard a gentle voice beside us. 'You're asking about the Ostlers?' I turned to see Martin Wayfield, the Classics Professor, who had stolen up on us, his fingers still keeping his place in some dusty volume of textual criticism. 'It's all a lot of nonsense but I can tell you a bit about them. I was once coming out of the gents in the Gunster Arms hotel . . .'

'Professor Wayfield! Silence, please!' the Librarian interrupted him in a panic-stricken whisper. 'You know the rules of the library.'

'Oh, all right. Come over to my room. We don't want to wake up the students, do we?'

Wayfield's room, a bleak modern office mercifully buried in

★ See 'Rumpole and the Summer of Discontent'.

books, piles of papers, files, reproductions of busts from the British Museum, fading photographs of other antiquities and posters for cruises round Greece and Turkey, seemed a haven of civilization in the grim Gunster desert. When we had settled there, he encouraged Mizz Probert to boil a kettle and make tea, filled an old pipe, lit it and said, 'What were we talking about?'

'Something that interested me strangely,' I reminded him. 'You were just coming out of the Gunster Arms gents . . .'

'Ah, yes.' He took up his story again. 'And there was one of these fellows, wearing a leather apron and gauntlets, with a bloody great gilded horseshoe hung round his neck, just about to slink into the private dining-room to swear some terrible oath of secrecy and offer to have his throat cut if he ever let on what they were up to. They do that, apparently. Well, I recognized him as a chap who used to be' – here he started to. laugh – 'the University Registrar. So I called out, "Hullo, Simkins! Your old lady cast a shoe, has she?" And he bolted like a rabbit!'

I laughed with him and then became serious. 'Hayden Charles, the late Vice-Chancellor,' I asked, 'was he one of the brotherhood?'

'Hayden always laughed about them. No. I'm sure he wasn't. You know, he got appointed because he was well in with the Ministry at that time. It almost seemed a condition of our grant to have Hayden. Some of the dedicated Ostlers were furious about it.' Then he became serious also. 'So you're defending Clive Clympton. Think you'll get him off?'

'Everyone's asking that. I don't know. Do you think he pushed the Vice-Chancellor over the staircase?'

'Who can tell what anyone'll do? When they're in a temper.' Wayfield was opening a battered carton of milk to add to our tea. It looked sour, so I said I'd have mine black and then I asked if my client was popular around the University.

'The leftie students love him and there are plenty of those,' Wayfield told us.

'And the old dons must hate him?' Liz Probert suggested.

'Not really. He's pretty universally respected. Even by Sir

Dennis Tolson, although they're chalk and cheese, politically.' He relit his pipe which never kept going for very long. 'You've probably heard stories about his private life?'

'You think they're true?' I knew what he was talking about, of course.

'Why not? Mercy Charles is a very attractive woman.'

'Everyone says that. And she finds the Professor a very attractive man?'

'"*Sed mulier cupido quod dicit amanti. In vento et rapida scribere oportet aqua*",' Wayfield replied unhelpfully. 'Not everyone says that.' And I had to ask him, 'What does it mean?'

'"But a woman's sayings to her lusting lover should be written in wind and running water." It's all there. In the Latin. But it's going to be forgotten when they abolish the Classics. I ought to get back to my Catullus.' He looked longingly at the book he had brought with him from the library. So I stood up and thanked him, rather glad to be dismissed before we had experienced his tea. Then I held out my hand, two fingers extended, the rest folded into my palm. Wayfield looked sympathetic. 'You've hurt your hand?' he asked.

'Not at all.' I opened my hand. 'Nothing wrong with it at all.' And the head of the Classics Department gave me a firm, strong, but quite normal, handshake.

Back in London, Uncle Tom was, as usual, practising putts with an old mashie niblick into the clerk's room waste-paper basket, when Claude Erskine-Brown approached him in a conspiratorial fashion. My account of the conversation that follows is derived from Uncle Tom's memory of it, so I cannot vouch for its total accuracy. However, it went somewhat along these lines. Claude opened the bowling by saying, 'Uncle Tom, I've got something very important to tell you. I'd be glad of your full attention.'

'Not offering me a brief, are you?' Uncle Tom asked nervously. 'I'm not sure I remember what to do with a brief.'

'No, Uncle Tom. I want you to understand this perfectly clearly. You see, I wanted to take you to the Opera.'

'No, you didn't!' The old golfer was clear about that. 'I did,'

Claude assured him, 'on your birthday. I met you in the street and I wanted to ask you.'

'And if you had, I wouldn't have gone! I don't care for opera. Now if it'd been a musical comedy, it might have been different.'

'Well, this was a sort of musical comedy' – Claude smiled as though to a child – 'called *Tristan and Isolde*.'

'I remember old Sneaky Purbright used to be in these Chambers . . .' Uncle Tom helped out a difficult conversation with a reminiscence. 'Before your time. Sneaky had tickets for a musical comedy. They were reviving *The Bing Boys*. It was a most delightful evening.' And here he broke into song, '"If you were the only girl in the world, And I was the only boy . . ."'

'Well, I wanted to give you a most delightful evening,' Claude assured him. 'But I couldn't because I was taking someone else.'

'Sneaky wanted to take someone else too, but his wife wouldn't have liked it. So he took me. To *The Bing Boys*.'

'Well, that's just it! I wanted to take someone else to Covent Garden and I did. But my wife wouldn't have liked it. So I told her I took you.'

Uncle Tom thought this over carefully and came out with 'Funny thing to say. When you didn't.'

'Well, I know. But, please, Uncle Tom. If anyone asks you – particularly if anyone called Phillida Erskine-Brown asks you – if you went to the Opera House with me, I beg you to say yes.'

'Oh, I see.' Somewhere deep within Uncle Tom a penny dropped. 'I see exactly what's going on!'

'Thank God for that!' Claude seemed greatly relieved.

'Oh, yes I wasn't born yesterday, you know! Sneaky Purbright was having hanky-panky with old Mat Mattingley's secretary in King's Bench Walk. That meant he was out of Chambers a lot, so whenever Sneaky's wife rang up we had to say, "He's gone over to the library to read Phipson on Evidence."'

'But this time it's the Opera,' Claude was anxious to explain, 'and absolutely nothing occurred.'

'So. In the fulness of time' – Uncle Tom ignored the interruption–'our phrase for hanky-panky in Chambers became "reading Phipson on Evidence". That was our expression for hanky-panky. I mean, "reading Phipson" meant you know what.'

'Please, Uncle Tom, I'd be very grateful. It's really quite innocent.'

'If you ask me, I'm to say I went to the Opera with you.' Uncle Tom was keen to cooperate.

'No,' Claude was still patient, 'if *my wife* asks you.'

'Absolutely,' Uncle Tom agreed. 'I'll tell Mrs Erskine-Brown it was a most delightful evening.' He started to play golf again, singing the while, '"Nothing else would matter in the world today,/We would go on loving in the same old way./ If you were the only girl in the world . . ."'

'I don't know how to thank you, Uncle Tom,' Claude said, but the old man was busy completing the ditty. '". . . and I was the only boy."'

Mr Justice Oliphant, known, not particularly affectionately, to the legal profession as 'Ollie' Oliphant, hailed from somewhere near Gunster and had done his practice in the deep North. He was a pallid, shapeless, rubbery sort of man, and every movement he made seemed to cost him considerable effort. As he made a note he would purse his lips, frown, suck in his breath, concentrate visibly, and then, when he read through what he had written, he would rub his eyes with his fist and gasp with surprise. He was fond of treating us like a lot of Southern layabouts, full of far-fetched fantasies, who eat grapes to the sound of guitars and take siestas. He was always telling us about his down-to-earth, North Country common sense and he was proud of calling a spade a spade, usually long before anyone had proved it was a toothpick. Perhaps because he knew the area, he was chosen to preside over the Gunster murder trial at the Old Bailey. The Prosecution was represented by Mordaunt Bissett, Q.C., a large, florid man with a plummy voice, who hunted every weekend in the season and was said to be extremely 'clubbable'. (There were many occasions in Court when I could have clubbed the fellow, if a suitable blunt instrument were handy. He had a talent for jumping over the rules of evidence as though they were low hedges in the Bicester country.) He was assisted by a junior whose name I now forget and whose only task seemed to be fetching coffee for his learned leader when we retired to the Bar mess. The Defence was in the more than capable hands of Mr Horace Rumpole and Mizz Liz Probert.

The trial was well attended by members of the press and, in the public gallery, I spotted a number of interested academics, including Martin Wayfield, the Professor of Classics. Let me begin my account of the proceedings at the point when Mrs O'Leary, the late Hayden Charles's housekeeper, was in the witness-box and Mordaunt Bissett, examining her in chief, began a question, 'Now tell us, when you were in the kitchen on the night of the murder . . .'

'My Lord, I object!' I was on my feet with the agility that constantly surprises my opponents. 'No one's proved it was a murder! It might be anything from manslaughter to accident.'

'Oh, come, come, Mr Rumpole.' The voice of the North Country comedian on the Bench tried to stifle my protests. 'The Jury and I will use our common sense. Mr Mordaunt Bissett is just using the word in the indictment your client faces.'

'To use that word before it's been proved isn't common sense. It is uncommon nonsense,' I insisted, at which Ollie became testy. 'If the Defence is going nit-picking, Mr Rumpole, we'll call it an "incident". Will that satisfy you?'

'It's not me that has to be satisfied, my Lord,' I answered grandly, 'it's the interests of justice!'

I sat down then and the Judge said, in his best down-to-earth manner, 'come along, Mr Mordaunt Bissett. Let's get back to work, shall we, now Mr Rumpole's had his say.' At which the mighty hunter smiled in an ingratiating sort of way and said to the witness, 'During the "incident" you could distinguish some of the words the man on the stairs was shouting. You told us you heard him say something about "licking the Chancellor's boots"?'

'I heard that. Yes,' Mrs O'Leary agreed.

'Could you recognize the man's voice?'

'I was sure I could.'

'Whose was it?' Mrs O'Leary looked at the tall, red-bearded man in the dock as though she regretted the abolition of the death penalty. 'It was *his* voice,' she said.

'You mean it was the voice of Professor Clympton?' Bissett was one for hammering home the message, and Mrs O'Leary obliged again with 'I'm sure it was.'

At this point Bissett sat and closed his eyes, as though the verdict was no longer in doubt. Ollie Oliphant made a note of the witness's last answer, pursed his lips, gasped for air like a porpoise and underlined the words heavily with a red pencil in a way the Jury couldn't help noticing. Then he asked me if I had any questions for Mrs O'Leary in a way which meant 'Do have a go, if you think it will do you the slightest good, young fellow, my lad!'

'Mrs O'Leary' – I rose to my feet, more slowly this time – 'Did you hear any other words you could distinguish, from Mr Charles's attacker?'

'Only a few, my Lord.'

'What were they?'

'I didn't think they were important. I couldn't make sense of them, anyway.'

'Let's see if we can.'

'I heard him say "oh!" loudly.'

'Oh, and then what?'

'Well, it sounded like "temporary". And then another "oh!" And then, I think I heard, "more is" . . .'

'Does all this make sense to you, Mr Rumpole?' his Lordship asked.

'Not at the moment, my Lord,' I admitted.

'So this evidence is merely brought out to puzzle the Jury?'

'Or perhaps, my Lord,' I suggested, 'to test their powers of deduction.' And then I turned my attention to the witness again. 'You say you heard the man shout something about licking the Chancellor's boots?'

'She's told us that!' The good old North Country patience was running out fast.

'Yes, but let me suggest *when* you heard it, Mrs O'Leary.

You heard it at tea-time, did you not? When you were helping serve sandwiches to the graduates and their families. Professor Clympton said the Vice-Chancellor licked the Chancellor's boots. It was said quite clearly.'

'Mr Rumpole! How do you know it was said clearly? You weren't there, were you?' Ollie Oliphant grinned at the Jury, clearly feeling he was on to a good thing. I hated to disappoint him. 'As a matter of fact I was,' I told the Court. 'But I'm not here to give evidence. This lady is. You heard that at tea-time, didn't you, Mrs O'Leary?'

'Yes, I did. And I thought it was a disgusting thing to say about Mr Charles.'

'So when you heard those words again from the hallway at about 10 p.m., you naturally thought it was Professor Clympton shouting them?'

'I thought so. Yes.' The answer was only a shade less confident.

'Because that was something you'd *already heard him* say?'

'I had. Yes.'

'And if someone *else* had used the same words at night time, a man you never saw perhaps, you'd be likely to assume it was Professor Clympton?'

There was a long pause. The Jury looked interested, Mordaunt Bissett, Q.C. still feigned sleep and the Judge didn't risk my wrath by putting in his two penn'orth.

'I suppose so,' the witness said at last.

'Even though you couldn't really recognize his voice?' I asked her. There was another long pause, and then she said, with even less certainty, 'I *think* I recognized it.'

'You *think* you recognized it.' I gave the Jury a look which was more triumphant than I felt. 'Thank you very much, Mrs O'Leary.' I sat down, having done all that was possible in the circumstances. Whereupon Mr Justice Oliphant set about trying to undo all the good I had done the Professor.

'Mrs O'Leary,' the Judge began in his most down-to-earth manner, 'let's use our common sense about this. You told Mr Mordaunt Bissett you were sure it was Professor Clympton's voice?'

'Yes.'

'And you told Mr Rumpole you *think* it was.'

'That's right.'

'So does it come to this, you *think* you're sure?'

'Yes. I suppose so,' the witness agreed reluctantly and the Judge looked pleased with himself. 'Common sense, Members of the Jury,' he said, with great satisfaction, 'it always does it.'

The next witness was young Christopher Perkins, the student who had just graduated when the 'incident' took place, and while he was being summoned and sworn, I took the opportunity of speaking to the beefy Prosecutor. 'Mordaunt, old darling,' I whispered, 'a word in your shell-like. Why did the Prosecution start this case in London?'

'We've got you a North Country judge,' he answered, as though that were some kind of compensation.

'Thank you very much but the Defence sometimes asks for cases to be moved because of local prejudice against the accused. Did you think some of the Jury might be prejudiced in favour of the Professor if he'd been tried in Gunster?'

Mordaunt Bissett gave me a smiling 'no comment' and rose to examine the young man in the neat blue suit, with slicked-down hair, rimless glasses and a minute moustache, who had sworn to tell nothing but the truth. 'Are you Christopher Perkins?'

'Yes, sir.'

'Did you graduate with first-class honours in Business Studies last July?'

'Yes, I did.'

'On the night of the incident, were you crossing the quadrangle past Tolson buildings?'

'Yes, I was.'

'Did you see Professor Clympton?'

'Don't lead,' I growled and Bissett smiled tolerantly and changed the question to 'What did you see?'

'I'd looked at my watch as I was due to meet a friend in the J.C.R. It was just nine fifteen. Then I saw Professor Clympton coming out of his rooms. He seemed to be in a hurry. He was carrying a bag, I remember.'

'Thank you, Mr Perkins.' Bissett sat down satisfied and I climbed to my feet with a new interest in the evidence. 'We haven't heard about the bag,' and I asked, 'Can you describe it?'

'Just an ordinary zipper holdall. I thought he was on his way to play squash or something.'

'On his way to play squash at that time of evening?'

'Well, I didn't know where he was going, did I?'

'Of course not.' The Judge was, as always, reluctant to exercise his right to silence.

'Well, I hope no one's suggesting he was carrying special equipment for pushing people downstairs,' I said, and couldn't resist adding, 'After all, we've got to use our common sense about this, haven't we, Members of the Jury?'

It was a time when everyone seemed to be carrying mysterious luggage. When I got back to Chambers I telephoned young Audrey Wystan, who was still in residence in Gunster, working at some thesis on the importance of cosmetics in metaphysical poetry, or something of the sort, by which she hoped to further her academic career. I asked her if she wanted to help the Professor and, when I got an enthusiastic and breathless 'yes', I gave her certain instructions about getting into his rooms on some pretext and conducting a search.

When I left Equity Court I saw a familiar figure hurrying through the gloaming. It was Soapy Sam Ballard, and in his hand was his tartan zipper-bag, the piece of luggage which had been the subject of so much speculation. I must confess that my curiosity overcame me and, instead of heading straight for Pommeroy's Wine Bar as I had intended, I set out, like that irreplaceable sleuth Fig Newton, to tail Ballard. I wanted to know where he was going and what he did with the mysterious holdall.

Keeping a discreet distance between us, I followed him across Fleet Street, down Fetter Lane and through some of the narrow and dingier lanes behind Holborn. At last we came to an anonymous and gloomy building, which might have been a converted warehouse. Windows on the first floor were lit up, and the regular pulse of loud disco music was audible in the street below. Moving quickly and, I thought, furtively, Ballard sneaked in through the swing-doors of this establishment. I loitered in the street and lit a small cigar.

After a decent interval I followed our Head of Chambers' footsteps in at the door and climbed a stone staircase to the first floor and the source of the music which was, by now, almost deafening. There was another pair of doors on the landing, over which a notice was fixed which read alliteratively ANNIE ANDERSON'S AEROBOTICS ATELIER. SESSIONS TWICE NIGHTLY. I approached the doors with a good deal of natural hesitation and found that they had small, circular windows in them. Peering through, I was able to discern a hefty blonde, no doubt Annie herself, clad in a yellow track-suit, leaping up and down and shouting commands in time to the music. The corybants she commanded were mainly young, but among them I spotted a breathless Ballard, pale and eager, leaping as best he could, clad in a bright purple track-suit and elaborately constructed plimsolls that had no doubt been the secret contents of his much discussed holdall. If I was laughing, my laughter was happily drowned by the dreadful sound of the musical accompaniment.

At about the same time as I was watching Ballard trip the heavy and fantastic toe at Annie Anderson's Aerobotics Atelier, young Audrey Wystan had entered Professor Clympton's rooms in Gunster. He had left a key with the porter and Audrey had borrowed it, saying that Clympton needed some things urgently for his trial. She was so anxious to help him that she practised this small deception on my express instructions. She went through his study without finding what I had sent her to look for, but at last she opened a big built-in cupboard in the bedroom. There was a zipper-bag on the floor, beneath the hanging suits and academic gowns, and when she opened it she found it to contain, to her bewilderment, a gilded horseshoe on a chain and a leather apron. She telephoned me and I got on to the indrustious Beazley to tell him to get out a witness summons for the man we should have to call the next day, with the permission of the Judge.

★

So, much to his obvious irritation, a reluctant witness, looking, at that moment, like an extremely displeased frog, was called to the witness-box and I asked him, as soothingly as possible, whether he were Sir Dennis Tolson.

'I am.'

This simple question an answer produced an outcry from the dock, where my client, foregoing his right to silence at last, began to utter fruitless cries of 'No! I forbid it!', 'I'm not having it!' and 'Stop it, Rumpole! What the hell do you think you're doing?' What I was hoping to do was to get the Professor off, despite all his efforts to land himself in the slammer for life. Fortunately Ollie Oliphant did something useful at last. 'Mr Rumpole,' he said, showing a rare grasp of the facts of the case, 'your client is creating a disturbance!'

'Is he really, my Lord?' I tried to keep calm in spite of the Professor. 'It's these literary chaps, you know. Very excitable natures.'

'Well, he's not getting excitable in my Court. Do you hear that, Clympton? Any more of this nonsense and you'll be taken down to the cells. Now' – here the Judge smiled winsomely at the witness – 'did you say, *Sir* Dennis Tolson?'

'Yes, my Lord.'

'Some of us do our weekly shop at Tolson's Tasty Foods. Don't we, Members of the Jury?' A few of the more sycophantic jury members nodded and Ollie started to exchange reminiscences with the fat little fellow in the witness-box. 'Sir Dennis, it may interest you to know, I come from your part of England.'

'Is that so, my Lord?' Tolson sounded as though he had received more fascinating information.

'I used to practise often at the old Gunster Assizes,' the Judge went on. 'Never dreamt I'd find myself sitting down here, at the Old Bailey.' I refrained from telling the old darling that it came as a bit of a shock to us too, and asked Sir Dennis if he attended by summons.

'It was served on me last night,' he told us. 'It was most inconvenient.'

'I'm sorry, but it would be most inconvenient for my client

to have to go to prison for a crime he didn't commit. Are you an Ostler?'

'A what, Mr Rumpole?' Ollie was clearly having difficulty keeping up.

'A member of the Ancient Order of Ostlers,' I explained. 'An organization with considerable power and influence in the City of Gunster.'

At which point the witness raised his arm in what looked like a mixture between a benediction and a Fascist salute and intoned, 'By the Great Blacksmith and Forger of the Universe . . .'

'That means you are?' I assumed.

'He doesn't permit me to answer that question.' Sir Dennis was also having a go at the right to silence.

'Don't bother about the Great Blacksmith for a moment,' I told him. 'His Lordship is in control here and he will direct you to answer my questions.'

'Provided they're relevant!' Ollie snapped like a terrier at my heels. 'What've you got to say, Mr Mordaunt Bissett?'

'I think the Defence should be allowed to put its case, my Lord.' The not very learned Prosecutor showed some unusual common sense. 'We have to consider the Court of Appeal.' Now, if there's anything which makes Ollie wake up in a cold sweat in the middle of the night it's the fear of being criticized by that august assembly. 'The Court of Appeal? Yes,' he agreed hastily. 'You're quite right. Get on with it then, Mr Rumpole. The Jury don't want to be kept here all night, you know.'

'Are most of the important people in Gunster members of the Ostlers?' I asked the witness.

'We are sworn to secrecy.'

'Are they members?' I was prepared to go on asking the question all day if I didn't get an answer.

'Our Ostlers are men of talent and ambition. Yes.' I got a sort of an answer.

'And is membership a path to promotion in local government, for instance, and in the University?'

'An Ostler will do his best to help another Ostler, yes. All things being equal.'

'And all things being equal, an ambitious English Professor might do well to join you, if he had his eyes on becoming Vice-Chancellor. In the fulness of time?'

There was a long silence then. I saw my client sit with his arms crossed, his eyes on the ground. He only lifted his head to look at the witness with an unspoken protest when he answered, 'Professor Clympton was one of our members. Yes. If that's what you're getting at.'

'Thank you, Sir Dennis.' I was genuinely grateful. 'That's exactly what I was getting at. Now did you, by any chance, have a meeting on the night Hayden Charles met his death?'

'As a matter of fact we did.'

'What time did that meeting begin?'

'Our normal time. Nine thirty.'

'Where was it?'

'The usual place.'

'The Gunster Arms hotel?' I remembered Wayfield's story.

'Yes.'

'And when did Professor Clympton arrive?'

'About ten minutes before the meeting was due to begin.'

'That's nine twenty. When Hayden Charles was still alive. When did he leave?'

'We broke up around midnight. We had a few drinks when the meeting was over.'

'And by eleven o'clock the police had found Hayden Charles dead. And Professor Clympton was with you all the time? From nine thirty to midnight?'

'Yes. He initiated a couple of candidates and . . .'

'Thank you, Sir Dennis' – I was prepared to spare the witness further embarrassment – 'you can keep the rest of your secrets intact.'

I sat down and Mordaunt Bissett got up to start a quite ineffective attempt to repair the fatal damage done to his case. While this was going on, Mizz Probert asked me in a whisper what on earth a decent left-wing professor thought he was doing with a lot of old businessmen in aprons.

'He was ambitious,' I told her. 'But he'd rather be suspected of murder than let it be known just how ambitious. Perhaps that's why he'll never thank me. He's lost the young.' And looking behind me at the man in the dock, I saw his face back in his hands, his shoulders bowed and felt some pity for him, but more for young Audrey Wystan who had so admired his outspoken independence of the University establishment.

The case of Claude Erskine-Brown was not going so happily. He and Uncle Tom were both in our clerk's room when Dianne announced that Mrs Erskine-Brown was on the phone and wanted to speak to the aged golfer in the corner. I was just back from a day's work at the Bailey and I saw Uncle Tom take the call, and was a witness to the agony of Erskine-Brown as he heard how it was going.

'Oh, Mrs Erskine-Brown. Where are you? Winchester Crown Court. Just checking up? Oh.' And then Uncle Tom obliged Claude by saying, 'When you were in Hong Kong, your husband did take me to a show. It was very kind of him indeed. It was my birthday. What was the show called? Just a moment . . .' Here he put his hand over the instrument and whispered to Claude, 'What was it called?' And received the answer, '*Tristan and Isolde.*'

'Oh, yes.' Uncle Tom was back in contact with our Portia. '*Tristan* and somebody else. No. Claude's not here at the moment. I think he's over in the library. Reading Phipson on Evidence. Yes. It was a most delightful show. *Tristan*, yes. I'm very fond of a musical, d'you see?'

'Uncle Tom!' Claude, in spite of himself, cried out, fearing what was coming. 'The tunes are unforgettable, aren't they?' Uncle Tom blundered on. 'I was singing to myself all the way home.' And here he burst into song with 'Nothing else would matter in the world today,/We would go on loving in the same old way,/If you were the only girl in the world . . .'

This is not, of course, the best-known number from Wagner's *Tristan*. Uncle Tom's voice faded as the phone was put down at the other end, and he turned to Claude and asked, amazed that his deception hadn't met with more success, 'Did I say something wrong?'

All over the place the truth was emerging despite the

conspiracy of silence. Walking to the bus stop, I caught up with Ballard, and greeted him with a cry of 'Hop, skip and jump!'

'What?' Our leader look startled.

'Or can't you do it without the purple jump-suit?' I asked politely. 'I bet that garment skips of its own accord.'

'Rumpole!' Ballard looked stricken. 'You know everything!'

'Pretty well.'

'Marguerite was so insistent that I should get what she calls my "naughty tummy" down,' he began to explain his extraordinary behaviour, 'she practically talked of nothing else.'

'I know.' I understood.

'At last I could stand it no more. I saw an advertisement for this "studio". It seemed so jolly. Music and . . .'

'. . . Young ladies?'

'That's why I kept it from Marguerite. I thought she might not appreciate . . .'

'You skipping about with young ladies? I think she'd admire your heroism, Bollard. Tell her you made the supreme sacrifice and got into a purple jump-suit, just for her. And you've lost weight?'

'A few inches.' He sounded modestly pleased. 'As I told you, my trousers hang loose.'

'Superb! Tell her, Bollard. Boast of it to her.'

'That's really your advice to me, Rumpole?'

'Why not? Bring it all out into the open, old darling. The time for secrets is over.'

'Although steps may be taken soon to bring the law into line with good, old-fashioned common sense, Members of the Jury' – Ollie Oliphant's summing up was drawing to a close – 'Professor Clympton has chosen not to enter the witness-box and give evidence. But you have had the testimony of Sir Dennis Tolson.' He said this as though the Holy Ghost had given tongue in Number One Court at the Old Bailey. 'Sir Dennis and I come from the same part of England. We have a rule up there in the North, Members of the Jury, Use your common sense. Sir Dennis isn't a stranger to us, is he? I expect some of you brought your sandwiches in Tolson's bags, didn't you? And Sir Dennis is quite sure the Professor was at the meeting when the deceased man fell from the stairs. Has he any reason for inventing? Use your common sense, Members of the Jury! Now. Take all the time you need to consider your verdict.'

With these words ringing in their ears, the Jury retired and I went out into the corridor to light a small cigar, walk up and down and hope for victory. As I was so engaged I met the Professor of Classics wandering vaguely, and I offered to buy him a coffee in the Old Bailey canteen. This fluid now comes from a machine which also emits tea, cocoa and soup, these beverages being indistinguishable. We sat at a table in a corner of the big room, among the witnesses, families, barristers and police officers engaged in other cases, and I said, 'You're taking a lot of interest in these proceedings?'

'Why not?' Wayfield filled his pipe but didn't get around to lighting it. 'Clive Clympton's a valued colleague.'

'Hayden Charles wasn't such a valued colleague, was he?'

'What do you mean?' Wayfield frowned, as though over a particularly obscure Latin text.

'I've been thinking about those odd words Mrs O'Leary heard. "Oh, temporary", she said, if you remember. "Oh, more is" ... As I told you. I don't know much Latin, but didn't Cicero express his disgust with the age he lived in? Didn't he say, "*O tempora, O mores!*"? Oh, our horrible times and our dreadful customs! – or words to that effect?'

'Cicero said that. Yes.'

Wayfield seemed surprised I knew such things, and I wouldn't have done had I not spent a good ten minutes with *The Oxford Dictionary of Quotations.*

'And did a Classics Professor,' I asked him then, 'shout it on the staircase, furious with the man who was going to stop its study at Gunster University?'

'I don't understand what you're saying, Mr Rumpole.' For once in his life, I thought, Martin Wayfield wasn't telling the truth. He lied without any talent.

'Don't you, Professor Wayfield? "Licking the boots of the Chancellor" and turning Gunster into a training-ground for bankers and accountants? You heard Clympton say that and you thought it was a pretty good description of Charles's activities. So good, in fact, that it was worth shouting at him again on the stairs.'

'Mr Rumpole, you argued Clive's case very well, but . . .' Wayfield tried an unconvincing bluster which also didn't suit him.

'But the Vice-Chancellor was seized by the throat with a strong grasp. I've felt your handshake, Professor. He was thrown against the banister by someone who thought all he believed in, his whole life, was threatened. Isn't that possible?'

'Just who is suggesting that?'

'Oh, no one but me. If anyone else does, I'll make them prove it. There's really no evidence, except for a rough translation from the Latin.'

Wayfield said nothing to that, but he took out his diary, tore a scrap of paper out of it and wrote something down. 'Look, if you're ever in Gunster again,' he said, 'do ring me. We could have dinner. I'll give you my number.'

'Thank you, Professor. I think I'll give Gunster a wide berth from now on.'

'Here's the number, anyway.' And he handed me the scrap of paper, just as Mizz Liz Probert, whom I had left downstairs to await events, came to tell us that the Jury were back with a verdict.

'I suppose I'm expected to thank you.' Clive Clympton parted from me with a singular lack of grace.

'No need. I get people off murder charges every day of the week. It's just part of the Rumpole service.'

'Couldn't you have done it without Tolson?'

'Probably not. Silence may be golden but it can also be extremely dangerous. It tends to give people ideas.'

So Professor Clympton went back to Gunster. Whether or not he ended up with Mercy Charles I don't know, but young Audrey Wystan took up a teaching job in America and we didn't see her again. In due course Martin Wayfield retired to Devon to write a new life of Cicero, but died before the task could be completed. Claude Erskine-Brown's difficulties were solved more easily. He told me that Phillida and he were on excellent terms again. 'How did you manage that?' I asked him. 'Did you teach Uncle Tom to sing the love duet?'

'Oh, no. I told her the truth. I said you'd persuaded me to take Liz Probert secretly to the Opera to settle a problem in Chambers. I made it perfectly clear that the whole wretched business was entirely your fault.' It is the touching loyalty of my fellow hacks that's such a feature of the great camaraderie of the Bar.

On the day I won *R. v. Clympton*, the Gunster murder, I returned home to the mansion flat, went into the kitchen, poured myself a sustaining glass of Château Fleet Street, and hoped to enjoy a post-mortem on my triumph with She Who Must Be Obeyed as she prepared supper for the hero of Court Number One.

'You know what first gave me the idea?' I told her. 'When the Prosecution moved the case to London. It wasn't for the Professor's benefit; they were afraid of Ostlers on the Jury who might let their fellow Ostler off. You see the point, don't you, old thing?' Hilda answered with a stunning silence.

'Secrets! It's extraordinary, Hilda. The secrets people think important. Take my Professor, now. He'd rather risk prison than break his oath of secrecy to a lot of middle-aged businessmen tricked out in fancy dress in a hotel dining-room. You follow me?' But once again, answer came there none. 'Of course, he wanted it all ways. He wanted to be the hero of the young. And he wanted the secret help of the Ancient Order of Ostlers. Do you see the point?' I sent out words like soldiers to battle and they never returned. 'Oh, thanks,' I said, 'always glad of your opinion, Hilda. So he resorted to silence. It's what everyone does when life gets too difficult. Take cover in silence. Wrap silence round your ears like a blanket. If you say nothing, you can't come to any harm. But no one can keep silent forever. You get lonely. You have to say something some time. Unless you're struck dumb by some unfortunate disease. Is that your problem, Hilda?' But my wife, peeling potatoes, seemed unaware of my existence.

'And what about the other Professor? The Latin scholar. He didn't say much, but I could see he found it difficult to keep quiet, extremely difficult. Look at this.' I showed her Wayfield's diary page and got no reaction. 'He gave me his number and wrote something on it. A Latin quotation. Of course. *Atque inter silvas Academi quaerere verum.* I might find my old school dictionary.' I went and found a Latin dictionary on a shelf in the living-room. It still smelled of ink and gob-stoppers. When I returned to the kitchen, the telephone on the wall was ringing. Hilda held it to her ear and said, 'Yes. Oh, hello, Marguerite.'

'A miracle,' I muttered, as I looked up the Latin words, 'she speaks!' In fact Hilda was talking quite jovially to the telephone. 'Rumpole told Sam to confess it all to you, *he* did that?' There was a further miracle. She Who Must Be Obeyed was smiling. 'Gymnastics? Lost four inches . . .? Plimsolls in the bag? Well, that is a relief, dear, isn't it?'

I had made sure that *silva* was a wood, and *quaerere* meant to seek, when Hilda put down the telephone and said, 'I hear you told Sam Ballard you didn't believe in secrets between married people.'

'Secrets between married people? Perish the thought!' I protested and went back to the dictionary. '*Verum* . . . Well, that's obvious.'

'Sam's trousers hang loose.' Hilda had got on to a sensitive subject. 'Your trousers don't hang loose, do they, Rumpole? Take up gymnastics. Lose four inches round the waist like Sam Ballard!'

'You want me to hop around in a bright purple jump-suit? To the sound of disco music. Perish the thought!' I repeated. And then I tried a rough translation of Wayfield's message: '"And seek for truth in the groves of Academe . . ." You see? Even the Professor of Classics couldn't keep things to himself.'

Rumpole at Sea

Mr Justice Graves. What a contradiction in terms! Mr 'Injustice' Graves, Mr 'Penal' Graves, Mr 'Prejudice' Graves, Mr 'Get into Bed with the Prosecution' Graves – all these titles might be appropriate. But Mr 'Justice' Graves, so far as I'm concerned, can produce nothing but a hollow laugh. From all this you may deduce that the old darling is not my favourite member of the Judiciary. Now he has been promoted, on some sort of puckish whim of the Lord Chancellor's from Old Bailey Judge to a scarlet and ermine Justice of the Queen's Bench, his power to do harm has been considerably increased. Those who have followed my legal career will remember the awesome spectacle of the mad Judge Bullingham, with lowered head and bloodshot eyes, charging into the ring in the hope of impaling Rumpole upon a horn. But now we have lost him, I actually miss the old Bull. There was a sort of excitement in the corridas we lived through together and I often emerged with a couple of ears and a tail. A session before Judge Graves has all the excitement and colour of a Wesleyan funeral on a wet day in Wigan. His pale Lordship presides sitting bolt upright as though he had a poker up his backside, his voice is dirge-like and his eyes close in pain if he is treated with anything less than an obsequious grovel.

This story, which ends with mysterious happenings on the high seas, began in the old Gravestones' Chambers in the Law Courts, where I was making an application one Monday morning.

'Mr Rumpole' – his Lordship looked pained when I had outlined my request – 'do I understand that you are applying to me for bail?' 'Yes, my Lord.' I don't know if he thought I'd just dropped in for a cosy chat.

'Bail having been refused,' he went on in sepulchral tones, 'in the Magistrates Court and by my brother judge, Mr Justice Entwhistle. Is this a frivolous application?'

'Only if it's frivolous to keep the innocent at liberty, my Lord.' I liked the phrase myself, but the Judge reminded me that he was not a jury (worse luck, I thought) and that emotional appeals would carry very little weight with him. He then looked down at his papers and said, 'When you use the word "innocent", I assume you are referring to your client?'

'I am referring to all of us, my Lord.' I couldn't resist a speech. 'We are all innocent until found guilty by a jury of our peers. Or has that golden thread of British justice become a little tarnished of late?'

'Mr Rumpole' – the Judge was clearly unmoved – 'I see your client's name is Timson.'

'So it is, my Lord. But I should use precisely the same argument were it Horace Rumpole. Or even Mr Justice Graves.' At which his Lordship protested, 'Mr Rumpole, this is intolerable!'

'Absolutely intolerable, my Lord,' I agreed. 'Conditions for prisoners on remand are far worse now than they were a hundred years ago.'

'I mean, Mr Rumpole,' the Graveyard explained, with a superhuman effort at patience, as though to a half-wit, 'it's intolerable that you should address me in such a manner. I cannot imagine any circumstances in which I should need your so-called eloquence to be exercised on my behalf.' You never know, I thought, you never know, old darling. But the mournful voice of judicial authority carried on. 'No doubt the Prosecution opposes bail. Do you oppose bail, Mr Harvey Wimple?'

Thus addressed, the eager, sandy-haired youth from the Crown Prosecution Service, who spoke very fast, as though he wanted to get the whole painful ordeal over as quickly as possible, jabbered, 'Oppose it? Oh, yes, my Lord. Absolutely. Utterly and entirely opposed. Utterly.' He looked startled when the Judge asked, 'On what precise grounds do you oppose bail, Mr Wimple?' But he managed the quick-fire answer, 'Grounds that, if left at liberty, another offence might be committed. Or other offences. By the defendant Timson, my Lord. By him, you see?'

'Do you hear that, Mr Rumpole?' The Judge re-orchestrated the piece for more solemn music. 'If he is set at liberty, your client might commit another offence or, quite possibly, offences.'

And then, losing my patience, I said what I had been longing to say on some similar bail application for years. 'Of course, he might,' I began. 'Every man, woman and child in England might commit an offence. Is your Lordship suggesting we keep them all permanently banged up on the off-chance? It's just not on, that's all.'

'Mr Rumpole. What is not "on", as you so curiously put it?' The Judge spoke with controlled fury. It was a good speech, but I had picked the wrong audience. 'Banging up the innocent, my Lord.' I let him have the full might of the Rumpole eloquent outrage. 'With a couple of psychopaths and their own chamber-pots. For an indefinite period while the wheels of justice grind to a halt in a traffic jam of cases.'

'Do try to control yourself, Mr Rumpole. Conditions in prisons are a matter for the Home Office.'

'Oh, my Lord, I'm so sorry. I forgot they're of no interest to judges who refuse bail and have never spent a single night locked up without the benefit of a water closet.'

At which point, Graves decided to terminate the proceedings and, to no one's surprise, he announced that bail was refused and that the unfortunate Tony Timson, who had never committed a violent crime, should languish in Brixton until his trial. I was making for the fresh air and a small and soothing cigar when the Judge called me back with 'Just one moment, Mr Rumpole. I think I should add that I find the way that this matter has been argued before me quite lamentable, and very far from being in the best traditions of the Bar. I may have to report the personal and improper nature of your argument to proper authorities.' At which point he smiled in a nauseating manner at the young man from the Crown Prosecution Service and said, 'Thank you for *your* able assistance, Mr Harvey Wimple.'

★

'Had a good day, Rumpole?' She Who Must Be Obeyed asked me on my return to the mansion flat.

'Thank God, Hilda,' I told her as I poured a glass of Pommeroy's Very Ordinary, 'for your wonderful sense of humour!'

'Rumpole, look at your face!' She appeared to be smiling brightly at my distress.

'I prefer not to. I have no doubt it is marked with tragedy.' I raised a glass and tried to drown at least a few of my sorrows.

'Whatever's happened?' She Who Must Be Obeyed was unusually sympathetic, from which I should have guessed that she had formulated some master plan. I refilled my glass and told her:

> 'I could a tale unfold', Hilda, 'whose lightest word
> Would harrow up thy soul, freeze thy young blood,
> Make thy two eyes, like stars, start from their spheres,
> Thy knotted and combined locks to part,
> And each particular hair to stand on end,
> Like quills upon the fretful porpentine: . . .'

'Oh come on, I bet it wouldn't.' My wife was sceptical. 'What you need, Rumpole, is a change!'

'I need a change from Mr Justice Graves.' And then I played into her hands, for she looked exceptionally pleased when I added, 'For two pins I'd get on a banana boat and sail away into the sunset.'

'Oh, Rumpole! I'm so glad that's what you'd do. For two pins. You know what I've been thinking? We need a second honeymoon.'

'The first one was bad enough.' You see I was still gloomy.

'It wouldn't've been, Rumpole, if you hadn't thought we could manage two weeks in the South of France on your fees from one short robbery.'

'It was all I had about me at the time,' I reminded her. 'Anyway, you shouldn't've ordered lobster.'

'What's the point of a honeymoon,' Hilda asked, 'if you can't order lobster?'

'Of course, you can *order* it. Nothing to stop you ordering,' I conceded. 'You just shouldn't complain when we have to leave three days early and sit up all night in the train from Marseilles. With a couple of soldiers asleep on top of us.'

'On our second honeymoon I shall order lobster.' And then she added the fatal words, 'When we're on the cruise.'

'On the *what*?' I hoped that I couldn't believe my ears.

'The cruise! There's still a bit of Aunt Tedda's money left.' As I have pointed out, Hilda's relations are constantly interfering in our married lives. 'I've booked up for it.'

'No, Hilda. Absolutely not!' I was firm as only I know how to be. 'I know exactly what it'd be like. Bingo on the boat deck!'

'We need to get away, Rumpole. To look at ourselves.'

'Do you honestly think that's wise?' It seemed a rash project.

'Moonlight on the Med.' She Who Must became lyrical. 'The sound of music across the water. Stars. You and I by the rail. *Finding* each other, after a long time.'

'But you can find me quite easily,' I pointed out. 'You just shout "Rumpole!" and there I am.'

'You said you'd sail away into the sunset. For two pins,' she reminded me.

'A figure of speech, Hilda. A pure figure of speech! Let me make this perfectly clear. There is no power on this earth that's going to get me on a cruise.'

During the course of a long and memorable career at the Bar, I have fought many doughty opponents and won many famous victories; but I have never, when all the evidence has been heard and the arguments are over, secured a verdict against She Who Must Be Obeyed. It's true that I have, from time to time, been able to mitigate her stricter sentences. I have argued successfully for alternatives to custody or time to pay. But I have never had an outright win against her and, from the moment she suggested we sail away, until the time when I found myself in our cabin on the fairly good ship S.S. *Boadicea*, steaming out from Southampton, I knew, with a sickening certainty, that I was on to a loser. Hilda reviewed her application for a cruise every hour of the days that we were together, and at most hours of the night, until I finally threw in the towel on the grounds that the sooner we put out to sea the sooner we should be back on dry land.

The *Boadicea* was part of a small cruise line and, instead of flying its passengers to some southern port, it sailed from England to Gibraltar and thence to several Mediterranean destinations before returning home. The result was that some of the first days were to be spent sailing through grey and troubled waters. Picture us then in our cabin as we left harbour. I was looking out of a porthole at a small area of open deck which terminated in a rail and the sea. Hilda, tricked out in white ducks, took a yachting cap out of her hat box and tried it on in front of the mirror. 'What on earth did you bring that for?' I asked her. 'Are you expecting to steer the thing?'

'I expect to enter into the spirit of life on shipboard, Rumpole,' she told me briskly. 'And you'd be well advised to do the same. I'm sure we'll make heaps of friends. Such nice people go on cruises. Haven't you been watching them?'

'Yes.' And I turned, not very cheerfully, back to the porthole. As I did so, a terrible vision met my eyes. The stretch of deck was no longer empty. A grey-haired man in a blue blazer was standing by the rail and, as I watched, Mr Justice Graves turned in my direction and all doubts about our fellow passengers, and all hopes for a carefree cruise, were laid to rest.

' "Angels and ministers of grace defend us!" It can't be. But it *is*!'

'What is, Rumpole? Do pull yourself together.'

'If you knew what I'd seen, you wouldn't babble of pulling myself together, Hilda. It's *him*! The ghastly old Gravestone in person.' At which I dragged out my suitcase and started to throw my possessions back into it. 'He's come on the cruise with us!'

'Courage, Rumpole' – Hilda watched me with a certain contempt – 'I remember you telling me, is the first essential in an advocate.'

'Courage, yes, but not total lunacy. Not self-destruction.

Life at the Bar may have its risks, but no legal duty compels me to spend two weeks shut up in a floating hotel with Mr Justice Deathshead.'

'I don't know what you think you're going to do about it.' She was calmly hanging up her clothes whilst I repacked mine. 'It's perfectly simple, Hilda,' I told her, 'I shall abandon ship!'

When I got up on the deck, there was, fortunately, no further sign of Graves, but a ship's officer, whom I later discovered to be the Purser, was standing by the rail and I approached him, doing my best to control my panic.

'I've just discovered,' I told him, 'I'm allergic to graves. I mean, I'm allergic to boats. It would be quite unsafe for me to travel. A dose of sea-sickness could prove fatal!'

'But, sir,' the purser protested. 'We're only just out of port.'

'I know. So you could let me off, couldn't you? I've just had terrible news.'

'You're welcome to telephone, sir.'

'No, I'm afraid that wouldn't help.'

'And if it's really serious we could fly you back from our next stop.' And he added the terrible words, 'We'll be at Gibraltar in three days.'

Gibraltar in three days! Three days banged up on shipboard with the most unappetizing High Court judge since Jeffreys hung up his wig! I lay on my bed in our cabin as the land slid away from us and Hilda read out the treats on offer: '"Daily sweepstake on the ship's position. Constant video entertainment and films twice nightly. Steam-bath, massage and beauty treatment. Exercise rooms and fully equipped gymnasium" – I think I'll have a steam-bath, Rumpole – "First fancy-dress ball immediately before landfall at Gib. Live it up in an evening of ocean fantasy. Lecture by Howard Swainton, world-famous, best-selling mystery novelist, on 'How I Think Up My Plots'."'

'Could he think up one on how to drown a judge?'

'Oh, do cheer up, Rumpole. Don't be so morbid. At five thirty this evening it's Captain Orde's Welcome Aboard Folks cocktail party, followed by a dinner dance at eight forty-five. I can wear my little black dress.'

'The Captain's cocktail party?' I was by no means cheered up. 'To exchange small talk and Twiglets with Mr Justice Deathshead. No, thank you very much. I shall lie doggo in the cabin until Gibraltar.'

'You can't possibly do that,' She told me. 'What am I going to tell everyone?'

'Tell them I've gone down with a nasty infection. No, the Judge might take it into his head to visit the sick. He might want to come and gloat over me with grapes. Tell them I'm dead. Or say a last-minute case kept me in England.'

'Rumpole, aren't you being just the tiniest bit silly about this?'

But I stuck desperately to my guns. 'Remember, Hilda,' I begged her, 'if anyone asks, say you're here entirely on your own.' I had not forgotten that Graves and She had met at the Sam Ballard–Marguerite Plumstead wedding, and if the Judge caught sight of her, he might suspect that where Hilda was could Rumpole be far behind? I was prepared to take every precaution against discovery.

During many of the ensuing events I was, as I have said, lying doggo. I therefore have to rely on Mrs Rumpole's account of many of the matters that transpired on board the good ship *Boadicea*, and I have reconstructed the following pages from her evidence which was, as always, completely reliable. (I wish, sometimes, that She Who Must Be Obeyed would indulge in something as friendly as a lie. As, for instance, 'I do think you're marvellous, Rumpole,' or 'Please don't lose any weight, I like you so much as you are!') Proceedings opened at the Captain's cocktail party when Hilda found herself part of a group consisting of the world-famed mystery writer, Howard Swainton, whom she described vividly as 'a rather bouncy and yappy little Yorkshire terrier of a man'; a willowy American named Linda Milsom, whom he modestly referred to as his secretary; a tall, balding, fresh-complexioned, owlish-looking cleric wearing gold-rimmed glasses, a dog-collar and an old tweed suit, who introduced himself as Bill Britwell; and his wife, Mavis, a rotund grey-haired lady with a face which might once have been pretty and was now friendly and cheerful. These people were in the act of getting to know each other when the Reverend Bill made the serious mistake of asking Howard Swainton what he did for a living.

'You mean you don't know what Howard does?' Linda, the secretary, said, as her boss was recovering from shock. 'You ought to walk into the gift shop. The shelves are just groaning with his best-sellers. Rows and rows of them, aren't there, Howard?'

'They seem to know what goes with the public,' Swainton agreed. 'My motto is keep 'em guessing and give 'em a bit of sex and a spot of mayhem every half-dozen pages. I'm here to research a new story about a mysterious disappearance on a cruise. I call it *Absence of Body*. Rather a neat title that, don't you think?'

'Howard's won two Golden Daggers,' Linda explained. 'And *Time* magazine called him "The Genius of Evil".'

'Let's say, I'm a writer with a taste for a mystery.' Swainton was ostentatiously modest.

'I suppose' – Bill Britwell beamed round at the company – 'that since I've been concerned with the greatest mystery of all, I've lost interest in detective stories. I do apologize.'

'Oh, really?' Swainton asked. 'And what's the greatest mystery?'

'I think Bill means,' his wife explained, 'since he's gone into the Church.'

'What I've always wanted,' the Reverend Bill told them, 'after a lifetime in insurance.'

'So you've joined the awkward squad, have you?' Swainton was a fervent supporter of the Conservative Party on television chat shows, and as such regarded the Church of England as a kind of Communist cell.

'I'm sorry?' Bill blinked, looking genuinely puzzled.

'The Archbishop's army of Reverend Pinkos' – Swainton warmed to his subject – 'always preaching morality to the Government. I can't think why you chaps can't mind your own business.'

'Morality *is* my business now, isn't it?' Bill was still looking irrepressibly cheerful. 'Of course, it used to be insurance. I came to all the best things late in life. The Church and Mavis.' At which he put an arm round his wife's comfortable shoulder.

'We're on our honeymoon.' Hilda told me that the elderly Mrs Britwell sounded quite girlish as she said this.

'Pleasure combined with business,' her husband explained. 'We're only going as far as Malta, where I've landed a job as padre to the Anglican community.'

And then Hilda, intoxicated by a glass of champagne and the prospect of foreign travel, confessed that she was also on a honeymoon, although it was a second one in her case.

'Oh, really?' Swainton asked with a smile which Hilda found patronizing. 'And which is your husband, Mrs –?'

'Rumpole. Hilda Rumpole. My husband is an extremely well-known barrister. You may have read his name in the papers?'

'I don't spend much time reading,' Swainton told her. 'I'm really too busy writing. And where is your Mr Rumbold?'

'Oh, well,' Hilda had to confess, 'he's not here.'

'You mean?' – Swainton was smiling and inviting the group to enjoy the joke – 'you're having a second honeymoon with a husband who isn't here?'

'No. Well. You see something rather unexpected came up.'

'So, now' – and Swainton could barely conceal his mirth – 'you're having a second honeymoon on your own?'

But Hilda had to excuse herself and hurry away, as she had seen, through the window of the saloon in which the Captain's cocktail party was taking place, stationed on a small patch of windy and rain-beaten deck, Rumpole signalling urgently for supplies.

What had happened was that, being greatly in need of sustenance and a nerve-cooling drink in my Ducal Class dug-out (second only to the real luxury of Sovereign Class), I had rung repeatedly for a steward with absolutely no result. When I telephoned, I was told there would be a considerable delay as the staff were very busy with the Captain's cocktail party. 'The Captain's cock up, you mean,' I said harshly, and made my way to the outskirts of the port (or perhaps the starboard) deck, where it took me considerable time to attract Hilda's attention through the window. 'Make your mind up, Rumpole,' She said when she came out. 'Are you in hiding or aren't you?' and 'Why don't you come in and meet a famous author?'

'Are you mad? *He's* in there.' I could see the skeletal figure of Graves in the privileged party around Captain Orde. He was no doubt entertaining them with an account of the Rumpole clientele he had kept under lock and key.

'Really,' Hilda protested, 'this is no way to spend a honeymoon. Mr Swainton looked as though he thought I'd done you in or something. Apparently he's doing research on a new book called *Absence of Body*. He says it's all about someone who disappears during a cruise.'

'Hilda,' I said, 'couldn't you do a bit of research on a glass or two of champagne? And on what they've got on those little bits of toast?'

So She Who Must Be Obeyed, who has her tender moments, went off in search of provisions. I watched her go back into the saloon and make for the table where the guzzle and sluice were laid out. As she did so, she passed Mr Justice Graves. I saw him turn his head to look at her in a stricken fashion, then he muttered some apology to the Captain and was off out of the room with the sudden energy of a young gazelle.

It was then I realized that not only was Rumpole fleeing the Judge, the Judge was fleeing Rumpole.

Back in the cabin, Hilda put on her dress for the dinner dance and added the finishing touches to her *maquillage*, whilst I, wearing bedroom slippers and smoking a small cigar, paced my confinement like a caged tiger. 'And you'll really like the Britwells,' she was saying. 'He's going to be a parson in Malta. They're quite elderly, but so much in love. Do come up to dinner, Rumpole. Then we could dance together.'

'We did that on our first honeymoon!' I reminded her. 'And it wasn't an astonishing success, so far as I can remember. Anyway, do you think I want Gravestone to catch me dancing?'

'I don't know why you're so frightened of him, quite

honestly. You don't exactly cower in front of him in Court from all you tell me.'

'Of course I don't cower!' I explained. 'I can treat the old Deathshead with lofty disdain in front of a jury! I can thunder my disapproval at him on a bail application. I have no fear of the man in the exercise of my profession. It's his friendship I dread.'

'His friendship?'

'Oh, yes. That is why, Hilda, I have fled Judge Graves down the nights and down the days.' And here I gave my wife a heady draught of Francis Thompson:

> 'I fled Him, down the arches of the years;
> I fled Him, down the labyrinthine ways
> Of my own mind; and in the mist of tears
> I hid from Him, and under running laughter.'

'Well, there's not much running laughter for me' – Hilda was displeased – 'going on a second honeymoon without a husband.'

When Hilda was made-up, powdered and surrounded with an appropriate fragrance, she left me just as the Britwells were emerging from the cabin opposite. They were also in evening-dress and were apparently so delighted to see my wife that they cordially invited her to inspect the amenities which they enjoyed. As the Britwell berth seemed in every way a carbon copy of that provided for the Rumpoles, Hilda found it a little difficult to keep up an interesting commentary or show any genuine surprise at the beauty and convenience of their quarters. At a loss for conversation she looked at their dressing-table where, she told me, two large photographs in heavy silver frames had been set up. The first was a recent wedding portrait of the Reverend and Mrs Britwell standing proudly together, arm-in-arm, outside a village church. The bride was not in white, which would have been surprising at her age, but she wore what Hilda called a 'rather ordinary little suit and a hat with a veil'. The other was a studio portrait of a pretty, smiling young girl in a sequined evening-gown. She asked if that were Bill's daughter, to which he laughed and said, 'Not exactly.' Before she could inquire further I whistled to Hilda from our door across the corridor as I had an urgent piece of advice for her.

'For God's sake, if you see the Judge,' I warned her through a chink in our doorway, 'don't encourage the blighter. Please, don't dream of dancing with him!'

I was not in the least reassured when She answered, 'You never know what I might dream of, Rumpole.'

Hilda didn't dance with the Judge that night. Indeed Mr Injustice Graves didn't even put in an appearance at the function and was busily engaged in lying as low as Rumpole himself.

Most of the dancing was done by the Britwells, who whirled and twirled and chasséed around the place with the expertise of a couple of ballroom champions. 'Aren't they good?' Hilda was playing an enthusiastic gooseberry to Swainton and his secretary, Linda. 'Don't you think he dances rather *too* well?' Swainton sat with his head on one side and looked suspiciously at the glittering scene.

'I don't know exactly what you mean.' Hilda was puzzled, but Linda told her, 'Howard looks below the surface of life. That's his great talent!'

When the husband and wife team came off the floor, perspiring gently after the tango, Howard Swainton repeated, 'We were saying you dance unusually well, Britwell, for a vicar.'

'Don't forget I wasn't always a vicar. I spent most of my life in insurance.'

'Oh, yes. I remember now. You told us that.' Howard Swainton seemed to be making a mental note.

Hilda said, 'Do men in insurance dance well?'

'Better than vicars!' Mrs Britwell was laughing. The elderly newly-weds did seem an ideally happy couple.

'I was in insurance and Mavis ran a secretarial agency.' Bill was telling the story of his life. 'Of course, I married her for her money.' He raised his glass of wine to his wife and drank her health.

'And I married him for his dancing!' Mavis was still

laughing. 'Why don't you let Bill give you a slow foxtrot, Mrs Rumpole?'

'Oh, that would be very nice' – Hilda had not had a great deal of practice at the foxtrot – 'but not this evening, perhaps.' She was looking anxiously about the room, a fact which the sleuth Swainton immediately noticed. 'Are you looking for someone?' he asked.

'Oh. Oh, well. A judge, actually. I happen to have met him before. I'm sure he was at the Captain's cocktail party but I don't seem to see him here.'

'A judge?' Swainton was interested.

'Oh, yes. He used to be just down the Bailey, you know,' Hilda told them. 'But now he's been put up to the High Court. Scarlet and ermine. A red judge. Sir Gerald Graves.'

'Graves?' Howard Swainton was smiling. 'That's a rather mournful name.' But the Reverend Bill didn't join in the laughter. He made a sudden movement and knocked over his glass of red wine. It spread across the tablecloth, Hilda told me, in words I was to remember, like blood.

> Swiftly, swiftly flew the ship,
> Yet she sailed softly too:
> Sweetly, sweetly blew the breeze –
> On me alone it blew.

It blew on me alone because I was taking a solitary stroll in the early morning before the waking hour of the most energetic judge. The good ship *Boadicea* clove the grey waters, seagulls chattered and soared in the sky behind us, hoping for scraps, and I trod carefully in the shadows of boats and deck buildings.

> Like one, who on a lonesome road
> Doth walk in fear and dread,
> And having once turned round walks on,
> And turns no more his head;
> Because he knows, a frightful judge
> Doth close behind him tread.

Coleridge's memorable lines were sounding in my ears as I

looked fearfully around me and then, almost too late, spotted an energetic old party in a blue blazer out for a constitutional. I ducked into the doorway of the Ladies Health and Beauty Salon, while Graves stopped and peered furtively into the window of the room where breakfast was being served to the Ducal passengers.

I know that he did this from the account that Hilda gave me later. She was at a table with Swainton and Linda Milsom, getting stuck into the coffee and eggs and bacon, when she saw the judicial features peering in at her. She only had time to say, 'Ah. There he is!' before the old darling vanished, and she said, 'He's gone!' Bill Britwell joined them with a plate of cornflakes he'd been fetching from a central table. 'Who's gone?' he asked.

'Mr Justice Graves. He must be an early bird.' The Reverend Bill sat and ate his breakfast and Swainton asked how Mavis, who was noticeably absent, was that morning.

'Well, not too good, I'm afraid. Mavis isn't quite the ticket.'

'The what?' Linda Milsom seemed to be listening to a foreign language.

'Not quite up to snuff.' Bill did his best to explain his meaning.

'He means she's sick,' Howard Swainton translated for Linda's benefit and his secretary looked deeply sympathetic. 'What, on her honeymoon?'

'Do tell her we're all so sorry for her.' Swainton was also solicitous, and then he turned his attention to Hilda and asked her, with obvious scepticism, 'And how's *your* husband, Mrs Rumpole? Have you heard from him lately?'

'Oh, yes, I have,' Hilda told him.

'Still busy, is he?'

'Well, he's on the move all the time.'

'Gee, I hope your wife gets better,' Linda was saying to Bill Britwell in a caring sort of way. 'I've got these great homoeopathic capsules. I could drop them into your cabin.'

'That's very kind of you but,' Bill told her firmly, 'I think she'd like to be left alone for the moment.'

'Such a terrible shame!' Hilda was also sympathetic. 'And she seemed so full of life last night.'

135

'Yes, that's exactly what I thought.' Howard Swainton was looking at the Reverend Bill as though he were an interesting piece of research and he repeated Hilda's words, 'So full of life!'

After funking a meeting with Hilda in the breakfast room, it seemed that Mr Injustice settled himself down in a deck-chair, with a rug over his knees, in a kind of passage on the upper deck between the side of the gymnasium and a suspended boat into which his Lordship, in time of trouble, ought, I suspected, to be ready to jump ahead of the women and children. There he sat, immersed in *Murder Most Foul*, the latest Howard Swainton, when, glancing up after the discovery of the fourth corpse, he saw Hilda standing at the end of the passage. His immediate reaction was to raise the alleged work of literature over his face, but he was too late. My wife gave a glad cry of 'Mr Justice Graves!' And, advancing towards him with indescribable foolhardiness, added, 'It is Sir Gerald Graves, isn't it? Hilda Rumpole. We met at Sam Ballard's wedding. You remember he got spliced to the ex-matron of the Old Bailey and astonished us all.' Whereupon she sat down in one of the empty chairs beside him and seemed prepared for a long chat.

'Mrs Rumpole' – Hilda, who is always a reliable witness, alleges that the old Deathshead here 'smiled quite charmingly' – 'of course, I remember. I had no idea you were on the boat.' And he added nervously, 'Are you here on your own?'

'Well, yes. On my own. In a sort of way.'

'Oh, I see. Oh, good!' His Lordship was enormously relieved, but then, Hilda told me, a sort of hunted look came into his eyes as he inquired anxiously, 'Your husband isn't about?'

'Not about? No. Well. Definitely not about. Of course, Horace's got a very busy practice,' Hilda explained. 'I believe you had him before you quite recently. I don't know if you remember?'

'Your husband's appearances before me, Mrs Rumpole,' Graves assured her, 'are quite unforgettable.'

'How sweet of you to say so.' She was gratified.

'In fact, we judges are all agreed,' Mr Justice added, 'there's simply no advocate at the Criminal Bar in the least like Horace Rumpole.'

'A "one off". Is that what you'd say about him?'

'Without doubt, a "one off". We're all agreed about that.'

'I'm sure you're right. That may be why I married him. He's a bit of a "one off" as a husband.' Hilda began, strangely enough, to treat the old Gravestone as a confidant.

'Forgive me, Mrs Rumpole' – Graves clearly didn't want to be let into the secrets of the Rumpole marriage – 'I have absolutely no idea what Rumpole is like as a husband.'

'No. Silly of me!' And here I believe that She laid a friendly hand on the old party's arm. 'Of course, you don't know what it's like to go on one honeymoon with him, let alone two.'

'No idea at all, I'm delighted to say.'

'But I'll tell him all the nice things you've said about him. About him being "unforgettable" and a "one off" and so on.'

'You'll tell him?' His Lordship's hunted expression returned.

'When I next see him.'

'Oh, yes, of course.' And he suggested hopefully, 'Back in England?'

'Or wherever. It may encourage him to break cover.'

'To do *what*, Mrs Rumpole?' There was a distinct note of panic in the judicial question.

'Well, to come out into the open a little more. Would it surprise you to know, Rumpole's really a very shy and retiring sort of person?'

By this time the shy and retiring Rumpole had outstayed his welcome in the entrance hall of the Ladies Health and Beauty Salon and I began to make my way back to the safety of our cabin, taking cover, from time to time, in such places as the children's play area (where I might have been spotted peering anxiously out from behind a giant cut-out clown) and the deck quoits' storage cupboard. Then, getting near to home, I glanced down a passage between a building and a boat and saw Hilda seated on a deck-chair, her knees covered with a rug. The back of the hanging boat prevented me seeing her companion, until it was far too late. 'Hilda!' I called. 'Yes, Rumpole. Here I am,' came the answer. And then, as I moved towards her, the sight I dreaded most hoved into view. We were forced together and there was no way in which a meeting between old enemies could be avoided. What was remarkable was that the Deathshead greeted me with apparent *bonhomie*.

'Rumpole!' He didn't rise from his seat but otherwise he was cordial. 'My dear fellow! This *is* a surprise. Your good lady told me that you weren't about.'

'Well,' I admitted, 'I haven't been about. Up to now.'

'What's up, old chap? Not got your sea legs yet? I always thought of you as a bit of a landlubber, I must say. Come along, then. Sit yourself down.'

I did so with a good deal of trepidation on the seaward side of She Who Must Be Obeyed.

'The Judge has been sweet enough to tell me that your appearances before him were "unforgettable",' Hilda said.

'Oh, yes? How terribly sweet of him,' I agreed.

'And like no one else.'

'And I honestly meant it, my dear old fellow,' Graves assured me. 'You are absolutely *sui generis*.'

'To name but a few?'

'Even if you have so very little Latin. What was the last case you did before me?'

'It was an application for bail.' And I added, with heavy irony, 'With the greatest respect, my Lord.'

'Of course it was!' Graves seemed to recall the incident with delight. 'You should have been there, Mrs Rumpole. We had great fun over that, didn't we, old fellow?'

'Oh, yes,' I assured him. 'It was a riot. Tony Timson's been laughing so much he could hardly slop out in Brixton.'

'He will have his joke, won't he, Mrs Rumpole?' The Judge's cheerfulness was undiminished. 'Your Horace is a great one for his little joke. Well, now I've met you both, there's no reason why we shouldn't have a drink together. After dinner in the Old Salts' bar at, shall we say, five minutes past nine exactly?'

At which point, the Gravestone took up his copy of *Murder*

Most Foul and left us to the sound of my, I hope derisory, 'If your Lordship pleases.' When he had withdrawn, I turned a tragic face to Hilda. 'The Old Salts' bar,' I repeated. 'At five past nine. *Now* look what you've done!'

'I had to flush you out somehow, Rumpole,' She said, unreasonably I felt. 'I had to get you to take part in your own honeymoon.'

But my mind was on grimmer business. 'I told you, it's the awful threat of his friendship. That's what I dread!'

That evening, in the privacy of our cabin, Hilda read out an account of the delights of the Old Salts' bar from the ship's brochure: '"Tonight and every night after dinner,"' she told me, '"Gloria de la Haye sings her golden oldies. Trip down Memory Lane and sing along with Gloria, or hear her inimitable way of rendering your special requests."'

'And that's not the only drawback of the Old Salts' bar,' I added. 'What about "Stiff sentences I have passed", the longplaying record by Mr Justice Gravestone?'

'Oh, do cheer up, Rumpole. We've got each other.'

'Next time you decide to go on a honeymoon, old thing,' I warned her, 'would you mind leaving him behind?'

'Poor Mavis Britwell getting sick like that!' Hilda's mind flitted to another subject. 'She'll be missing all the fun.'

'Tonight,' I told her, having regard to the rendezvous ahead, 'the sick are the lucky ones.'

When we left the cabin on our way to dinner, Hilda's mind was still on the misfortunes of Mavis, and she knocked on the door of the cabin opposite with the idea of visiting the invalid. After some delay, the Reverend Bill called from behind the door that he wouldn't be a minute. Then the little man I was to discover to be Howard Swainton, the famous author, came bouncing down the corridor, carrying a bunch of red roses and a glossy paperback of his own writing. 'Visiting the sick, are we?' he said. 'We all seem to have the same idea.'

'Well, yes. This is my husband.' Hilda introduced me and Swainton raised his eyebrows higher than I would have believed possible.

'Is it, really?' he said. 'I *am* surprised.'

'And this is Mr Howard Swainton,' Hilda went on, unde-terred, '*the* Howard Swainton.'

'How do you do. I'm *the* Horace Rumpole,' I told him.

'Your wife says you're a barrister.' Swainton seemed to find the notion somewhat absurd, as though I were a conjuror or an undertaker's mute. 'I am an Old Bailey hack,' I admitted.

'And we've all been wondering when you'd turn up.' Swain-ton was still smiling, and I asked him, 'Why? Are you in some sort of trouble?'

Before matters could further deteriorate, the vicar opened his cabin door and Hilda once again performed the introductions. 'I'm afraid Mavis is still feeling a little groggy,' Bill Britwell told us. 'She just wants to rest quietly.' Hilda said she understood perfectly, but Howard Swainton, saying, 'I come bearing gifts!' and calling out 'Mavis!', invaded the room remorselessly, al-though Bill protested again, 'I'm not sure she feels like visitors.'

We followed, somewhat helplessly, in Howard's wake as he forged ahead. The woman whom I took to be Mavis Britwell was lying in the bed furthest from the door. The clothes were pulled up around her and only the top of her head was visible from where we stood. Howard Swainton continued his ad-vance, saying, 'Flowers for the poor invalid and my latest in paperback!' I saw him put his gifts down on the narrow table between the two beds, and, in doing so, he knocked over a glass of water which spilled on to Mavis's bed. She put out an arm automatically to protect herself and I couldn't help seeing what Swainton must also have noticed: the sick Mrs Britwell had apparently retired to bed fully dressed.

'Oh, dear. How terribly clumsy of me!' Swainton was dab-bing at the wet bed with his handkerchief. But Mavis had drawn the covers around her again and still lay with her face turned away from us. 'Perhaps you could go now?' her husband said with admirable patience. 'Mavis does want to be perfectly quiet.' 'Yes, of course.' Swainton was apologetic. 'I *do* under-stand. Come along, the Rumpoles.'

We left the cabin then and Swainton soon parted from us to collect his secretary for dinner.

'She was dressed,' Hilda said when we were left alone. 'She was wearing her blouse and cardie.'

'Perhaps the Reverend Bill fancies her in bed in a cardie.'

'Don't be disgusting, Rumpole!' And then Hilda told me something else she had noticed. The two heavy silver-framed photographs, which had stood on the dressing-table when she first visited the Britwells' cabin, had disappeared. She Who Must Be Obeyed has a dead eye for detail and would have risen to great heights in the Criminal Investigation Department.

The Old Salts' bar was liberally decorated with lifebelts, lobster nets, ships in bottles, charts, compasses and waitresses with sailor hats. There was a grand piano at which a small, pink-faced, bespectacled accompanist played as Miss Gloria de la Haye sang her way down Memory Lane. Gloria, a tall woman in a sequined dress, who made great play with a green chiffon handkerchief, must have been in her sixties, and her red curls no doubt owed little to nature. However, she had kept her figure and her long-nosed, wide-mouthed face, although probably never beautiful, was intelligent and humorous. She was singing 'Smoke Gets in Your Eyes' and, with dinner over, we were awaiting our assignation with Gravestone in the company of Bill Britwell, Linda Milsom and Howard Swainton – Mrs Mavis Britwell still being, her husband insisted, unwell and confined to her room. Hilda was giving an account of what she would have it thought of as a happy meeting with Sir Gerald Graves.

'Is he someone you've crossed swords with?' Swainton asked me. 'In the Courts?'

'Swords? Nothing so gentlemanly. Let's say, chemical weapons. The old darling's summing up is pure poison gas.'

'Oh, go on, Rumpole!' Hilda was having none of this. 'He was absolutely charming to you on the boat deck.'

'What's the matter with the claret, Hilda? Glued to the table? – That was just part of his diabolical cunning.'

'Rumpole, are you sure you haven't had enough?' She was reluctant to pass the bottle.

'Of course, I'm sure. Coping with his lethal Lordship without a drink inside you is like having an operation without an anaesthetic.'

At which, dead on time, Mr Injustice berthed himself at our table, saying, 'You're remarkably punctual, Rumpole.'

'Oh, Judge! Everyone' – Hilda introduced the old faceache as though she owned him – 'this is Sir Gerald Graves. Howard Swainton, *the* Howard Swainton, Linda, his personal assistant, and Bill Britwell, the Reverend Bill. Sir Gerald Graves.'

'Five past nine exactly.' The Judge had been studying his watch during these preliminaries and I weighed in with 'Silence! The Court's in session.'

'Well, now. Our second night at sea. I'm sure we're all enjoying it?' Graves's face contorted itself into an unusual and wintry smile.

'Best time we've had since the Luton Axe Killing, my Lord,' I told him.

'What was that you said, Rumpole?'

'It's absolutely thrilling, my Lord,' I translated, a little more loudly.

'I'm afraid' – the Reverend Bill got up – 'you'll have to excuse me.'

'Oh. So soon?'

'Can't you relax, Bill? Forget your troubles.' Swainton tried to detain him. 'Enjoy a drink with a real live judge.'

'I must get back to Mavis.'

'It's his wife, Judge. She hasn't been well,' Howard Swainton said with apparent concern. And as Gloria switched from 'Smoke Gets in Your Eyes' to 'Thanks for the Memory', Bill agreed, 'Well, not quite the ticket.'

'I'm sorry to hear it.' Graves was sympathetic. 'Well, I do hope she's able to join us tomorrow.'

'I'm sure she hopes so too.' Swainton was smiling as he said it. 'Give her all our best wishes. Tell her the Judge is thinking of her.'

'Yes. Yes, I will. That's very kind.' And Bill Britwell retreated from the Old Salts' bar saying, 'Please! Don't let me break up the party.' Whereupon Swainton came, like the terrier

Hilda had described, bounding and yapping into the conversation with 'I say, Judge. Horace Rumpole was just talking about your little scraps in Court.'

'Oh, yes? We do have a bit of fun from time to time. Don't we, Rumpole?' Graves smiled contentedly but Swainton started to stir the legal brew with obvious relish. 'That wasn't exactly how Rumpole put it,' he said. 'Of course, I do understand. Barristers are the natural enemies of judges. Judges and, well, my lot, detective-story writers. We want answers. We want to ferret out the truth. In the end we want to tell the world who's guilty!'

'Well put, if I may say so, Mr Swainton!' Graves had clearly found a kindred spirit. 'In your tales the mysteries are always solved and the criminal pays –'

'Enormous royalties!' I chipped in, 'I have no doubt.'

'His heavy debt to society!' Graves corrected me and then continued his love affair with the bouncy little novelist. 'You always find the answer, Swainton. That's what makes your books such a thumping good read.'

Gloria had stopped singing now and was refreshing herself at the bar. Her plump accompanist was going round the tables with a pad and pencil, asking for requests for the singer's next number.

'Thank you, Judge. Most kind of you.' Howard Swainton was clearly not above saluting the judicial backside. 'But the Horace Rumpoles of this world always want to raise a verbal smokescreen of "reasonable doubt". Tactics, you see. They do it so the guilty can slide away to safety.'

'*Touché*, Rumpole! Hasn't Mr Swainton rather got you there?' Graves was clearly delighted by the author's somewhat tormented prose.

'Not *touché* in the least!' I told him. 'Anyway, I've heard it so many times before from those who want to convict someone, anyone, and don't care very much who it is. There speaks the voice of the Old Bill.'

'But I don't understand. His name's Howard.' Miss Linda Milsom, however rapid her shorthand, was not exactly quick on the uptake.

'Detective Inspector Swainton' – I was now in full flood – 'distrusts defending counsel and wants all trials to take place in the friendly neighbourhood nick. He's so keen on getting at the truth that, if he can't find it, he'll invent it – like the end of a detective story.'

'Is this how he goes on in Court?' Swainton asked with a smile to the Judge, who assured him, 'Oh, all the time.'

'Then you have my heartfelt sympathy, Judge,' Swainton said, and I could scarcely withhold my tears for his poor old Lordship. 'Thank you,' Graves said. 'Tell me, Swainton, are you working on some wonderful new mystery to delight us?'

Then my attention was distracted by the little accompanist, who asked me if I'd care to write down a request for Gloria. I looked across at the tall, sequined woman, apparently downing a large port and lemon, and I was whisked back down the decades to my carefree bachelor days. I was leaving Equity Court, when the Chambers were then run by Hilda's Daddy, C. H. Wystan, for a chop and a pint of stout at the Cock tavern, and had decided to give myself a treat by dropping in to the Old Metropolitan music hall, long since defunct, in the Edgware Road. There I might see jugglers and adagio dancers and Max Miller, the 'Cheeky Chappie', and . . . At this point I scribbled a song title on the accompanist's pad. He looked at it, I thought, with some surprise, and carried it back to Gloria. And then, bringing me painfully back to the present, I heard Swainton tell us the plot of his latest masterpiece.

'In *Absence of Body*,' he said, 'I am now thinking along these lines. A woman, a middle-aged woman, perfectly ordinary, is on a cruise with her new husband. He's a fellow who has taken the precaution of insuring her life for a tidy sum. He tells everyone she's ill, but in fact she's lying in bed in their cabin' – here Swainton leant forward and put a hand on Graves's knee for emphasis – 'fully *dressed*.'

'I see!' Graves was delighted with the mystery. 'So the plot thickens.'

'It's the truth, you understand,' Swainton assured him. 'It's so much stranger than fiction. Rumpole was a witness to the fact that when we called on Mrs Mavis Britwell in her cabin, she was lying in bed with her clothes on! I don't know why it is, but I seem to have a talent for attracting mysteries.'

'You mean she wanted you to believe she was ill?' Graves asked.

'Or *someone* wanted us to believe she was ill,' Swainton told him. 'Of course, one doesn't want to make any rash accusations.'

'Doesn't one?' I asked. 'It sounds as though one was absolutely longing to.' But Mr Justice Graves was clearly having the time of his old life. 'Swainton,' he said, 'I'd very much like to know how your story ends.'

'Would you, Judge? I'm afraid we'll all just have to wait and see. No harm, of course, in keeping our eyes open in the meanwhile.'

At which moment, the accompanist pounded some rhythmic chords on the piano and Gloria burst into the ditty whose words I could still remember, along with long stretches of *The Oxford Book of English Verse*, better than most of the news I heard yesterday:

> 'Who's that kicking up a noise?
> My little sister!
> Whose that giggling with the boys?
> My little sister!
> Whose lemonade is laced with gin?
> Who taught the vicar how to sin?
> Knock on her door and she'll let you in!
> My little sister!
> Who's always been the teacher's pet?
> Who took our puppy to the vet?
> That was last night and she's not home yet!
> My little sister!'

'What an extraordinary song!' Hilda said when my request performance was over.

'Yes,' I told her. 'Takes you back, doesn't it? Takes *me* back, anyway.'

When the party in the Old Salts' bar was over, Hilda slipped her arm through mine and led me across the deck to the ship's rail. I feared some romantic demonstration and looked around for help, but the only person about seemed to be Bill Britwell, wrapped in a heavy raincoat, who was standing some way from us. It was somewhat draughty and a fine rain was falling, but there was a moon and the sound of a distant dance band. Hilda, apparently, drew the greatest encouragement from these facts.

'The sound of music across the water. Stars. You and I by the rail. Finding each other . . . Listen, Rumpole! What do you think the Med. is trying to say to us?'

'It probably wants to tell you it's the Bay of Biscay,' I suggested.

'Is there nothing you feel romantic about?'

'Of course there is.' I couldn't let that charge go unanswered.

'There you are, you see!' Hilda was clearly pleased. 'I always thought so. What exactly?'

'Steak and kidney pudding.' I gave her the list. 'The jury system, the presumption of innocence.'

'Anything else?'

'Oh. Of course. I almost forgot,' I reassured her.

'Yes?'

'Wordsworth.'

There was a thoughtful silence then and Hilda, like Gloria, went off down Memory Lane. 'It doesn't seem so very long ago,' she said, 'that I was a young girl, and you asked Daddy for my hand in marriage.'

'And he gave it to me!' I remembered it well.

'Daddy was always so generous. Tell me, Rumpole. Now we're alone' – Hilda started off. I'm not sure what sort of intimate subject she was about to broach because I had to warn her, 'But we're not alone. Look!'

She turned her head and we both saw Bill Britwell standing by the rail, staring down at the sea and apparently involved in his own thoughts. Then, oblivious to our existence, he opened his coat, under which he had concealed two silver-framed photographs, much like those Hilda had seen on the dressing-table on her first visit to his cabin. He looked at them for a moment and dropped them towards the blackness of the passing sea. He turned from the rail then and walked away, not noticing Hilda and me, or Howard Swainton, who had also come out of the Old Salts' bar a few minutes before and had been watching this mysterious episode with considerable fascination.

Time, on a cruise ship, tends to drag; watching water pass by you slowly is not the most exciting occupation in the world. Hilda spent her time having her hair done, or her face creamed, or taking steam-baths, or being pounded to some sort of pulp in the massage parlour. I slept a good deal or walked round the deck. I was engaged in this mild exercise when I came within earshot of that indefatigable pair, Graves and Swainton, the Judge and the detective writer, who were sitting on deck-chairs, drinking soup. I loitered behind a boat for a little, catching the drift of their conversation.

'Photographs?' The Judge was puzzled. 'In silver frames? and he threw them into the sea?'

'That's what it looked like.'

'But why would a man do such a thing?'

'Ask yourselves that, Members of the Jury.' I emerged and posed the question, 'Is the Court in secret session or can anyone join?'

'Ah, Rumpole. There you are.' Graves, given a case to try, seemed to be in excellent humour. 'Now then, I believe you were also a witness. Why would a man throw photographs into the sea? That is indeed the question we have to ask. And perhaps, with your long experience of the criminal classes, you can suggest a solution?'

'I'm on holiday. What Britwell did with his photographs seems entirely his own affair.' But Swainton clearly didn't think so. 'I can offer a solution.' He gave us one of his plots for nothing. 'Suppose the Reverend Bill isn't a Reverend at all. I believe a lot of con men go on these cruises.'

'That is an entirely unfounded suggestion by the Prosecution, my Lord.' I had the automatic reaction of the life-long defender, at which moment the steward trundled the soup trolley up to me and Graves, by now well in to presiding over the upper-deck Court, said, 'Please, Mr Rumpole! Let Mr Swainton complete his submission. Your turn will come later.'

'Oh, is that soup?' I turned my attention to the steward. 'Thank you very much.'

'Suppose Bill Britwell wanted to remove all trace of the person in the photographs?' Swainton suggested.

'Two persons,' I corrected him. 'Hilda told me there were two photographs. One was Bill Britwell and his wife. The other was of a young girl. Are you suggesting he wanted to remove all trace of two people? Is that the prosecution case?'

'Please, Mr Rumpole, it hasn't come to a prosecution yet,' Graves said unconvincingly.

'His wife? This is *very* interesting!' Swainton yelped terrier-like after the information. 'One picture was of his wife. Now, why should he throw that into the sea?'

'God knows. Perhaps it didn't do her justice,' I suggested, and Swainton looked thoughtful and said, in a deeply meaningful sort of way, 'Or was it a symbolic act?'

'A what?' I wasn't following his drift, if indeed he had one. 'He got rid of her photograph,' Swainton did his best to explain, '*because he means to get rid of her*.'

'That is a most serious suggestion.' Graves greeted it with obvious relish, whilst I, slurping my soup, said, 'Balderdash, my Lord!'

'What?' The little novelist looked hurt.

'The product of a mind addled with detective stories,' I suggested.

'All right!' Swainton yapped at me impatiently. 'If you know so much, tell us this. Where do you think Mrs Mavis Britwell is? Still in bed with her clothes on?'

'Why don't you go and have a peep through the keyhole?' I suggested.

'I wasn't thinking of that, exactly. But I was thinking . . .'

'Oh, do try not to,' I warned him. 'It overexcites his Lordship.'

'The steward does up the cabins along our corridor at about

this time,' Swainton remembered. 'If we happened to be passing, we might just see something extremely interesting.'

'You mean we might take a view?' The Judge was clearly enthusiastic and I tried to calm him down by saying, '– Of the scene of a crime that hasn't been committed?'

'It's clearly our duty to investigate any sort of irregularity.' Graves was at his most self-important.

'And no doubt your delight,' I suggested.

'What did you say, Rumpole?' The Judge frowned.

'I said you're perfectly right, my Lord. And no doubt you would wish the Defence to be represented at the scene of any possible crime.'

'Have you briefed yourself, Rumpole?' Swainton gave me an unfriendly smile. I took a final gulp of soup and told him, 'I certainly have, as there's no one else to do it for me.'

When we got down to the corridor outside the cabins, the trolley with clean towels and sheets was outside the Graves's residence, where work was being carried out. We loitered around, trying to look casual, and then Bill Britwell greatly helped the Prosecution by emerging from his door, which he shut carefully behind him. He looked at Graves in a startled and troubled sort of way and said, 'Oh. It's you! Good morning, Judge.'

'My dear Britwell. And how's your wife this morning?' The Judge smiled with patent insincerity, as though meaning, We certainly don't hope she's well, as that would be far too boring.

'I'm afraid she's no better,' Britwell reassured them. 'No better at all. In fact she's got to stay in bed very quietly. No visitors, I'm afraid. Now, if you'll excuse me.' He made his way quickly down the corridor and away from us on some errand or other, and Hilda opened the door of our cabin which, you will remember, was dead opposite the berth of the Britwells. 'Ah, Mrs Rumpole.' His Lordship was delighted to see her. 'Perhaps you'd allow us to be your guests, just for a moment?' and, although I gave Hilda a warning about helping the Prosecution, She eagerly invited the judicial team in, although she asked them to forgive 'the terrible mess'. 'Oh, we can put up with any little inconvenience,' the Judge boomed in his most lugubrious courtroom accent, 'in our quest for the truth!'

So the search party took refuge in our cabin until the steward pushed his trolley up to the Britwells' door, unlocked it with his pass key and went inside, leaving the door open. Graves waited for a decent interval to elapse and then he led Swainton and me across the corridor and through the door, while the steward was putting towels in the bathroom. There was no one in either of the twin beds, and only one of them seemed to have been slept in. There was no powder, make-up or perfume on the dressing-table and, so far as one quick look could discover, no sign of Mrs Mavis Britwell at all.

'Can I help you, gentlemen?' The steward came in from the bathroom, surprised by the invasion. 'Oh, I'm sorry!' Swainton apologized with total lack of conviction. 'We must have got the wrong cabin. They all look so alike. Particularly,' he added with deep meaning, 'those with only a *single* occupant.'

That night, in the Old Salts' bar, Graves and Swainton were seated at the counter, and Gloria was drawing towards the end of her act, when I intruded again on their discussion of the state of the evidence.

'Britwell told us a deliberate lie,' the Judge was saying.

'He distinctly said she was in the room,' Swainton agreed.

'In my view his evidence has to be accepted with extreme caution,' Graves ruled. 'On any subject.'

'I don't see why.' I put my oar in and Swainton gave a little yapping laugh and said, 'Here comes the perpetual defender.'

'We all tell the odd lie, don't we?' I suggested, and then I ordered a large glass of claret, which I had christened Château Bilgewater, from Alfred, the barman.

'Speak for yourself, Rumpole.' Graves looked at me as though I was probably as big a liar as the Reverend Bill. I wasn't going to let him get away with that without a spot of cross-examination, so I put this to his Lordship. 'When you met my wife on the deck the other morning, didn't you tell her that you had no idea she was on the boat?'

'I *may* have said that,' the Judge conceded.

'And I distinctly saw you at the Captain's cocktail party the night before. You caught sight of Mrs Hilda Rumpole and went beetling out of the room because you recognized her!'

'Rumpole! That is . . .' The Judge seemed unable to find words to describe my conduct so I supplied them for him. 'I know. A grossly improper argument. You may have to report it to the proper authorities.'

'Gentlemen!' Swainton was, unusually, acting as a peace-maker. 'We may all tell the odd white lie occasionally, but this is a far more serious matter. We have to face the fact that Mrs Britwell has apparently disappeared.'

'In the midst of the words she was trying to say,' I suggested:

> 'In the midst of her laughter and glee,
> She softly and suddenly vanished away
> For the Snark *was* a Boojum, you see.'

'The question is' – Swainton was in no mood for Lewis Carroll – 'what action should we take?'

'But who exactly *is* the Boojum – or the Snark, come to that?' This, I felt, was the important question.

'The circumstances are no doubt very suspicious.' Graves had his head on one side, his lips pursed, his brandy glass in his hand, and was doing his best to sound extremely judicial.

'Suspicious of what?' I had to put the question. 'Is the theory that Bill Britwell pushed his wife overboard for the sake of a little life insurance and then kept quiet about it? What's the point of that?'

'It's possible he may have got rid of her,' Swainton persisted, 'for whatever reason . . .'

'If you think that, stop the boat,' I told them. 'Send for helicopters. Organize a rescue operation.'

'I'm afraid it's a little late for that.' Swainton looked ex-tremely serious. 'If he did anything, my feeling is, he did it last night. In some way, I think, the event may have been connected with the photographs that were thrown into the water.'

So they sat on their bar stools and thought it over, the Judge and the fiction writer, like an old eagle and a young sparrow on their perches, and then Graves rather lost his bottle. 'The circumstances are highly suspicious, of course,' he spoke carefully, 'but can we say they amount to a certainty?'

'Of course we can't,' I told them, and then launched my attack on the learned Judge. 'The trouble with the Judiciary is that you see crime in everything. It's the way an entomologist goes out for walks in the countryside and only notices the beetles.'

Graves thought this over in silence and then made a cautious pronouncement. 'If we were sure, of course, we could inform the police at Gibraltar. It might be a case for Interpol.' But Swainton had dreamed up another drama. 'I have a suggestion to make, Judge. If you agree. Tomorrow I'm giving my lecture, "How I Think Up My Plots". I presume you're all coming?' 'Don't bet on it!' I told him. But he went on, undeterred. 'I may add something to my text for Britwell's benefit. Keep your eyes on him when I say it.' 'You mean, observe his demeanour?' The Judge got the point.

Looking down the bar, I saw Gloria talking to Alfred, the barman, while beside me Swainton was babbling with delight at his ingenious plan. 'See if he looks guilty,' he said. 'Do you think that's an idea?'

'Not exactly original,' I told him. 'Shakespeare used it in *Hamlet*.'

'Did he, really?' The little author seemed surprised. 'It might be even better in my lecture.'

By now I had had about as much as I could take of the Judge and his side-kick, so I excused myself and moved to join Gloria, who was giving some final instructions to the barman. 'A bottle of my usual to take away, Alfred,' I heard her say. 'The old and tawny. Oh, and a couple of glasses, could you let us have? They keep getting broken.'

'Miss Gloria de la Haye?' I greeted her, and she gave me a smile of recognition. 'Aren't you the gentleman that requested my old song?'

'I haven't heard you sing it for years,' I told her. 'Music halls don't exist any more, do they?'

'Worse luck!' She pulled a sour face. 'It's a drag, this is, having to do an act afloat. Turns your stomach when the sea gets choppy, and there's not much life around here, is there?' She looked along the bar. 'More like a floating old people's home. I'm prepared to scream if anyone else requests "Smoke Gets in Your Eyes". I want to say it soon will, in yours, dear, in the crematorium!'

'I remember going to the Metropolitan in the Edgware Road.'

'You went to the old Met.?' Gloria was smiling.

'"Who's that kicking up a noise?"' I intoned the first line of the song and she joined me in a way that made the Judge stare at us with surprise and disapproval:

> 'Who's that giggling with the boys?
> My little sister!'

'That was my act, the long and short of it,' Gloria confirmed my recollection. 'Betty Dee and Buttercup. I was Buttercup's straight man.'

'Wasn't an alleged comic on the same bill?' I asked her. 'Happy Harry someone. A man who did a rather embarrassing drunk act, if I remember.'

'Was there?' Gloria stopped smiling. 'I can't recall, exactly.'

'And about Buttercup?' I asked. 'Rather a pretty girl, wasn't she? What's happened to her?'

'Can't tell you that, I'm afraid. We haven't kept in touch.' And Gloria turned back to the barman. 'My old and tawny, Alfred?' She picked up the bottle of port and the glasses the barman had put in front of her and went out of the bar. I let her get a start and then I decided to follow her. She went down corridors between cabin doors and down a flight of stairs to a lower deck where a notice on the wall read SECOND-CLASS PASSENGERS. From the bottom of the stairs I watched as she walked down a long corridor, a tall, sequined woman with a muscular back. Then she opened a cabin door and went inside.

In the normal course of events, a lecture 'How I Think Up My Plots' by Howard Swainton would have commanded my attention somewhat less than an address by Soapy Sam Bollard to the Lawyers As Christians Society on the home-life of the Prophet Amos. However, Swainton's threatened re-enactment of the play scene from *Hamlet* seemed likely to add a certain bizarre interest to an otherwise tedious occasion, so I found myself duly seated in the ship's library alongside Hilda and Judge Graves.

Bill Britwell, whom Swainton had pressed to attend, was a few rows behind us. Dead on the appointed hour, the best-selling author bobbed up behind a podium and, after a polite smattering of applause, told us how difficult plots were to come by and how hard he had to work on their invention in order to feed his vast and eager public's appetite for a constant diet of Swainton. An author's work, he told us, was never done, and although he might seem to be enjoying himself, drinking soup on the deck and assisting at the evening's en-tertainment in the Old Salts' bar, he was, in fact, hard at work on his latest masterpiece, *Absence of Body*, the story of a mysterious disappearance at sea. This led him to dilate on the question of whether a conviction for murder is possible if the corpse fails to put in an appearance.

'The old idea of the *corpus delicti* as a defence has now been laid, like the presumably missing corpse, to rest.' Swainton was in full flow. 'The defence is dead and buried, if not the body. Some years ago a steward on an ocean-going liner was tried for the murder of a woman passenger. It was alleged that he'd made love to her, either with or without her consent, and then pushed her through a porthole out into the darkness of the sea. Her body was never recovered. The Defence relied heavily on the theory of the *corpus delicti*. Without a body, the ingenious barrister paid to defend the steward said, there could be no conviction.'

At this, Graves couldn't resist turning round in his seat to stare at Bill Britwell, who was in fact stirring restlessly. 'The Judge and the Jury would have none of this,' Swainton went on. 'The steward was condemned to death, although, luckily for him, the death sentence was then abolished. This case gave me the germ of an idea for the new tale which I am going to introduce to you tonight. Ladies and Gentlemen. You are privileged to be the first audience to whom I shall read chapter one of the brand-new Stainton mystery entitled *Absence of Body*.' He produced a wodge of typescript and Linda Milsom gazed up at him adoringly as he started to read: '"When Joe Andrews suggested to his wife that they go on a cruise for their honeymoon, she was delighted. She might not have been so pleased if she had had an inkling of the plan that was already forming itself at the back of his mind . . ."' At which point there was the sound of a gasp and a chair being scraped back behind us. Obediently playing the part of guilty King Claudius, Bill Britwell rose from his seat and fled from the room.

'You saw that, Rumpole,' the Judge whispered to me with great satisfaction. 'Isn't that evidence of guilt?'

'Either of guilt,' I told him, 'or terminal boredom.'

The ship's gift shop, as well as stocking a large selection of Howard Swainton, and others of those authors whose books are most frequently on show at airports, railway stations and supermarket checkouts, sold all sorts of sweets, tobacco, sun oil (not yet needed), ashtrays, table mats and T-shirts embellished with portraits of the late Queen Boadicea, giant pandas and teddy bears, cassettes and other articles of doubtful utility. On the day of the first fancy-dress ball, which was to take place on the evening before our arrival at Gibraltar, the gift shop put on display a selection of hats, false beards, noses, head-dresses and other accoutrements for those who lacked the skill or ingenuity to make their own costumes. In the afternoon the shop was full of passengers in search of disguises in which they could raise a laugh, cut a dash, or realize a childhood longing to be someone quite different from whoever they eventually turned out to be.

'Rumpole,' Hilda was kind enough to say, 'you look quite romantic.' I had put a black patch over one eye and sported a three-cornered hat with a skull and cross-bones on the front. Looking in the shop mirror, I saw Jolly Roger Rumpole or Black Cap'n Rumpole of the Bailey. And then She looked across the shop to where the Reverend Bill was picking over a selection of funny hats. 'You wouldn't think he'd have the nerve to dress up this evening, would you?' She said with a disapproving click of her tongue. I left her and joined Britwell. I spoke to him in confidential but, I hope, cheering tones. 'You must be getting tired of it,' I said sympathetically.

'Tired of what?'

'People asking "How's your wife?"'

'They're very kind.' If he were putting on an act, he was doing it well. 'Extremely considerate.'

'It must be spoiling your trip.'

'Mavis being ill?' He beamed at me vaguely through his spectacles. 'Yes, it is rather.'

'Mr Justice Graves,' I began and he looked suddenly nervous and said, 'The Judge?' 'Yes, the Judge. He seems very worried about your wife.'

'Why's he worried?' Britwell asked anxiously.

'About her illness, I suppose. He wants to see her.'

'Why should he want that?'

'You know what judges are,' I told him. 'Always poking their noses into things that don't really concern them. Shall we see your wife tonight at the fancy-dress party?'

'Well. No. I'm afraid not. Mavis won't be up to it. Such a pity. It's the sort of thing she'd love so much, if she were only feeling herself.' And then Hilda joined us, looking, although I say it myself, superb. She was wearing a helmet and breastplate and carrying a golden trident and a shield emblazoned with the Union Jack. Staring at my wife with undisguised admiration, I could only express myself in song:

> 'Rule Britannia!
> Britannia rules the waves, (I warbled)
> Britain never, never, never shall be . . .'

'Is it going too far?' She asked nervously. But I shook my head and looked at Bill Britwell as I completed the verse:

> 'Marri–ed to a mermai–ed,
> At the bottom of the deep blue sea!'

There was a sound of considerable revelry by night and as that old terror of the Spanish Main, Pirate Cap'n Rumpole made his way in the company of assorted pierrots, slave girls, pashas, clowns, Neptunes and mermaids towards the big saloon from which the strains of dance music were sounding, I passed an office doorway from which a Chinese mandarin emerged in the company of Captain Orde, who was attending the festivities disguised as a ship's captain. As I passed them I heard Orde say, 'The police at Gib have the message, sir. So if he can't produce the lady . . .' 'Yes, yes, Captain.' The mandarin, who looked only a little less snooty and superior than Mr Justice Graves in his normal guise, did his best to shut the officer up as he saw this old sea-dog approaching from windward. 'Why there you are, Rumpole! Have you had some sort of an accident to your eye? Nothing serious, I hope.'

Hilda and I have not danced together since our first honeymoon. As I have already indicated, the exercise was not a startling success and that night, with all the other excitement going on, she seemed content not to repeat the experiment. We sat in front of a bottle of the Bilgewater red, to which I had grown quite attached in an appalling sort of way, and we watched the dancers. Howard Swainton, as an undersized Viking, was steering the lanky Linda Milsom, a slave girl, who towered over him. It might be an exaggeration to say his eye-level was that of the jewel in her navel, but not too much of one. Across the room we could see the Reverend Bill holding a glass and admiring the scene. He was wearing a turban, a scimitar and a lurid beard. 'Bluebeard!' Hilda said. 'How very appropriate.'

'Oh, for heaven's sake!' I told her, 'don't *you* start imagining things.' And then a familiarly icy voice cut into our conversation. 'Mrs Rumpole,' said the ridiculously boring mandarin, 'might I ask you to give me the honour of this dance?' She Who Must Be Obeyed, apparently delighted, said, 'Of course, Judge, what tremendous fun!' My worst fears were confirmed and they waltzed away together with incomprehensible zest.

In due course, Swainton and his houri came to sit at our table and, looking idly at the throng, we witnessed the entry of two schoolgirls in gym-slips and straw hats. One was tall and thin and clearly Gloria. The other, small and plump, wore a schoolgirl mask to which a pigtailed wig was attached. Swainton immediately guessed that this was Miss de la Haye's little accompanist in disguise. 'Betty Dee and Buttercup,' I said, only half aloud, as this strange couple crossed the room, and Linda Milsom, who was having trouble retaining the liverish-looking glass eye in her navel, said, 'Some people sure like to make themselves look ridiculous.' A little time passed and then Swainton said, 'Well, that beats everything!' 'What?' I asked, removing my nose from my glass and shifting the patch so that I had two eyes available.

'An alleged vicar dancing with a bar pianist in drag.' It was true. The Reverend Bill and the small schoolgirl were waltzing expertly. 'I think,' I said, 'I could be about to solve the mystery of the Absent Body.'

'I very much doubt it.' Swainton was not impressed with my deductive powers.

'Would you like me to try?' And, before he could answer, I asked Linda to cut in and invite Bill Britwell for a dance.

'Oh,' she appealed to her boss, 'do I have to?' 'Why not?' Swainton shrugged his shoulders. 'It might be entertaining to watch Counsel for the Defence barking up the wrong tree.'

When instructed by the best-selling author, Miss Milsom acted with decision and aplomb. I saw her cross the floor and speak to Bill Britwell. He looked at his partner, who surrendered more or less gracefully and was left alone on the floor. Before the small schoolgirl could regain the table where Gloria was waiting, Cap'n Rumpole had drawn up alongside.

'I'm afraid I'm no dancer,' I said. 'So shall we go out for a breath of air?' Without waiting for a reply, I took the schoolgirl's arm and steered her towards the doors which led out to the deck.

So there I was by the rail of the ship again, in the moonlight with music playing in the background, faced, not by Hilda, but by a small, round figure wearing a schoolgirl mask.

'Betty Dee and Buttercup,' I said. 'You were Buttercup, weren't you? The little sister, the young girl in the photograph

Bill Britwell threw into the sea? Not that there was any need for that. No one really remembered you.'

'What do you want?' A small voice spoke from behind the mask.

'To set your mind at rest,' I promised. 'No one knows you've been part of a music-hall act. No one's going to hold that against you. Bill can preach sermons to the Anglicans of Malta and no one's going to care a toss about Betty Dee and Buttercup. It's the other part you were worried about, wasn't it? The part you played down the Old Bailey. A long time ago. Such a long time. When we were all very young indeed. Oh, so very young. Before I did the Penge Bungalow Murders, which is no longer even recent history. All the same I was at the Bar when it happened. You know, you should've had me to defend you. You really should. It was a touching story. A young girl married to a drunk, a husband who beat her. Who was he? "Happy" Harry Harman? He even did a drunk act on the stage, didn't he? Drunk acts are never very funny. I read all about it in the *News of the World* because I wanted the brief. He beat you and you stabbed him in the throat with a pair of scissors. You should never have got five years for manslaughter. I'd've got you off with not a dry eye in the jury-box, even though the efficient young Counsel for the Prosecution was a cold fish called Gerald Graves. It's all right. He is not going to remember you.'

'Isn't he?' The small voice spoke again.

'Of course not. Lawyers and judges hardly ever remember the faces they've sent to prison.'

'Are you sure?'

I was conscious that we were no longer alone on the deck. Bill Britwell had come out of the doors behind us, followed by Graves and Howard Swainton, who must have suspected that the drama they had concocted was reaching a conclusion. 'Oh, yes,' I said, 'you can come out of hiding now.'

She must have believed me because she lifted her hands and carefully removed the mask. She was only a little nervous as she stood in the moonlight, smiling at her husband. And the Judge and the mystery writer, for once, had nothing to say.

'Such a pleasure, isn't it,' I asked them, 'to have Mrs Mavis Britwell back with us again?'

The Rock of Gibraltar looked much as expected, towering over the strange little community which can be looked at as the last outpost of a vanishing Empire or as a tiny section of the Wimbledon of fifty years ago, tacked improbably on to the bottom of Spain. The good ship *Boadicea* was safely docked the next morning and, as the passengers disembarked for a guided tour with a full English tea thrown in, I stood once more at the rail, this time in the company of Mr 'Miscarriage of Justice' Graves. I had just taken him for a guided tour round the facts of the Britwell case.

'So she decided to vanish?' he asked me.

'Not at all. She went to stay with her old friend, Miss Gloria de la Haye, for a few days.' And then I asked him, 'She didn't look familiar to you?'

'No. No, I can't say she did. Why?'

'"Old men forget"' – I wasn't about to explain – '"yet all shall be forgot."'

'What did you say?' His Lordship wasn't following my drift.

'I said, "What a load of trouble you've got."'

'Trouble? You're not making yourself clear, Rumpole.'

'You as good as accused the Reverend Bill of shoving his dear wife through the porthole.' I recited the charges. 'You reported the story to the ship's captain, who no doubt wired it to the Gibraltar police. That was clear publication and a pretty good basis for an action for defamation. Wouldn't you say?'

'Defamation?' The Judge repeated the dread word. 'Oh, yes,' I reminded him, 'and juries have been quite absurdly generous with damages lately. Remember my offer to defend you?' My mind went back to a distant bail application. 'Please call on my services at any time.'

'Rumpole' – the Judicial face peered at me anxiously – 'you don't honestly think they'd sue?'

'My dear Judge, I think you're innocent, of course, until you're proved guilty. That's such an important principle to keep in mind on all occasions.'

And then I heard a distant cry of 'Rumpole!' Hilda was kitted out and ready to call on the Barbary apes.

'Ah, that's my wife. I'd better go. We're on a honeymoon too, you see. Our second. And it may disappoint you to know, we're innocent of any crime whatsoever.'

Rumpole and the Quacks

There is, when you come to think about it, no relationship more important than that of a man with his quack – or 'regular medical attendant', as Soapy Sam Ballard would no doubt choose to call him. A legal hack relies on his quack to raise him to his feet, to keep him breathing, to enable him to cross-examine in a deadly manner and then, gentle as any sucking dove, move the Jury to tears. Without the occasional ministrations of his quack, the criminal defender would be but a memory, an empty seat in Chambers to be filled by some white-wig with a word processor, and a few unkind anecdotes in the Bar mess. There might be tears shed around Brixton and the Scrubs, but the Judiciary would greet my departure with considerable relief. In order to postpone the evil hour as long as possible, I am in need of the life-support of a reasonably competent quack.

Mind you, I do a great deal for my own health by what is known in the Sunday papers as a 'sensible life-style'. I am careful to take, however rough and painful the experience may be, a considerable quantity of Pommeroy's Very Ordinary, which I have always found keeps me astonishingly regular. I force myself to consume substantial luncheons of steak and kidney pud and mashed potatoes in the pub opposite the Old Bailey, and I do this in order to ward off infection and prevent weakness during the afternoon.

My customary exercise consists of a short stroll from the Temple tube station to Equity Court, and rising to object to impertinent questions put by prosecuting counsel. I avoid all such indulgences as jogging or squash – activities which I have known to put an early end to many a promising career at the Bar.

The quack By Appointment to the House of Rumpole used to be a certain Dr MacClintock, a Scot of the most puritanical variety, who put me on the scales and sentenced me to a spell on nothing more sustaining than a kind of chemical gruel called Thin-O-Vite. He did this with the avowed intent of causing a certain quantity of Rumpole to vanish into thin air and leave not a wrack behind. I never felt that this was a scheme likely to contribute to anyone's good health, and readers of these chronicles will recall that MacClintock kicked the bucket not long after prescribing it.* The poor old darling was your pessimistic brand of quack who foresees death following hard upon your next slap-up tea of crumpets and Dundee cake.

So you don't want a quack who is too gloomy and turns your mind to being carried downstairs in your box by sweating undertaker's men complaining of the weight. On the other hand, the quack who tells you there's absolutely nothing wrong with you and that you've got the liver of a five year old and you'll probably go on forever is also disconcerting. Does he protest too much? Is he just trying to keep up your spirits? And has he secretly informed She Who Must Be Obeyed that you have, at the best, two more weeks to live? On the whole, and to sum up, all you can say is that a man's relationship with his quack is a matter of mutual confidence and judicious balance.

When Dr MacClintock was translated to the great geriatric ward in the skies, the responsibility for the health and well-being of the Rumpoles eventually passed to Dr Ghulam Rahmat. Dr Rahmat had been highly spoken of by Mac-Clintock, who had made him a partner in that small quackery which served the area around Froxbury Mansions. He was a short, thick-set man, perhaps in his late forties, with greying hair and large, melting brown eyes behind heavy spectacles. He was the most optimistic, indeed encouraging, quack I have ever known.

* See 'Rumpole and the Quality of Life' in *Rumpole and the Age of Miracles*, Penguin Books, 1988.

'How are you, Rumpole?'

'I am dying, Egypt, dying.' She Who Must Be Obeyed, whose title, as you will know, derives from the legendary and all-powerful Queen Cleopatra, answered me with a brisk 'Then we'd better call the Doctor.'

'Call nobody,' I warned her, wincing at the deafening sound of my own voice. 'I am returning to my bed. There's nothing on today except a Chambers meeting to consider the case of a Mrs Whittaker who wants to come in as a pupil to Erskine-Brown. That's something worth missing. If Henry telephones tell him that Rumpole's life is ebbing quietly away.'

'Stuff and nonsense, Rumpole. You drank too much, that's all.'

Was that all? My head felt as though I had just received a short back-and-sides from the mad axe-man of Luton and a number of small black fish seemed to be swimming before my eyes. No doubt it was all because the Lord Chancellor, in a moment of absent-mindedness, had decided to make Hoskins a circuit judge. Hoskins, the colourless and undistinguished member of our Chambers, mainly concerned with the heavy cost of educating his four daughters, had never found it easy to come by or do his briefs. Now, presumably on the basis that if you can't argue cases you'd be better off deciding them, Hoskins had been elevated to the Circus Bench. The net result was a party in Chambers, at which the large and hungry-looking Misses Hoskins appeared and giggled over their sherry. This soirée was followed by a longer and more serious session in Pommeroy's, which had ended once again, I regret to say, with Henry and me recalling the great hits of Dame Vera Lynn. So now I turned my face to the wall, closed my eyes and knew what it was like to stand loitering on the edge of eternity.

'And how is the great barrister-at-law feeling now?'

I was awoken from a troubled doze by a voice which sounded like that of an actor playing the part of an Indian doctor. His dialogue also had the sound of words invented to create a character. This was my first meeting with him, but in all our subsequent encounters I felt that there was something unreal, almost theatrical, about Ghulam Rahmat, and the way he pronounced the absurd title he always insisted on giving me, 'barrister-at-law'.

'I am,' I confessed to the smiling character at my bedside, 'feeling like death.'

'Temporary, sir. A purely temporary indisposition. No need to fly the flag over the Old Bailey at half-mast yet awhile. Tomorrow there will be rejoicing there. The crowds in the street will be cheering. Word will go round. The great barrister-at-law is returned to us, stronger than ever. I have told your good lady while you were sleeping, sir. From the look of him, your husband strikes me as strong as a horse.'

Now I had a lifetime's experience of the evil after-effects of over-indulgence in Pommeroy's plonk, but they had, up till now, not included the presence of an Asian quack doing Peter Sellers impressions at the Rumpole bedside. I appealed to Hilda, who had joined the party.

'Did you tell Doctor . . .'

'Rahmat, sir. Ghulam. Medical doctor, Bachelor of Arts of the University of Bombay. A professional like you, sir. But not with a title so imposing and universally feared as barrister-at-law.'

'Did you tell Dr Rahmat that I felt near to death?' I asked Hilda.

'We are all near to death.' The thought seemed to cause the Doctor a good deal of amusement. He began to laugh, but suppressed the sound as though it were somehow impolite, like a belch. 'But, no doubt, Mr Rumpole will survive us all. Sit up, please. Will you do me the honour to let me listen to your chest? What a lung you have there, sir! It's a pleasure to listen to your hearty breathing. No doubt about it. You will go on forever.'

'Really?' I must say the man had cheered me up considerably. 'So there's nothing seriously wrong?'

'Nothing at all. I diagnose a severe attack of the collywobbles brought on by food-poisoning, perhaps?'

'*Food*-poisoning?' She Who Must repeated with an unbelieving sigh.

'For which I prescribe two Alka-Seltzers in a glass of water, strong black coffee, a quiet day in bed and even more than the usual kindness and consideration from your lady wife. And tomorrow we shall say the barrister-at-law is himself again!'

When she had seen the medical man off the premises and returned to the sick-room, I restrained myself from telling Hilda that for her to treat me with more than her usual kindness and consideration wouldn't greatly tax her ingenuity. Instead, I gave her a weak smile and quaffed the Alka-Seltzer. 'What a very charming and sensible quack,' I said as I effervesced quietly.

But events were soon to occur which placed considerable doubt on the charm and good sense of Dr Ghulam Rahmat.

The following facts emerged during the subsequent proceedings. At 10.30 a.m. on the day in question, the waiting-room in the local surgery was full of assorted bronchials, flus, eczemas, rheumatics, carbuncles and suspected and feared anti-social diseases. The receptionist, a Miss Dankwerts, was seated behind her desk, in charge of the proceedings. The names of the doctors were written upon an electric device on the wall behind her, and beside each name a red light flashed if they were engaged or a green if they were available. At the moment with which we are concerned Dr Rahmat's light was red as he was seeing a Miss Marietta Liptrott, who had been waiting to be treated for a sore throat. She had previously been a patient of Dr Cogger, but as he was busy she had asked specifically for the Indian doctor. Miss Liptrott had been closeted with her chosen quack for about ten minutes when a scream was heard from behind Dr Rahmat's door. With her clothes somewhat disarrayed, she flew past the assorted complaints and the startled receptionist and, crying, 'The beast! The beast!', rushed out of the building and into the wastelands around the Gloucester Road. The doctors were accustomed to press their buttons as soon as a patient left, but Dr Rahmat's light remained red for some time after Miss Liptrott ran out. When it changed to green and his next patient, a Mrs Rodway, was admitted she found the Doctor nervous, apparently unable to concentrate on her urticaria and looking, so the witness was to testify, as though 'he'd had the fright of his life'.

Towards the end of the afternoon surgery on that day, that is to say shortly after six o'clock, I happened to call in to get a prescription for She Who Must Be Obeyed (whose blood pressure is inclined to rise, especially if I have overstayed my allotted time in Pommeroy's). The surgery was almost empty, but a youngish man in a blue suit was opening his brief-case on the receptionist's desk and I saw it contained a number of printed folders, pill bottles and a portable telephone. I took him to be the rep for a firm of manufacturing chemists and he was rattling on about the wonders of a miracle cure for something or other when Dr Cogger's light went green and he shot out of his door and recognized me.

'Hullo there, Mr Rumpole.' Tim Cogger had treated me on a couple of occasions for temporary voice loss, the occupational hazard of Old Bailey hacks and opera singers. He was considerably younger than old MacClintock, but he seemed to have inherited the leadership of the practice. Cogger was the hearty type of quack who once played rugby football for Barts and seemed to believe in the short, sharp shock treatment for most illnesses. He was continually complaining that his patients were 'typical National Health pill-scroungers' and, on my rare visits to him, he seemed to regard a head cold as the mark of a wimp. 'You're looking well!' he told me, as though daring me to complain of anything.

'I was looking for Dr Rahmat,' I said. 'He promised my wife a prescription.'

'Oh, I'm afraid Rahmat's gone home.' Dr Cogger seemed to know all about something extremely serious. 'He may not be back at work for a day or two. If it's for Mrs Rumpole, perhaps I could help?' Dr Cogger then got the receptionist to look up Hilda's records and scribbled a new prescription in the most obliging manner. I then knew nothing of the dramatic event of the morning, but by the evening it was certainly service with a smile down at the local quackery.

In due course Miss Marietta Liptrott sent in a complaint to

the General Medical Council, alleging approaches made to her by Dr Rahmat far beyond the call of medical duty. With the ponderous tread which characterizes all judicial proceedings, that august body began to move towards the trial of my encouraging quack for serious professional misconduct. Meanwhile life in Equity Court continued as usual without any earth-shaking changes. Uncle Tom perfected his putts in the clerk's room, where Henry and Dianne did their best to control their emotions and only allowed themselves a few covert glances of mutual adoration as they unwrapped their sandwiches at lunchtime. Mizz Liz Probert tried to start a movement to turn Chambers into a cooperative dedicated to the entirely fallacious principle that all barristers are created equal, but whenever she brought up the subject, Claude Erskine-Brown stuffed bits of his Walkman into his ears and she was left listening to the distant twittering of *Die Walküre*. Phillida Erskine-Brown, our Portia, continued to star in a number of *causes célèbres* and enjoyed a success which Claude took with manful resignation. Sam Ballard made out a list of do's and don'ts for members of Chambers, which he pinned up on the notice-board in the clerk's room. This included such precepts as: DO NOT ALLOW SUCH ARTICLES AS SOLICITORS' LETTERS OR WITNESS STATEMENTS TO BE DROPPED INTO THE UPSTAIRS LAVATORY. Well, sometimes there seems to be no other place for them. DO NOT BE SEEN DRINKING WITH A LAY CLIENT IN A FLEET STREET WINE BAR. THIS SORT OF THING BRINGS CHAMBERS INTO DISREPUTE. Well, it had been the fortieth anniversary of Fred Timson's first Court appearance under my auspices. Finally, to show that Ballard was deeply concerned about the environment, DO REMEMBER THE FORESTS. SAVE PAPER. To which I had added, on my return from Pommeroy's after the glass or two with Fred, AND DON'T WASTE IT ON BLOODY SILLY NOTICES IN THE CLERK'S ROOM. After which the list vanished mysteriously, no doubt to be re-cycled and re-emerge as a Green Party newsletter.

'Rumpole. A word with you.' Sam Ballard accosted me one morning. 'I wanted to let you know. Heather Whittaker has joined us as Erskine-Brown's pupil.' He uttered this news with a good deal of awe and wonder, as though announcing that the Queen Mother had agreed to drop in afternoons to answer the telephone. 'I just wanted to explain this to you. She's not young. She's taking up the Bar in middle life. And she is a thoroughly nice type of person.'

'Oh, good,' I told him. 'We could do with a few of those around here.'

'I think you were away when we had the Chambers meeting and agreed to take her.'

'Yes,' I remembered, 'I was dying.'

'Oh, really?' I was afraid I detected, in Soapy Sam's eye, a glimmer of hope.

'Yes. But I changed my mind. I'm not dying any more. Sorry to disappoint you.'

'Well, I want to make this quite clear to you. Mrs Whittaker is, well, not the sort of person who would enjoy rough behaviour in Chambers. Members coming in, perhaps from some wine bar, singing and so on.'

'You mean she doesn't like Dame Vera Lynn?'

'And I don't suppose she'd relish a working environment where people scribble obscenities on notices pinned up in the clerk's room.'

'Does it occur to you, Ballard, that the Whittaker woman may have joined the wrong profession?'

'She was at Girton' – this news seemed to me quite irrelevant – 'with my cousin Joyce.'

'Well, this isn't Girton. She'll be in daily contact with murder, grievous bodily harm and indecent exposure. She'll have to take in incest, adultery and dubious magazines with her tea and buns. You're not seriously suggesting she's going to scream with horror at a bit of graffiti on the notice-board? Anyway, it wasn't obscene.'

'I'm glad you admit you wrote it!' Ballard looked triumphant.

'I admit nothing,' I said. 'So what's this new pupil going to specialize in? The theft of knitting patterns? Excuse me, Bollard. I'm off to confer about a bit of gross indecency on the

National Health. Don't tell La Whittaker. She might have a fit of the vapours.'

In fact I had a conference in a type of litigation new to me. During a life spent earning my crusts before some pretty unlikely tribunals, I had never yet appeared before the General Medical Council. But Dr Rahmat had telephoned me and told me he was in trouble. I had fixed him up with the dependable Bernard as an instructing solicitor and he was even then waiting for me in my consulting room – an ailing medic who hoped that Rumpole would work the miracle cure.

'In all my troubles and tribulations I had one thought to comfort me. I know an absolutely wizard barrister-at-law!'

Dr Rahmat was no longer smiling. He sat in my client's armchair, looking somewhat thinner and older than when he had stood at my bedside. But he was still playing the Indian doctor in a way which he seemed to hope I would find entertaining. 'How could I be accused of such a dreadful thing? Me, Ghulam Rahmat? All my life I have been a peaceful fellow. I have been anxious to please and to make trouble for no one!'

Perhaps you were too anxious to do what you thought would please Miss Liptrott, I felt like saying. Instead, I asked him to tell me about himself. He told me about his training in Bombay, his coming to England and discovering there was a vacancy in old MacClintock's practice.

'Dr MacClintock was a man who showed no prejudices at all. I said, "Do you mind taking on an Indian doctor in your very British practice?" "Certainly not," he told me. "You can be as Indian as you damn well please."' I looked at the smiling client and had the strange idea that the exaggerated accent and vocabulary had been put on to oblige Dr MacClintock, who wanted to demonstrate his open-mindedness. 'And how are things,' I asked, 'since Dr Cogger's taken over?'

'Just the same.' The smile continued. 'Dr Tim Cogger is a thoroughly good man. A chap with a fine sense of humour. You know what they say of him at Barts? He was a great practical joker. Perhaps not a brilliant doctor but . . .'

'Are you?'

'What?'

'A brilliant doctor?'

'Most of us are not. Most of us are at a loss, more than we like to admit. But we try to be kind and cheerful and wait for the disease to go away. To be perfectly frank, that is how I treated the great barrister-at-law.'

'I'm afraid' – I had to break the news to him – 'Miss Marietta Liptrott doesn't seem likely to go away.'

'No, dash it all.' His cheerfulness, which had come back as he described his professional life so candidly, had drained away like bathwater, leaving him disconsolate again. 'What a pain in the neck. If I can be so jolly rude about a young lady.'

'Had you seen her before?'

'No. And if I have to be honest with you, I hope and pray I never see her again.'

'What did she look like?'

For an answer he took out his wallet and handed me a cutting from the *Daily Beacon*. 'First time,' he said ruefully, 'that I ever got my name in the paper.' INDIAN DOCTOR TRIED TO STRIP AND MAKE LOVE TO ME. NANNY TELLS OF SURGERY ANTICS blared the headline. The story went on:

Children's nurse, Marietta Liptrott, 27, who works for a wealthy Kensington family, only had a sore throat but Dr Rahmat had his own ideas about treatment. He made her lie down on a couch, she said in her complaint to the General Medical Council, and wanted her to pull down her knickers. Dr Ghulam Rahmat, 50, who only came to England 12 years ago said, 'I have the best barrister in the country and I shall fight this every inch of the way.'

I was looking at Miss Liptrott's photograph: a pale face with large, trusting eyes and an upper lip drawn over slightly protruding teeth. This gave her a breathless and eager look.

'I never took a shine to her, Mr Rumpole, to be perfectly frank with you.'

'What's your situation, Doctor? Have you a wife?'

'Had, Mr Rumpole. There is poor hygiene in some of our

171

hospitals and I lost her. My son is in Bombay, studying. He hopes, in his humble way, to be a barrister-at-law, third-class merely. Not in your league, I may say.' To my embarrassment I saw tears in the eyes behind his heavy spectacles. We hacks see clients at their most emotional moments, but remain oddly embarrassed when they start weeping.

'So. What's our defence?' I was anxious to get back to business.

'The same,' he announced with great satisfaction, 'as in E. M. Forster's fine work, *A Passage to India*.'

When I was up at Oxford, studying night and day for my record-breaking fourth in law, I remembered a chap called Perkins, who greatly admired this Forster. He told me that personal relationships were all important and if he had to choose between betraying his country or Rumpole, he hoped he'd choose his country. Happily, Perkins became a clergyman in Wales and didn't have to make this agonizing decision, but he did get me to read *A Passage to India*, the gist of which had, I was ashamed to say, now slipped my mind.

'Of course,' I said, 'just remind me of the plot.'

'This English lady accuses an Indian doctor of raping her in the Marabar caves,' the Doctor reminded me.

'Ah, yes, of course. It all comes back to me. And what was his defence exactly?'

'That it all went on in her fevered imagination.'

'I see.' I was a little doubtful. 'And how did it work out?'

'He was acquitted! You will enjoy a similar triumph, great barrister-at-law.'

'Well, let's hope so.' I was by no means convinced. 'We've got to remember that was a work of fiction.' I then brought the Doctor down to earth by trying to get his exact clinical reasons for asking a patient who had come in to complain of a sore throat to remove her knickers.

When Dr Rahmat had left me he was in a mood of unbridled optimism. I wandered out into the passage with my mind set on a little refreshment at Pommeroy's. The door of Erskine-Brown's room opened and out stepped a well-groomed, neatly dressed, grey-haired lady, who greeted me with a friendly smile and carefully controlled cry of 'Mr Rumpole, isn't it?'

'A piece of him,' I told her.

'I've been so longing to meet you. I'm Heather Whittaker, Erskine-Brown's pupil. I've taken to the Bar rather late in life I'm afraid.'

'It's probably a profession for the aged,' I consoled her. 'The young can't stand the pace.'

'You're a legend, Mr Rumpole. Of course you know that. I'm absolutely dying to hear you on your feet.'

'Well,' I said hospitably, 'why not pop along to the General Medical Council? I've got a doctor in trouble.'

'Oh, I'd love that.' She seemed genuinely enthusiastic. 'Of course, I've heard Erskine-Brown on his feet.'

'Oh, really? And did you manage to keep awake?'

'Just about.' She allowed herself a small but charming giggle. 'With you I'm sure I should be on the edge of my seat. What's your doctor been up to?'

'I'd better not tell you. Our Head of Chambers says you shock easily.'

'What nonsense!' Her smile widened. 'I want to know all the gory details.' I must say that Ballard was right about one thing. Our new pupil, Mrs Heather Whittaker, seemed a nice type of person.

My life at that time was bedevilled by women. Not only had a person of that persuasion got my unfortunate doctor in trouble, but a client of mine, similarly constituted, was becoming a pain in my neck.

'So. She's been ringing up again,' said She Who Must Be Obeyed in threatening tones as I got home that evening.

'She?' I asked with carefully simulated innocence. 'Who on earth's she?' Of course, I knew perfectly well. She was the worst driver who ever skidded her gleaming white Volkswagen off the Uxbridge Road, mounted the pavement, terrorized the passers-by, hit a municipal waste disposal bin and someone's mobile shopping-basket, and finally crashed into a lamp-post.

The driver's name was Mrs Bambi Etheridge. Only

Rumpole's skill, and the fact that the chief prosecution witness lectured the lady Chairman of the Bench on the hopeless incompetence of woman drivers, led to her triumphant acquittal on the grounds of poor road surface and fast oncoming traffic. Whatever might be said of her as a driver, Mrs Etheridge was a social menace. She was a generously built lady who, as she moved, clattered with what I believe is known as costume jewellery and gave off a deafening smell of what she was at pains to tell me was Deadly Sins by St Just. Her hair was unconvincingly blonde and her make-up strove to represent the effect of too much sunbathing in Florida. She spoke as though she were trying to attract the attention of a deaf and uncooperative waiter on the far side of a noisy dining-room.

'Mr Rumpole,' she bellowed, as we came out of Court 'you are an absolute sweetie. How can I reward you, Mr Rumpole, darling?' I told her that it was normal to do it with a cheque sent through her solicitors.

'But I mean something more personal. What about a naughty lunch? Just the two of us. Could you get a long afternoon off? And do you enjoy scrumptious desserts as much as I do? Oh, good. All men enjoy scrumptious desserts, don't they? That's settled then. I'll give you a tinkle. Are you in the book? I'm sure you are.'

'Lunch,' I said regretfully, for I'm particularly fond of lunch, 'no, I'm afraid that's impossible. The pressure of work, you see.'

'Oh, come on, Mr Rumpole. Give yourself a bit of fun, why don't you? Has anyone ever told you, you're a very cuddly sort of barrister?'

My blood ran cold. I saw Mr Bernard, our admirable instructing solicitor, avert his eyes in shame. And this woman was going in search of my telephone number. I fervently wished I had lost her case and she was even now being led off to the dungeons.

'Mrs Etheridge, please don't trouble yourself to telephone. I'm afraid I rarely lunch out nowadays. In fact I do nothing except work.'

'All work and no play makes Mr Rumpole a dull boy.' She

slapped my wrist lightly. 'And I'm sure you're not that, are you? Be seeing you!'

And with that she was gone, with a whiff of Deadly Sins, a carillon of costume jewellery and the relentless beat of her high heels on the entrance hall of the Uxbridge Magistrates Court. Three evenings later the telephone rang in Froxbury Mansions. Hilda answered it, frowned with extreme displeasure and handed me the instrument with a grim 'There's a woman asking for you who rejoices in the name of Bambi Etheridge.'

'Oh,' I said weakly, 'what does she want?'

'God knows what she wants with you, Rumpole. You'd better ask her.'

'Yes!' I barked into the instrument in a way which I hoped would put an end once and for all to the hideous notion that I am in the least cuddly. 'Rumpole speaking.'

'Oh, dear.' The Etheridge menace appeared to coo down the line. 'Is it a bad moment? Are you with your wife? Ought I to have pretended to be the Water Board or something?'

'No,' I said firmly, 'I don't think you can.'

'Can what, Mr Rumpole? What are you suggesting? I only rang to invite you to lunch.'

'I don't think you can get costs against the police. Yes. I know you won. But you did hit a lamp-post. It was quite a reasonable prosecution to bring. I'm sorry. That's my final legal opinion.'

'Oh, of course,' Bambi purred understandingly. 'You can't talk now, can you? I'll ring again.'

'Don't do it,' I said. 'You'll be throwing good money after bad by appealing.'

'What a thing to say! You're not bad money are you, Mr Rumpole? I said I'll ring again when you're not in the bosom of your family. By-ee.'

'Stupid woman!' I said when I put the phone down. 'She wants to appeal on costs.'

'Oh, yes?' Hilda looked at me with profound disbelief. 'Is that why she called you my lovely husband?'

'She didn't?'

'She did to me. I said, "Hilda Rumpole speaking," and she said, "Oh, yes. And is your lovely husband about by any chance?"'

'Look' – I felt called on to defend myself on a most serious charge of which I was undoubtedly innocent, having been put in the frame by the appalling Bambi – 'she's only a customer.'

'Well, that poor girl was only a customer of Dr Rahmat's, wasn't she? And look what happened to her!' And She Who Must Be Obeyed adjourned for supper, clearly having made up her mind without the need for further argument.

I did get taken out for an expensive lunch not long after that fatal phone call, and I was invited by a lady whose brains and beauty far exceeded the modest attainments in either of those departments by Bambi Etheridge. Mrs Phillida Erskine-Brown, Q.C., our Portia, knocked at my door in Chambers late one morning and said, 'Come on, you old devil. I'm taking you out to lunch.' Expecting a couple of sandwiches at Pommeroy's, I was surprised when she said, 'Savoy Grill suit you, would it?'

'Well,' I admitted, 'if we're really roughing it. But what's come over you, Portia? Are they putting you on the High Court Bench?'

'They're not putting me anywhere. The question is, where am I putting myself? I'm just about fed up, Rumpole. I've had it up to here. So we're going out to spend what's left of Claude's money and I hope he finds *that* boring!' With which enigmatic statement she set off along the Strand at a pace so brisk that I had to break into a trot to keep up with her.

It was not until we were seated on the plush and had our hands round a couple of cocktails that Phillida started to unburden herself. 'Rumpole,' she said, 'tell me honestly. Am I boring?'

'Whatever gave you that idea?'

'Am I a rut?'

'Scarcely.'

'Humdrum? Would you call me humdrum?'

I looked at our Portia. Her hair was reddish, inclined to

gold. Her face, that of one of the most intelligent Pre-Raphaelite models, had grown, I thought, finer in the years since I had known her. The formal white blouse and dark suit, combined with the horn rims she used to read the menu, merely added to that charm which had, in the past, completely turned the heads of such connoisseurs of feminine beauty as the Hon. Mr Justice Featherstone. As I looked at her, the only wonder was how, all those years ago, she had been put in the club and then married by a character as un-exotic as my learned friend, Claude Erskine-Brown.

'Run of the mill. Am I run of the mill?'

'You are certainly not.'

Apart from her beauty, Mrs Erskine-Brown has brains. Not for nothing had I named her Portia. When she spoke up for the Defence the general opinion in the jury-box was that if a nice girl like that was on his side, the villain in the dock couldn't be nearly as black as he was painted. When prosecuting, she could pot the prisoner with all the aplomb of the Avenging Angel on a good day.

'Men,' she now said, 'are all the same!'

'Are we? I'm not sure I'm exactly like Claude.'

'Perhaps not you, Rumpole. You're not really interested, are you?'

'Not interested in what?'

'In what everyone else who happens to be male seems to spend their time thinking about, sex.'

'Oh, that,' I said, and gave a small shudder of fear at the thought of returning home to be cooed at over the telephone by Bambi.

'They're all the same. Take that wretched doctor of yours.'

'Dr Rahmat?'

'A woman only has to wander into his surgery with a sore throat and he's trying to get into her knickers. Just like Claude.'

'Claude looks after people with sore throats?' I wasn't following her drift.

'I'll get him, though. I'll cross-examine the life out of him. He'll be struck off for ten years.'

'Claude?'

'No. Dr Rahmat.'

'What's Dr Rahmat got to do with it?'

'I'm prosecuting him before the General Medical Council.'

'First rate!' I tried to sound enthusiastic, but I saw the unhappy doctor's hopes fading rapidly. 'I'll have a foeman worthy of my steel. Foe-woman, I'm sorry. You have to be so careful when you talk to lady barristers nowadays.'

'I don't know how you could defend a person like that.'

'You know I have to defend a person like anyone.'

'But you couldn't defend a real snake.'

'Dr Rahmat?'

'No!' And she added in such a tone that I came to the conclusion that hell hath absolutely no fury like a Mrs Phillida Erskine-Brown, Q.C. scorned, 'Claude!'

'All right,' I said. 'What's Claude done now?'

As the waiter had set smoked salmon and Sancerre before us, it seemed a suitable moment to get on with putting the indictment. By way of answer, Mrs Erskine-Brown opened the slender black brief-case she had brought with her and produced a copy of a somewhat lurid magazine called *Casanova*. On the cover of this publication a bikini-clad young woman disported herself with a medicine ball, both articles looking as though they had been inflated with a bicycle pump.

'Let me read you this.' Phillida flicked through what were, no doubt, distressing pages of photographs and came to rest among the advertisements which, when I got a chance to examine them at my leisure, were mostly of the lonely hearts variety.

'"Barrister. Good-looking and young at heart,"' Phillida read in tones of such disgust that they almost put me off my lunch. '"In a rut. Bored with the humdrum of married life. Seeks a new partner for the occasional fling. Country walks, opera-going, three-star restaurant treats and all the other pleasures of life. Tall and slender preferred. Write with a photograph, if possible, to . . ." And there's a box number. There you are! Read it for yourself if you want to.' She almost threw the exhibit at me, drained her wine glass at a gulp and ordered us both a refill from the waiter. I glanced at it as I asked, 'So how do you connect this with Claude?'

'It's obvious, isn't it? He's a barrister and "opera-going".'

'There are about four thousand barristers and some of them must go to the Opera. I don't think, Mrs Erskine-Brown, that your evidence is absolutely conclusive.'

'I found this in his room in Chambers, Rumpole,' Phillida said between gritted teeth. 'Now. What further proof do you want?'

'I see.' This last piece of testimony did seem to have landed the unfortunate Claude in the manure. 'Well,' I admitted, 'things are beginning to look rather black for the accused.' As I said this, I was glancing further down the page of *Casanova* and found boxes announcing the service of 'escorts' and ladies equipped to give massage treatment 'in the hotel or home'. These announcements were embellished with photographs and one struck me as familiar. It was under the heading NAUGHTY MARIETTA WILL KEEP YOU COMPANY AT DINNERS OUT OR BUSINESS FUNCTIONS. There was a snap of this companionable girl. Her hair had been done over more elaborately than when she appeared in the *Daily Beacon*, but there was no mistaking the wide eyes and small, even features and slightly protruding teeth of Miss Liptrott, the girl who was about to bring about the downfall of Doctor Rahmat.

During the beef and Beaujolais, our Portia rattled on about her husband's character defects and his pathetic failure even to be unfaithful without advertising for it in the public prints. Then, perhaps, feeling she had confided too much, she remembered a conference in Chambers, paid the bill and left me. She went so hurriedly, in fact, that I found myself still in possession of the copy of *Casanova*, and I finished the Brouilly, which would never have been seen dead in Pommeroy's, and again contemplated the features of the undoubted Miss Liptrott. Dr Rahmat's case seemed to follow me around that day, for, glancing across the restaurant, I spotted the large, muscular and jovial figure of Dr Tim Cogger, lunching profusely with someone I recognized as the fellow with the brief-case, who had apparently been trying to flog his pills and potions around the quackery. I raised what remained in my glass in salutations but Dr Rahmat's senior partner, although he glanced in my direction, seemed not to have noticed me at all.

When I got back to my room in Chambers, I propped *Casanova* up on my desk, got a line from Henry and started to dial. I heard a ringing tone and, as I was saying, 'Is that the Naughty Marietta escort service?', I was aware of the door opening and our Head of Chambers sidled into the room and stood agape as I heard the whispered reply, 'Yes. This is Marietta speaking.'

'Marietta Liptrott, I presume?'

'Who are you? Are you the newspapers?'

'No, I promise you. Just someone in need of an escort. I heard from a friend that you were a very companionable young lady.'

'Oh, well. Yes. I suppose that's all right.' There was a pause but no denial of the name. 'When's the function?'

'It's not for me, actually.' I raised my voice slightly and turned to smile at the intruder. 'It's for a friend of mine. He wants to take you along to add a little colour to a ladies' night at the Lawyers As Christians Society. Call you back with the details. Nice to talk to you, Miss Liptrott.' I put down the telephone.

'Rumpole! Is that your idea of a joke?'

'Well, you shouldn't have been standing there listening to a private conversation.'

'I couldn't help hearing that you were using Chambers telephone facilities to call up an escort agency.'

'Of course, you could help it. You could have beaten a hasty retreat.'

'Rumpole. You're a married man.'

'That has not escaped my attention.'

'I don't ask why you should feel the need to do that sort of thing . . .'

'Good. Nice to chat to you, Bollard. Now, if you don't mind closing the door on your way out . . .'

He moved towards the exit and then paused. 'Rumpole,' he said solemnly, 'don't you think you ought to make a clean breast of it to Hilda?'

'A clean breast of what?'

'The fact that you're troubled by those sort of, well, needs.'

'Ballard' – I looked at the man with pity – 'when you next feel the need to talk absolute balderdash, why don't you make a clean breast of it to Matey?'

He went then but was back in a twinkling, his head round the door. 'I forgot why I dropped in,' he confessed.

'On the chance of earwigging a salacious phone call?' I suggested.

'No, it wasn't that. Now I remember. I've had a word with Mrs Whittaker. It seems you've asked her to take a note for you in that G.M.C. case of yours. Are you sure it's not distasteful in any way?'

'I promise. She can resort to ear-plugs for the more sensational parts of the evidence.' When I was finally relieved of Bollard's company, I continued a close study of infectious mononucleosis in the *Principles and Practice of Medicine* I had got out of the library. Then I called on Mrs Erskine-Brown to return the incriminating magazine she had left with me in the restaurant.

'There you are,' I said, when I entered the comfortably appointed Q.C.'s room Phillida inhabited apart from her husband. I dropped the distasteful magazine on her desk. 'You left the vital evidence in the restaurant. What are you going to do to the unfortunate Claude? Confront him with it?'

'No good at all.' She came to a quick legal decision. 'He'd only say it wasn't him or something equally devious. No. I shall trap him with it. Leave him absolutely no way of escape.'

Traps were being set all around by Phillida, not only for Claude but for the unfortunate Dr Rahmat as well.

'There are some exquisite echoes in India; there is the whisper round the dome at Bijapur; there are the long, solid sentences that voyage through the air at Mandu, and return unbroken to their creator.' So wrote old E. M. Forster, whose work I had turned to, together with the *Principles and Practice of Medicine*, by way of preparation for the struggle ahead. The old literary darling might well have had something to say about the echoes that the accusation against Dr Rahmat sent reverberating round the small world of Rumpole, to be half heard, mainly misunderstood and set up fresh rumours. One evening as we sat over our chops in Froxbury Mansions, Hilda, who had apparently caught one such echo said, 'I've arranged for you to see Dr Cogger.'

'Why on earth?'

'Well, you certainly can't see Dr Rahmat. I don't know why on earth you're defending him.'

'I'm defending him because he's in trouble.'

'Anyway, that Marguerite Ballard rang up and said Sam was worried about you and that you'd seemed rather strange lately. What were you doing strange, Rumpole?'

'I suppose phoning up escorts,' I answered her through a certain amount of chop and mashed potato.

'What did you say?'

'I said I suppose I was feeling out of sorts.' I had changed my mind about taking Hilda into my confidence. It would have taken too long and she might well not have accepted my evidence.

'Well, if you're feeling out of sorts, stop complaining to *me* about it. Go and see Dr Cogger tomorrow evening, on your way home from Chambers. Do try and have a bit of sense, Rumpole.'

So evening surgery found me, ever obedient, waiting for the green light to flash beside Dr Cogger's name. I sat among people with varying degrees of illness, coughing and sneezing their way through outdated copies of *Punch*, the *Sunday Fortress* cooking supplement, *Good Housekeeping* and the *Illustrated London News*. Pale children played with the broken-down toys provided, an antique Chinaman clutched the handle of his walking-stick and muttered ferociously to himself, a very thin girl bit her lip and sat holding her boyfriend's hand. The flats and bedsits around the Gloucester Road had handed over their sick and dying. Then I put down the back number of *Country Life* which hadn't been holding my attention and saw what surely must have been an unusual sight in a doctor's waiting-room, the lurid cover of *Casanova*.

'Do you take this regularly?' I approached the receptionist with the dubious periodical in my hand.

'Not at all. It shouldn't have been left out there. Of course it'd upset the old people.'

From Miss Dankwerts's look of pity, I could see I was being taken for one of the easily upset old people. 'You mean' – my curiosity was aroused – '*Casanova* isn't normally available in the waiting-room?'

'Of course not. As a matter of fact,' she gave a small smile at the expense of the medical men from whom she obviously felt as aloof as she did from her patients, and whispered, 'the cleaning lady found it in one of the doctors' rooms. It should never have been put out.'

'Of course. The advertisements are rather interesting though. You might find a friend.' And, before she could deal with this outrageous suggestion, the green light flashed and I was admitted into Dr Cogger's presence with the folded *Casanova* swelling my jacket pocket.

'Well, Mr Rumpole. What seems to be the trouble?' The Doctor was as cheerful and hearty as ever.

'I don't know. Failing eyesight, perhaps. I thought I saw you having lunch in the Savoy Grill, but I must've been mistaken. You didn't seem to recognize me when I raised my glass to you.'

'The Savoy Grill?' He smiled at me, a big man with huge hands and a surprisingly gentle voice. 'That's a bit out of the class of a struggling G.P.'

'So it wasn't you then?'

'I hardly think so.' He shook his head. 'Now' – he was turning over my notes – 'it seems your wife made this appointment. What does she think is wrong with you?'

'Someone told her I was behaving rather strangely in my Chambers.'

'Behaving strangely?' He was adding these words to the log of Rumpole's weaknesses, where they would be immortalized together with my weight. 'What sort of strangeness?'

'Well, ringing up escort agencies.'

'Escort agencies? But, Mr Rumpole, why ever should you do that?'

'I suppose they thought I was looking for escorts.'

'You mean, young girls to take out to dinner? That sort of thing?'

'That sort of thing. Yes.'

'My dear Mr Rumpole' – he leant back in his chair and his smile was entirely kindly – 'I shouldn't let that worry you in the least. A lot of men, perfectly decent chaps, in my experience, feel the need of young, fresh – well, young company. It doesn't mean they're sick in any way. It's perfectly natural.'

'Is that what you think?'

'Oh, yes. I do, quite honestly.'

'I thought it might be.'

'Oh, did you?' His smile faded and he gave me a look, I thought, of some unease. Of course, that may have been because I was being such a terse and unforthcoming patient.

'Yes. When I saw that magazine *Casanova* in your waiting-room.'

'Oh, that!' He was smiling again, at full beam. 'I can't think how it got there.'

'It's full of advertisements for escorts, companions, people for nights out on the town. All that sort of thing.'

'Is it? I didn't look. It seems to have interested you.'

'Yes, it did. Your receptionist said it was found in one of the doctors' rooms.'

'Well, Mr Rumpole, my partners are big boys now. I really can't be expected to nanny them. Perhaps I should have, though. When I think of the trouble poor old Rahmat's got himself into – Now' – he looked at his watch and seemed to decide that his time was being wasted in idle chatter – 'what would you say your problem is, medically?'

'Medically,' I told him, 'I can't sleep. I seem to wake up around one o'clock in the morning and worry about poor old Rahmat, as you rightly call him.'

'My dear Mr Rumpole. Why should *you* worry?'

'I suppose, because I'm defending him.'

For the first time Dr Cogger looked startled and unsure of himself. 'You are?' He frowned. 'I hadn't realized that. Perhaps we shouldn't have been talking about it. I've been asked to give evidence.'

'For the Doctor? I didn't think we'd asked you.'

'No. Well, for the Council. I just told them what I knew. I certainly don't want to make things any more difficult for Rahmat. Look. I'll write you out some pills. Perfectly harmless. Just take one when you wake up in the middle of the night. At least that should stop you worrying.'

'About Dr Rahmat?'

'If you can manage it. I know. It's distressing for all of us when a doctor goes off the rails.'

'Rumpole, I'm terribly worried.'

'Oh, dear.'

'Worried and frankly mystified.' It didn't take much to mystify Erskine-Brown, and as we sat together in Pommeroy's, our day's work done, I waited to hear what detail of our life on earth was puzzling him at the moment.

'It's about Philly. She's taken to calling herself "The Rut".'

'The what?'

'The Rut! I come home and there'll be a note: GONE ROUND TO MARGOT'S, SO I DON'T BORE YOU TO DEATH. "THE RUT". Why do you think she calls herself "The Rut"?'

'I have no idea.'

'Do you think it has some amorous significance? I looked it up in *The Oxford English* in the Bar library. It refers, Rumpole, to periods of sexual excitement in certain animals.'

'Didn't you ask your wife what she meant?'

'Of course.'

'What did she say?'

'That I should know, if anyone did.'

'And you found that reply enigmatic?'

'I certainly did.'

I looked at the man. I wouldn't have thought Claude had any special talent for lying, but he spoke with apparent conviction and not an eyelid was batted.

'She's also begun to ask me about country walks.'

'Say again.'

'She says, "When are you going out for another country walk, Claude?" She knows that country walks are just not my scene.'

'I shouldn't have thought so.'

'They tire you out and you get your shoes dirty. Whatever gave her the idea I want to go tramping around the country-side?'

'Are you sure *you* didn't?'

For an answer he shook his head sadly and said, 'Do you know I really am worried about Philly. Do you think she ought to see a doctor?'

'I think,' I told him, 'that she's about to see about a dozen of them. In the General Medical Council. And I'm sure she'll do this case like she does all her cases – brilliantly.' And she'll have you stitched up too, Claude, I thought as I looked at the man who still seemed to be seeing his perilous situation through a glass darkly.

I left Pommeroy's and when I disembarked from the bus and was making my way towards the mansion flat, I saw Dr Rahmat hurrying along the street in front of me. I called out and he turned like a startled hare and then managed a smile of greeting. 'The barrister-at-law. And looking extremely fit, if I may say so.'

'I wanted to see you. There's a question that I should have asked. Mr Bernard was trying to get hold of you at the sur-gery.'

'Alas, I am seldom there now. The patients don't seem too dead keen on seeing me. But shall we walk along? I have an ap-pointment.'

'All right. It's about Dr Cogger,' I said, when we were on the move. 'Did you and he ever quarrel about anything?' Dr Rahmat walked a few steps in silence and I prompted him, 'If I'm going to defend you, you'd better trust me.'

'Well,' he admitted, 'we had a few words once. About the drugs.'

'What about the drugs?'

'He was always wanting me to prescribe . . .' Here he men-tioned a number of long, Latinized trade names which went, I have to confess, in at one of my ears and out at the other. 'They were very expensive drugs, most of them from March-main's, and I told him that my patients would be just as well off with a few kind words and a couple of aspirins.'

'How did he react to that?'

'Badly. He got in a most terrible bait. He went so far as to say that he didn't want partners who were so pig ignorant on the subject of new drugs. I'm sure it was said in the heat of the moment and he didn't mean it exactly.'

We had reached the Star of Hyderabad, our local Indian eatery, and Dr Rahmat stopped in front of its red and gold door. 'I am most reluctant to part from you, great barrister-at-law, but, alas, I have an appointment.'

'I'll come in with you for a moment. You can buy me a beer.'

'It would be a pleasure, but some other time, I'm afraid. This is an appointment of a private nature.' He then bolted into the Star of Hyderabad and, resisting all temptations to peer in and see who he was dating, I headed off to an empty house, for it was one of the nights when Hilda was at her bridge lesson with Marigold Featherstone.

At about nine o'clock the phone rang and a familiar voice said, 'Is Horace there? It's Bambi.' 'This is a recorded message,' I answered in a nasal and mechanical tone. 'I'm afraid we are not available at the moment, but if you will leave your name and telephone number, we will get back to you as soon as possible. Please speak after the tone. *Bleep*.' I then held the instrument at arm's length and, when it had finished twittering, laid it to rest. I woke up at one in the morning with Dr Rahmat's case going round and round in my head. I wondered about mononucleosis, Dr Cogger's strange reluctance to be recognized in the Savoy Grill and his practical jokes at Barts. What exactly had he done there? I imagined in those feverish hours a live lady, substituted for a corpse on the dissecting table, who sat up suddenly and made several students faint. I imagined trying to connect an escort agency with a row about prescribing expensive drugs with long names – and sleep eluded me. At about two thirty I took one of Dr Cogger's pills, which had no effect on me at all.

*

The General Medical Council rules from an imposing head-quarters in that mecca of doctors, the purlieus around Harley Street. I crossed Portland Place, walked down Hallam Street, and entered, wigless and without gown, the building in which the top medics, playing, for a while, the parts of judges, decide the fate of their fellow quacks.

Up the stairs I found an imposing square chamber, decorated with the portraits and busts of solemn, whiskered old darlings who, no doubt, bled their customers with leeches and passed on the information to alarmed small boys that self-abuse leads to blindness. A large stained-glass window bore the image of a ministering angel and two balconies, decorated with Adam-style plaster-work, held up the visiting public and a large body of journalists from such scandalsheets as the *Daily Beacon*, whose ears were pricked up for all the details of Dr Rahmat's unusual medical treatment. At tables round three sides of a rectangle sat the eleven judges, a few of whom were not doctors, but lay brothers or sisters from allied worlds, such as nursing or sociology. Presiding at the top table was a lean and elderly Scot, the distinguished saw-bones, Sir Hector MacAuliffe, who looked as though he would have found Calvin himself a bit of a libertine.

I found myself seated at a small table, as in an American courtroom, with Dr Rahmat in embarrassing proximity to me. I have always found it a great advantage to sit as far away from clients as possible, as their suggestions on how to conduct the trial, if adopted, almost always prove fatal. On my other side, Mrs Whittaker, grey-haired and clad in a decent black suit, was ready to take a note – a task she was to perform with admirable efficiency.

At a table opposite me sat our Portia and the prosecution team. Between us, in the wide open spaces of the room, was the solitary chair and small table at which the witnesses gave evidence in some comfort. We were all provided with heavy-duty microphones, so that our voices boomed and echoed as though we were in a swimming-pool.

'Yes, Mrs Erskine-Brown.' Sir Hector gave a nod of encouragement to the opposition and Claude's Philly stood up and, with an almighty swipe, drove straight down the fairway. 'This, sir, is a flagrant and distressing case of a doctor's violent and unprovoked sexual assault upon a young woman. When you have heard all the evidence, we have little doubt that you will find the charge of professional misconduct proved against Dr Rahmat beyond any shadow of reasonable doubt.' So Phillida went on to tell the story of this young children's nurse (making Naughty Marietta sound like some kind of junior Florence Nightingale) who called in to the surgery with a sore throat and was told to lie on the couch and, when her knickers were removed, Dr Rahmat 'thrust his hand between her legs, tried to kiss her and suggested that there was time for a quick one'.

'Meaning sexual intercourse?' Sir Hector was clearly not about to take the view that my client was offering his patient a small sherry.

'That is what we ask the committee to infer.' Phillida went on, 'Miss Liptrott screamed and had to struggle to free herself from the Doctor's embraces. She pulled her clothes back on and she was still screaming, "The beast! The beast!" as she ran into the reception area. There she was seen by the waiting patients and by a Miss Dankwerts. After the incident she suffered extreme bouts of nervous depression and was treated for that complaint by Dr Cogger, a senior member of the practice, whom I shall be calling as a witness.'

'Very fair. She puts the case most fairly. And old Tim Cogger. He will be fair to me also.' Dr Rahmat, since he arrived in Court, had seemed in a confident mood. Now his optimistic words were caught up by the microphone, causing a glare of disapproval from Sir Hector and an ironic smile from Phillida, which seemed to promise stormy weather to come.

I imposed a vow of silence on my client until he came to give his evidence, and then I heard Phillida ask if she might call Dr Cogger first as he was a busy man and had to get away to his practice. To this I readily agreed, as it would suit me very well to put the case I had worked out in the early hours to the senior doctor before I came to cross-examine the mysterious Marietta.

Dr Cogger was apparently well known to Sir Hector, and to

several members of the committee to whom he nodded in a friendly fashion as he settled himself in the witness's chair. Yes, he told Phillida, he had known Dr Rahmat since he joined the practice and always found him a pleasant and hard-working colleague 'within his limitations'. He had been shocked at the complaint Miss Liptrott made when he treated her for nervous depression, following the incident in the surgery. Finally, with great seriousness, Mrs Erskine-Brown asked, 'And tell us, Dr Cogger, if a young woman came to you with a sore throat, can you think of any reason for asking her to lie on a couch and remove her knickers?'

There was a certain amount of chortling from the Press Gallery, at which an attendant in a commissionaire's uniform shouted, 'Silence!' Sir Hector glared savagely upwards and Dr Cogger shrugged his muscular shoulders and said, with apparent sorrow, 'I'm afraid I can't.'

'Dr Cogger. You are no doubt familiar with infectious mononucleosis, commonly known as glandular fever?' I began my cross-examination.

'Of course.'

'Is it not so prevalent among young people that it is sometimes called the "kissing disease"?'

'I think you may take it, Mr Rumpole' – Sir Hector spoke whilst still gazing up at the ceiling, apparently bored – 'that we all know what glandular fever is.'

'Well, I should have thought so, sir.' I tried a charming smile which he didn't notice. 'That's why I can't understand why anyone should find Dr Rahmat's method of examination in the least peculiar. Is not a symptom of glandular fever' – I turned to the witness – 'a sore throat?'

'It can be,' Dr Cogger agreed reluctantly.

'In fact, the patient may complain of a sore throat only?'

'That may happen.'

'But if you suspect glandular fever you may look for the other symptoms, such as swellings in the armpits and the groin?'

'You might.'

'A competent doctor would do so?'

'If he suspected mononucleosis. Yes.'

'So when a young woman, who complained of a sore throat, came to a competent doctor, he might ask her to lie on the couch and remove her knickers so that he could examine her groin?'

'It's possible.'

'Dr Cogger. Are you trying to assist this committee by telling us the truth?'

'Yes. Of course.'

'Then why did you tell my learned friend, Mrs Erskine-Brown, that you could think of no reason why Dr Rahmat should examine this young lady in the way described?'

'Steady on, Mr Rumpole!' Dr Rahmat did his best to keep his whisper away from the microphone, but he was clearly agitated. 'You don't mean to attack Tim Cogger, do you? Such a decent fellow!'

'I mean to win this case for you, if you'll only shut up,' I whispered back, and wished my client would go for a walk in the park until it was all over. 'Well, what's the answer?'

'I suppose the complaint you're suggesting didn't occur to me.'

'You mean, you're a good doctor, like Dr Rahmat, within your limitations? One limitation being you forget the odd disease occasionally?'

Dr Cogger flushed and moved restlessly, looking as though he'd have liked to have got me out on the rugger field and done for me in the scrum. Rahmat whispered, 'Don't be so merciless, Rumpole,' and Sir Hector came to the witness's rescue with 'I hope you're not suggesting that a routine examination includes the doctor trying to kiss his patient and suggesting there might be "time for a quick one"?' The lugubrious Scot had, unhappily, put his finger on the weakness of our case.

Instead of arguing, I decided that the best form of defence was the attack which I had planned during the sleepless watches of the night and which, in daylight and under the cold eyes of the hostile medics, seemed even more perilous. And my client was probably going to hate it.

'Dr Cogger. You say you treated Miss Liptrott for nervous tension. What did you give her? A couple of aspirins?'

'No. I prescribed Phobomorin, so far as I can remember.'

'Is that an expensive drug?'

'I believe it's fairly expensive. I haven't looked up the price lately.'

'Is it supplied by the firm of manufacturing chemists whose representative buys you lunch at the Savoy Hotel?'

The question took the witness by surprise and he seemed to feel in danger. He had denied he'd ever been at such a lunch to me, but now, on his oath, he seemed to feel an unexpected compulsion to tell the truth. He did his best by smiling confidentially at Sir Hector and saying, 'Peter Kellaway of Marchmain's is a personal friend. We lunch together occasionally.'

'And when you last lunched together who paid?'

'I can't remember.'

'Try to think.'

'It may have been Peter.'

'Or may it have been his company, Marchmain's? The manufacturing chemist?'

'Mr Rumpole' – Sir Hector spoke as though I was a backward medical student who insisted on asking questions about housemaid's knee in the brain surgery class – 'we are here to decide if your client made a sexual assault on his patient. What on earth have Dr Cogger's lunches at the Savoy got to do with it?'

'I quite agree, sir. These questions can't possibly be relevant.' Counsel for the Prosecution arose in all her glory.

'One at a time, please, Portia.' I managed a resonant whisper across the room and then turned on the elder of the kirk. 'It is a well-known fact that in any trial questions which may seem irrelevant at first lead straight to the truth, however deeply it is buried. Therefore wise judges are extremely reluctant to interrupt a cross-examination by the Defence. Less experienced tribunals are, of course, frequently tempted to do so.'

I got a look from the presiding Scot which seemed to indicate a desire to sentence me to a long stretch in the Aberdeen Home for Incurables, but then he conferred with his legal assessor, a balding barrister in mufti, and decided to let me go on. 'Continue, Mr Rumpole, provided the next question shows some relevance to this case.'

'You said Dr Rahmat had his limitations?' I attacked the witness again. 'Did you mean that he was unwilling to agree to prescribe certain drugs?'

'We had some disagreements about drugs. Yes. I thought his treatment often old-fashioned.'

'You mean he wouldn't prescribe expensive drugs from Marchmain's?'

In the silence that followed, Sir Hector at last leant forward attentively and the other doctors appeared interested. I thought they'd known cases of drug companies offering sweeteners to medical practitioners.

'Some of the drugs I thought we should use came from Marchmain's, I suppose.'

'Yes, I suppose so. Tell me, did you only get expensive lunches out of it, or did a little cash change hands occasionally?'

'Hold on, Mr Rumpole! This is quite unnecessary.' My client was clearly upset.

'Oh, do shut up, Rahmat!' Hostile witnesses can be coped with, but mutinous clients are intolerable. Then I regained my composure and smiled quite winsomely at Dr Cogger. 'Well, Doctor. Would you care to answer the question?'

'Perhaps' – Phillida rose and smiled at the seat of judgment in a way which was far more winsome than anything I could have managed – 'the witness should be warned that he needn't answer questions which might, well' – she picked up and inserted the distasteful words as though with a delicate pair of forceps – 'incriminate him.'

This was a grave tactical error by the fair prosecutor because Sir Hector duly warned the witness and Dr Cogger came to the conclusion that it was a question which, with the best will in the world, he preferred not to answer. From then on, of course, his credibility content sank rapidly.

'Quite right!' Rhamat's behaviour was extraordinary. 'No need at all for Tim to answer such an impertinent question!'

'You can't make an omelette without breaking eggs,' I told him, and then turned to the witness. 'And because he refused to take part in your prescription racket' – Rahmat winced and sighed with disapproval again – 'you wanted to get him out of the practice?'

'It's very hard to get rid of a partner as you know, Mr Rumpole.' Dr Cogger may have thought his answer clever. In fact, it was unwise in the extreme.

'Very hard,' I agreed, 'unless you can get him found guilty of professional misconduct.'

'Mr Rumpole!' Dr Cogger leaned back in his witness's chair, all his self-confidence returned as he said with great good humour, 'You're not suggesting I went into Dr Rahmat's room and tempted him into seducing *me*, are you?'

'Don't ask me questions!' I tried the snub brutal and was pleased to see that the Judges around us had been less than amused by Dr Cogger's fantasy seduction. 'Just look at *this*, will you.'

This was a document unhappily familiar to the Prosecutor – another copy of that issue of *Casanova*, which had turned up both in Erskine-Brown's room and Dr Cogger's surgery. It was carried to the witness by one of the aged commissionaires, with a marker in the relevant page. 'Do you see an advertisement there, headed NAUGHTY MARIETTA?'

'What on earth has this got to do with the case we're trying?' Sir Hector had noticed the cover of *Casanova* and knew the devil's work when he saw it.

'If you listen,' I told him, 'you will soon discover the answer.' And I asked the witness if it didn't appear to be an advertisement for an escort service.

'It would seem so.'

'And do you see a photograph of the young lady who calls herself Naughty Marietta?'

'Yes, I do.'

'Is that Miss Marietta Liptrott? The lady you treated for a nervous disorder and the complainant in this case?'

There was a long silence. Sir Hector looked at the ceiling. Other doctors examined their finger-nails or sat with their pencils poised waiting to write down the answer. Portia looked at me with a half-smiling tribute to Rumpole's ability to pull something out of the hat in the most unlikely cases and Rahmat, of course, whispered, 'Stop the attack on poor Tim, Mr Rumpole. It is quite uncalled for.'

'It looks like her,' Dr Cogger admitted at last.

'It *is* her,' I said. After all, I had confirmed that fact on the telephone. 'This children's nurse we've heard about goes out to dinner for money. Rather like you, Dr Cogger.'

'Just what are you suggesting?'

'You know quite well, don't you? I'm suggesting you paid this girl to stage the scene in Dr Rahmat's consulting room. The scream, the rushing out into the waiting-room, the complaint and the nervous disorder. It was all an act. A put-up job. So you could get Dr Rahmat out of your practice. Because he wouldn't cooperate. Did you suggest she should complain of a sore throat, or was it just a bit of luck that Dr Rahmat suspected glandular fever?'

'That's absolutely ridiculous! I didn't know of the existence of Miss Liptrott until after the incident took place.'

'Did you not? This incident, we've heard, took place on March 13th of this year. Will you look at the cover of that *Casanova*? What is the date on it?'

Dr Cogger took the magazine with some reluctance and announced with even more hesitation, 'January of this year.'

'And you know where this magazine was found, don't you? We can ask Miss Dankwerts, if you don't wish to answer.'

'I know.'

'Will you tell the tribunal?'

'Apparently it was found in the waiting-room.'

'Of *your* surgery?'

'Yes.'

I sat down then next to a client, who, far from congratulating me on a cross-examination of even more than my usual brilliance, sat with his head in his hands, murmuring, 'Oh, Mr Rumpole. You shouldn't have put poor old Tim through the mill like that. There was no need, I told you that. No need whatsoever.'

'Nonsense, old darling. Pull yourself together. You can't make an omelette without breaking eggs, as I told you.' And then I had to leave him to stew because Miss Liptrott, who had come into the room and was taking the oath, now demanded my full attention.

The complainant was not, in any sense, beautiful, but she was young, her eyes were bright, her jeans clean and well-ironed, and she seemed, even in the circumstances in which she found herself, unexpectedly cheerful. She admitted, in answer to Portia's gentle questioning, that she was a children's nurse who often went out in the evenings, as one of a number of friends who had got together to form an escort agency, which they had named – and this seemed to give her particular pleasure – after her.

Looking at Miss Liptrott, I was discouraged to see what appeared to be an honest witness. I had fired all my ammunition at Dr Cogger and, although severely holed below the water-line, he had not quite sunk. He had not admitted the conspiracy and I would need to get Marietta to crumble if Dr Rahmat were to be back plying his stethoscope as usual. All right, I guessed the more sensible doctors on the committee were thinking to themselves, perhaps she is an escort, which may mean she's a call girl. She's still entitled to have her sore throat seen to without being molested.

Carefully, slowly, and with extreme tact my opponent took the girl through her story. Now we were in the consulting room and Dr Rahmat had asked her to lie on the couch.

'And what happened then?'

'He said he just wanted to see if I had any swellings and asked if I'd mind him feeling.'

'Did he remove your knickers?'

'No. I think I may have pulled them down.'

'And then? What happened then?'

'I am not . . . quite sure.' The witness frowned slightly and seemed to be doing her very best to remember. 'I think he went to a basin in the corner of the room to wash his hands.'

'And what did you do?'

'Oh, I ran screaming out of the door.'

Marietta smiled at Sir Hector as though inviting him to join her in laughing at the silliness of her behaviour.

'What made you do that?' Phillida was still admirably patient.

'I don't know, really. I'd been up late with a very boring gentleman who kept me up talking half the night about the mortgage rates. I was overtired, I think. My nerves were bad. I suppose I just lost control of myself.'

'Had Dr Rahmat tried to kiss you?'

'Don't lead,' I grumbled, but the protest was unnecessary. Whatever lead Phillida gave, the girl was clearly not going to follow it.

'I'm . . . I'm sure he hadn't.'

'Did he put his hand between your legs?'

'Oh, no!' Miss Liptrott looked shocked. 'I'm sure he didn't do that either.'

'You apparently ran out of the room shouting, "The beast! The beast!" Do you remember that?'

'Not really. If I did, I wasn't talking about Dr Rahmat. I'd met some other people who weren't very nice.'

'Miss Liptrott' – Sir Hector looked like an elder of the kirk who has just been reliably informed that there is no such thing as hell and that sin is now permissible – 'you made a statement to the General Medical Council to the effect that Dr Rahmat made improper advances to you.'

I looked round the Court in the pause that followed. Dr Cogger was now in the public gallery, leaning forward in his seat, looking as mystified as everyone except the witness, who seemed to find her behaviour perfectly natural.

'Well. I'd made such a fuss in the surgery. I felt I had to give some reason for it, otherwise you'd have thought me very silly, wouldn't you? But I always meant to tell the truth when I got here.'

'And what is the truth, Miss Liptrott?' Phillida's line sounded less like a question than a cry for help; but help for the prosecution case was not forthcoming.

'The truth' – Marietta now seemed to have no doubt about the matter – 'is that Dr Rahmat always behaved like a perfect gentleman.'

It was at this point that Phillida, after a whispered

consultation with her instructing solicitor, threw in the towel. 'In view of the evidence which has just been given, we do not feel it would be right to continue with the case against Dr Rahmat.' The battle was over and I had no idea how I had come to gain such a decisive victory.

'Mr Rumpole' – Sir Hector was looking at me with slightly less than his usual disgust – 'during the course of your cross-examination you made certain serious allegations against Dr Cogger. As I understand it, you suggested he joined with this young lady in a conspiracy to "frame", if I may use a common expression . . .'

'Oh, by all means, sir. "Frame" puts it very nicely.'

'Very well then. To "frame" Dr Rahmat. In view of the evidence we have just heard, may we take it that all such allegations are now withdrawn?'

I was about to open my mouth when Dr Rahmat was up beside me, standing to attention and saying at the top of his voice, 'Unreservedly withdrawn, sir. Dr Tim Cogger is a fine man. He leaves this Court without a stain on his character. My barrister-at-law will confirm this without a moment's delay.'

'Do you agree, Mr Rumpole?'

'Oh, yes.' I may have sounded a little mournful as my brilliant defence went out of the window, but I resigned gracefully. 'I agree. Not a stain on the Doctor's character.'

'*A Passage to India*' – I reminded Dr Rahmat when we went for a celebratory bottle of plonk in a wine bar off the Marylebone Road – 'ends with the girl, who's meant to have been raped by the Indian doctor, withdrawing her whole story in Court.'

'Such a brilliant writer, old E.M.F.,' Dr Rahmat agreed. 'Always so true to life.'

'Do you think the Naughty Marietta's read the book?'

'Well, sir, perhaps.'

There was a pause as I filled my mouth with the wine, product, perhaps, of the same sun-starved vineyard which grew the Château Thames Embankment grape. Then I said, 'Who do you think put her up to it?'

'Oh, Tim Cogger, undoubtedly.' Dr Rahmat smiled tolerantly. 'He wanted to get rid of me, you see. He thought I had tumbled to why he was wanting us all to use the Marchmain drugs.'

'You think he hired Marietta?' I looked at the man, amazed at his conversion to my view of the case.

'Oh, I'm sure he did so.'

'How are you sure?'

'She told me.'

I finished the glass. Soon I should finish the bottle.

'You've talked to her about it?'

'Oh, certainly. I have taken her out to dinner on a number of occasions. We go to the Star of Hyderabad. It was not something I thought you would wish to know.'

'Why?'

'I knew I had the most brilliant barrister-at-law. I knew you would win my case, but I didn't want to win by rubbishing poor old Tim Cogger. I want to keep my partnership, you know. I want to get on well with all the chaps in the surgery, Dr Tim included. So it seemed the best way out was to persuade Miss Liptrott to tell the truth, which is that nothing happened. It seemed to me such an easy way to win the case, but far too unsubtle, of course, for a brilliant barrister-at-law like yourself. But at least I managed, sir, to make an omelette without the breaking of a single egg!'

I looked at the chap with a sinking feeling. What if the infection spread and all clients got themselves off without any help from the learned friends? The future of the legal profession began to look bleak.

'There's one other thing you might tell me,' I asked, as I stared at the quack in amazement. 'How much did you give the lady to persuade her to tell the truth?'

'I gave her, as you might say, sir, all my worldly goods.'

'What are you talking about? Don't babble!'

'To be honest with you, Mr Rumpole, I do not babble. Miss Marietta Liptrott is as charming and honest as she is beautiful. She has done me the honour of agreeing to be my wife. The ceremony will be at the mosque in Regent's Park, with a reception to follow at the Star of Hyderabad in the Gloucester Road. You and your good lady are cordially invited.'

'And Dr Cogger, of course.' I began to get the picture.

'Oh, yes, indeed. All the surgery will come. And I hope that Tim Cogger will propose the toast to the happy couple. I shall certainly ask him.'

'And in all the circumstances,' I thought it fair to say, 'I don't see how he can refuse.'

'Rumpole. Something distinctly peculiar has happened.'

'You mean you lost "Rahmat", Portia? Not your fault, I assure you. That case took on a life of its own. We were both left with omelettes on our faces, in a manner of speaking.'

'No, it's not that exactly. Look. I'd better tell you and see if you can offer any sort of explanation. You know I was going to lay a trap for Claude?'

'You told me. And I trembled for the fellow.'

'Well. It didn't really come off.' Our Portia settled herself in the client's chair in my room. I lit a small cigar and prepared to listen to her account which went more or less as follows. She had written an answer to the advertisement in *Casanova* to the box number indicated, in the following terms:

Dear Barrister bored with married life, I am slim, intelligent and considered attractive. I am more than ready for the occasional fling, but I can think of better ways of spending an evening than going to the Opera. Sorry I haven't got a photograph, but I've had no complaints about my looks. Suggest we meet at a place convenient to you, in the Temple churchyard by Oliver Goldsmith's tomb, 5.30 next Thursday week. We'll both wear red carnations. I look forward eagerly to the ensuing fun and games. I'm also in a rut and bored to tears with married life!

She sent this missive, sure that it would trap the errant Claude and when he showed up, over-excited, with a flower in his button-hole, she would let him have it to some considerable effect. 'The odd thing is, Rumpole, I went to the churchyard with my red carnation and Claude never turned up. Do you think he'd got wind of what I was up to? You didn't say anything to him, did you?'

'Now, Portia. Would I?'

'I don't know. You men always stick together. I waited for about half an hour. In the drizzle. The churchyard was empty.'

'No one came?'

'Well, I didn't see a soul. Except that new pupil here. What's her name?'

'Mrs Whittaker.'

'Yes. She was hanging about, looking at the inscriptions on the tombs and, you know, it was rather a coincidence. She was wearing a red carnation.'

'Did you speak?'

'I think I said "hello" and she wandered off. Perhaps she'd been to a wedding or something.'

'Perhaps.' And then a vague memory struck me. I looked up Claude's alleged advertisement in the copy of *Casanova* I had brought back with my papers in the Rahmat case and read it through carefully. Then I read it through again.

'Portia,' I said, 'you're a brilliant advocate and your court-room manner is irresistible. But it's no good lightly skimming the written evidence. You haven't read every word, every letter. Just look at this again.' I handed her the document. 'Read it aloud, if you'd be so kind.'

'Barrister. Good-looking and young at heart. In a rut. Bored with the humdrum of married life . . .'

'Just look carefully after the word barrister. Isn't there a small letter in brackets?'

'Well, yes. It looks like an "f".'

'It is an "f". You were so sure you had Claude in the frame that you didn't notice it. "F" for female. It's a lady barrister in search of adventure. A lady barrister who shares Claude's room, which is why you found the magazine there. So it was a lady barrister who turned up wearing a carnation. I'm sorry, Portia. I'm afraid you disappointed her.'

'Mrs Whittaker?'

'The evidence seems conclusive. Poor old Mr Whittaker. He

must be of the humdrum persuasion. You know, perhaps we should take out a subscription to *Casanova*. We've learnt a good deal, haven't we, from a single issue?'

But Portia was off, smiling now, in search of her husband. She might even be going to buy him lunch at the Savoy. People only seek out Rumpole when they're in trouble.

There is little more to tell. Bambi rang once more to tell me that she had had another little mishap with the white Volkswagen and was being done for dangerous driving. 'Can't help, I'm afraid,' I told her. 'What you need for that is a brilliant Q.C. Only way to get off with your record. There's an absolutely scintillating silk called Sam Ballard. I might get him to take you on.'

'Oh, really? Is he cuddly?'

'Sam Ballard? Well known for it.' And I told her, 'He cuddles for England. And there's something else, he's in a rut. Bored to tears with married life.'

A week later I was in the clerk's room, talking to Uncle Tom, who, as usual, was practising putts into the waste-paper basket, when there was a tintinnabulation of costume jewellery, a clatter of high heels and Mrs Bambi Etheridge passed through on her way to Ballard's room. She flashed me a smile, but her mind was clearly on higher things, and she went up to her assignation leaving us with her lingering perfume.

'Odd sort of pong.' Uncle Tom was thoughtful. 'A bit reminiscent of the red light district of Port Said.'

'It's Deadly Sins,' I told him, 'by St Just.'

'Is it, really? Of course, I've never been to Port Said. I say, Rumpole. What a lot you know about women!'

'Not much,' I admitted. 'I am continually surprised.'

'I say' – Uncle Tom became so entranced by the thought that he failed to hole into the waste-paper basket in one – 'I wonder if Ballard'll make a play for her, and she'll come out screaming like the girl in your case! That'd liven things up a bit.'

'I'm afraid' – and I was already feeling a touch of pity for Soapy Sam – 'that Ballard'll be the one who comes out screaming.'

But all was silent from upstairs. I could only think I had brought two people together who needed, and deserved, each other.

Rumpole for the Prosecution

As anyone who has cast half an eye over these memoirs will know, the second of the Rumpole commandments consists of the simple injunction 'Thou shalt not prosecute.' Number one is 'Thou shalt not plead guilty.' Down the line, of course, there are other valuable precepts such as 'Never pay for the drink Jack Pommeroy is prepared to put on the slate', 'Never trust a vegetarian', 'If Sam Ballard thinks it, then it must be wrong', 'Never go shopping with She Who Must Be Obeyed', 'Don't ask a question unless you're damn sure you know the answer', 'If a judge makes a particularly absurd remark, rub his nose in it, i.e. repeat it to the Jury with raised eyebrows every hour on the hour' and 'Never ask an instructing solicitor if his leg's better'. This last is as fatal as asking a client if he happens to be guilty; you run a terrible danger of being told.

But the rule against prosecuting has been the lodestar of my legal career. I obey this precept for a number of reasons, all cogent. It seems to me that errant and misguided humanity has enough on its plate without running the daily risk of being driven, cajoled or hoodwinked into the nick by Rumpole in full flood, armed with an unparalleled knowledge of blood-stains and a remarkable talent for getting a jury to see things his way. As everyone – except a nun in a Trappist order and the Home Secretary – now knows, the prison system is bursting at the seams and it would be out of the question for even more captives to arrive at the gates thanks to my forensic skills.

Then again, prosecuting counsel tend to be fawned on by Mr Justice Graves and his like, characters whom I prefer to keep in a state of healthy hostility. Finally, I should point out that it is the task of prosecuting counsel to present the facts in

a neutral manner and not try to score a victory. This duty (not
always carried out, I may say, by those who habitually per-
secute down the Old Bailey) takes the fun out of the art of
advocacy. There are many adjectives which might be used to
describe Rumpole at work but 'neutral' is not among them. It
is a sad but inescapable fact that as soon as I buckle on the wig
and gown and march forth to war in the courtroom, the old
adrenalin courses through my veins and all I want to do is win.

Bearing all this in mind, you may find it hard to understand
how, in the case that came to be known as the 'Mews Murder',
I took the brief in a private prosecution brought by the dead
girl's father.

'All right, Mr Rumpole. You're out to protect the underdog,
I understand that. I might say that I find it very sympathetic.
You attack the establishment. Tease the judges. Give the
police a hard time. Well, doesn't my daughter deserve defending as much as any of your clients?'

I looked down at the pile of press-cuttings on my desk and at
the photograph of Veronica Fabian. She was a big, rather
plain girl in her early twenties. I imagined that she had a
loud laugh and an untidy bedroom. There was also, in spite
of her smile, a look of disappointment and a lack of confidence about her, and I thought she might have been a girl
who often fell unhappily in love. Whatever she had been
like, she had died, beaten to death in an empty mews house
in Notting Hill Gate. I didn't altogether understand what I
could do in her defence, or how such an earthbound tribunal
as a judge and jury down the Old Bailey could now pass
judgment on her.

'You want me to defend your daughter?'

'Yes, Mr Rumpole. That's exactly what I want.'

Gregory Fabian, senior partner in the firm of Fabian &
Winchelsea, purveyors of discreet homes to the rich and
famous, dealers in stately homes and ambassadorial dwellings,
had aged, I imagined, since the death of his daughter. There is
something squalid about murder which brings a sense of shame
to the victim's as well as the killer's family. In spite of this,

Fabian spoke moderately and without rancour. He was a slim man, in his early sixties, short but handsome, clear-featured, with creases at the sides of his eyes and the general appearance of someone who laughed a good deal in happier times.

'Isn't it a little late for that? To defend her, I mean?'

'There's no time limit on murder is there?' He smiled at me gently as he said this, and I was prepared to accept that his interest went beyond mere revenge.

'Justice! We haven't had much of that, sir. Not since they decided not to charge Jago. We just wanted to know how much that cost him. Whatever it was, he could probably afford it.' Up spoke young Roger Fabian, the dead girl's brother and the one who, being very close in appearance to his father, seemed to have inherited all the good looks in the family and left little for his sister. He looked what he probably had been, the most popular boy in whatever uncomfortable and expensive public school he had attended; but he bore his good fortune modestly, and even managed to slander the fair name of the serious crimes squad with a certain inoffensive charm. His habit of calling me 'sir' made me feel uncomfortably respectable. I wondered if all prosecuting counsel get called 'sir' at conferences.

'Why did the police let him go? That's what we want you to find out.'

'You were recommended to us as a barrister who didn't mind having a go at a man like Detective Chief Inspector Brush.'

Brush? The very copper who, in his salad days, had been the hammer of the Timsons and my constant sparring partner down the Bailey, now promoted to giddy heights in charge of a West London area, where he had brilliantly failed to solve the 'Mews Murder' and let Christopher Jago, the number one suspect, out of his clutches.

'They say you'll never be a judge, so you're not afraid of going for the police, Mr Rumpole.' Fabian senior managed to make it sound like a compliment.

'They said we weren't to mind about the soup on the tie or

the cigar ash down the waistcoat.' Fabian junior was even more complimentary. 'And you don't care a toss for the establishment.'

'They said you'd do this job far better than the usual sort of polite and servile Q.C.' And when I asked George Fabian who they were, who spoke so highly of Rumpole, and he gave the name of Pyecraft & Wensleydale, our instructing solicitor and one of the poshest firms in the city, I could hardly forbear to preen myself visibly.

In answer to repeated inquiries from Pyecraft, Detective Chief Inspector Brush and his men had disclosed the gist of Christopher Jago's statement to them. He said he was a local estate agent, who had seen the For Sale notices outside 13A Gissing Mews, off Westbourne Grove, and wanted to view the property for a client of his own. He had rung Fabian & Winchelsea, and been put through to a young lady, believed to have been Veronica Fabian, who worked with her brother and father in the family business. He made an appointment to meet her at the house in question at eight thirty the following morning. The time was set by Jago, who was leaving that day to do a deal in some time-share apartments on the Costa del Sol. When Jago got to 13A Gissing Mews, the front door was open. He went in, expecting to meet Miss Fabian, whom he told the police he had never met before. The little mews house was still half-furnished and decorated, apparently, with African rugs and carvings. There were some spears fixed to the wall of the hallway, and a weighted knobkerrie, a three-foot black club, had been torn down and caused the fatal blow to the girl. Jago said he had knelt beside her body and tried to raise her head, during which operation his cuff had become smeared with blood.

Then there followed the events which might have made any family feel that they had good reason to suspect Christopher Jago. He said he panicked. There he was with a dead girl whose blood was on his clothing and he felt sure he would be accused of some sort of sex killing – one of the murders which had recently terrified the neighbourhood. He left the house, drove to the airport and went on his way to Spain. Two hours later, the owner of the mews called to collect some of his possessions, found the body and called the police. Veronica Fabian had died from extensive wounds to her skull. The only real clue was the name she had written against her eight thirty appointment in her desk diary: Arthur Morrison. The police spent a great deal of time trying to find or identify the man Morrison but without success.

As luck would have it, Jago had parked his car on a resident's parking place in the mews, and the irate resident had taken its number. When he got back to England, Jago was questioned as a possible witness. He immediately admitted that he had found the dead girl, panicked and run away. However, after several days when he was assisting the police with their inquiries (often a euphemism for getting himself stitched up) Jago was released to the surprise and fury of the surviving members of the Fabian family.

'You'd've charged him at least, Mr Rumpole, wouldn't you?' Fabian *père* sounded, as ever, reasonable.

'Perhaps. But I've grown up with the awkward habit of believing everyone innocent until they're proved guilty.'

'But you'll take it on for us, won't you? At least let a jury decide?'

'I'll have to think about it.' I lit a small cigar and blew out smoke. If Fabian *fils* had come expecting ash down the waistcoat I might as well let him have it. It's a curious English system, in my view, which allows private citizens to prosecute each other for crimes with the aim of sending each other to chokey, and I wasn't at all sure that it ought to be encouraged. I mean, where would it end? I might be tempted to draft an indictment against Sam Ballard, the Head of our Chambers, on the grounds of public nuisance. I had caught this soapy customer ostentatiously pinning up NO SMOKING notices in the passage outside my door.

'But we've got to have justice, Mr Rumpole. Isn't that the point?'

'Have we? "Use every man after his desert," as a well-known Dane put it, "and who should escape whipping?"' I puffed out another small cigar cloud, hoping it would eventually waft its way in the general direction of our Head of Chambers who would, no doubt, go off like a fire alarm. I was thinking of the difficulty of having a client I could never meet in this world, whom I could never ask what happened when she went to the mews house to meet this mysterious and vanished Morrison or, indeed, whether she wanted such secrets as she may have had to be dragged out in a trial which could no longer have any interest for her.

'The power of evil is everywhere, Rumpole. And I'm afraid everywhere includes our own Chambers at Equity Court. That is why I have sought you out, although one doesn't like to spend too much time in these places.'

'Does one not?' I consider any hour wasted which is not passed with a hand round a comforting glass of Château Thames Embankment in Pommeroy's haven of rest.

'Passive alcoholism, Rumpole.' Sam Ballard, who, I imagine, gets his hair-shirts from the Army & Navy Stores and whose belligerent puritanism makes Praise-God-Barebones look like Giovanni Casanova, had crept up on me at the bar and abandoned himself to a slimline tonic. 'You've heard of passive smoking, of course?'

'I've heard of it. Although, I have to say, I prefer the active variety.'

'Passive alcoholism's the same thing. Abstainees can absorb the fumes from neighbouring drinkers and become alcoholics. Quite easily.'

'Is that one of Matey's medical theories?' Sam Ballard, of course, had fallen for the formidable Mrs Marguerite Plumstead, the Old Bailey matron, and made her his bride, an act which lends considerable support to the theory that love is blind.

'Marguerite is, of course, extremely well informed on all health problems. So now, when we ask colleagues to dinner, we make it clear that our house is an alcohol-free zone.'

This colleague thought, with some gratitude, that the Bollard house in Waltham Cross would also be Rumpole-free in the future. 'But that wasn't why I wanted a word in confidence, Rumpole. I need to enlist your help, as a senior, in years anyway, a very senior member of Equity Court. A grave crime has been committed.'

'Oh my God!' I did my best to look stricken. 'Some bandit hasn't pinched the nail-brush again?'

'I'm afraid, Rumpole' – Bollard looked as though he were about to announce the outbreak of the Black Death, or at least the Hundred Years War – 'this goes beyond pilfering in the downstairs toilet.'

'Not nail-brush nicking this time, eh?'

'No, Rumpole. This time it would appear to be forgery, false pretence and obtaining briefs by fraud.' I lit another small cigar which had the desired effect of making Bollard tell his story as rapidly as possible, like a man with a vital message to get out before the poison gas rises above his head. It seemed that Miss Tricia Benbow – a somewhat ornate lady solicitor in whom Henry finds, when she enters his clerk's room with the light behind her, a distinct resemblance to the late Princess Grace of Monaco – had sent a brief in some distant and unappetizing County Court (Snaresbrook, Luton or Land's End, for all I can remember) to young David Inchcape whose legal career was in its tyro stages. Someone, as this precious brief was lying in the clerk's room, scratched out Inchcape's name and substituted that of Claude Erskine-Brown, who duly turned up at the far-flung Court to the surprise of Miss Benbow who had expected a younger man. An inquiry was instituted and, within hours, Sherlock Ballard, Q.C. was on the case. Henry denied all knowledge of the alteration, which seemed to have occurred before he entered the brief in his ledger, young Inchcape looked hard-done-by, and Claude Erskine-Brown, whose performances in Court were marked by a painstaking attention to the letter of the law, emerged as public enemy number one.

'That quality of evil is all pervasive.' The slimline tonic seemed to have gone to Ballard's head. He spoke in an impressive whisper and his eyes glittered with all the enthusiasm of a Grand Inquisitor preparing for the *auto-da-fé*. 'In my view it has entered into the character of Erskine-Brown.'

Not much can be said in criticism of that misguided, and

somewhat fatuous, old darling with whom I have shared Chambers at Equity Court for more years than we like to remember. Claude's taste for the headier works of Richard Wagner fills him with painful longings for young ladies connected with the legal profession, whom he no doubt sees as Rhine Maidens or mini-Valkyries in wig and gown. In Court his behaviour can vacillate between the ponderous and the panic-stricken, so those who think unkindly of him, among whom I do not number myself, might reasonably describe him as a pompous twit. All that having been said, the soul of Claude Erskine-Brown is about as remote from evil as Pommeroy's plonk is from Château Latour.

'Claude would be flattered to hear you say he was evil,' I told our Head of Chambers. 'He might feel he'd got a touch of the Nibelungens or something.'

'I noticed it from the time we did that case about the dirty restaurant. He wanted to conceal the fact that he'd been dining there with his female instructing solicitor. From what I remember, he wanted to mislead the Court about it.'*

'Well, that's true,' I conceded. 'Old Claude, so far as I can see, conducts his love life with the minimum of sexual satisfaction and the maximum amount of embarrassment to all concerned. If you want to call that evil . . .'

'A man who wishes to deceive his wife is quite capable of deceiving his Head of Chambers.' For a moment I caught in Ballard's voice an echo of that moral certainty which characterizes the judgments of She Who Must Be Obeyed.

'How do you know he'd deceive you? Have you asked him if he put his name on the brief?'

'I'm afraid Erskine-Brown has added perjury to his other offences.'

'You mean he denied it?'

'Hotly.'

'No one in the clerk's room did it?'

'Henry and Dianne say they didn't and I'm prepared to accept their evidence. Rumpole, when it comes to crime, you have considerably more experience than any of us.'

* See 'Rumpole à la Carte'.

'Thank you very much.'

'I want to undertake a thorough investigation of this matter. Examine the witnesses. And if Erskine-Brown's found guilty . . .'

'What, then?'

'You know as well as I do, Rumpole. There is no place in Equity Court for fellows who pinch other fellows' briefs.'

I gave Soapy Sam the chance of a little passive enjoyment of the heady fumes of Château Fleet Street and thought the matter over. Poor old Claude was probably guilty. The starring role played by his wife, Phillida, now luxuriously wrapped in the silk gown of Q.C., in so many long-running cases must have made him despondent about his own practice, which varied between the second-rate and the mediocre. The sight of a brief delivered by a solicitor he fancied sufficiently to fill up with priceless delicacies at La Maison Jean-Pierre to a white-wig must have wounded him deeply.

Moreover, it had to be remembered that he had admitted young Inchcape to our Chambers under the impression that he was thereby proving his tolerance to those of the gay persuasion, only to discover that Inchcape was in fact a closet heterosexual and his successful rival for the favours of Mizz Liz Probert.* All these were mitigating factors which would spring instantly to the mind of one who always acted for the Defence. They were already outweighing any horror I might have felt at the crime he had probably committed.

'I'm sorry, Bollard.' Our leader was still alongside me, his nose pointedly aimed from the direction of the glass that contained my ever-diminishing double red. 'I can't help you. It's the second time today I've been asked; but prosecution isn't my line of country. Rumpole always defends.'

Not long after that events occurred which persuaded me to change my mind, with results which may have an incalculable effect on whatever is left of my future.

*

* See 'Rumpole and the Quality of Life' in *Rumpole and the Age of Miracles*, Penguin Books, 1988.

It was that grim season of the year, which now begins around the end of August and reaches its climax in the first week of December, known as the 'build-up to Christmas'. I have often thought that if the Son of Man had known what he was starting he would have chosen to be born on a quiet summer's day when everyone was off on holiday on what the Timson family always refers to as the Costa del Crime. As it was, crowds of desperate shoppers were elbowing their way to the bus stops in the driving rain. More crammed aboard as we crawled through the West End, where the ornamental lights had been switched on. I sat contemplating the tidings of great joy She Who Must Be Obeyed had brought to me a few weeks earlier. That very night her old school friend, Charmian Nichols, was to arrive to spend the festive season *à côté de chez* Rumpole in the Gloucester Road.

Readers of these chronicles will only have heard, up till now, of one of the old girls who sported with my wife, Hilda, on the fields of Bexhill Ladies College when the world was somewhat younger than it is today. You will recall the redoubtable Dodo Mackintosh, painter in watercolour and maker of 'cheesy bits' for our Chambers parties, who regards Rumpole with a beady, not to say suspicious, eye, whenever she comes to call. Dodo's place, on this particular Christmas, had been taken by Charmian Nichols. Charlie Nichols, no doubt exhausted by the wear and tear of marriage to a star, who had been not only a monitor and captain of hockey, but winner of the Leadership and Character trophy for two years in succession, had dropped off the twig quite early in the run up to Christmas and the widowed Charmian wrote to Hilda indicating that she had nothing pencilled in for the festive season and was inclined to grant us the favour of her company in the Gloucester Road. She added, in a brief postscript, that if Hilda had made a prior commitment to that 'dowdy little Dodo Mackintosh' she would quite understand. She Who Must Be Obeyed, in whose breast Mrs Nichols was able to awaken feelings of awe and wonder which had lain dormant during our married life, immediately bought a new eiderdown for the spare bedroom and broke the news to Dodo that there would be no room at the inn owing to family commitments. You see it took the winner of the Leadership and Character trophy to lure Hilda to perjury.

'Hilda, dear. Why ever can't you persuade Howard to buy a new Crock-a-Gleam? Absolutely no one plunges their hands into washing-up bowls any more. Of course, it is rather sweetly archaic of you both to still be doing it.'

The late Dean Swift, in one of those masterpieces of English literature which I shall never get around to reading, spoke of a country, I believe, ruled by horses, and there was a definite air of equine superiority about La Nichols. She stood, for a start, several hands higher than Rumpole. Her nostrils flared contemptuously, her eyes were yellowish and her greying mane was carefully combed and braided. She was, I had noticed, elegantly shod and you could have seen your face in her polished little hooves. She would, I devoutly hoped, be off with a thoroughbred turn of speed as soon as Christmas was over.

'You mean, get a dishwasher?' Hilda no longer trusted me to scour the plates to her satisfaction and Charmian had taken my place with the teacloth, dabbing a passable portrait of the Tower of London at our crockery and not knowing where to put it away. 'Oh, Rumpole and I are always talking about that, but we never seem to get around to buying one.' This was another example of the widow's fatal effect on She's regard for the truth; to the best of my recollection the word 'dishwasher' had never passed our lips.

'Well, surely, Harold,' Charmian whinnied at me over the glass she was polishing mercilessly, 'you're going to buy Hilda something white for Christmas?'

'You mean handkerchiefs? I hadn't thought of that. And the name is Horace, but as you're here for Christmas with the family you can call me Rumpole.'

'No, white! A machine to wash plates and things like that? Charlie had far too much respect for my hands to let them get into a state like poor Hilda's.' At this, she looked at my wife with deep sympathy and rattled on, 'Charlie insisted that I could only keep my looks if I was fully automated. Of course I just couldn't have lived the life I did without our Plan-ahead "archive" freezer, our jumbo-microwave and rôtisserie.' Something snapped beneath the teacloth at this point. 'Oh, Hilda. One of your glasses gone for a Burton! Was it terribly precious?'

'Not really. It was a Christmas present from Dodo. From what I can remember.'

'Oh, well then.' Charmian shot the shattered goblet, a reasonably satisfactory container for Pommeroy's Perfectly Ordinary, into the tidy-bin. 'But surely Hammond can afford to mechanize you, Hilda? He's always in Court from what you said in your letters.'

'Legal aid defences,' Hilda told her gloomily, 'don't pay for much machinery.'

'Legal aid!' Charmian pronounced the words as though they constituted a sort of standing joke, like kippers or mothers-in-law. 'Isn't that a sort of National Health? Charlie was always really sorry for our poor little doctor in Guildford who had to pig along on that!'

I wanted to say that I didn't suppose old Charlie had much use for legal aid in his stockbroking business, but I restrained myself. Nor did I explain that our budget was well off balance since our cruise,* which had taken a good deal more than Hilda's late aunt's money, that legal aid fees had been cut and were paid at the pace of a handicapped snail, and that whenever I succeeded in cashing a cheque at the Caring Bank I had to restrain myself from making a dash for the door before they remembered our overdraft. Instead, I have to admit, something about the condescending Charmian, as she looked with vague amusement around our primitive kitchen equipment, made me want to impress her on her own, unadmirable terms.

'As a matter of fact,' I said, casually filling one of Dodo's remaining glasses, 'I don't only do legal aid defences. I get offered quite a few private prosecutions. They can be extremely lucrative.'

'Really, Rumpole. Just how lucrative?' Hilda stood

* See 'Rumpole at Sea'.

transfixed, her rubber gloves poised above the bubbling Fairy Liquid, waiting for the exact figures. The next morning, when I arrived at my Chambers in Equity Court, Henry told me.

'Two thousand pounds, Mr Rumpole. And I've agreed refreshers at five hundred a day. They've promised to send a cheque down with the brief.'

'And it's a case likely to last a day or two?' I stood awestruck at the price put upon my prosecution of Christopher Jago.

'We have got it down, Mr Rumpole, for two weeks.' I did some not so swift calculations, mental arithmetic never having been my strongest point, and then came to a firm decision. 'Henry,' I said, 'your lady wife, the Mayor of Bexleyheath . . .'

'No longer, Mr Rumpole. Her year of office being over, she has returned to mere alderman.'

'So you, Henry' – I congratulated the man warmly – 'are no longer Lady Mayoress?'

'Much to my relief, Mr Rumpole, I have handed in my chain.'

'Henry, you'll be able to tell me. Does the alderman ever plunge her ex-mayorial hands into the Fairy Liquid?'

'Hardly, Mr Rumpole. We have had a Crock-a-Gleam for years. You know, we're fully automated.'

Well, of course, I might have said, on a clerk's fees you would be, wouldn't you? It's only penurious barristers who are still slaving away with the dishcloth. Instead I made an expansive gesture. 'Go out, Henry,' I bade him, 'into the highways and byways of Oxford Street. Order up the biggest, whitest, most melodiously purring Crock-a-Gleam that money can buy and have it despatched to Mrs Rumpole at Froxbury Mansions with the compliments of the season.'

'You're going to prosecute in Jago then, Mr Rumpole?' Henry looked as surprised as if I had announced I meant to spend Christmas in a temperance hotel.

'Well, yes, Henry. I just thought I'd try my hand at it. For a change.'

Finally, my clerk declined a trip up Oxford Street but Dianne, who was busily engaged in reading her horoscope in *Woman's Own* and decorating her finger-nails for Christmas, undertook to ring John Lewis on my behalf. At which moment my learned friend Claude Erskine-Brown entered the clerk's room looking about as happy as a man who has paid through the nose for tickets for *Die Meistersinger von Nürnberg* and found himself at an evening of 'Come Dancing'. He noted, lugubriously, that there were no briefs in his tray – even those with other people's names on them – and then drew me out into the passage for a heart to heart.

'It's a good thing you were in the clerk's room just then, Rumpole.'

'Oh, is it? Why exactly?'

'Well. Ballard says he doesn't want me to go in there unless some other member of Chambers is present. What's he think I'm going to do? Forge my fee notes or ravish Dianne?'

'Probably both.'

'It's unbelievable.'

'Perhaps. We've got to remember that Ballard specializes in believing the unbelievable. He also thinks you're sunk in sin. He's probably afraid of getting passive sinning by standing too close to you.'

'Rumpole. About that wretched brief in the Rickmansworth County Court . . .'

'Oh, was it Rickmansworth? I thought it was Luton.' I was trying to avoid the moment that barristers dread – when your client looks at you in a trusting and confidential manner and seems about to tell you that he's guilty of the charge on which you've been paid to defend him.

'Rumpole, I wanted to tell you . . .'

'Please, don't, old darling,' I spoke as soothingly as I knew to the deeply distressed Claude. 'We all know the feeling. Acute shortage of crime affecting one's balance of payments. Nothing in your tray, nothing in the diary. The bank manager and the taxman hammering on the door. The VAT man climbing in at the window. Then you wander into the clerk's room and all the briefs seem to be for other people. Well, heaven knows how many times I've been tempted.'

'But I didn't do it, Rumpole. I mean I'd've been mad to do it. It was bound to get found out in the end.'

Many crimes, in my experience, are committed by persons undergoing temporary fits of insanity, who are bound to be found out in the end but I didn't think it tactful to mention this. Instead I asked, 'What about the handwriting on the changed brief?'

'It's in block letters. Not like mine, or anyone else's either. All the same, Ballard seems to have appointed himself judge, jury and handwriting expert. Rumpole' – Claude's voice sank in horror – 'I think he wants me out of Chambers.'

'I wouldn't be surprised.'

'What on earth's Philly going to say?' The man lived in growing awe of Phillida Erskine-Brown, Q.C., the embarrassingly successful Portia of our Chambers. 'I should think she'd be very glad to have you at home to do the washing up,' I comforted him. 'That is, unless you have a Crock-a-Gleam like the rest of us.'

'Rumpole, please. This is no joking matter.'

'Everything, in my humble opinion, is a joking matter.'

'I want you to defend me.'

'Do you? Ballard's asked me to fill an entirely different role.'

'You!' The unfortunate Claude gave me a look of horror. 'But you don't ever prosecute, do you?'

'Well' – I did my level best to cheer the man up – 'hardly ever.'

I passed on up to my room, where I lit a small cigar and reopened the papers in the Jago case, which I read with a new interest since Henry had dealt with the little matter of my fee. I looked at the photograph of the big, plain victim and thought again how little she looked like her trim and elegant father and brother. I went through the account of Jago's statements, and decided that even the clumsiest cross-examiner could ridicule his unconvincing explanations. I turned the pages of a photostat of Veronica Fabian's diary and learnt, for the first time, that she had had six previous appointments with the man called Arthur Morrison, and I wondered why the name seemed to mean something to me. Then the door was flung open and an extremely wrathful Mizz Liz Probert came into my presence.

'Well,' she said, 'you've really deserted us for the enemy now, haven't you, Rumpole.'

'I haven't been listening to the news.' I tried to be gentle with her. 'Are we at war?'

'Don't pretend you don't know what I mean. Henry's told me all about it. In my opinion it's as contemptible as acting for a landlord who's trying to evict a one-parent family on supplementary benefit. You've gone over to the Prosecution.'

'Not gone over' – I did my best to reassure the inflamed daughter of Red Ron Probert, once the firebrand leader of the South-East London Labour Council – 'just there on a visit.'

'Just visiting the establishment, the powers that be, the Old Bill. Just there on a friendly call? How comfortable, Rumpole. How cosy. You know what I always admired about you?'

'Not exactly. Do remind me.'

'Oh, yes. No wonder you've forgotten, now you've taken up prosecution. Well, I admired the fact that you were always on the side of the underdog. You stopped the Judges sending everyone to the nick. You showed up the police. You stood up for the underprivileged.' Liz Probert was using almost the same words as the Fabians, but now she said, 'And you, of all people, are being paid by some posh family of ritzy estate agents to cook up a case against a bit of a naff member of their profession. They're narked he's been let free just because there isn't any evidence against him.'

'Let me enlighten you.' My tone, as always, was sweetly reasonable. 'There is plenty of evidence against him.'

'Like the fact that he never went to a "decent public school" like the Fabians?'

'And like the fact that he scooted out of the country when he found the body instead of telephoning the police.'

'Oh, I'm sure you'll find lots of effective points to make against him!' Hell hath no fury like an outraged radical lawyer, and Mizz Probert's outrage did for her what a large Pommeroy's plonk did for me – it made her extremely eloquent. 'You'll be able to argue him into a life sentence with a twenty-five-year recommendation. Probably you'll get the thanks of the Judge, an invitation to the serious crimes squad dinner dance and a weekend's shooting at the Fabians' place in Hampshire. I don't know why you did it – or, rather, I know only too well.'

'Why, do you think?'

'Henry told me.' Then she took, as I sometimes do, to poetry: '"Just for a handful of silver he left us." You're always quoting Wordsworth.'

'I do. Except that's by Browning. *About* Wordsworth.'

'About him, is it? "The Lost Leader"? Well. No wonder you like Wordsworth so much.'

All this was hardly complimentary to Rumpole or, indeed, to the Old Sheep of the Lake District whose job in the stamp office had earned him the fury of the young Robert Browning. I wasn't thinking of this, however, as Liz Probert continued her flow of denunciation. I was thinking of the unfortunate Claude Erskine-Brown and the way he had spoken to me in the passage. He had seemed angry, puzzled, depressed, but not, strangely enough, guilty.

It's rare for a criminal hack to be invited into his customer's home. We represent a part of their lives they would prefer to forget. Not only do they not ask us to dinner, but when catching sight of us at parties years after we have sprung them from detention they look studiously in the opposite direction and pretend we never met. No one, I suppose, wants the neighbours to spot the sturdy figure of Rumpole climbing their front steps. I may give rise to speculation as to whether it's murder, rape or merely a nice clean fraud that's going on in their family. The Fabians were different. Clearly they felt that they had, as representatives of law and order, nothing to be ashamed of, indeed much to be proud of in the way they were pursuing justice, in spite of the curious lassitude of the police and the Director of Public Prosecutions. Mrs Fabian, it seemed, suffered from arthritis and rarely left the house so my discreet and highly respected solicitor, Francis Pyecraft (of Pyecraft & Wensleydale), and my good self were invited there for drinks. The dead girl's mother wanted to look us over and grant us her good housekeeping seal of approval.

'It's not knowing, that's the worst thing, Mr Rumpole,' Mrs Fabian told me. 'I feel I could learn to live with it, if I knew just *how* Veronica died.'

'You mean who killed her?'

'Yes, of course, that's what I mean.'

I didn't like to tell her that a criminal trial, before a judge, who comes armed with his own prejudices, and a jury, whose attention frequently wanders, may be a pretty blunt instrument for prising out the truth. Instead, I looked at her and wondered if couples are attracted by physical likeness. Mrs Fabian was as small-boned, clear-featured and neat as her husband and son. And yet they had produced a big-boned and plain daughter, who had stumbled, no doubt, unwittingly, on death.

'Perhaps you could tell me a little more about Veronica. I mean about her life. Boyfriends?'

'No.' Mrs Fabian shook her head. 'That was really the trouble. She didn't seem to be able to find one. At least, not one that cared about her.' We sat in the high living-room of a house overlooking the canal in Little Venice. Tall bookshelves stretched to the ceiling, a pair of loud-speakers tinkled with appropriate baroque music. The white walls were hung with grey drawings which looked discreetly expensive. Young Roger moved among us, replenishing our glasses. The curtains hadn't been drawn and Mrs Fabian sat on a sofa looking out into the winter darkness, almost as though she was still expecting her daughter to come home early on yet another evening without a date. Veronica's mother, father and brother, I imagined, never found it difficult to find people who cared about them. Only their daughter had to get on without love.

'She worked in your firm. What were her other interests?'

'Oh, she read enormously. She had an idea she wanted to be a writer and she did some things for her school magazine, which were rather good, I thought,' Gregory told me.

'*Very* good.' Mrs Fabian gave the dead girl her full support.

'She never got much further than that, I'm afraid. I suggested she came and worked for us, and then she could write in her spare time. If she seemed to be going to make a success of it – the writing, I mean – of course, I'd've supported her.'

'Just do a little estate agency, darling, until you publish a bestseller.' I could imagine the charm with which Gregory Fabian had said it, and his daughter, unsure of her talent, had agreed.

A fatal arrangement; if she had stuck to literature, she would never have kept an appointment in a Notting Hill Gate mews.

'What did she read?'

'Oh, all sorts of things. Mainly nineteenth-century authors. She used to talk about becoming a novelist.'

'Her favourites were the Brontës,' Mrs Fabian remembered.

'Oh, yes. The Brontës. Charlotte, especially. She had a very romantic nature.' Veronica's father smiled, I thought, with understanding.

'This man Morrison,' I said, 'whoever he may be, keeps turning up in the desk diary. No one in the office's ever heard of him. He's never been a client of yours?'

'Not so far as I've been able to discover. There's no correspondence with him.'

'You don't know a friend of hers by that name?'

'We've asked, of course. No one's ever heard of him.'

I got up and crossed to the darkened window. Looking out, all I could see was myself reflected in the glass, a comfortably padded Old Bailey hack with a worried expression, engaged in the strange pursuit of prosecution.

'But in her diary she seems to have had six previous appointments with him.'

'Of course' – Mrs Fabian was smiling at me apologetically, as though she hardly liked to point out anything so obvious – 'we don't know everything about her. You never do, do you? Even about your own daughter.'

'All right, then. What do you know about Christopher Jago? You must have come across him in the way of business.'

'Not really.' Gregory Fabian stopped smiling. 'He has, well, a different type of business.'

'And does it in a different sort of way,' his son added.

'What does that mean?'

'Well, we've heard things. You do hear things . . .'

'What sort of things?'

'Undervaluing houses. Getting their owners to sell cheap to a chap who's really a friend of the agent. The friend sells on for the right price and he and the agent divide up the profits.'

'We've no evidence of that,' Gregory told me. 'It wouldn't

be right for you to assume that's what he was doing. Apparently he's rather a flashy type of operator, but that's really all we know about him.'

'He's a cowboy.' Roger was more positive. 'And he looks the part.'

They were silent then, it seemed, for a moment, fearful of the mystery that had disturbed their gentle family life. Roger crossed the room behind me and drew the curtains, shutting out the dark.

'She wasn't robbed. She hadn't been sexually assaulted. So far as we know she hadn't quarrelled with anyone and Jago didn't even know her. Why on earth should he want to kill her?' I asked the Fabians and they continued to sit in silence, puzzled and sad.

'The police couldn't answer that question either,' I said. 'Perhaps that's why they let him go.'

I left the house on my own, as Pyecraft was staying to discuss the effect of the girl's death on certain family trusts. Gregory came down to the hall and, as he helped me on with my coat, he said quietly, 'I don't know if Francis Pyecraft explained to you about Veronica.'

'No. What about her?'

'As a matter of fact she's not our daughter.'

'Not?'

'No. After Roger was born, we so wanted a girl. Evelyn couldn't have any more children, so we adopted. Of course, we loved her just as much as Roger. But now, well, it seems to make it even more important that she should be treated justly.' Again, I thought, he was talking as though Veronica were still alive and eagerly awaiting the result of the trial. Then he said, 'There's always one child that you feel needs special protection.'

Christmas came and we sat in the kitchen round the white coffin of the Crock-a-Gleam which flashed, sighed, belched a few times and delivered up our crockery. As I rescued the burning-hot plates from a cloud of steam, the widow Charmian said, 'At least I've made Howard cough up a dishwasher for you, Hilda. I've managed to do that.'

'It wasn't you' – I had long given up trying to persuade our visitor to use my correct name – 'that made me buy it.' 'Oh?' Charmian was miffed. 'Who was it, then?'

'I suppose whoever killed Veronica Fabian.' I don't know why it was that Charmian gave me a distinct touch of the Scrooges. Later, when we opened our presents in the sitting-room, I bestowed on Hilda the gift of lavender water, which I think she now uses for laying-down purposes, and I discovered that the three pairs of darkish socks, wrapped in holly-patterned paper, were exactly what I wanted. Hilda opened a small glass jar, which contained some white cream which smelled faintly of hair oil and vaseline.

'Oh, how lovely.' She Who Must Be Obeyed was doing her best not to sound underwhelmed. 'What is it, Charmian?'

'Special homoeopathic skin beautifier, Hilda dear.' Charmian was tearing open the wafer-thin china early-morning tea set on which we had, I was quite convinced, spent far too much. 'We've got to do something about those poor toil-worn hands of yours, haven't we? And is this really for me?' She looked at her present with more than faint amusement. 'What funny little cups and saucers. And how very sweet of you to go out and buy them. Or was it another old Christmas present from Dodo Mackintosh?' It says a great deal for the awe in which Hilda held her, and my own iron self-control, that neither of us got up and beaned the woman with our Christmas tree.

After a festive season of this nature, it may not surprise you to know that I took an early opportunity to return to my place of business in Equity Court, where I found not much business going on. Such few barristers and clerks as were visible seemed to be in a state of somnambulism. I made for Pommeroy's Wine Bar, where even the holly seemed to be suffering from a hangover and my learned friend Claude Erskine-Brown was toying, in a melancholy and aloof fashion, with a half bottle of Pommeroy's more upmarket St-Emilion-type red.

'You're wandering lonely as a Claude,' I told him. 'Did you come up to work?'

'I came,' he said dolefully, 'because I couldn't stay at home.'

'Because of Christmas visitors?'

'No. Because of the shrink.'

I didn't catch the fellow's drift. Had his wits turned and did he imagine some strange diminution in size of his Islington home, so he could no longer crawl in at the front door?

'The what?'

'The shrink. Phillida knows all about the case of the altered brief. Ballard told her.'

'Ah, yes.' I knew my Soapy Sam. 'I bet he enjoyed that.'

'She was very understanding.'

'You said you were innocent, and she believed you?'

'No. She didn't believe me. She was just very understanding.'

'Ah.'

'She said it was the mid-life crisis. It happens to people in middle age. Mainly women who pinch things in Sainsbury's. But Philly thinks quite a lot of men go mad as well. So she said it was a sort of cry for help and she'd stand by me, provided I went to a shrink.'

'So?'

'It seemed easier to agree somehow.' Poor old Claude, the fizz had quite gone out of him and he had volunteered to join the great army of the maladjusted. 'She fixed me up with a Dr Gertrude Hauser who lives in Belsize Park.'

'Oh, yes. And what did Dr Gertrude have to say?'

'Well, first of all, she had this rather disgusting old sofa with a bit of Kleenex on the pillow. She made me lie down on that, so I felt a bit of a fool. Then she asked me about my childhood, so I told her. Then she said the whole trouble was that I wanted to sleep with my mother.'

'And did you?'

'What?'

'Want to sleep with your mother.'

'Of course not. Mummy would never have stood for it.'

'I suppose not.'

'Quite honestly, Rumpole. Mummy was an absolute sweetie in many ways, but – well, no offence to you, of course – she was *corpulent*. I didn't fancy her in the least.'

'Did you tell Gertrude that?'

'Yes. I said quite honestly I wouldn't have slept with Mummy if we'd been alone on a desert island.'

'What did the shrink say?'

'She said, "I shall write down 'fantasizes about being alone with his mother on a desert island'." Quite honestly, I can't go and see Dr Hauser again.'

'No. Probably not.'

'All that talk about Mummy. It's really too embarrassing. She'd have hated it so, if she'd been alive.'

'Yes, I do see. Excuse me a moment.' I tore myself away from the reluctant patient to a corner in which I had seen Mizz Liz Probert settling down to a glass of Pommeroy's newly advertised organic plonk (the old plonk, I strongly suspected, with a new bright-green label on the bottle). There was a certain matter about which I needed to ask her further and better particulars.

'Look here, Liz.' I pulled up a chair. 'How did you know all that about Christopher Jago?'

'You can't sit there,' she said. 'I'm expecting Dave Inchcape.'

'Just until he comes. How did you know that Jago didn't go to a public school, for instance?'

'He told me.'

'You met him?'

'Oh, yes. Dave and I got our flat through him. And I have to tell you, Rumpole, that he was absolutely honest, reliable and trustworthy throughout the whole transaction.' I had forgotten that Liz and Dave were now co-mortgagees and living happily ever after somewhere off Ladbroke Grove.

'What do you mean, he was honest and reliable?'

'Well. We got our place pretty cheaply, compared to the price Fabian & Winchelsea were asking for the other flats we saw. He never put up the price or let us be gazumped by other clients and he helped us fix up our mortgage. Oh, and he didn't conk me on the head with a Zulu knobkerrie.'

'Yes. I can see that. What else about him? Did he have a wife, girlfriend – anything like that?'

'Hundreds of girlfriends, I should think. He's rather attract-ive. Tall, fair and handsome. So you see, I shan't be giving evidence for the Prosecution.'

'I imagine from what you said, you wouldn't come and take a note for me? Act as my junior?'

'You must be joking!' Mizz Liz took a gulp of the alleged organic brew and looked at me with contempt.

'I'll have to ask your co-habitee.'

'Save your breath. Tricia Benbow's already briefed Dave for the Defence. He knows I'd never speak to him again if he took part in a prosecution.'

'Christopher Jago's gone to La Belle Benbow?'

'Oh, yes. He asked me if I knew a brilliant solicitor and said he preferred women in his life, so I sent him off to her.'

'But Dave Inchcape's not doing the case alone? I mean no offence to him but he's still only a white-wig.'

'He's got a leader.'

'Who?' A foeman, I rather hoped, worthy of my steel. Liz looked at me in silence for a moment, as though she was relishing the news she had to impart.

'Our Head of Chambers,' she told me.

'Heavens above!' I nearly choked on my non-organic chemi-cally produced Château Ordinaire. '"Thus the whirligig of time brings in his revenges." Rumpole for the Prosecution and Ballard for the Defence. He'd better sit close to me. He might catch some passive advocacy.'

On my way out, I had a message for Claude Erskine-Brown, who was still palely loitering. 'Come and help me in the "Mews Murder",' I said. 'Be my hard-working junior. Take your mind off your mother.'

'Rumpole!' The man looked pained and I hastened to com-fort him. 'At least you'll find someone who's deeper in the manure than you are, old darling,' I said.

Being in possession of two such contradictory views of Chris-topher Jago as those provided by the Fabians and Mizz Liz Probert, I decided that a little investigative work was neces-sary.

I could hardly ask Francis Pyecraft to hang round such pubs and clubs as Jago might frequent, so I called in the services of my old friend and colleague, Ferdinand Isaac Gerald Newton, known as Fig Newton to the trade. You could pass through many bars and hardly notice the doleful, lantern-jawed figure, sitting in a quiet corner, nursing half a pint of Guinness and apparently engrossed in *The Times* crossword puzzle which he solves, I am ashamed to say, in almost less time than it takes me to spot the quotations. But he hoovers up every scrap of gossip and information dropped within a surprisingly wide radius. You can't make bricks without straw and Fig is straw-purveyor to the best Old Bailey defenders. Now he would have a chance, as I had, of seeing life from the prosecution side.

I met him a couple of weeks later in Pommeroy's. He was suffering, as usual, from a bad cold, having been up most of the night keeping watch on a block of flats in a matrimonial matter, but between some heavy work with the handkerchief he was able to tell me a good deal. Our quarry lived in a 1930s house near Shepherd's Bush Road, the ground floor of which served as his office. He drove an electric blue Alfa-Romeo, the car which had led to his arrest. He was well known in a number of pubs round Maida Vale and Notting Hill Gate, where many of the properties he dealt in were situated. He was unmarried but went out with a succession of girls, his taste running to young and pretty blonde secretaries and receptionists. None of them lasted very long and in the Benedict Arms, one of his favourite resorts near the Regent's Canal, the bar staff would lay bets on how soon any girl would go.

There was one notable exception, however, to the stage army of desirable young women. On half a dozen occasions, the suspect had come into the Benedict Arms with a big, awkward, pale and rather unattractive girl. They had sat in a corner, away from the crowd, and appeared to have had a lot to say to each other. When Fig told me that, the penny dropped. I smote the table in my excitement, rattling the glasses and attracting the stares of the legal hacks busy drinking around us. I had just remembered what I knew about Arthur Morrison.

On my way home I went to check the facts in the library, for Veronica Fabian had no doubt known a great deal more than I did about minor novelists in the last century. Arthur Morrison, a prolific author, was born in 1863 and lived on into the Second World War. His best-known book about life in the East End of London was published in 1896. It was called *A Child of the Jago*.

I put the *Companion to English Literature* back on the library shelf with a feeling of relief. God was in his heaven: the widow Charmian, despite a pressing invitation to stay from Hilda, had gone back to Guildford, and the first prosecution I had ever undertaken seemed likely to be a winner. As I have said, I find it very difficult to embark on any case without being dead set on victory.

'May it please you, my Lord, Members of the Jury. I appear in this case with my learned friend, Mr Claude Erskine-Brown, for the Prosecution. The Defence of Christopher Jago is in the hands of my learned friends, Mr Samuel Ballard and Mr David Inchcape.' As I uttered these unaccustomed words, I had the unusual experience of the scarlet Judge on the Bench welcoming me with the sort of ingratiating smile he usually reserved for visiting Supreme Court justices or extremely pretty lady plaintiffs entering the witness-box.

'Did you say you were here to *prosecute*?'

'That is so, my Lord.'

'Members of the Jury' – Mr Justice Oliphant, as was his wont, spoke to the ladies and gents in the jury-box as though they were a group of educationally subnormal children with hearing defects – 'Mr Rumpole is going to outline the story of this case to you. In perfectly simple terms. Isn't that right, Mr Rumpole?'

'I hope so, my Lord.'

'So my advice to you is to sit quietly and give him your full attention. The Defence will have its chance later.' This reference caused Soapy Sam Ballard to lift his posterior from the bench and smile winsomely, an overture which Mr Justice 'Ollie' Oliphant completely ignored. Ollie comes from the northern circuit and prides himself on being a rough diamond who uses his robust common sense. I hoped he wasn't going to try to help me too much. Most acquittals occur when the Judge sickens the Jury by over-egging the prosecution pudding.

So we went to work in Number One Court. The two neat Fabians, father and son, sat in front of me. The man in the dock couldn't have been a greater contrast to them. He was tall, two or three inches over six feet, with a winter suntan that must have been kept going with a lamp, as well as visits to Marbella. His hair, clearly the victim of many hours' work with a blow-drier, was bouffant at the front and, at the back, swept almost down to his shoulders. His drooping moustache and the broad bracelet of his watch were the colour of old gold and his suit, like his car, might have been described as electric blue. He looked less like the cowboy Roger Fabian had called him than a professional footballer whose private and professional life is in a continual mess. He lounged between two officers in the dock, with his long legs stuck out in front of him, affecting alternate boredom and amusement. Underneath it all, I thought, he was probably terrified.

So there I was, opening my case to the Jury in as neutral a way as I knew how. I described the little mews house as I remembered it when I went to inspect the scene of the crime: the cramped rooms, the chill feeling of the home unused, the African carvings and weapons on the wall. I asked the Jury to picture the girl from the estate agents' office, who was waiting in the hallway, with the front door left open, to greet the man who had telephoned her.

Who was it? Was it Mr Morrison? Or was that a name she used to hide the identity of someone she knew quite well? I took the Jury through my theory that the literate Veronica had picked the name of the author of a book with Jago in the title. Then I waited for Ballard to shoot to his feet, as I would have done had I been defending, and denounce this as a vague and typical Rumpolean fantasy. I waited in vain. Ballard was inert, indeed there was an unusually contented smile on his face as he sat, perhaps deriving a little passive sensual satisfaction from the close and perfumed presence of his instructing solicitor, Miss Tricia Benbow.

'The Defence will no doubt argue that there is a real Arthur Morrison who met Veronica Fabian in the mews and killed her before Jago arrived on the scene.'

Once again Ballard replied with a deafening silence as he stared appreciatively at the back of his solicitor's neck. My instincts as a defender got the better of me. Jago may have been a crooked estate agent with a lamentable private life and an appalling taste in suits, but he deserved to have the points in his favour put as soon as possible. 'That's what you're going to argue, Ballard, isn't it?' I said in a *sotto voce* growl.

'Oh, yes.' Ballard shot obediently to his feet. 'If your Lordship pleases. It will be my duty to submit to your Lordship, in the fulness of time and entirely at your Lordship's convenience, of course, that the Jury will have to consider Morrison's part in this case very seriously, very seriously indeed.'

'If there is a Morrison, Mr Ballard. We have to use our common sense about that, don't we?' His Lordship intervened.

'Yes, of course. If your Lordship pleases.' Ballard subsided without further struggle. The Judge's intervention had somewhat unnerved me. I felt like a tennis player, starting a friendly knock up, who suddenly sees the referee hurling bricks at his opponent.

'Of course, I can concede that we may be wrong about the reasons Veronica Fabian used that name when entering her eight thirty appointment.'

'Use your common sense, Mr Rumpole. Please.' His Lordship's tone became distinctly less friendly. 'Mr Ballard hasn't asked you to concede to anything. Your job is to present the prosecution case. Let's get on with it.'

The Fabians, father and son, were looking up at me, and it was their plea for justice, rather than the disapproval of Oliver Oliphant, which made me return to the attack. 'In any event, Members of the Jury, we intend to call evidence to prove that Jago was seeing the dead girl quite regularly, meeting her in a public house called the Benedict Arms and having long, intimate conversations with her. There will also be evidence that he told the police . . .'

'That he'd never seen her before in his life!' Mr Justice Oliphant was like the helpful wife who always supplies the punchline to the end of her husband's best stories.

'I was coming to that, my Lord.'

'Come to it then, Mr Rumpole. How long is this case expected to last?'

My reaction to that sort of remark was instinctive. 'It will last, my Lord, for as long as it takes the Jury to consider every point both for and against the accused, and to decide if they can be sure of his guilt or not.' I felt happier now, at home in my old position of arguing with the Judge. Ollie opened his mouth, no doubt to deliver himself of a little more robust common sense, but I went on before he could utter.

'The police decided not to charge Jago because there was no apparent motive for the crime. But if he knew Veronica Fabian, if they had some sort of relationship, they may have had to consider why he ran from that house, where Veronica was lying dead, and told no one what he had seen. Finally, Members of the Jury, it's for you to say why he lied to the police and said he never met her.' And then I repeated the sentence I had used so often from the other side of the Court. 'You won't convict him of anything unless you're certain sure that the only answer is he must be guilty. That's what we call the golden thread that runs through British justice.'

So we began to call the evidence, produce the photographs and listen to the monotonous tones of police officers refreshing their memories from their notebooks. When I was defending, such witnesses presented a challenge, each to be lured in a different way, with charm, authority or lofty disdain, to produce some fragment of evidence which might help the customer in the dock. Now all I had to do was let them rattle on and so prosecuting seemed a dull business. Then we got the scene of the crime officer, who produced the fatal knobkerrie, its end heavily rounded, still blood-stained and protected by cellophane, as was the three-foot black handle. Ballard, who had sat mum during this parade of prosecution evidence, showed no interest in examining this weapon and said he had no questions.

'What about the finger-prints?' I could no longer restrain myself from hissing at my so-called opponent, a foeman who, at the moment, was hardly being worthy of my attention, let alone my steel.

'What about them?' Ballard whispered back in a sudden panic. 'Jago's aren't there, are they?'

'Of course not!' By now my whisper had become entirely audible. 'There are no finger-prints at all.'

'Mr Rumpole,' the voice of robust common sense trumpeted from the Bench, 'I thought you told us you appeared for the *Prosecution*. If Mr Ballard wants to ask a question for the Defence no doubt he will get up on his hind legs and do so!' I rather doubted that but, in fact, Soapy Sam unwound himself, drew himself up to his full height and said, as though a brilliant idea had just occurred to him, 'Officer. Let me put this to you. There are absolutely no finger-prints of Christopher Jago's on the handle of that weapon, are there?'

'There are no finger-prints of any sort, my Lord.'

'I'm very much obliged. Thank you, officer.' Ballard bowed with great satisfaction and as he sat down I heard him tell his junior, Inchcape, 'I'm glad I managed to winkle that out of him.'

Later we got the officer who had been in charge of the investigation, Detective Chief Inspector Brush, and even though he was, for the first time, in recorded history, my witness, I couldn't resist teasing him a little.

'Tell me, Chief Inspector. After the body was found, you spent a good deal of time and trouble looking for Arthur Morrison.'

'We did, my Lord.'

'In fact Morrison was always your number one suspect.'

'He still is, my Lord.'

'You don't accept that Arthur Morrison and Jago were one and the same person?'

There was a pause and then 'I suppose that may be a possibility.'

'And that Arthur Morrison is nothing but a dead author.'

'I don't know much about dead authors, Mr Rumpole.' There, at least the Detective Chief Inspector was telling the truth.

'If you'd known that, whether or not Morrison existed, Jago had been meeting the dead girl regularly, would that have made any difference to the decision not to charge him?'

There was a long silence and then Brush admitted, 'Well, yes, my Lord. I think it might.'

'Let's use our common sense about this, shall we? Don't let's beat about the bush,' Ollie intervened. 'Jago told you he'd never met the girl. If you'd known he was lying, you'd've charged him.'

'Yes, my Lord.'

'Well, there we are, Members of the Jury. We've got that clear at last, thanks to a little bit of down-to-earth common sense.' Mr Justice Oliphant had joined me as leader of the Prosecution. And that might have been that, but there was one other question someone had to ask and I couldn't rely on Ballard.

'You first questioned Mr Jago because you had discovered that his car had been parked outside 13A Gissing Mews at the relevant time.'

'Yes.'

'You had no idea that he had been into the house and found the body?'

'At that time. No.'

'So he volunteered that information entirely of his own accord?'

'That's right.'

'Was that one of the reasons he wasn't charged?'

'That was one of the reasons we thought he was being honest with us, yes.'

I sat down, having made Ballard's best point for him. Of course he had to totter to his feet and ruin it.

'And, so far as that goes, Chief Inspector' – Ballard stood, pleased with himself, rocking slightly on the balls of his feet – 'do you still think he was being honest with you about the way he found the girl?'

'I'm not sure.' Brush paused and then gave it back to the poor old darling, right between the eyes. 'If he was lying to us about not knowing the girl, I can't be sure about any of his evidence, can I?' Mr Justice Oliphant wrote down that answer and underlined it with his red pencil. The Fabians looked as though they were slightly more pleased with the way Ballard was doing his case than with my performance, but no doubt they'd be too polite to say so.

At the end of our evidence we called my old friend, Professor Andrew Ackerman, Ackerman of the Morgue, with whom I have spent many fascinating hours discussing bloodstains and gun-shot wounds. He testified that Veronica Fabian had died from a heavy blow to the frontal bone of the skull, consistent with an attack by the knobkerrie, Exhibit P.1. I asked him if this must have been a blow straight down on her head, and he ruled out the possibility of it having been struck from either side. From the position of the wound it was clear to him that the club had been held by the end of the handle and swung in an upward trajectory. I felt that his evidence was important, but at the moment he gave it I didn't realize its full significance.

'So you're defending? I expect you have Mizz Liz Probert's full approval?' I was disarming in the robing-room, taking off the wig and gown and running a comb through what remains of my hair, when I found myself sharing a mirror with young Dave Inchcape.

'What do you mean?'

'Well, she thinks prosecuting's as bad as aiding merciless landlords evict their tenants.'

'I know she doesn't think you should be prosecuting.'

'And I rather think,' I told him as I got on the bow-tie and adjusted the silk handkerchief, 'that Mr Justice Ollie Oliphant would agree with her.'

'By the way, I think we're doing pretty well for Chris, don't you? He's promised us a great party if we get him off.' Dave Inchcape had fallen into the defender's habit of first-name familiarity with alleged criminals. I wondered if it were ever so and the robing-room once rang with cries of 'I think we're going to get Hawley off – Hawley Crippin, of course.'

I walked back to Chambers with the still despondent Erskine-Brown, who had just been cut dead by Ballard and La Belle Benbow as they were coming out of the Ludgate Circus Palais de Justice.

'By the way, Claude,' I said, 'what was that case you're meant to have pinched from Inchcape all about?'

'Please' – the man looked at a passing bus, as though tempted to dive under it – 'don't remind me of it.'

'But what was the subject matter? Just the gist, you understand.'

'Well, it was a landlord's action for possession. Nothing very exciting.'

'He wanted to turn out a one-parent family?'

'No. I think they were a couple of ladies in the Gay Rights movement. He said they were using the place to run a business. Why do you ask?'

'Because,' I tried to encourage him, 'the evidence you have just given may be of great importance.' But Claude didn't look in the slightest cheered up.

No two characters could have been more contrary than Christopher Jago and his defence counsel. Jago lounged in the witness-box, flashed occasional smiles at the Jury, whose female members looked embarrassed and the males stony-faced. He was a bad witness, truculent, defensive and flippant by turns, and Soapy Sam was finding it hard to conceal his deep disapproval of the blow-dried, shiny-suited giant he was defending.

As I had called several witnesses, who said they had seen him with Veronica in the Benedict Arms, Jago no longer troubled to deny it. He said he first saw her in the pub at lunchtime with another girl from Fabians' whom he knew slightly and he bought them both a drink. Some time after that he saw her eating her lunch in a corner, alone with a book, and he talked to her.

'What did you talk about?' I asked when I came to cross-examine.

'The house business. Prices and that around the area. I didn't chat her up, if that's what you're suggesting. She wasn't the sort of girl I could ever fancy, even if I weren't pretty well looked after in that direction.' He gave the Jury one of his least endearing grins.

'So why did you meet her so often?'

'I just happened to bump into her, that's all.'

'It's not all, is it? Your meetings were planned. She entered five or six appointments with Morrison in her diary.'

To my surprise he didn't answer with a blustering denial that he and Morrison were one and the same person. Had he forgotten his best line of defence, or was he overcome by that strange need to tell the truth, which sometimes seems to attack even the most unsatisfactory witnesses? 'All right then,' he admitted. 'She seemed to want to see me and we made a few dates to meet for a drink round the Benedict.'

'Why did she want to see you?'

'Perhaps she fancied me. It has been known.' He looked at the Jury, expecting a sympathetic giggle that never came. 'I don't know why she wanted us to meet. You tell me.'

'No, Mr Jago. You tell us.'

There was a silence then. Jago looked troubled and I thought that he was afraid of the evidence he would have to give.

'She was a bit scared to tell me about it. She said it would mean a lot of trouble if it got out.'

'What was it, Mr Jago?' I was breaking another of my rules and asking a question without knowing the answer. At that moment I was in search of the truth, a somewhat dangerous pursuit for a defence counsel, but then I wasn't defending Jago.

He answered my question then, quietly and reluctantly. 'She was worried about what was happening at Fabians'.'

I saw my clients, the father and son, listening, composed and expressionless. They didn't try to stop me and by now it was too late to turn back. 'What did she say was happening at Fabians'?'

'She said they gave the people who wanted to sell their houses very low valuations. Then they sold to some friend who looked independent, but who was really in business with them. The friend sold on at the proper price and they shared the difference. She reckoned they'd been doing that for years. On a pretty big scale, I imagine.'

Gregory Fabian was writing me a note quite impassively. His son was flushed and looked so angry that I was afraid he was going to shout. But his father put a hand on his son's arm before he passed me his message. I remembered that Roger had said Jago practised the same fraud the Fabians were now being accused of.

'Why do you think she told you that?' I read Gregory's note then: HE'S TRYING TO RUIN US BECAUSE WE KNOW HE KILLED VERONICA. STOP HIM DOING IT.

'She told me because she was worried. I was in the same business. She wanted my advice. Like I said, perhaps she fancied me, I don't know. She said she hadn't got anyone else, no real friends, she could tell about it.'

I thought of the lonely girl who was trapped in a business she couldn't trust, pinning her faith on this unlikely companion. Perhaps she thought her confidences would bring them together. At any rate they were an excuse to meet him.

'Mr Jago, when you called at Gissing Mews that morning . . .'

'Like I told you. I was interested in the place for a client. I phoned Veronica and . . .'

'And you kept the appointment and found her dead in the hallway.'

'Yes.'

'Why didn't you telephone the police?'

'Because I was afraid.'

'Afraid you'd be arrested for her murder?'

'No. Not afraid of that.'

'Of what then?'

There are moments in some trials when everyone in Court seems to hold their breath, waiting for an answer. This was such an occasion and the answer when it came was totally unexpected.

'I thought she'd been done over because she'd told me what

the Fabians were up to. I thought, that might be you, Christopher, if you get involved any more.'

'*You* killed her!' Roger Fabian couldn't restrain himself now. Ollie Oliphant uttered some soothing words about understanding the strength of the family feelings, but urged the young man to use his common sense and keep quiet. I did my best to pull myself together and behave like a prosecuting counsel. I asked Jago to take Exhibit P.1 in his hand, which he did without any apparent reluctance.

'I'm bound to put it to you,' I said, 'that you and Veronica Fabian quarrelled that morning when you met in the mews house. You lost your temper and took that knobkerrie off the wall. You swung it up over your head . . .'

'Like that, you mean?' He lifted the African club and as he did so all the odd pieces of the evidence came together and locked into one clear picture. Christopher Jago was innocent of the murder we had charged him with, and, from that moment, I was determined to get him off.

The case began and ended in the little house in Gissing Mews. I asked Ollie Oliphant to move the proceedings to the scene of the crime as I wished to demonstrate something to the Jury, having taken the precaution of telling my opponent that if he wanted to get his client off, he'd better support my application. So now the cold, gloomy mews house, with its primitive carvings and grinning African masks, was crammed to the gunwales with legal hacks, jury members, court officials and all the trimmings, including, of course, Jago and the Fabians. In one way or another, as many of us as possible got a view of the hall, where I stood by the telephone impersonating, with only a momentary fear that I might have got it entirely wrong, the victim of the crime. I got Jago to stand in front of me and swing the club, P.1, again in order to strike my head. I was not entirely surprised when neither Sam Ballard, Q.C. nor Mr Justice Oliphant tried to prevent my apparent suicide, although Claude Erskine-Brown did have the decency to mutter, 'Mind out, Rumpole. We don't want to lose you.'

Everyone was watching as the tall, flamboyant accused lifted

the knobkerrie and tried to swing it above his head. He tried
and failed. When I was cross-examining him, I remembered
the cramped rooms and low ceilings of the mews cottage. Now
as the club bumped harmlessly against the plaster, everyone
present understood why Jago couldn't have struck the blow
which killed Veronica Fabian. Whoever killed her must have
been at least six inches shorter.

It was my first prosecution and I had managed, against all
the odds, to secure an acquittal.

'You got him off?'

'Yes.'

A few days, it seemed a lifetime, later, I was alone with
Gregory Fabian in his white, early Victorian house in Little
Venice.

'Why?'

'Did you want an innocent man convicted? That's a stupid
question. Of course you did.'

He said nothing and I went on, as I had to. 'You said there's
always one child who needs protecting, but you weren't thinking of Veronica, were you? You were talking about your son.'

'What about Roger?'

'What about him? Odd, his habit of accusing other people of
the things he did himself.'

'What did he do?' Gregory was quiet, unruffled, still carefully courteous, in spite of what I'd done to him.

'I think you know, don't you? The racket of undervaluing
homes, so you could sell them to your secret nominees. He
accused Jago of doing that, just as he accused him of Veronica's
murder.'

The house was very quiet. Mrs Fabian was upstairs somewhere, resting. God knows where Roger was. Even the traffic
sounded far away and muted in the darkness of an early
evening in January.

'What are you trying to tell me?'

'What I think. That's all. I'm not setting out to prove
anything beyond reasonable doubt.'

'Go on then.' He gave a small sigh, perhaps of resignation.

'Veronica discovered what was going on and didn't like it. She asked Jago's advice, and I expect he told her to keep him well-informed. No doubt so he could make something out of it when it suited him to do so. Then I think Roger found out what his sister was doing. Well, she wasn't his real sister, was she? She was the loved girl, who had arrived after he was born, the child he was always jealous of. I expect he found out she had a date to meet Jago at the mews house. He went after her to stop her. I don't think he meant to kill her.'

'Of course he didn't.' The father was still trying, I thought, to persuade himself.

'He lost his temper with her. They quarrelled. She tried to telephone for help and he ripped out the phone. Remember that's how they found it. Then he took the knobkerrie off the wall. He's short enough to have been able to swing it without hitting the ceiling. But you know all that, don't you?' Gregory Fabian didn't answer, relying, I suppose, on his right to silence.

'You wanted Roger to be safe. You wanted him to be protected, forever. And the best way of doing that was to get someone else found guilty. That's what you paid me to do. To be quite technical, Mr Fabian, you paid me to take part in your conspiracy to pervert the course of justice.'

'You said,' he sounded desperately hopeful, 'that you couldn't prove it . . .'

'It's not my business to prosecute. It never has been. And it's not my business to take part in crime. I told Henry to send your money back.'

He stood up then and moved between me and the door. I thought for a moment that the repressed violence of the Fabians might erupt and he would attack me. But all he said was 'Poor Roger.'

'No, Poor Veronica. You should never have stopped her becoming a novelist.'

I walked past him and out of the house. I heard him call after me 'Mr Rumpole!' But I didn't stop. I was glad to be out in the darkness, breathing in the mist from the canal, away from a house silenced by death and deception.

*

I decided to walk a while from the Fabian house, feeling I had, among other things, to think over what remained of my life. 'Mr Rumpole, although briefed for the Prosecution and under a duty to present the prosecution case to you, took it into his head, no doubt because of the habit of a lifetime, to act for the Defence. So, the basis of our fine adversarial system, which has long been our pride, has been undermined. Mr Rumpole will have to consider where his future, if any, is at the Bar. In the absence of a prosecutor, you and I, Members of the Jury, will just have to rely on good old British common sense.' These were the words with which Ollie sent the Jury out to consider its verdict, which turned out to be a resounding not guilty for everyone, except Rumpole whose conduct had been, according to his Lordship, in his final analysis, 'grossly unprofessional'.

It was while I was brooding on these judicial pronouncements that I heard the sound of revelry by night and noticed that I was passing a somewhat glitzy art nouveau pub, picked out in neon lights, called the Benedict Arms. I remembered that this was the night of Christopher Jago's celebration party, to which he had invited not only his defenders, but, and in all the circumstances of the case, this was understandable, the prosecution team as well. I had persuaded Claude not to sit moping at home and I'd promised to meet him there. Accordingly I called into the saloon of the Benedict and was immediately told that Chris's piss-up was on the first floor.

I climbed up to a celebration very unlike our Chambers parties in Equity Court. Music, which sounded to my untrained ear very like the sound produced by a pneumatic drill pounding a pavement, shook the windows. There were a number of metallically blonde girls in skirts the size of pocket handkerchiefs and tops kept up by some stretch of the imagination and a fair number of men with moustaches, whom I took for downmarket estate agents. Like dark islands in a colourful sea, the lawyers had clearly begun, with the exception of the doleful Erskine-Brown, to enjoy the party.

'Thanks for coming.' Jago stood before me. 'Do you always work for the other side? If you do, I'm bloody glad I didn't have you defending me.' It was the sort of joke I could do without and then, to my astonishment, I saw him put an arm around Mizz Liz Probert and say, 'You know this little legal lady, I'm sure, Mr Rumpole? I told her she can have my briefs any day of the week, quite honestly!' And I was even more astonished to see that Mizz Liz, far from kneeing this rampant chauvinist in the groin, smiled charmingly at the man she thought had been saved from a life sentence by the efforts of her co-mortgagee.

Wandering on into the throng of celebrators, I saw Bollard in close proximity to his grateful instructing solicitor, Tricia Benbow. It seemed to me that Soapy Sam had been the victim of much passive alcoholism, no doubt absorbed from the glass he held in his hand.

Then, under the sound of the pneumatic drill, I heard the shrilling of a telephone and I was hailed by Jago, who had answered it.

'Mr Rumpole. It's your clerk. He says it's urgent.'

'All right. For God's sake, turn off the music for five minutes.' I took the telephone from him. 'Henry!'

'I've got an awkward situation here, Mr Rumpole. The truth of the matter is Mrs Ballard is here.'

'Oh. Bad luck.'

'She happened to come out of her sprains and fractures refresher course and she wanted to meet up with her husband. She said –' Henry's voice sank to a conspiratorial murmur in which I could detect an almost irresistible tendency to laughter – 'he told her he was going to a Lawyers As Christians Society meeting tonight and might be late home. But she wants to know where the meeting's being held so she can join him, if at all possible.'

'Henry, you didn't tell her he was at a piss-up in the Benedict Arms, Maida Vale?'

'No, sir. I didn't think it would be well received.'

'Why involve me in this sordid web of intrigue?'

'Well, we don't want to land the Head of Chambers in it, do we, Mr Rumpole? Not in the first instance, anyway.' Our clerk was positively giggling.

'Where is the wife of Bollard now?'

'She's in the waiting-room, sir.'

'Put me through to her, Henry. Without delay.' And when Mrs Ballard came on the line, I greeted her warmly.

'Matey . . . I mean, Marguerite. This is Horace Rumpole speaking.'

'Horace! Whatever are you doing there? And where's Sam?'

'Oh, I'm afraid brother Ballard can't come to the phone. He's busy preparing to induct a new member.'

'A new member. Who?'

'Me.'

'You, Horace?' The ex-Matron sounded incredulous.

'Of course. I have decided to put away the sins of the world and lead a better, purer life in future.'

'But where are you meeting?'

'I'm afraid that can't be divulged over the telephone.'

'Why ever not?'

'For your own safety I think it's better for you not to know. We've had threatening calls from militant Methodists.'

'Horace. Are you sure Sam's all right? I can hear a lot of voices.'

'Oh, it's a very full house this evening. Hold on a minute.' I held the phone away from my ear for a while and then I told her, 'Sam really can't get away now. He says he'll see you back in Waltham Cross and don't wait up for him. He'll probably be exhausted.'

'Exhausted?' She sounded only a little suspicious. 'Why?'

'It's the spirit,' I said. 'You know how it tires him.'

'Is he filled with it?' Her suspicions seemed gone and her voice was full of admiration.

'Oh, yes,' I assured her, 'right up to the brim.'

I put down the phone and the blast of road-mending music was restored. I then approached our Head of Chambers, who was standing with Dave Inchcape – Tricia, the solicitor, having danced away with her liberated client.

'That was your wife on the phone,' I told him.

'Good heavens.' The man was still sober enough to panic. 'She's not coming here?'

244

'Oh, no. I gave you a perfect alibi. Tell you about it later. I'll also tell you my solution to the Case of the Altered Brief. I'm getting into the habit of solving mysteries.'

'I'd better go and find Liz.' Inchcape seemed anxious to get away.

'No, you stay here, David.' I spoke with some authority and the young man stood, looking anxious. 'We're all but toys in the hands of women and your particular commander-in-chief is Mizz Liz Probert. I know you come into the clerk's room early to see what's arrived in the post, all white-wigs do. To your horror you found you'd been engaged by a flinty-hearted landlord to kick two ladies, active in Gay Rights, out of house and home. How could you face your co-habitee, if you did a case like that? It was a matter of a moment, Members of the Jury,' I addressed an imaginary tribunal, 'for David Inchcape to scratch out his name and write Mr Claude Erskine-Brown in block capitals.'

'Is this true?' Ballard tried his best to look judicial, although he was somewhat unsteady on his pins.

David Inchcape's silence provided the answer.

I was rather late home that evening and climbed into bed beside Hilda's sleeping back. I had no professional duties the next day and wandered into the kitchen in my dressing-gown and with a head still throbbing from the pile-driving music at Jago's celebration. I found Hilda in a surprisingly benign mood, all things considered, but I also noticed something missing from our home.

'Where's the Crock-a-Gleam?' I said. 'You haven't pawned it? I know things aren't brilliant but . . .'

'I sent it back to John Lewis,' Hilda told me. 'We might get a little something for it.'

'Why?' I felt for a chair and lowered myself slowly into it. 'What's it done wrong?'

'Nothing, really. It just takes about twice as long to do the washing up as even you do, Rumpole. That's not it. It's *her*.'

'Her?'

'Charmian Nichols. She wrote to Dodo and said Christmas

with us was about as exciting as watching your finger-nails grow. And when I think of what we spent on her wretched tea set. "Charming Knickers", that was her nickname at school. We got her completely wrong. There wasn't anything charming about her.'

'How do you know what she wrote about Christmas?'

'Dodo sent me her letter, of course. Well, after that, I couldn't sit and look at the dishwasher you bought just to please her.'

Wonderfully loyal group, your old school friends, I thought of saying that but decided against it. Then Hilda changed the subject.

'Rumpole,' she said, 'are things very bad?'

'No one wants to employ me. Not since I changed sides in the middle of a case.'

'You did what you thought was right,' she said, surprisingly sympathetically. But then she added, 'Do be careful not to do what you think's right again. It does seem to have disastrous results.'

'I can't promise you that, Hilda.' I made my bid for independence. 'But I can promise you one thing.'

'What's that?'

'From now on, old thing, I promise you, Rumpole only defends.'